# THE THUNDER WARRIOR

## BOOK TWO – LORDS OF THUNDER TRILOGY

## A MEDIEVAL ROMANCE

## BY

# KATHRYN LE VEQUE

ISBN: 978-1508736028
Print Edition

Text by Kathryn Le Veque
Cover by Kathryn Le Veque

Note: All Kathryn's novels are designed to be read as stand-alones, although many have cross-over characters or cross-over family groups.

Novels that are grouped together have related characters or family groups.

Series are clearly marked. All series contain the same characters or family groups except the American Heroes Series, which is an anthology with unrelated characters.

There is NO particular chronological order for any of the novels because they can all be read as stand-alones, even the series.

# TABLE OF CONTENTS

# AUTHOR'S NOTE

The Lords of Thunder Trilogy takes place in the year 1258, which was the year that saw Simon de Montfort come to power in his struggle against Henry III. It is a pivotal year in English history and Simon de Montfort was a true visionary on how government should be run. Did you know that an image of him is in the United States House of Congress? He is considered the man who held the first democratic gathering (at least as democratic as Medieval England can get!).

Maximus' story takes place during the month of May, the month that Simon de Montfort held what was referred to as the "Mad Parliament". It's a fairly complex period in time and there were a lot of measures and provisions leveled against the King by de Montfort and his supporters, but the Mad Parliament was a gathering that really set forth rules against the king that defined the next several years of his reign.

In this novel, you will hear the characters refer to de Montfort's "gathering" quite a bit – it's the Mad Parliament they are referring to. Although I don't have a scene involving this parliament, as this would really make this book more of a history lesson and less of a romantic novel, the Mad Parliament is an underlying plot set against the love story of Maximus and Lady Courtly Love de Lara.

There are less politics in this book than in Gallus' book, THE THUNDER LORD, because Gallus' book was essentially establishing the foundation of the series and the political upheaval that was going on at the time. This book is much more about Maximus and how a man, so dedicated to war and politics, can fall in love – and fall hard. While Gallus' book was spread out over four months, Maximus' is a snapshot of his life during the month of May. It is much different from Gallus' book but just as exciting and complex, if not more so.

Happy reading!

Hugs,
*Kathryn*

# BOOK TWO

LORDS OF THUNDER TRILOGY:
THE DE SHERA BROTHERHOOD

THE THUNDER WARRIOR:
WHEN THUNDER STRIKES

# PART ONE

## WINDS OF FATE

### MAY

*"In days of old,*
*With men so bold,*
*A storm was brewing brightly.*
*These men, it was told,*
*As knights so bold,*
*Were known to tame the lightning"*

*~ 13th century chronicles*

# CHAPTER ONE

*Year of our Lord 1258 A.D.*
*Reign of Henry III*
*Oxford, England*

I T WAS A day of days, a mild spring day that was perfect in every fashion. The sun was brilliant against the deep, blue expanse of sky with nary a cloud to hamper the view. Days like this were rare, neither hot nor cold, but in that perfect temperature that seemed to bring out the best in both man and beast. A breeze, as soft and caressing as a child's whisper, whistled through the busy and proud town of Oxford.

The Street of the Merchants was a bustling road that was lined on both sides by close-quarters buildings, stalls and shops that were manned by aggressive salesmen determined to push their wares upon a spend-happy public. Between St. Clement's Church and the castle stretched the main thoroughfare through the town, and travelers spilled into the Street of the Merchants, just off the main road. This created a crowded bottleneck at the head of the street.

Four armed knights pushed themselves through the bottleneck and ended up in the crowds shopping along the avenue. The smells from the bakers on the next street wafted heavily in the air, the scent of yeast and of hard, brown crusts making for hungry shoppers at this time in the morning. Near the middle of the avenue near a fabric vendor's stall, a man playing what looked like a crudely made *vielle* stood in the tiny gap between two buildings while his daughter, a round girl with a big mouth, sang quite loudly and somewhat off key. All of it, the sights and smells of the day, contributed to the hurried setting.

"Licorice root, wasn't it?" one of the knights asked the group. "And spiced wine?"

The knight in the lead, a very large man with massive shoulders and a crown of dark, wavy hair replied. "Wine with marjoram," he said. "She was specific. It settles her stomach, as does the licorice."

The knight who asked about the licorice root made a face. "Have you ever tasted licorice?" he asked. "It is most foul and turns your tongue black."

The knight in the lead turned to look at the licorice-hating knight, who was now sticking his tongue out to demonstrate his aversion. Sir Maximus de Shera, a brawny beast of a man with enormous shoulders and a granite-square jaw, shook his dark brown head at his younger brother's antics.

"It does not matter what you or I think of it," he said. "Jeniver is feeling ill from her pregnancy and Gallus asked us to find her some."

Sir Tiberius de Shera put his tongue back in his mouth but he still wasn't convinced. The very tall, lean, muscular brother was animated to a fault and opinionated until the very end.

"The spiced wine would do better," he said. "Moreover, why are *we* running Gallus' errands for him? His wife is the one feeling ill. He should be the one to come and fish for stinking roots and rotten wine for her."

Maximus grinned. "Will you tell him that to his face?"

Tiberius shook his head. "Not me," he said. "Much like you, I do as I am told by our illustrious, older brother. Let us get this over with. I will head down to the end of the avenue and see if I can find an apothecary. You stay here and see if you can locate the wine with all of the dried weeds in it."

Maximus merely waved Tiberius on and the man headed down the street with another knight in tow. Maximus cocked an eyebrow.

"He does not understand," he said to the knight who had remained with him. "He is not yet old enough to realize that a man will do anything for the woman he loves. He's not yet had experience with love like that."

The knight who had remained with him, a hulking man named Sir Garran de Moray, glanced at Maximus with his onyx-black eyes.

"You speak as if you have known an affair such as that," he said. "I did not know that about you, Max."

Maximus pulled his muscular rouncey to a halt and dismounted. "It was a long time ago," he said, muttering, as if he did not want to spare thought to those memories. "I was seventeen years of age and she was fourteen. We were madly in love."

"What happened?"

Maximus grunted. "A de Shera cannot marry below his station," he said, somewhat sarcastically. "She was the smithy's daughter. When my father found out, he sent both her and her father away. I heard that she died later that year of a fever. I have always wondered if…."

He trailed off, disinclined to continue, as he tethered his horse to the nearest post. Garran dismounted beside him, unwilling to push the subject of his young and tragic love. Garran had known Maximus and this was the first time he'd heard such a thing, but he wasn't surprised. Maximus tended to keep silent on personal matters. He wasn't one to wear his heart on his sleeve or speak on things even remotely private. Keeping that in mind, Garran pointed to the building in front of them.

"A wine and spice merchant," he said, changing the subject. "It is my guess we will be able to find a myriad of things to settle Lady de Shera's belly. If the wine doesn't make her drunk enough to forget her ills, then we shall find a spice that will make her giddy enough to not care."

Smirking, Maximus moved into the shop with Garran on his heels. Inside, it was dark, cluttered, and smelled of great and exotic lands. Mustard, nutmeg, and cardamom were in great baskets lining the walls, and there were spices from The Levant, Egypt, and darkest Africa. It made him sneeze. The merchant, a fat man dressed in silks and speaking with an odd accent, tried to sell them all manner of mysterious ingredients, including flakes of gold that were said to ward off the demons of sickness.

Maximus didn't want golden medicine. He simply wanted licorice root for his brother's wife's nausea. The merchant, however, steered him towards chamomile and assured him that it would soothe an upset belly, so he ended up buying that as well. As the merchant tried to interest him in some dark seeds that looked like bugs, seeds that also promised to ease Lady de Shera's bellyache, screams could be heard out on the avenue.

At first, Maximus didn't pay any attention although Garran did. As Maximus paid the spice vendor for the products he had acquired, Garran went to the door of the stall and casually looked out to see what the fuss was about. He caught sight of it about the same time a massive wave of smoke blew into the spice merchant's stall, catching Maximus' attention.

"What is it?" he said to Garran. "Where is the smoke coming from?"

Garran's features were bordering on concern as he pointed to the south. "A building is on fire," he said. "It looks as if people are trapped."

Thanking the merchant, Maximus went to the door, looking in the direction that Garran was indicating. Across the avenue and on the corner of the street where several hostels were located, smoke was billowing out of the first floor of a three-storied building. The entire area was filling up quickly with smoke and people were beginning to panic. A fire such as that, in the cramped quarters of the city, could spread quickly. Already, merchants were starting to pack up their wares with the intention of fleeing. As people began to run away from the fire, Maximus handed his recent purchase back to the merchant for safekeeping as he and Garran headed towards the flames.

As the knights drew closer, they could see that the first floor of the building was quickly becoming engulfed. A layer of heavy smoke was clogging the avenue and they could see through the haze that there were people on the second and third floors of the building that was burning. There didn't seem to be any flame on those levels but it was only a matter of time. Smoke was already filling the rooms, swirling from the windows as the people inside began to throw their possessions out the windows. In fact, people were starting to come out of the windows as well.

Two women and a small child jumped onto the street below, suffering no injuries by pure fortune. The crowd gathered at the base of the building was carrying buckets to extinguish the fire, encouraging the people trapped inside to jump. As Maximus and Garran came to the west side of the building, the side that fronted the Street of the Merchants, a young woman and a girl appeared on the third floor above.

The young woman, coughing as the smoke swept upward, had what looked to be a rope of material of some kind in her hands. It was clear that she had tied items together to form a rope, a very clever and resourceful action, and Maximus and Garran ran towards the rope as she lowered it.

"Make sure you secure the end of it," Maximus shouted up to the young woman. "Tie it tightly. We will help you!"

As the young girl cowered in the window, the woman disappeared inside and they could feel the cloth rope tugging.

"Hopefully she is tying it to something sturdy," Garran said, squinting up at the smoke-filled window. "What is this place, anyway?"

Maximus, holding on to the end of the rope, glanced about. "I am not sure," he said. "A hostel, mayhap? People are throwing capcases and satchels out into the street."

Garran glanced around, too, and was forced to agree. There were possessions strewn out all over the avenue. As he watched, a pair of children stole a few items in the mud and ran off with them, disappearing into the quagmire of alleyways and avenues beyond. Garran cocked a disapproving eyebrow.

"And they are making it easy for thieves," he commented, returning his attention to the women above them. "She had better hurry, the fire is gaining. It will reach the upper floor soon."

He was correct. It had already reached the second floor and had engulfed at least two of the rooms. More people were jumping, landing in the mud and hard-packed earth of the avenue below, but those on the third floor, as this woman and girl were, had a bit more of a challenge. It was more of a jump. As they seriously began to wonder what happened to the young woman, she suddenly appeared into the window next to the girl.

"Hurry down the rope!" Maximus yelled up to her. "Send the little one down first!"

Already, the young woman was rushing the girl onto the rope, but the girl was frightened. She wept and struggled a bit, fearful of the general chaos going on around her. The young woman was firm, however, and she coughed, laboring against the smoke, as she forced the girl onto the linen rope.

Once the girl was on the rope, she froze, crying, as the young woman encouraged her to slither down. Garran, seeing that the girl was very uncertain on the rope, positioned himself underneath her should she fall. His instincts had been correct, for the girl had hardly moved at all before she lost her grip and, screaming, tumbled right into his arms. A flailing fist caught Garran in the mouth, drawing blood, but he didn't utter a word about it or even acknowledge it as he carried the girl away from the burning building. He was well clear when he set the terrified child to her feet.

"Are you well, lass?" he asked her, not unkindly. "Did you hurt yourself?"

The girl sniffled, wiping her running nose with the back of her hand. "N-Nay," she stammered. "I did not hurt myself. But you must help my sister!"

She was pointing to the third floor where the young woman was trying to mount the rope. The smoke was thicker now, billowing out of the window in great, black clouds and swirling around the young woman as she tried to get a good grip on the rope, repeatedly trying to gain purchase on it. It became evident that her palms were sweating, or perhaps injured, because she was having a difficult time grasping it. The more she tried, the more it seemed to slip through her fingers.

Maximus was standing directly beneath the rope that the young girl had attempted to use. He could see that the woman was nearly swamped with smoke at this point and flames were beginning to shoot from the windows of the chamber next to hers. There was no more time to delay, sweating palms or no, and he took hold of the end of the linen rope, holding it steady.

"Lass!" he boomed up to her. "Come now! Use the rope!"

The woman was hurrying. He could see it. Her movements

were quick, determined, yet futile in most instances. Maximus could see the orange glow behind her now as the flames made their way into her chamber and the woman, feeling the heat behind her, made a desperate leap onto the rope.

Unfortunately, her grip wasn't very strong. As the flames began to flick out from the window, the woman tried to lower herself down the rope. She slipped, but caught herself, desperately attempting to hold on to the linen that seemed as slippery as silk. Maximus held on to the other end of it, holding it steady, as she lowered herself slowly and precariously.

"That's it, lass," Maximus called up to her, encouragingly. "One hand over the other. Do not panic, steady, lass, steady."

The woman was able to lower herself to the second floor level, which was a miracle considering her weak grip and uneven progress. She was valiantly trying to descend and Maximus watched her with some concern as she made progress. Gazing up at her feet and at the dark green surcoat as it blew about in the wind that the firestorm was creating, he realized he could see up her skirt and was trying not to look at her very shapely legs. He could also see the hem of her fine white shift and, as it billowed about, he'd caught a glimpse of naked buttocks.

Maximus wasn't hard-pressed to admit that he found the show tantalizing, but he knew his thoughts were grossly out of place considering the circumstances. Therefore, he tried to focus on her hands and the upper, well-covered portion of her torso. Anything to keep his gaze from wandering to her legs and smooth arse. Unfortunately, the Winds of Fate had other ideas.

Abruptly, the linen rope went slack as the fire burned through whatever the young woman had anchored it to. All Maximus could see was the woman as she came sailing down upon him. The skirt, caught by the wind as she fell, belled out and Maximus soon found his head covered by it. Her feet hit his shoulders and glanced off, her heels sliding down his shoulder blades as her bum came to rest on his collarbone.

It was a hard hit against his throat and he pitched backwards with the momentum of her fall, realizing that a woman's pink, tender center was suddenly in his face. It was the only thing he could see. As he hit the ground, the woman fell atop him, her fuzzy notch squarely on his face.

Maximus lay there as the woman essentially knelt over him in an extraordinarily provocative position. From the way they had fallen, her skirts were tangled around them so she couldn't rise immediately. He was trapped, his face against that sensual core, and in spite of the circumstances, it was the most arousing experience he'd ever known. Had he stuck out his tongue, he could have easily lapped her. But she was grunting unhappily, struggling to climb off him, and Maximus had to pull himself away from that rather beautiful sight to restore the woman's dignity. He shifted so she could at least pull her skirts out from underneath him.

"Sirrah!" the woman gasped, trying to yank her tangled skirt away from his head. "Let me *go!*"

Maximus realized that his arms were tangled in her skirts as well. "I am trying, my lady," he assured her. "Kindly push yourself up and I will be able to move."

Evidently, the woman could feel his hot breath against her woman's core as he spoke because she suddenly shrieked and began pummeling his head, still half-wrapped up in her skirts.

"You beast!" she cried. "You dirty, foul beast! Remove yourself!"

She was landing some heavy blows to his head and Maximus put his hands up, grabbing her fists as they swung at them. He could only see her with one eye because of the skirts still around his head, but that one eye was glaring.

"You will cease your fit," he growled. "I am not here by choice, lady. *You* fell on top of *me*. If anyone should be angry between us, it

THE THUNDER WARRIOR     11

should not be you. Now, stop beating me and pull your skirts away from my head unless you wish to remain in this position for the rest of your life."

The young woman was embarrassed and frustrated. Maximus could see it in her expression. She was also the most utterly beautiful woman he had ever laid eyes on. With long, blond hair secured in a braid, she had a sweet oval face, lush lips, and big eyes the color of a hot, summer sky. She was absolutely ravishing. But that beautiful face was twisted into a serious frown.

Grunting miserably, the woman yanked at her skirts, trying to push herself off of him. Maximus was able to get his arms free and he reached out, taking her by the waist as he sat up. He was able to set her to her feet before rolling over and rising to his knees. He watched as the woman ran over to the young girl, pulling the child into a relieved embrace.

"Are you well, Issie?" she asked softly. "Did you hurt yourself?"

The young girl shook her head, holding tightly to the woman. "Nay," she replied, looking at Garran, who was standing a few feet away. "He... he saved me."

The young woman looked at the big, black-eyed knight. "You have my thanks," she said sincerely. Then, she reluctantly turned to Maximus, who was just rising to his feet and brushing the dirt off his leather breeches. It was clear that she was torn between her embarrassment and her gratitude. "And to you, sirrah... I suppose I should thank you also. Had you not been here, the outcome might have been considerably different for my sister and me."

Maximus moved away from the flaming structure, which was starting to collapse. Pieces of building were falling onto the avenue and, silently, he and Garran moved the women away from the danger to the other side of the street. It was a chivalrous habit to protect the weaker, female sex and had nothing to do with his overall concern for the women. Considering the ungrateful lady had beat him around the head, he would just as soon leave her where she stood.

"Your gratitude is unnecessary," he said, realizing he was having difficulty looking her in the eye and not thinking of that sweet morsel between her legs that had presented itself so unexpectedly to him. "If you are uninjured and do not require further assistance, then we shall be along our way."

He didn't even wait for an answer. He found that he was increasingly confused as to his reaction to the woman, as if she had somehow cast a spell over him. Something about her was pulling him towards her whether or not he wanted to and he didn't like it, not one bit. As he and Garran turned away, heading back for the Street of the Merchants and to the business they were there to conduct, the young woman's soft voice called after him.

"Sirrah," she said. "I should like to know your name so that I may tell my father. He will want to thank you."

Maximus paused and he turned to face her. Her voice had a silky, sensual quality, something he found quite alluring. *A siren's song*, he thought ominously. *She is trying to bewitch me with that honeyed tone.*

"As I said, gratitude is not necessary," he said somewhat stiffly. "We were honored to be of assistance."

He turned to leave but, again, the woman stopped him. "Wait, please," she said. By the time he turned around with some impatience to look at her, she was walking towards him, clutching the little girl beside her. Her lovely features were considerably softer. "I… I am sorry I became angry with you when you were only trying to help. I am afraid that my fear got the better of me. If you would forgive my behavior, I would consider it a personal favor."

Lord, but that tone was smooth and gentle. He almost closed his eyes to it, letting it flow over him, infiltrate him, and he knew that if he let himself go that she could talk him into anything with those dulcet tones. He wanted to walk away from her and away from the situation. He truly did. He had no involvement here and was anxious to be about his business. But gazing into those bright, blue eyes, he realized he couldn't simply walk away from her. Something about her had reached out to grab him.

"There is nothing to forgive, my lady," he said, less stiffly. "Your fright is understandable."

She smiled faintly and Maximus went weak in the knees. He simply couldn't help it. He'd never seen such a beautiful smile. "You are too gracious," she said. Then, she indicated the girl in her grasp. "This is my sister, Lady Isadora de Lara. I am Lady Courtly. My father is Kellen de Lara. Mayhap you know of him."

Maximus cocked an eyebrow. "The Lord of the Trilateral Castles?" he asked. "Trelystan, Hyssington and Caradoc Castles. Your father is Viscount Trelystan."

Courtly nodded. "He is, indeed," she said, surprised that the man should know her father in such detail. "Then you know him?"

Maximus nodded. "I do," he replied. He had a mind like a steel trap and never forgot anything once he'd learnt it. "The Marcher lords of de Lara hold nearly the entire southern portion of the Welsh Marches as the Lord Sheriffs. Everyone knows of your family, my lady. They are great and powerful. And I know your father well. He is a fine and just man."

Courtly's smile grew. "Thank you," she said sincerely. "I should like to tell him who saved my sister and me from certain death."

Maximus hesitated for a moment. A modest man, he wasn't one to easily accept praise or accolades, but he saw no harm in giving the lady his name. Moreover, he wanted her to know it. As foolish as it was, he wanted her to know *him*.

"De Shera," he replied. "I am Maximus de Shera and my counterpart is Garran de Moray."

He was pointing to Garran beside him but Courtly didn't look at Garran. She was focused on Maximus as the smile faded from her face.

"De Shera," she murmured, mulling the name over. "I believe I have heard my father speak of you. You have brothers, do you not?"

"Two."

She nodded as her recollection returned. "Indeed, I have heard my father speak of you and your brothers," she said. "One of your brothers is an earl, is he not?"

"The Earl of Coventry."

"My father says the de Sheras are de Montfort's muscle."

Maximus shrugged. "De Montfort has many men that fit that description," he replied humbly. "We are simply part of a group under de Montfort's command."

Courtly eyed the very big, very broad knight. He had brown hair, close-cropped, and a neatly trimmed beard and mustache that embraced his square-jawed face. His eyes were a very dark green, a color of the jade stone she had seen once on a piece of jewelry her father had given her mother. His features were even and well-formed, and he had shoulders so broad that she was sure the man couldn't fit through a doorway with ease. His hands were the size of trenchers.

He was exceptionally handsome, which did nothing to ease the embarrassment of what had happened when the linen rope had given way and she had fallen on top of him. The man's face had been pressed right up against her genitals. She could still feel his scratchy beard against her tender core. The recollection of it sent shivers through her body, a quivering she did not understand, but all she knew was that it fed her embarrassment and caused her palms to sweat. Or perhaps there was more to it than simply embarrassment, something primal and wanting. She simply didn't know. All she knew was that she'd never known anything like it.

"I am sure you are being modest," she finally said. "I am not even a warrior, yet I have heard the de Shera name frequently. I am honored and fortunate that you were here to save my sister and me. It will make a fine story to tell my friends, in any case. They will be quite envious."

A flicker of a smile twitched on Maximus' lips. "I hope it does not cause them all to run out and set buildings on fire, hoping I will come around to save them."

Courtly laughed softly, displaying lovely, white teeth. "Would it be such a burden, then?" she teased. "You are a hero, after all."

He shook his head firmly. "I am nothing of the sort," he said. "I happened to be here at the right time and that is all."

Courtly's eyes glimmered. "As I said, we were most fortunate."

Maximum simply nodded. The conversation was dwindling but he didn't want it to. He rather liked talking to her. Her voice was like music to his ears and her smile made him forget all time and space and reason. It was hypnotic. He could have spent all day listening to her laugh. If she were a siren, then he was gladly, and quite happily, succumbing to her deadly charms. He didn't care in the least. But he didn't want to make a fool of himself by lingering over a dying conversation so he cleared his throat softly, sorry to see it end.

"I will take no more of your time, my lady," he said, eyeing the little girl clutched against her sister. "Before I go, however, tell me where your father is so I may send him word of your predicament. Surely he will want to know."

Courtly looked at the hostel, which was now crumbling with flame and ash. Men were attempting to douse the fire with buckets of water, sending great plumes of white smoke into the air.

"I am not entirely sure where he is," she said. "He said he had business to attend this morning but did not say where. My sister and I have nowhere to go at the moment. I suppose we should simply wait here for him to return."

Maximus, too, watched men struggle to put out the flame. The building was a total loss as people scrambled to keep the fire from spreading to the other closely-crowded buildings surrounding it.

"Have you no one to wait with you?" he asked. "No servants or soldiers? None of your father's men?"

Courtly shook her head. "He took his men with him," she replied. "My sister and I had a secured room and our nurse has gone to do some shopping. We were alone when the fire started."

Maximus turned to look at her. "Do you know how it started?"

Again, she shook her head. "I do not," she replied. "We heard the shouts and I went to open the door to the corridor and found it was filled with smoke. That is when I tied the bed linens together to make a rope."

Maximus was intently studying her lovely face as she spoke. He realized that she had a slight lisp, which he found very sweet. There was nothing imperfect about the woman as far as he was concerned.

"That was very resourceful of you," he said. "Not many women would have had the presence of mind to do that."

Courtly smiled bashfully. "It seemed the right thing to do," she said. "I certainly wasn't going to wait for the flames to consume us. I had to save my sister."

He nodded his approval. "And you did," he said. "I shall wait with you until your father returns. That is the least I can do for the woman who saved her sister."

Courtly was back to laughing softly, now feeling giddy in his presence. She'd never felt giddy in her entire life so this was something new and rather thrilling. Contrary to their embarrassing introduction, she was quickly overcoming it and was now feeling at ease with the man. He was kind and considerate. She rather liked talking to him.

"Truly, that is not necessary," she said. "I am sure my father will return any moment."

Maximus simply nodded. "And I will leave when he comes," he said, eyeing her. "But not before."

Courtly wasn't sure what to say to that. She was very flattered that he should take it upon himself to remain with her until her father returned. She wanted to pretend he was doing it because there was something about her personally that he liked, not simply because he felt a sense of chivalry towards her, but it was a foolish hope and she knew it. Still, it was fun to pretend. She would probably never see him again after this so she would take what time she could with him, a handsome and honorable knight of the highest order, and make the most of it.

"You are kind, my lord," she said, looking away rather coyly when he turned his gaze to her. "Now I am feeling quite guilty for having called you a foul beast. You are nothing of the kind."

Maximus suppressed a grin. "You have already apologized for that."

She glanced at him. "I realize that, but I want to make sure you understand that I am truly sorry," she said. Then her focus moved to the building in front of them, now a heap of flaming ruins. She sighed heavily. "Oh, dear… all of our possessions were in there. I did not even have time to throw them into the street. I suppose I really did not think to because it all happened so fast."

Garran, standing on the other side of the ladies, heard her. "Mayhap it is good that you did not, my lady," he said. "There were thieves running off with the possessions that had been thrown out into the streets. Had they run off with yours, we would have had to tear apart the northern end of the city looking for them."

Courtly looked at the big, broad knight with the black eyes. "I would not have asked that of you, I assure you," she said. "But I find it quite sad that people must steal because they do not have food to eat or clothing to wear. That is why they steal, you know.

They have nothing else."

Garran glanced at Maximus over the lady's blond head, seeing his own thoughts reflected in Maximus' eyes. *She is naïve, this one.* A crystal princess raised in a crystal palace with the only true grasp of the world being what she had been told. Women such as Lady Courtly rarely had a true idea of the evils of the world, protected as they were. Garran cleared his throat politely.

"Mayhap, my lady," he replied. "But it is also equally as likely that they are simply greedy or wicked. It could be any number of reasons."

Courtly was still watching the smoldering ruins. "Poverty does terrible things to people."

Maximus was looking at her. There was something sad in her tone. "Poverty and greed drive men to do bold and wicked things," he said, changing the subject because he didn't want to debate the morals of mankind with her. He'd seen far more than this guileless lady could ever lay claim to. "I seem to recall that the de Laras have a townhome in Oxford. Why is it that you did not stay there instead of this hostel?"

If Courtly noticed the obvious change in focus, and she would have had to have been daft not to, she didn't comment on it. She smiled politely.

"You know a great deal about us, Sir Maximus," she said. "I wonder what else you know?"

He gave her a half-grin. "I have always been one to remember tiny, little details," he said. "Once I hear or read something, I never forget it. It is a gift or a curse, depending on how one looks at it."

"How do you look at it?"

"It depends upon the information."

Courtly's smile turned genuine. "I think it is a wonderful gift," she said. "As for the de Lara home, we have one in Kennington, which is a few miles south of Oxford. However, my father's sister is in residence right now and he dislikes her intensely, so we must stay in town."

Maximus snorted. "I had an uncle like that," he muttered. "My father could not stand to be around him for a variety of reasons. He is the uncle that we used to... well, it does not matter what we used to do. In any case, it is a pity your stay in town resulted in the loss of your possessions, but at least you retained your lives. That is what matters most, is it not?"

Courtly was watching him intently. "What did you used to do to your uncle?"

Maximus shook his head. "Childhood antics, my lady. Not worth mentioning."

"Will you tell me if I ask very nicely?"

"Nay."

"Why not?"

"Because we were terrible children and I do not want you to think ill of me."

Courtly laughed softly. "I would never do that," she said, a mischievous glimmer in her eye. "I will beg you if I have to."

"Do not beg."

"I will. I am about to do it. I swear, I will."

Maximus was trying not to grin, trying not to look at her, but she was being very charming. It was extremely difficult to resist.

"Beg all you like," he said, turning away from her so he wouldn't have to look at that lovely, charming face. "I will never tell you. I would rather die than tell you."

Courtly could sense a game afoot. "That seems rather harsh," she said, feigning seriousness. "Did you steal from him, then?"

"Nay."

"Beat him?"

"Nay."

She sighed deeply. "Then I cannot guess what it is," she said, pretending to be resigned and miserable. "It would seem that I must go to my grave not knowing what you and your brothers did to this uncle. It is a terrible curse you have put upon me. Do you not know that a woman's curiosity must be satisfied or else?"

He looked at her then, grinning. "Or else what?"

She could see she had his interest and she looked away, being playful. "I cannot tell you," she said, turning the tables on him. "You would not like the answer."

"Tell me."

She shook her head. "I would rather die than tell you," she said, using his own words. "And do not beg because it will not do any good."

She was clever, this one. Maximus appreciated her quick wit very much, seeing how she had turned the tables against him. Oddly, it made him respect her, for this was no simple-minded woman. She was sharp. With that in mind, he sighed in contemplation.

"Very well, then," he said, folding his arms across his broad chest and pretending to be cross. "I will tell you what my brothers and I did to our uncle if you will tell me what happens when a woman's curiosity is not sated."

Courtly looked at him, pointing a finger at him. "Quickly," she hissed. "Tell me swiftly. It will be less painful that way. *Hurry!*"

Maximus did as he was told without hesitation. "My uncle would fart uncontrollably when he slept and my brothers and I would light his farts a-fire," he said. "One time, we burned up his breeches."

Courtly burst out in a loud guffaw, slapping her hand over mouth to stifle the laughter. "You didn't!"

"We did."

She snorted into her hand, laughing deeply, but Maximus feigned a scowl at her. "Stop laughing," he muttered swiftly.

"Quickly, tell me what would have happened had I not sated your curiosity."

Courtly removed her hand from her mouth, displaying her lovely smile in full bloom. "Nothing," she said, throwing up her hands. "I simply said that so you would feel sorry for me and tell me what I wanted to know."

Maximus pretended to be very cross when, in truth, he was swept up in her gentle flirt as surely as a leaf swept up in a breeze. He had no control over anything at the moment. He was purely at her mercy.

"You are a terrible woman to tease me like that," he said. "Can you not see how gullible I am?"

Courtly's smile never left her face, her gaze riveted to him as if he were the only man in the entire world. "I cannot imagine the great Maximus de Shera to be gullible," she said. "I would imagine you are the smartest brother of all. You said so yourself."

He shook his head. "I did not say I was the smartest brother," he corrected her. "I simply said that I remember everything I am told. If my brothers heard me say that I was the smartest of all of them, they would beat me and roll me in pitch."

Courtly giggled at his admission. She was coming to find the man very humorous and very delightful. As she opened her mouth to reply, a distant shouting stopped her. Both she and Maximus turned in the direction of the avenue leading from St. Clement's Church in time to see well-armed men on expensive horses heading in their direction. Maximus recognized the de Lara bird of prey immediately.

Through the smoke and ash, armored men surrounded them and the man in the lead, riding a big, dappled charger, leapt from his steed. His gaze was on the women and on Maximus in particular. His confusion, and his concern, was apparent.

"De Shera?" he addressed Maximus, his brow furrowed, before

looking to Courtly. "Court, what has happened? What goes on?"

Courtly pointed to the pile of smoldering ruins that had once been their hostel. "There was a fire, Papa," she told him seriously. "Sir Maximus and Sir Garran saved our lives. We had to jump from the window and they were here to save us."

Kellen de Lara, Viscount Trelystan and Lord Sheriff of the Southern Marches, looked at his eldest daughter with horror. A man in his early forties, he was fair and handsome, his face weathered from the years of harsh elements and harsh campaigns. His gaze moved between the smoking building and his daughter's earnest face. Stunned, he simply shook his head.

"Sweet Jesù," he murmured, reaching out to grasp his daughters, the both of them. "Is this true?"

"It is."

"And you jumped from the building?"

"Aye, Papa."

Kellen was nearly beside himself. "Are you well?" he demanded softly. "Did you hurt yourself in any way?"

Courtly shook her head. "We are well," she replied, her gaze moving to Maximus. "It is Sir Maximus you must thank, Papa. He was a hero."

Maximus, embarrassed by the praise, was already shaking his head even as Kellen turned to him. "It was not as much as that, my lord," he said. "Your daughter was quite resourceful and constructed a rope from bed linens, using it to lower herself with. All we did was hold the rope steady and make sure she and her sister came to no harm."

Kellen was pale with shock. "I can never thank you enough, Sir Maximus," he said. "What you have done… you have saved my children. I am in your debt."

Maximus shook his head, uncomfortable. "That is unnecessary, my lord," he assured the man. "I was happy to help. But now that you are here, I must go about my business. I did not want to leave your daughters unescorted until you returned."

Kellen was overwhelmed with the situation and with Maximus' chivalry. He knew the man in name and reputation only, as he'd never had the opportunity to work closely with him. De Montfort kept the de Shera brothers close to him, like personal attack dogs, so it wasn't often that the brothers mingled with the other barons. Now, Maximus was in his midst and had evidently done him a great service. He owed the man.

"Again, you have my deepest thanks," he said. "You as well, Sir Garran, have my thanks. May I at least invite you both to sup with us this eve? I should like to demonstrate my thanks for your heroics. Invite your brothers as well. I've not had the opportunity to converse with the three of you other than cursory discussions."

Maximus was hesitant. "Your offer is generous, my lord, but my brothers may have other plans," he said. Then, he caught a glimpse of Courtly's hopeful expression and he knew that, come what may, he was going to accept de Lara's invitation. It would give him another opportunity to see Courtly again. "I, however, have no such plans. I would be happy to sup with you."

Kellen smiled and Courtly positively beamed. "Excellent," Kellen said. Then, he turned to eye the heap of ashes behind him. "We have been supping at the hostel but it would seem our dining hall has been burned to the ground. Come out to Kennington House, south of Oxford, and we shall dine tonight in the halls of my ancestors. We shall put on such a feast as to impress even the likes of you. Will you come, then?"

Maximus nodded, trying not to stare at Courtly, who was smiling at him quite openly. "I will be honored, my lord," he said. "I will see you this eve."

With that, he nodded his farewells to the de Lara group, excusing himself, and together he and Garran headed back down the avenue, back to the spice merchant to reclaim the licorice root and other things he had purchased. Already, he was thinking on the evening and the time he would spend gazing at Courtly de Lara's magnificent face. Already, he was missing her as he headed back down the avenue.

It was an effort not to turn around and look at her, but he didn't want to do it and seem over-eager. His thoughts, however, lingered on the lovely Courtly as her father took charge of both her and her sister, ushering them onto horses and making their way to Kennington House where the vile de Lara aunt resided.

Even as they reached the spice vendor, Maximus was thinking on gold-spun hair and on luminous, blue eyes. As Garran collected the packages they had already paid for, Maximus caught sight of an entire shelf of perfumed oil. He gazed at it, a thought coming to him, as Garran headed out of the stall.

"We must find Ty," Garran said, squinting down the avenue to see if he could catch sight of the youngest de Shera brother. "We need to get this stuff to Lady de Shera."

Maximus was still looking at the perfumed oil, breaking from his train of thought as Garran spoke. He eyed Garran, eyed the oil, and then pretended to look at other things.

"Go and find my brother," he instructed. "I will look the wares over one more time to see if there is something else we can purchase to help Jeniver's belly."

Garran went without another word. Maximus peered from the doorway of the stall, casually, watching the knight head down the avenue in search of Tiberius. When he was positive that Garran wasn't going to turn around and head back in his direction, he went straight to the spice merchant and pointed to the perfumed oils on the shelf.

A few minutes later, a beautifully wrapped phial of rose-scented oil was tucked safely in Maximus' tunic, intended for a certain young lady when he saw her at sup that night.

# CHAPTER TWO

*Kennington House*
*Oxford South*

KENNINGTON HOUSE HAD been built the previous century and had come into the de Lara clan through marriage. It had originally been a de Vere property those years ago and the de Veres had spared little expense for it; a very large and lavish hall was attached to a two-storied secondary building that contained four smaller chambers on the bottom floor and a massive, master's chamber on the upper floor. The house itself was shaped like a "T", with the window of the master's chamber facing the church across the road because the pious de Veres liked it that way.

In the smaller chamber on the ground floor, Courtly sat on a simple, oak chair, working on a piece of embroidery that wasn't her own. Her aunt, Lady Ellice, had given it to her when they had arrived at Kennington House earlier that day and had told her to finish it. The woman had given her and Isadora no greeting other than to hand them projects to complete, for her attention was fully on her younger brother, Kellen, and the distinct distaste they had for one another. A childless spinster, Ellice had no patience for children or even for people in general. She was a bitter, nasty shrew.

Therefore, while Ellice and Kellen went through the motions of a stiff greeting as Kellen explained the reason behind their arrival at Kennington, Courtly and Isadora disappeared into the house and into the small bedchamber they usually slept in during the times they had visited. Neither girl wanted to be around their father and aunt when the conversation turned nasty, which it usually did fairly quickly. It had, for as long as the girls could remember, an underlying hatred and bitterness from Ellice towards her brother, although that underlying hatred had never been explained. It was simply the way of things.

As Courtly sat on the chair, in a linen surcoat that smelled of smoke, working on the small piece of embroidery that was a hummingbird upon a flower, she could hear her father's agitated voice and Ellice's low, threatening one, both of them still out in the small courtyard. She sighed heavily as she listened. She didn't understand how siblings could not get on with one another and it was like this every time they visited.

"Shall we stay here with Auntie now that our lodging has burned?" Isadora asked. She had a pair of Ellice's stockings in her hand and had been commanded to sew a hole in the heel. "Court, I do not wish to stay here. I do not like staying with Auntie in the least."

Courtly looked at her younger sister. At eleven years of age, Isadora was a frail, delicate thing. She was also quite smart and quite vocal, which could get her into trouble at times. With light brown hair and her sister's big, blue eyes, she looked like a little, porcelain doll, and Courtly was the only mother she had ever known. Given that the girls' mother had perished of a fever when Isadora had been two years of age, the task of raising the toddler had been given over to Courtly until she went to foster and she was, naturally, very protective of the girl, and especially protective from their shrewish aunt.

"Nor do I," Courtly said patiently. "But until Papa can make other arrangements, we must stay where he tells us. For tonight, it will be here."

Isadora didn't want to sew the hole in her aunt's smelly stocking. She threw it onto the bed.

"Why does Auntie make us do her terrible chores?" she demanded. "Her stockings stink of rot and I do not want to mend them."

Courtly extended the half-finished bird embroidery. "Would you rather work on this?"

Isadora frowned, crossing her arms stubbornly over her chest. "Nay," she said. Then, she threw herself onto the small, spartanly-covered bed. "I do not want to stay here at all!"

Courtly watched her sister verge on a tantrum. "You may as well accept that we will at least stay the night here," she said. "Fussing over it will not change things. Besides, Sir Maximus and Sir Garran are to join us tonight for sup. We cannot leave before we properly thank them for saving us."

Isadora rolled over onto her back, eyeing her sister. Her tantrum was forgotten as she thought on the powerful knights who had saved them from certain death. Her thoughts lingered particularly on the de Shera brother and the way her usually-reserved sister had interacted with him. Courtly was usually quite controlled and not willing to give members of the opposite sex her attention, but she had clearly broken that rule for Sir Maximus. It was an intriguing thought.

"You like Sir Maximus," she said bluntly. Tact was not her strong suit. "I could tell. You smiled at him a lot."

Courtly kept her head down, resuming her embroidery. "I must be polite to him," she said evenly. "What would you have me do? Be rude to the man who saved us?"

"You fell on his head."

Courtly couldn't help it, then. Her cheeks flushed a deep red as she thought on the very embarrassing position she found herself in when she had plunged from the makeshift rope. She could not have planned that fall to be any worse than it had been. She had hit him at precisely the right angle to make her legs split and go along his shoulders, his head right in between them. She could still feel his hot breath against her tender core and it caused bolts of shock to race up her spine at the mere hint of the memory.

"It was an accident, I assure you," she told her sister, not looking at her. "Believe me when I say that if I'd had another choice on the manner in which I landed on him, I more than likely would have taken it."

Isadora could see that her sister was humiliated by the event but, instead of avoiding the subject, she grinned. It wasn't often that she got a rise out of her serious sister.

"Your skirt was around his head," she giggled. "You sat right on his head!"

Courtly rolled her eyes with some misery. "Aye, I did, you little goat," she snapped softly. "I will hear no more about it, do you understand? If I do, I shall spank you soundly."

Isadora continued to giggle, not at all fearful of Courtly's threat. She rolled around on the bed, silly and snorting, kicking her legs up in the air.

"He is very handsome," she said. "I like his beard. When he smiles, his eyes crinkle."

Courtly was growing flustered as she continued with her embroidery. "No more talk of Sir Maximus," she snapped but it was without force, although her mind was inevitably lingering on the very big knight with the well-trimmed beard. Indeed, he was quite handsome. "We will be seeing him tonight and that will be the end of it."

Isadora stopped kicking her legs in the air and rolled onto her side, propping her head up on her hand. "Is that what you want?"

she asked. "Never to see him again?"

Courtly eyed her sister. "Mayhap not," she admitted. "I... I suppose I would like to see him again. But you know how Papa is. He does not like men around us. I have had six suitors and he has chased them all off."

Isadora shrugged. "But he cannot chase Sir Maximus off," she said. "He is bigger than Papa and more frightening. Mayhap he will be the one man Papa does not chase off."

Courtly shook her head, looking back to her embroidery. "I would not stake my life on that," she said, sounding defeated already. She would not have been opposed to Sir Maximus being the one man her father couldn't chase off, but alas, she was sure it was not to be. She paused before stabbing into the material again, her expression wistful. "But I do wish... I wish that, just once, he would not chase off a suitor. I will never marry if he does that."

Isadora sensed something in her sister, a longing she had never seen before. Courtly usually didn't care about the men their father chased off, but perhaps Sir Maximus was different. He certainly seemed different.

"Mayhap if you speak to Papa," she said helpfully. "Mayhap if you tell him you do not wish for him to chase away Sir Maximus, then he will not."

Courtly shook her head, firmly. "He will not listen," she said. "You know how he is. All men are evil and only have lust of the flesh on their mind. Therefore, I am afraid you and I will either be destined to be spinsters our entire lives or destined for the nunnery. That will be our only choices should Papa continue his ways, and I do not wish to end up at a nunnery."

Isadora gazed at her sister, her young thoughts lingering on the bearded knight. "Would you be Lady de Shera, then?"

Courtly shrugged coyly. "Mayhap."

Isadora was interrupted from replying when the chamber door

jerked open and a rather large woman stood in the doorway. Lady Ellice de Lara, a fair-haired and somewhat masculine woman, eyed her nieces with something just short of hostility. But that was usual with her, an embittered woman with a nasty attitude, particularly towards her brother's children. At the sight of the woman, Isadora sat bolt upright and grabbed the smelly hose she was supposed to be mending, grabbing for the needle and, in her haste, stabbing herself. The girl yelped and put the offended finger in her mouth as Ellice entered the room. Her gaze was mostly on Courtly.

"Well, well," she said, her eyes lingering on Courtly's fair head. "Busy at work, I see. Lady Courtly Love de Lara and her sister, Lady Isadora Adoration de Lara. Such grand names for rather small and insignificant ladies."

Courtly forced a smile at her aunt. "It is nice to see you again, Auntie," she said politely, not reacting to the insult dealt. "Did Papa tell you what happened in town? Issie and I were nearly killed in a fire. We lost all of our possessions."

Ellice looked her niece over, critically. "You seem well enough to me," she said. "And before you go begging for more clothing or other foolish trinkets, know that I have nothing for you. You will make do with what you have."

"We *have* nothing."

Ellice eyed her niece, snorting rudely after a moment, before turning her gaze to Isadora. "And you?" she said, eyeing the child. "You had better mend that stocking before nightfall or there will be consequences."

Isadora cowered as Courtly spoke up. "Auntie, she will have it done," she said, rather firmly. "You need not threaten her."

Ellice looked at Courtly, her eyes narrowing. "You accuse me of threatening her?"

"You just did."

Ellice didn't like being questioned in the least. She lived at

Kennington and ruled it with an iron fist, verbally abusing cringing servants. Her eldest niece was questioning that omnipotent power and that did not set well with her.

"Your mother," she finally snorted. "You look and act just like her. She did not know when to control her mouth, either."

Courtly didn't want to back down from the woman but she had no desire to fight with her, either. There was something very petulant and wicked about Ellice at times, something Courtly didn't want to tangle with. It would only come to no good end, mostly hers. Therefore, she lowered her gaze and turned back to her sewing.

"Thank you for providing us with shelter tonight, Auntie," she said politely. "If we could have some soap sent to us so that we may wash the smoke smell away, we would be grateful."

"I have no soap for you."

Courtly didn't acknowledge the nasty retort. "Then we will see you this evening at sup. Good day, Auntie."

She was essentially dismissing her aunt but doing in the nicest possible way. It was gaining the upper hand without obviously gaining it. Everyone in the room knew she was sending the woman on her way. Ellice frowned at her niece. She rather liked verbally sparring, even if she didn't like insolence, and was somewhat disappointed that Courtly had backed down. It frustrated her.

"Courtly Love," she scoffed as she turned away. "It is a foolish name. I told my brother it was a foolish name when you were born but your mother insisted. She said it was the embodiment of what a true lady should be; chaste and virtuous. What a foolish, foolish woman your mother was."

She was muttering as she turned for the door, heading out of the room without even shutting the ornately carved door panel of darkly stained oak. As the woman wandered down the corridor, Isadora leapt up from the bed and slammed the door, throwing the bolt.

"I do *not* want to stay here tonight!" she declared again. "Auntie is an evil witch!"

In spite of her tense expression, Courtly broke down into giggles. "Mayhap we shall not have to," she said. "Mayhap Papa is, even now, scouring the outskirts of Kennington for a place to stay. I am sure he does not wish to remain here as much as we don't."

Isadora remained by the door, listening to the corridor outside. She hissed. "I can still hear her," she said, frowning. "She is telling the servants not to bring us any soap!"

Courtly sighed heavily, shaking her head. "I shall speak with Papa," she said. "Not to worry. We shall have what we need. In fact, we should make a list of all we lost. Will you do that, Issie? Make a list?"

She proposed the list to distract her sister and the ruse worked. Isadora was flighty, and a bit dramatic, but she was also very intelligent. She nodded eagerly and came away from the door.

"I shall think of everything we had," she said. Then, her expression saddened. "I lost my pink, silk dress."

"And I lost my red brocade."

Isadora nodded, ticking off the contents of her bag in her head. She had been schooled by the monks at St. Mary's Church in the village of Trelystan when she had been younger, mostly because she had demanded of Kellen that she learn to read and write. With Courtly away fostering at the time, Kellen had been unable to deny his lonely, youngest daughter and took her to the monks at the church, whereupon they undertook the task of teaching the seven-year-old to write with the lure of much coinage donated by Kellen.

Four days a week, Kellen would take his daughter to the church and the monks would teach her how to read and write. Isadora, extremely bright, learned quickly and stopped going to the church after a year. At that point, Kellen should have sent her away to foster with her sister but found he simply couldn't bear to do it. His daughters reminded him of his wife, and he missed her greatly, so shortly after Isadora stopped going to the church, Kellen recalled Courtly from Prudhoe Castle. The older sister returned, reunited with her younger sibling, and Kellen proceeded to continue the girls' education himself.

The results were that the girls learned mathematics, military tactics, some literature, and military history. Kellen imparted upon them what he knew, that being mostly things that only knights would know from their schooling and fostering. Therefore, the girls were quite educated as a page or squire would be, and Courtly conveyed what she had learned at Prudhoe, so Isadora wasn't too one-sided. She could sew and sing, and knew how to run a household. But she liked mathematics and writing much better.

"I need parchment and quill!" Isadora announced as she hunted around the ill-furnished room. "What shall I use to write?"

Courtly glanced around. "I am not sure there would be anything here," she said. "Make a list in your mind and then we shall write it down later. For now, think on everything we had. That is a good start."

Isadora was already busy with her mental list. She began rattling off the contents of her satchel, counting the lost pieces on her fingers, and then prompting Courtly to do the same. As Courtly stitched the hummingbird and listed off the possessions she had lost, Isadora committed what she could to memory.

When she began speaking of her pink, silk dress and how she was determined to have another one made, Courtly's thoughts drifted to the red brocade she had lost and how she would not be able to wear it at the feast that night. All she would be able to wear for Sir Maximus was the smoke-stenched, dark green wool that she currently wore. It was all she had in the world.

So much for making an elegant impression on a man she realized that she wanted very much to impress.

# CHAPTER THREE

*The One-Eyed Raven Inn*
*Oxford proper*

"**K**ELLEN DE LARA is a man with a formidable reputation. Saving his daughters unquestionably puts you in his debt."

The words were spoken by Gallus de Shera, the eldest de Shera brother and the current Earl of Coventry. He was the intelligence behind the trio of brothers, men known as the Lords of Thunder, while Maximus was the muscle and Tiberius was the life force that kept them all bound together. These men, this tight-knit group, were some of the most powerful men in England.

All three brothers, and the entire House of de Shera, were staunch supporters of Simon de Montfort and his opposition to King Henry, and they were currently in Oxford because de Montfort was convening the greatest group of barons yet, men that would place demands upon a king who seemed more intent on deliberately forgetting all of the pledges he had made over the past several years to his barons, pledges that were extraordinarily complicated during this dark and complicated time. The gist of the situation was that de Montfort intended that in this place in time, and upon this country, there would be fairness and equality. He intended that the barons should have a say in how the country was run, among other things, and the de Shera brothers would be a part of that bold, new world, hence their presence in Oxford. They were here for a purpose, and that purpose was soon to come.

As the afternoon of the most eventful day began to wane towards evening, the three brothers and their four sworn knights sat in the common room of an inn they had taken over upon their arrival to Oxford four days earlier. There were gourd pitchers of cheap wine on the table before them and the remains of a few loaves of bread. The men-at-arms they had brought with them, at least most of them, were in various positions around the room, eating and drinking and cavorting with several women that could only be described as easy prey. In the smoke-hazed tavern, the knights ignored the antics of the men around them and settled in to discuss not only the events of the day, but future plans as well.

Called The One-Eyed Raven, the inn had a cavernous common room but only five sleeping rooms, all of which belonged to the de Shera party for the duration of their stay in Oxford. The main room was long, with two barkeep areas full of barrels of wine, cups, and other implements, and tables enough to seat up to sixty people at times. Most of the tables were crudely built and were tables in only the literal sense; whether or not they actually held together under the weight of food or wine was another matter entirely. A small hearth by the door and then another larger hearth about mid-point in the room kept the big chamber warm and smelling of acrid smoke. A large pack of dirty, mean dogs congregated near the bigger hearth, waiting for scraps of food to fall upon the uneven dirt floor.

In the midst of the noisy and smelly common room, the de Shera group listened to Gallus. Maximus sat next to his older brother, having just explained, between big gulps of wine, what had transpired with Kellen de Lara's daughters earlier that day. It had barely been a mention from Maximus during the course of a conversation that had been dominated by talk of de Montfort's parliament but Gallus thought it was a rather important event. He veered talk away from de Montfort's gathering for a few minutes to focus on his humble brother's heroics.

"Truly, Max," he said. "You saved the man's daughters. I seem to remember hearing that he only had two daughters and that his wife was long dead. It is a great thing you did."

Maximus didn't like praise. He simply shook his head. "Anyone would have done the same thing."

Gallus fought off a grin. Maximus was far too modest. "Mayhap," he concurred. "But it was you and Garran. What did de Lara say to you? Does he even know?"

Maximus nodded. "He knows," he replied. "I waited with the daughters until he returned from his errand. He thanked me profusely and told me that he is in my debt."

Gallus looked at the others. "You see?" he said. "The great Lord Sheriff of the Southern Marches is now indebted to my brother. That is a great ally to have, Max."

Maximus merely grunted, drinking of his wine. He wasn't thinking of the de Lara debt so much as he was thinking about the eldest de Lara daughter. He hadn't been able to get the woman out of his mind since he met her, and with the rose-scented oil tucked safely away in his tunic, the obsession with her was growing. The dulcet vision of silken blond hair and big, blue eyes was ingrained in his brain, something he could not and would not shake. But he was terrified to let on his thoughts, even to his brothers and trusted knights. He glanced around the table, and most especially at the men sworn to his family. The talent and bloodlines of de Shera knights ran deep.

*De Wolfe, de Moray, and du Bois.* The eldest sons of the great Wolfe of the North, William de Wolfe, served them. Scott de Wolfe was a big, brawny man with blond hair, greatly resembling his Scottish heritage and his twin, Troy, was dark and muscular like their father. Garran, of course, was the son of the mighty Bose de Moray, a former captain of the guard for Henry III, and Stefan du Bois rounded out the powerful group. Young, but extremely strong, big and intelligent, Stefan was descended from the great House of de Lohr on his mother's side and the formidable House of du Bois on his father's. Aye, 'twas a mighty stable the House of de Shera was privileged to command. Maximus considered himself extremely lucky.

But aside from the great bloodlines, the knights were also very trustworthy and Maximus considered them all close friends. Perhaps when he was willing to divulge what he was thinking about the eldest de Lara daughter, he would mention it to them. *Perhaps*. But he wasn't ready to take that step. Maximus had never been known to show attention to a woman, *any* woman, because he was more of a warrior than any of them. He breathed, slept, and ate the knighthood. He feared the shock of knowing the Thunder Warrior had an eye towards a certain lady might send them all into fits.

"We have been invited to sup with de Lara this eve," he finally said, watching a host of surprised faces turn to him. "He invited all of us. I told him I did not know of my brothers' plans but assured him that I would join him."

Tiberius looked at Gallus. "I have no plans," he said, already thinking on a fine meal at the de Lara table. It would undoubtedly be better than the meal at the inn. "What about you?"

Gallus shook his head. "I have no such plans, either," he replied, but instinctively, his attention turned to the rooms above them where his pregnant wife was resting. "However, I am not entirely sure how well Jeni feels. I am not sure if she will want to accompany us."

Maximus shrugged. "Then you should remain with her," he said. "Has the licorice root helped?"

Gallus nodded. "Somewhat," he replied. "The chamomile has helped even more. At least she has been able to eat something."

Maximus nodded. "I am glad it helped," he said. "Mayhap it is not my place to say so, but it might have been better for her had she remained at Isenhall."

Isenhall Castle near Coventry was their home and seat of the mighty Earl of Coventry. Gallus held the title and had since it had been passed down through their mother. In fact, thoughts of home brought about thoughts of their beloved mother, who had been quite ill as of late.

Any mention of Isenhall had their thoughts turning to Lady Honey de Shera, the matriarch of the family. Her given name was Charlotte, but Gallus' father had called her "Honey" because he had declared her as fine and as sweet as honey. Everyone called the woman Honey, including her sons. Moreover, they were very attached to her and her illness was weighing heavily upon them. Being away from her during this time did not bode well for any of them.

"Nay," Gallus finally muttered, his good humor fading as he toyed with his wine cup. "My wife wanted to come with me and I could not deny her. With her difficult pregnancy, it is my sense that remaining behind with Honey would have been more of a strain upon her. You know that she would want to tend Honey, or aid the physics at the very least, and that is too much for her at this time. And she cannot help Honey no matter how hard she would try. Nay, it is better to let her come with us and get away from the death vigil. But, with God as my witness, even though we are in Oxford for this great gathering, my heart is not here. It is back at Isenhall with our mother."

Maximus and Tiberius sobered greatly at the thought of their languishing mother; a cancer in her belly, the physics had said, and the woman had lain at death's door for more than a month. She was unconscious most of the time but had become vaguely lucid twice, at least enough so that they could communicate with her. The first time, only Gallus' wife had been with her but the second time, Maximus had been present. His mother's words of wisdom still rattled in his head.

"Honey knows how we feel," Maximus murmured as Tiberius took a very large drink of wine. Tiberius was more emotional than the rest of them and tended to weep at the mention of his dying mother. Maximus eyed his younger brother before continuing. "She knew about de Montfort's gathering in Oxford, the parliament that he is convening. She has known about it for months, before she fell terribly ill. When she awoke from her deep sleep and asked me what I was doing praying beside her bed, I told her that we would remain with her until the very end. Jeniver heard me, and your wife further heard when Honey told me that the world would not stop because of her. She told me that we had a responsibility to England and that we had to go with de Montfort. There was no arguing with her about it."

Tiberius, unable to contain his emotion, wiped at his eyes. "So we left her with only a physic for comfort," he said, grieved. "I did not want to come to Oxford. I told all of you as much. I wanted to remain with my mother."

Gallus and Maximus looked at their brother, not unsympathetic. "And risk Honey waking up to your face, seeing that you had not continued with your commitment to de Montfort and to England?" Gallus pointed out. "She would climb out of her deathbed and beat you with a switch, and you know it. We discussed this before we left, Ty. We can do nothing to help her. Our mother's fate is consigned to God. We are doing what she wants us to do. We are securing England's future, for us and for our children."

Tiberius wasn't happy but he understood. It was what their mother wanted, and no one disobeyed Honey and lived to tell the tale. With a heavy sigh, he poured himself more wine. Maximus watched his brother, knowing the man was hurting like they all were. There was nothing they could do for their mother and, for the powerful de Shera brothers, it was a difficult fact to accept. Resigned, he moved to pour himself more wine also, noting the expression of his knights across the leaning table. His gaze fell upon Scott.

"Your father should be in town," he said to the brawny knight, changing the subject away from the gloom of Honey de Shera. "He said he would meet us here from when we last saw him at Kenilworth. Has he contacted you yet?"

Drawn into the conversation, Scott shook his head. "He has not," he replied. "I am sure he will be here any day now."

Gallus nodded. "I have sent men out to scour the town, leaving word for him at other inns," he said. "He will know where to find us when he arrives."

"I expect my father to arrive shortly, also," Stefan spoke up from the end of the table. "You know he will want to be a part of this, on behalf of the Earl of Canterbury. David de Lohr is a very, very old man and does not travel, so he will send my father in his stead."

Gallus lifted his eyebrows. "I have not seen my uncle in many years," he said wistfully. "He is, in truth, my mother's uncle, but David is a living legend. I remember him well from my childhood, visiting Canterbury on two occasions. The man is well into his eighties by now."

Stefan grinned. "He is my great-grandfather," he said. "I grew up with the man. He celebrated his eighty-eighth year this past March but I would wager he could still take all of us on in a sword fight. Old de Lohr's never die. They live on and on until someone finally digs a hole in the ground and forces them into it. Even then, they will not go easily."

Gallus smiled knowingly at the knight who was his distant cousin. "My grandfather, Christopher de Lohr, passed away eleven years ago," he said. "The man lived a very long and very full life. His was a great loss."

Stefan's smile faded. "I do not believe my great-grandfather has gotten over it," he said. "I can still hear him sitting in his solar at Canterbury, speaking to an empty chair. My mother told me that he was speaking to his brother. He did that for years. He probably does it still."

Gallus thought on the legendary de Lohrs, as his mother was Christopher de Lohr's youngest daughter. He was very proud to carry those legendary bloodlines. As his thoughts lingered on his very big and very wise grandfather, a man he had much admired, Maximus finished what was left in his wine cup and set the empty cup on the table.

"As much as I would like to reminisce about our grandfather, I have other plans for this evening," he said, changing the subject back to the focus at hand. Then, he looked around the table. "Who is going with me to de Lara's table?"

The knights were already standing up, as was Tiberius, eager to experience something other than the stale food and stuffy atmosphere of The One-Eyed Raven. But Gallus remained seated, looking up at the group on their feet.

"I should remain with my wife," he said, with some regret. "If she is feeling better, mayhap we will come later. Where are you going, anyway?"

Maximus pointed towards the south. "Kennington House," he said. "Since their hostel burned, de Lara will evidently be staying there."

Gallus's eyebrows drew together. "Why were they staying in a hostel in the first place if they have a home outside of the city?"

Maximus snorted. "Lady Courtly told me that they do not stay there because her father's sister resides there and they cannot stand one another," he said, his grin breaking through. "This should be an interesting evening, then. Are you sure you do not want to come?"

"Nay."

"Not even for the entertainment value of de Lara fighting with his sister?"

Gallus grinned. "I will think on it," he said. "If it is a good fight, make sure to tell me about it."

Maximus shook his head. "I will not," he said. "If you cannot summon the will to come, why should I tell you anything? You will be left to wonder."

Gallus waved him off. "Go, then," he said, watching his brothers and knights turn for the door that would take them out to the livery. "And if the sister starts throwing pots, I hope you get caught in the crossfire."

He heard Maximus laugh all the way out the door.

*Kennington House*

COURTLY AND ISADORA sat in the massive hall, listening to their father and aunt screaming at each other in the kitchen that was across the yard from the hall. The small servant's door was open, the one that led to the yard, and they could hear every word spoken as the fight raged. From the gist of what was being spoken, it was apparent that Ellice had no intention of providing a meal to her brother's guests and Kellen was enraged. Since he controlled the de Lara fortune, he threatened to stop his support of Kennington if Ellice didn't produce a feast of epic proportions. Even with the warning, Ellice was still not inclined to do so.

The girls sat at a large table, one of four large tables in the massive dining hall of Kennington, surrounded by a cold room, dead hearth, and no food. It was dark outside, as night had fallen, so the ladies were essentially sitting in the dark and cold, wondering what was going to happen to the evening's meal. Guests were expected at any moment and they had nothing to offer.

At least, nothing to offer from Ellice, but Courtly had never been one to sit around and lament a situation. If there was something that could be done, she would find it. She was rather resourceful that way, as the bed-linen rope had proved earlier in the day. She was a thinker, a doer, and this situation simply wasn't acceptable. Her aunt was being stubborn and belligerent as far as she was concerned, and she was growing nearly as frustrated as her father as she sat there, arm around Isadora, listening to the battle.

Courtly didn't want to be embarrassed in front of a man she truly wanted to impress, but with her smoke-filled dress, she was already at a disadvantage. No food for a feast would be the last nail in the coffin. The man would run off and tell the world that the House of de Lara was filled with savages. Not that she cared what the world in particular thought, but she was greatly concerned with what Sir Maximus de Shera thought. It was an odd sensation to actually care what a man thought about her. She'd never experienced that before. Therefore, as she listened to her father scream at her aunt, she decided to take matters into her own hands. She would not let Aunt Ellice ruin her chance with Sir Maximus, which was exactly what would happen if she didn't do something.

"Come along," she said, standing up from the dark and cold table and taking Isadora by the hand. "We are going to the kitchen to see what we can do about preparing the evening meal."

Isadora was yanked along as they crossed the floor to the servant's entrance that led to the kitchen yard. "But what will we do?" Isadora asked, intimidated. "We cannot make Auntie change her mind!"

"I do not intend to make her change her mind. I intend to do her job."

"What do you mean?"

"We will cook if we have to."

"But I do not know how to cook!"

Courtly ignored her whining sister. They quit the hall, out into the cool, dark night with the kitchen directly across from them. Already, they could see Kellen and Ellice standing by the door, arguing in the dim light of the yard.

"I will tell you what to do," Courtly said as she eyed both her father and her aunt. "I learned a great deal about cooking at the kitchens of Prudhoe Castle. Lady d'Umfraville had fostered at a great house in France and she knew a good deal about cooking and food. It is very simple, truly."

Isadora was still fearful but she didn't argue. She simply allowed her sister to pull her along, stumbling across the rocky ground at times. By the time they reached Kellen and Ellice, who were standing in front of the kitchen door, the older adults were looking at them with varied degrees of curiosity, although Ellice's expression was mixed with hostility. At her limit of patience with her stubborn aunt, Courtly addressed the woman.

"Auntie, I mean no disrespect, but Papa invited a very important knight to sup with us this evening and I will not permit you to ruin it," she said flatly. "I do not know why you seem so willing to treat all of us as if we are your enemy, but it is ridiculous and selfish. If you are going to be nasty and rude, then do it with your own people. I will not permit you to ruin my reputation or Papa's reputation simply because you do not know what it means to be kind and generous. Now, get out of my way. I am going into the kitchen and see to the evening meal before all is lost."

Ellice looked at her with a great deal of shock and contempt. It wasn't the words that shocked her so much, but the look of steely determination coming from her niece. The woman meant what she said.

"You are not entering my kitchen, you little toad," Ellice snarled. "If you step one foot in there, I will beat you within an inch of your life."

"You will not," Kellen said, his voice low and threatening. "If you lay a hand on her, I will forget you are my sister and kill you where you stand. Is that in any way unclear?"

Ellice looked at her brother, her eyes narrowing. "You would not dare touch me."

"Try it and see."

Ellice's jaw worked furiously. It was clear that she was beyond fury but smart enough not to tempt fate. Her brother was bigger and stronger than she was and could quite easily carry out his threat. Now, she was losing ground in the argument and not liking it in the least. She had been holding her own until Courtly had appeared. Now, the volatile situation had taken an ominous turn and she was trying to figure out how to prevent it.

"Well?" Courtly said, breaking into Ellice's thoughts. "Will you move aside or will I push you aside?"

Ellice's venom turned back to her niece. "If you touch me, you will regret it."

Courtly smiled thinly. "If you touch me, *you* will regret it," she replied. "Papa has brought his men with him. They are camping in the courtyard and will take up residence in the hall shortly. You do not stand a chance against Papa and his men, so you may as well move aside before Papa has you physically removed from your own home. That would be shameful."

It was a dig at her aunt's obstinacy, something that did not go unnoticed by Ellice. She was so furious that her face had grown pale and her lips were drawn into a tight, ugly line. She knew she had no choice in the matter now that her niece was making demands and she furthermore knew that if she made any move to touch or push the woman, she could very well find herself with a broken neck because her brother was very protective of his daughters.

Jaw ticking, grinding her teeth, Ellice had no choice but to surrender. God, she hated that feeling. She took a small step away from the door, just enough so that Courtly and Isadora could slip inside. As the girls disappeared into the darkened structure, Ellice focused her hate on her brother.

"This is not over," she growled. "This is *my* home. You cannot come here and make demands, Kellen. You have been trying to control my life since we were small children and our parents let you. I came to Kennington to get away from you and your controlling ways. I will not let you give the commands at Kennington now. This is my home."

Kellen's expression was impassive. He knew what she was alluding to but he refused to comment on it. To do so would only create worse of an argument.

"It is *my* home," he said. "I only let you live here by my good graces. But I am coming to think that is a mistake. You are a nasty, embittered shrew, Ellice. God help you, for I cannot."

Ellice's jaw ticked and, for the first time since Kellen's arrival at Kennington, a measure of emotion flickered in the woman's eyes. Deep-seated resentment and deep, agonizing emotion. The reflection in her dark eyes was evident, hinting at old pain, long past.

"If I am a shrew, then it is of your making," she said hoarsely. "You have created what you see. This is *not* over, Kellen. It is not over in the least."

With that, she walked away from her brother, something she rarely did when they were arguing, and headed to the exterior stairs that led to the master's chamber of the manor. Kellen watched her go, surprised she had given up as she had. It wasn't like the woman to surrender an argument. But he let it go, mostly because he was glad she had acquiesced as she had. He didn't want to fight with her all night and by her final words, he suspected that was where they were headed before she abruptly turned away. Relieved, he went to check on his daughters.

Kellen stuck his head into the kitchen to see how the girls were getting along and noted that Courtly was on her knees in front of the hearth, trying to light it with a flint and stone. She was trying very hard but the flint was being stubborn and it was dark, making it difficult to see.

"Court?" he asked. "Do you require any assistance?"

Courtly nodded firmly. "Can you please start the fire, Papa?" she asked, handing the man the flint and stone as he ducked into the low-ceilinged room. "When you've done that, I will need help. Mayhap you can track down a serving woman or two. Also, Issie and I are in desperate need of soap. We smell like smoke and I cannot greet our guests smelling like a fire pit."

Kellen knelt down and expertly started the fire where his daughter had struggled. As the rather large hearth began to burn, he lay a good deal of wood and peat on top of it to spark up the blaze. The kitchen began to fill with warmth and light, illuminating a rather cramped and evidently well-stocked kitchen. There was food in its raw form everywhere.

"I will see what I can do for you," he said. "If I cannot find any soap, then I will send one of my men into town for it."

Courtly pleaded with him. "Then why not do that now?" she asked. "Do not waste time searching Kennington when Auntie has probably hid all of the soap, anyway. She knew we needed it."

Kellen nodded as he headed for the door. "Very well," he said. "Is there anything else you require?"

Courtly began to look around the kitchen. Fowl hung from the ceiling overhead, tied with hemp to the beams, and there was a massive, cooked leg of pork propped on a table that was shoved into a corner of the room. Furthermore, she could see sacks of something underneath another table and she went to it, opening the sack to find dried multi-colored beans inside. Another sack had sand-colored flour, half-empty. Quickly, she began calculating what she had to work with.

"Give me a few moments before you send the man off," she said to her father. "I may need something from town but, as of yet, I am not sure."

Kellen stood in the doorway. "Then I will wait," he said. "What do you intend to do?"

Courtly pointed at the leg of pork. "I can boil that with the beans to make a stew," she said. "There is flour here to make bread, but I need a few more things for the bread before I can actually make it. Papa, would you check and see if you can find a store of wine or ale? If not, then we will have to find some quickly."

Kellen went on the hunt as Courtly began pulling out the sacks from beneath the table. Isadora still stood over near the hearth, uncertain as she watched her sister work, and Courtly turned to the girl.

"Issie," she said. "Go and see if you can find any cheese or butter or even milk. I would hope there is some. And I need eggs. Find as many eggs as you can. Will you please do this?"

Isadora nodded and began her search, sticking her head under tables and into crevices as Courtly pulled a very large pot out from underneath a table and dragged it over to the hearth. There was a big, iron arm affixed to the mortar of the hearth, made to hold big pots, and she heaved the pot onto the arm. Now, it was time to go to work.

The well for the manor was just outside the door and Courtly filled several buckets, pouring the water into the pot and putting several pounds of beans in to soak. She managed to find great bunches of vegetables near a half-filled bowl of dirty water, baskets of carrots and little, brown onions that had been harvested but not cleaned. They were covered in mud. She set about cleaning them in the water she had drawn from the well, washing and re-washing until the dirt came off.

With the only knife she could find, she then chopped up the carrots and onions, putting the chunks of vegetables into the pot along with the beans. As she worked on the stew, Isadora returned with her hands full of small, brown eggs. She had located the chicken coop and had collected all of the eggs she could carry, but Courtly sent her back for more. Isadora fled out the door, frenzied, as only a young girl could be.

It was fortunate that Ellice's kitchen was well-stocked. Courtly was very thankful to come across a bag of salt and another sack half-full of peppercorns. Salt and peppercorns, smashed with the bottom of a small, iron pot, went into the stew pot, which was now starting to steam. The feast was on the fire but Courtly was feeling a distinct sense of urgency as she turned her attention towards the leg of pork. The guests would be arriving at any moment and the stew would take time to cook, so she fed off her sense of urgency, hurrying to put the meal together.

Using the dull knife she had used to chop up the vegetables, Courtly began cutting pieces of pork off of the leg and putting it all into the pot of beans and vegetables. The meat was shriveled and looked as if the household had been eating off of it for some time, but she didn't care. At this point, some meat was better than no meat, and she hoped that cooking it with the beans would give the pork new life. Throwing in more salt, she watched as the pot began to bubble.

As she watched the roiling in the pot grow livelier, she couldn't even think about disappointing a man she wanted to impress. She simply had to move onward and hope she could produce an appetizing and even tasty meal. As she continued to cut off more pork and Isadora shuffled back and forth between the chicken pen and the kitchen, bringing in more eggs, a timid servant girl appeared and declared that she had been sent by Kellen. Courtly put the woman in charge of making the bread, something she evidently knew nothing about, so Courtly switched places with her. As the servant gingerly cut away at the pork leg and threw the meat into the pot, Courtly went about trying to remember how to make bread.

Although Lady d'Umfraville had instructed her charges in how to run a kitchen and even how to cook items, Courtly's strong point had never been making bread. She knew that bread needed to be made with two- or three-day-old bread dough, so that it would rise, but neither she nor the servant girl could find anything that resembled old bread dough. The woman that usually worked in the kitchen was missing, obviously kept away by Ellice, so there was nothing to do but try to make a fair semblance of bread. Courtly prayed it would be acceptable. She had one chance to impress Sir Maximus and everything in the world seemed to be against her – her dress, her lack of an opportunity to clean herself or even brush her hair, and now the food. Everything was against her. But she wasn't going to give up, not in the least.

Pushing up the sleeves of her smoke-scented surcoat, she went to work.

# CHAPTER FOUR

**"T**HIS BELONGS TO de Lara?" Tiberius asked as they came upon the compact manor house, the windows emitting a glowing light in the dark of night. "This hardly looks like a property for the great marcher lords."

Maximus' gaze moved over the house. Surrounded by a wall that was part timber and part stone, the house itself was oddly shaped and rather small. There was a two-storied structure that he could see and then another single-storied wing that attached to it. He pulled his black and white Spanish Jennet to a halt and the knights around him followed suit. He and Tiberius sat a moment, looking at the distant structure, the only point of light and shelter in miles of darkened landscape.

"This has to be it," Maximus finally said. "The priest on the south side of Oxford said he knew the house and directed us down this road. There is nothing else *but* this house, so this has to be it."

Tiberius shrugged. He was hungry and somewhat irritable, so he spurred his big, brown warmblood forward.

"Come on, then," he said. "I am famished. I must eat before I collapse. But from the looks of that place, I don't suppose they will provide us more than a crust of bread and the dregs of the wine."

Maximus and the knights followed, loping down the road and closing the distance between them and the manor house. As they drew closer, the structure seemed to become somewhat bigger, but certainly not what they had expected from a great marcher lord. It was run-down and the walls seemed hardly enough to hold back an army of children, much less men with wicked intentions. The gate itself was very large and seemed to be made strictly of wide, hammered, iron strips that were held together with big, iron bolts. One could see right through the slats into the yard beyond, which would have been a horrible feature in the event of an attack. Arrows, arms, and weapons could come right through the gaps at the inhabitants inside.

Maximus and Tiberius dismounted their horses and approached the odd gate, looking inquisitively at the gathering of men beyond. There were a couple of fires and men milling about, tending horses or sitting by the fire mending clothes or weapons. It was all quite casual, as if they hadn't a care in the word. No sentries on duty, no guards. Tiberius and Maximus looked at each other curiously, shrugged, and then Maximus called out to the men.

"Greetings," he bellowed in the loud, deep voice that Maximus was so capable of. "I am de Shera. I have come at the invitation of Kellen de Lara."

Every man in the ward looked over at the gate as Maximus' voice echoed off the buildings. A few of the men even stood up, as if a challenge had been issued. Clearly, Maximus' voice was loud enough that it could be startling and he always sounded as if he were bellowing commands in battle. It was just his nature. But one of the men broke off from the group, a big, blond devil, and headed to the gate at a clipped pace. As he approached, he lifted a hand in greeting.

"Lord de Lara is expecting you," he said. "You will leave your weapons at the gate."

Maximus' expression was steely. "I will leave them inside the gate and not outside."

The man didn't reply other than to throw the big, iron bolts on the gate and yank it open. Creaking and groaning, the gate slowly opened as the man heaved.

Not wanting to seem as if they were trying to bust into the ward, Maximus didn't help the man as he struggled with the very big, very heavy gate. Finally, he opened it enough so that men were able to pass through, and Maximus and Tiberius did, followed by their knights. But once they were all inside the gate, they immediately began removing weapons.

"You will place someone to guard our possessions and weapons," Maximus instructed de Lara's man. "I do not want to return to find things missing."

De Lara's knight whistled sharply between his teeth and two men came away from the group in the ward, making their way over. The knight issued a few orders to the pair before returning his focus to Maximus.

"My name is St. Héver," the knight said. "I am Lord de Lara's second."

Maximus cocked an eyebrow. "The house of St. Héver?"

"Aye."

"I have heard of it."

The big knight dipped his head politely. "I am honored, my lord."

Maximus eyed the knight. He'd seen this man, too. He was a fighting man, a knight on the front lines, and Maximus remembered hearing somewhere that Kirk St. Héver was a fearsome fighter. He certainly seemed big and professional enough. After a moment of scrutinizing St. Héver, Maximus began to look around at the manor complex.

"Where is de Lara?" he asked. "Surely he was expecting me sooner than this. We were delayed when one of the horses came up lame and we had to return to the livery for another."

Kirk pointed to the long, single-storied building behind them by several dozen yards. It was at the far end of the ward.

"He is in the hall," he replied. "You may go to him."

Maximus pushed past the knight, heading towards the building indicated. He and his men had to pass by de Lara's men as they went and there were looks bordering on hostility as they passed. Maximus ignored them but Tiberius went so far as to sneer at a pair of young knights who were posturing angrily. He leaned into his brother's ear.

"Why are these men so hostile?" he hissed. "Have we unknowingly offended them?"

Maximus didn't know and he surely didn't care. "Idiots," he replied under his breath. "De Lara had better have a good meal to make up for the bad manners of his men."

Tiberius glanced over at the host of unfriendly faces. "We are allied with de Lara, are we not?"

"Both de Lara and I support de Montfort, so we are, in theory."

"I do not think his men know that."

Maximus wouldn't give a second thought to the soldiers who were watching him and his party trudge across the bailey towards the hall. While the bailey itself smelled of men and animals, of urine and animal dung, they were catching wafts of smells that were emerging from the hall and the scents upon the air were most appealing. He could most definitely smell bread and he thought he even smelled meat.

He was famished, that was true, but his stomach seemed to be nervous for other reasons. Every time he thought of that phial of rose oil in his tunic, that secret precious bottle, thoughts of the lovely Courtly filled his mind and he realized that he was anxious to see her again. Fearful, even. He wondered if she had only been kind to him at their first meeting earlier that day because he saved her life.

Self-doubt clutched at him as he patted the rose oil, wondering if he had acted too hastily in purchasing it. What if her smiles and pleasant conversation had only been out of gratitude and nothing more? Maximus wasn't in the habit of being attracted to women on a daily basis, so when he was attracted to one, it meant something to him. Certainly, other knights took whores or wives. Tiberius had a glut of women who lived or died by his smile and Gallus was now married, but Maximus had always been a warrior's warrior. He was a knight, a fighter, and that was what filled his time – thoughts and practice of how he could better himself as a warrior. His time had never been filled with the opposite sex. Until now. He secretly hoped that was about to change.

Entering the arched doorway that opened into Kennington's hall, he was met with a rather small and narrow common room with a dramatically arched ceiling constructed of big timbers. Immediately to his left was an alcove with a feasting table, evidently meant for the lord of Kennington and his family, and then there were two long, feasting tables, side by side, in the room. Instead of a hearth, there was a fire pit at one end of the room and the pitched roof had holes in it so that smoke could escape. The fire was lit and the room was quite warm, and quite pleasant, as Maximus and his men moved into the hall.

"Sir Maximus!"

The call came from the end of the hall with the fire pit and Maximus saw Kellen emerging from a small door. Dogs trailed after him as he headed in Maximus' direction, his expression far more pleasant than the expressions his men had presented outside.

"You have arrived," Kellen said, somewhat happily. "I am glad you could come. We have been looking forward to supping with you this eve. And you have brought your men?"

Maximus nodded, indicating the men to his right. "I do not believe you have met my brother, Tiberius," he said, indicating the tall, dark-haired brother. "And these are my knights, the de Wolfe brothers, de Moray, and du Bois."

Kellen's smile faded somewhat as he looked at the collection of knights. "De Wolfe?" he repeated. "William de Wolfe?"

Scott nodded. "Indeed, my lord," he said. "He is our father."

Kellen was visibly impressed. "Then the honor is mine to have the sons of the illustrious Wolfe under my roof," he said. Then, he indicated the tables. "Please sit. Food shall be brought about shortly."

Maximus and his men moved to the closest table. There was a wooden tray that had a pile of what looked to be some kind of dense, cream-colored bread upon it. That was where the heavy smell of bread was coming from. As Maximus took a seat, Tiberius reached out and took a hot piece of the bread, sniffing at it.

"What manner of bread is this?" Tiberius asked, biting into it. It was puffy, rather dense, and had an abundance of salt in it and on top of it. "It is delicious."

With that, the other knights grabbed at it, taking hunks for themselves. Kellen sat opposite Maximus and next to Troy de Wolfe. He seemed rather confused by the question.

"It is… truthfully, I am not sure," he said. "I will have to ask my daughter."

Maximus peered at the plate of bread. "Did she instruct the servants to bake it thusly?"

Kellen appeared uncomfortable in the slightest. "She created the recipe," he said, avoiding the question. He didn't want de Shera to know that his daughter had been working like a slave in the kitchen for the past two hours because Ellice was hiding most of the servants from him. The man didn't need to know his family's problems and, frankly, he was embarrassed by it. "Courtly fostered at Prudhoe Castle in the north and the lady of the castle was evidently quite adept in cookery. She learned in France and passed her knowledge along to my daughter. Therefore, my daughter is skilled in the art of fine cookery. You will be sampling it tonight."

That seemed to impress Maximus. "Where is your daughter?" he asked, looking around the room. "Will she join us?"

Kellen's discomfort grew. "She will, eventually," he said, trying to be delicate on how he explained things. "There was some trouble with the servants this evening and she is in the kitchen at the moment, overseeing things. But she will join us at some point."

Maximus watched Kellen as the man fidgeted a bit and had difficulty meeting his eye. He wondered why. Reaching out, he took a piece of the flat bread and bit into it. Tiberius had been correct. It was quite delicious.

"How are your daughters after their experience today?" he asked, chewing. "I hope they suffered no ill effects."

Kellen shook his head. "Fortunately not," he replied. "But all of their clothing and possessions were burned, so I will apologize in advance that neither one has had the opportunity to change into more appropriate clothing. Until I can secure a seamstress or material for them, they are forced to make do."

Maximus finished one piece of bread and reached for another. "That is very unfortunate," he said. "Had I known, I would have brought material with me. I would assume your daughters can sew."

Kellen nodded. "They can," he said. "Courtly can, anyway. Isadora does not have much interest in it."

"Oh?" Maximus said. "Why not?"

Before Kellen could reply, Isadora emerged from the small doorway on the other side of the fire pit, a pitcher in one hand and several small wooden cups in the other. She was trying to be very careful about not dropping anything and when Maximus saw her, he jumped up and went to her.

"Here, lady," he said, taking the pitcher. "Allow me to help you.

I fear the pitcher is much too heavy for you."

Isadora gazed up at the man who had a hand in saving her young life. She hadn't a chance to speak with him at all earlier, as Courtly had seemed to do all of the talking for them, so she was a bit shy to speak with him, and his chivalrous gesture had her cheeks flushing.

"I can carry it," she insisted.

Maximus could see that he'd either embarrassed or offended her and hastened to make amends. "Of course you can," he said. "I only meant to help. Forgive me for offering if you did not need it."

Isadora was growing more flushed by his sweet behavior and she smiled timidly. "I am not offended," she said, moving towards the table of men with the cups in her hands. "I was being very careful not to drop it."

Maximus nodded. "I could see that," he said. "You are quite strong. In fact, I do believe your muscles are bigger than mine."

Isadora's smile grew as she became flustered and flattered at the same time. "I am *not* too strong," she said. "You are teasing me."

Maximus grinned, the corners of his eyes crinkling just as Isadora said they did. "I never tease a lady," he insisted, although it was obvious he was jesting. "Well, not *much.*"

Isadora giggled. Much like her sister had been, she too was very quickly becoming enraptured by the big, handsome knight. "I must return to the kitchen and bring out more food," she said eagerly. "I will come back."

Maximus' confused expression returned. "Why must you get food?" he asked. "Why do you not sit down and join the conversation?"

Isadora spoke before her father could interject a tactful explanation. "Because we cannot find the servants," she told him with straight honesty as only a child could give. "It is only my sister and I, and one servant Papa managed to find."

Brow furrowed now, Maximus glanced at Kellen. "Where are your servants?" he asked the question to both of them. "Has something happened to them?"

Kellen was appalled that his youngest daughter had divulged the information he had been trying very hard not to disclose. Isadora was young, intelligent, and tactless.

"Nay, nothing has happened to them," he said quickly. "They belong to my sister and… you see, my sister has…."

"Auntie did not want to prepare a feast tonight," Isadora said helpfully because her father seemed to be stumbling. "She did not want to share her food or servants, so Papa became angry with her and she ran off and took her servants with her. Courtly and I have been working in the kitchen and cooking. She wanted to make a good meal for you and I have helped her."

She said it rather proudly as Kellen put a hand over his face, appalled at the words that had just come out of his daughter's mouth. That which he had been trying to conceal was now common knowledge for the entire room. He didn't dare look at Maximus, who was staring at Isadora as if attempting to comprehend what she had just told him.

"Your *sister* has been cooking?" he repeated. "Do you mean to tell me that she has actually cooked a meal?"

Kellen's hand came away from his face. "It is not as bad as it sounds," he insisted weakly. "Courtly is a fine woman, my lord. Cooking is a servant's task and she certainly would not do it habitually. She…."

Again, Isadora cut her father off, eager to tell Sir Maximus of Courtly's accomplishments. At least, Isadora *thought* they were great accomplishments.

"She wanted to make sure you were presented with a great feast," she said enthusiastically. "She did it herself, all of it. She made a stew with beans and pork, and she made a boil of vegetables that has vinegar and honey and pepper in it, and she also fried the pork and made a sauce of onions and butter to put on it. But she had trouble with the bread… it has eggs and milk and onions in it. She couldn't make it puff up like real bread."

Maximus listened to the child rattle on. He was stunned, but not for the reasons Kellen might have thought. True, it was shocking for a noblewoman to cook, but he was overcome with the fact that Courtly actually went to the trouble to do it. Once again, faced with a situation that was seemingly difficult, in this case an aunt running off with all of her servants, Lady Courtly showed her ingenuity by cooking a meal herself so that there would be food to eat for guests. *For him.* Truly, he was astonished by the lengths the woman went to in order to please her guests. The fact that cooking, by noblewomen, simply wasn't done had never even entered her mind.

"Where is your sister?" he asked after a moment.

Isadora pointed to the door near the fire pit. "In the kitchen."

Maximus' gaze found the door. It was difficult to read his thoughts for his expression remained neutral. He had learned long enough never to show his emotions. After a moment, he turned to Kellen, who was not so adept at hiding his thoughts. He spoke.

"You are ashamed of this." It was not a question.

Kellen was looking up at Maximus with some hesitance in his features. "I did not want you to think my daughter is anything other than a fine lady," he said. "Noblewomen do not spend time in the kitchen, cooking, and I do not want you to think I forced my daughter into some manner of servitude. It was her idea, I assure you. She simply did not want me to be embarrassed when you attended a feast with no food."

"So she cooked an entire meal by herself?"

Kellen nodded with some resignation. "She did," he said. "I apologize that I have no cook or servants to offer you this evening. Although it is unseemly, it would seem my daughters must do the work tonight. I pray you can overlook that breach of etiquette."

Maximus just looked at the man. Then, he moved away from the table and headed for the small door near the fire pit. Isadora, not to be left behind, trotted after him. When they disappeared through the door, Kellen turned his perplexed expression to Tiberius.

"Where did he go?" he asked. "Surely he does not intend to humiliate or berate my daughter."

Tiberius wasn't sure where Maximus had gone but he shook his head firmly in response. "Never," he said firmly. "My brother would not do that. I am sure he intends to thank the lady for her efforts."

Kellen, now concerned over Maximus and his daughters, alone in a kitchen, returned his focus to the small kitchen door. "Then mayhap I should go also."

He started to rise but Tiberius put out a hand, forcing the man to stop. "No need," he said evenly. "I am sure Maximus will return shortly. Meanwhile, you will tell me of Kennington House. I have never heard of it before, you know. How long has it been in the de Lara family?"

Kellen allowed himself to be reluctantly engaged in a conversation about the history of Kennington House, but the truth was that his thoughts were on the kitchen where Maximus had gone. He didn't like the idea of the man being alone with his eldest daughter, even if Isadora was present. There was something unsettling and unseemly about it. He didn't like men around his daughters as it was, not even men who had saved their lives, so it was very difficult for him to remain and allow himself to be engaged by Tiberius de Shera. All the while, he kept wondering what Maximus was doing, speaking to Courtly, unchaperoned. Nay, he didn't like it at all. Men were only after one thing, even men like Maximus de Shera.

The more Tiberius talked and the more time passed with Maximus missing, the unhappier he became.

"GREETINGS, MY LADY."

Courtly heard the voice, deep and gentle, coming from behind. She had been bent over a boiling pot of vegetables and she turned, startled, to see Maximus standing in the doorway. Overwhelmed by the unexpected sight of him, she couldn't even manage to find her tongue. She simply stared at him, wooden spoon in hand, and her mouth hanging open. She was trying to think of something to say to the man, for surely, he was expecting some manner of response, but through it all, she could only think one thing – *Sweet Jesú, the man is more handsome than I remember!*

Seeing Courtly's obvious shock, Maximus grinned. "Please tell me that you remember me," he said, sounding as if he were pleading. "Surely you have not forgotten my name."

Red-faced from having been bent over a boiling pot, Courtly lowered the spoon. "Of course I have not forgotten, my lord," she said. "I… uh… well, the cook is out in the yard and I was simply… helping so that…."

Maximus cut her off gently. "Your father told me what happened," he said quietly. He could see that she was deeply shaken from his unexpected appearance. "In fact, he said you have cooked the entire meal."

Courtly glanced around the kitchen. The big, simmering pot of beans and pork rested over the fire and a pile of bread was on the table. It would be difficult to deny such a thing and she supposed that it was too late to run off and hope he forgot he ever saw her in the kitchen. She was deeply surprised her father should tell Sir Maximus what had occurred and rather embarrassed that she had tried to lie to him about it.

"I… I did, my lord," she finally said, sighing. "He really told you that?"

Maximus nodded, his eyes never leaving her face. "Aye," he said. "Your father said that your aunt fled and took the servants with her. I came to tell you that I am deeply honored that you would go to so much trouble to feed me and my men. Is there anything I can do to help you?"

Stunned at not only the generous offer but also by the man's attitude towards the dirty grind of kitchen work, Courtly had no idea what to say to him. The question seemed genuine but certainly he couldn't have meant it. Not only was it woman's work, but it was something only servants and peasants would do. After a moment, she simply shook her head.

"You are a guest," she said. "I would not dream of letting you help. But you are kind to offer."

Maximus couldn't take his eyes off her. With her cheeks red, her hair mussed, and her hands dirty, she was still the most beautiful woman he had ever seen. He thought that maybe their first meeting had been an illusion of sorts, that she really wasn't the angel he'd built up in his mind. But seeing her at this moment, at probably what she considered to be her worst, all he could think was how utterly marvelous she was. She was better than he had remembered.

"But you have no one to help you other than Lady Isadora, who is doing a fine job," he said, watching Isadora grin as the girl gathered more bread and rushed out to take it to the hall. "I am relatively strong and follow commands well. If you just tell me what to do, I will do it."

So he *had* meant his offer and Courtly was off-guard by his chivalry. She wasn't used to a man offering himself in servitude to her, a man she had been counting the minutes until she saw again. Now, here he was, unwilling to leave her alone as she worked hard to prepare his meal. He was offering to help. But the mere thought was distressing.

*Sweet Jesú*, she wanted so badly to impress him. She wanted him to think she was a lady and meaningful of his attention. But here she was, in her dirty, smoke-smelling dress, her hair askew and her cheeks flushed from the heat. She knew she looked terrible. Her heart began to beat faster in her chest and her breathing began to quicken. Emotions she couldn't control were bubbling up in her chest, embarrassment and disappointment and longing. Aye, she longed for him, longed to see him again, and longed to be a woman worthy of a de Shera. But she wasn't. In her present state, she knew she wasn't. She looked like the lowliest peasant, dirty and smelly. After this night, she was sure she would never see him again.

"You do not need to help," she said softly, defeat in her voice. "You are my father's guest and he would become enraged if he saw that you were to help me. It is bad enough that his daughter has been forced to cook the meal. I cannot even imagine what you must think of me, Sir Maximus. When you first saw me, I fell out of a window and landed on your head. Now, you see me working in a kitchen. I do not blame you if you think the de Laras are terribly uncivilized and uncouth people. We have shown you little else."

Maximus gazed steadily at her. There was a faint smile on his face and an expression he'd never had before. Something like understanding with an inkling of adoration thrown in. He just couldn't stop staring at her. Her words, for him, had no meaning. She had no idea what he was thinking because he didn't really know himself, but he knew that it wasn't disgust or disappointment. It was something he'd never before known. It was warmth, liquid and viscous, like honey flowing through his veins. It made his heart pound and his hands sweat. Reaching into his tunic, into the pouches sewn on the inside, he pulled forth the small, silken purse with the phial inside.

"This is what I think of you," he said quietly, extending the purse. "I brought this to thank you for being so kind to have me to sup. I brought it as a gift for you. I hope that you do not think me too forward."

Shocked, Courtly looked at the small, silk purse. It was a moment before she reached out, hesitantly, to accept it. But she didn't open it. She simply stared at it.

"For me?" she asked, as if she hadn't heard him correctly.

Maximus nodded. He found that he was fairly eager for her to open it. "Indeed," he said. "It is not unheard of to give a gift to the hostess of a feast."

Courtly was still looking at it. "Does Papa know you brought this?"

"He does not."

Her eyes came up, studying him. "I am not entirely sure he would allow me to accept a gift from you, Sir Maximus. Papa is rather… odd about those things."

Maximus snorted. "Why?" he asked. "It is not as if I am giving you a jewel, for Christ's sake. It's simply a… a gift. You do not have to tell your father if you wish."

Courtly's lips twitched with a smile as she gazed up at him. "I am glad you said that," she said, "for I very much want to keep it, but I fear that Papa will make me give it back if he knows."

"Then do not tell him," Maximus told her. "Now, open it quickly before he comes in here, sees the gift, and berates us both – me for giving it and you for accepting it."

Courtly laughed softly as she rapidly untied the purse and pulled forth the alabaster phial. She gasped softly when she saw it, with great pleasure, and when she pulled out the stopper and inhaled the rich, rose scent, she sighed again. Her face lit up with a bright, grateful smile, a gesture that sent Maximus' heart fluttering wildly.

"Thank you, Sir Maximus," she said sincerely. "Perfumed oil, isn't it?"

Maximus nodded. He was trying very hard not to grin like an idiot because her reaction had pleased him so. "Do you like it, then?"

"I love it," she said, nodding firmly. "It is the most wonderful gift I have ever received. I cannot thank you enough for your thoughtfulness. You truly must be a very generous and kind man."

Maximus was starting to feel a bit embarrassed with her gratitude. He didn't like recognition, or praise, but she was giving it to him in great doses and he was starting to feel uncomfortable, as if he didn't know how to gracefully accept it. Her thanks had been enough but her praise had made him self-conscious. He was mesmerized by her happy expression and wanted very much to be gracious in return, but he had no idea where to begin. He pointed at the delicate phial.

"You should hide it now," he said. "If your father finds it, he will want to know where you got it and I do not wish to lie to him."

Courtly cocked her head, eyeing him as she sniffed at the oil again. "Would you lie to him on my behalf?"

Maximus pursed his lips, clasping his hands behind his back and kicking at the dirt of the kitchen floor in a sweetly coy gesture. "I suppose I would have to," he said. "I gave it to you, after all. I should not like for him to become enraged at you for something I did."

Courtly smiled at him as she put the phial back into the purse and shoved the entire thing into a pocket in the waistline of her surcoat. When she was finished tucking it away, she returned her focus to Maximus. He was watching her closely, and she took a moment to simply take in the man and his features; the square jaw covered by the neatly trimmed beard, the straight nose, the cropped hair. To think that such a handsome man would bring her a gift made her feel light and giddy, but it was more than that – he was showing depth that she had never seen in a man of his caliber. Working in a kitchen and an unkempt appearance didn't disturb him. Was it possible that Maximus de Shera was a man of true and noble character, more than she could possibly imagine?

"You are very gallant to want to protect me," she said after a moment. "Is that who you truly are, Sir Maximus? A protector of women who jump out of windows?"

He shrugged. "I am a protector of women who need it," he said. "You may need it should your father discover what I brought you."

"If he does, I will handle him. I would not want to trouble you with it."

"It would be no trouble, I assure you."

She laughed softly, mostly because he seemed so unsure of himself as they skirted the edge of a flirtatious exchange. "How can you say that to me?" she demanded lightly. "I smell of smoke, my face is red, and I am cooking like a common servant. I cannot comprehend that you would still be so gallant towards a woman who has done naught to impress you, in any fashion."

Maximus' smile faded as he gazed into her big, beautiful eyes. His guard was going down and he didn't even realize it. He wasn't practiced enough with women yet to truly know how to maintain a sense of self-protection. Whatever magic Courtly de Lara had, it was working on him. It was breaking him down, stone by de Shera stone.

"That is not true," he said quietly. "I knew when I met you this afternoon that you were a lady of breeding and beauty and honor. Even now, you cook a meal because there is no one left to do it. Rather than let us starve, you would make sure we do not. That speaks greatly for your character, my lady. You have impressed me deeply yet you do not even realize it."

Courtly could feel his sincerity. Something in his gaze was reaching out for her, touching her, like invisible fingers that would stroke her cheek or touch her hair. She could feel all of this from him and more, and her heart, much like his, began to race wildly. Could it be possible that the man was as interested in her as she was in him? She could not dare to hope but, evidently, it was true. She could read it in his expression and in everything about him. Her heart began to soar.

"If that is true, then I am honored and grateful," she said, feeling heat in her cheeks that had nothing to do with the heat of the kitchen. The heat came from Maximus' gaze. "At the very least, I have not offended you with my actions, and I am greatly relieved."

Maximus found himself inspecting the arch of her eyebrows and the pert tip of her nose. She had such a magnificent face. "Nay, lady, you have not offended me," he said, his tone gruff and soft. "You could never do such a thing. But as much as I would like to continue this conversation, mayhap we should take the food into the hall now so that my men will not faint away from hunger. My brother has come with me and he becomes quite cross when he is hungry, so do allow me to help you bring the meal to the table. It would be my honor."

Courtly wasn't sure she could deny his offer for help again. Truth was, she didn't want to deny him. He was being genteel and kind, and she liked it very much. She wanted to keep him with her, around her, even if that meant carrying trays of beans and pork. If he was willing, she would let him. She smiled in surrender.

"Very well," she said. "I should not like your brother to become angry because he is famished. I must carry this great pot out to the feasting hall so that we may distribute the stew from it. Will you help me with it?"

Maximus looked around the kitchen, noting there were no trenchers. "That is a very heavy and very hot pot," he said. "What did you plan to serve the stew in?"

Courtly sighed, the smile fading from her face. "There is no old bread or trenchers that I can find," she said. "However, I made bread and I thought… well, it seems barbaric for all of us to eat out of the pot, but I am not sure there is any choice."

Maximus began poking around the kitchen, looking for some-thing to serve guests with individual servings. Under the butcher's table, he found four wooden trays, which he pulled out and set upon the tabletop.

"We can use these," he said. "We can cover them with the bread you prepared and then put the stew on top of it. Do you have spoons?"

Courtly inspected the trays. "I am ashamed I did not find these before you did," she said, shrugging when he grinned at her. "They *are* rather dirty. Mayhap we can rinse them with water and use them as you have indicated. It is a brilliant idea. And I have indeed found some spoons to use."

"Excellent," Maximus said, picking up the trays. "Where is the well?"

Courtly pointed to the kitchen yard outside. "In the yard," she said. "I will see if I can find other things to use to serve the stew in."

Maximus winked at her and went out into the yard, drawing water in the darkness to rinse off the dirty trays. Still lingering on his wink, Courtly went about searching for other trays, stashed or hidden, and found six wooden bowls of varying sizes that had been kept under a smaller butcher's block. Maximus ended up rinsing those off as well, and when all was said and done, they had found eleven items that could be used to eat from.

Both Maximus and Courtly were people of thought, of re-sourcefulness, and in this small moment of time, in a smelly and smoky kitchen, they bonded over making the evening meal a success as neither of them had ever bonded with anyone else. It was an odd situation, to say the least, but one that brought out the best in both of them. Courtly started it when she decided not to let her dinner guests go hungry and Maximus helped ensure that Court-ly's efforts would be a success. By the time the food was actually brought to the table, in abundance, Courtly was actually proud of what she had done and Maximus admired the woman more than he could have expressed. He was the last one to be seated, ensuring that Courtly was seated and served before he was. It was a sweetly chivalrous gesture, one that didn't go unnoticed by anyone in the room, including Kellen.

But Kellen was the only one who wasn't touched by it. In fact, he could see that something was brewing between Maximus and his daughter and he silently scolded himself for inviting the man into his home where he could get his claws into Courtly. His daughter, however, didn't seem to mind in the least. She spent the entire evening smiling at Maximus and speaking to him on fairly frivolous things, to which he paid careful attention. Any other man would have ignored the topics she was discussing, but not Maximus. He was listening. Any man who would listen to talk of flowers and painting and art was a fool for a woman, indeed. Kellen cursed himself for not having seen any of this at the onset.

As the evening deepened and Kellen watched the interaction between the two, he knew that he could not let it go on. Whatever was happening had to be immediately stopped.

He would have to end it.

# PART TWO

## WINDS OF CHANGE

# CHAPTER FIVE

*The One-Eyed Raven Inn*

THE LADY JENIVER ferch Gaerwen de Shera sat across the table from her husband's brother at the morning meal, a surprising event considering her pregnancy often kept her in bed in the morning. But not this morning, she was actually hungry as she pulled bread apart as Gallus, Maximus, Tiberius, and the knights sat in the quiet common room of the old inn. Men were sleeping in various positions around the room, just beginning to stir, as the sun began to rise.

"Please tell me about your meal at Lord de Lara's last night, Max," Jeniver insisted as she popped a piece of warm bread into her mouth. "Ty said that the lord's daughter actually cooked the meal herself. Is this true?"

Maximus smiled weakly. He was exhausted because he hadn't slept all night. Thoughts of Courtly de Lara had been seared into his brain until there was nothing else he could think of. Her brilliant smile, her honeyed voice, and her magnificent beauty had him obsessed as he had never been obsessed with anything in his life. He'd only known the woman a day, but in that day, he'd come to discover a woman of humor, intelligence, determination, and compassion. There wasn't one aspect of the woman that he didn't like or wasn't attracted to.

"Aye," he said. "Evidently, her father and his sister hate one another. The sister resides at Kennington and when de Lara told her he'd invited guests for dinner, the woman ran off and took her servants. Rather than let her father be embarrassed in front of his guests, Lady Courtly cooked the meal herself to save the man's honor."

"And it was a damn fine meal," Tiberius, mouth full of bread, spoke. "She learned her craft at Prudhoe Castle and the meal was delicious. But I came to see last night that we may have a problem with the lovely Lady Courtly."

Jeniver's brow furrowed. "What problem is that?"

Tiberius eyed Maximus. "I think our dear, sweet Max is fond of the lady," he said. "She was the only one he spoke to all evening. It was as if there were only the two of them in the entire hall."

Shocked, Jeniver looked at Maximus. "Is this true?" she asked. "Are you fond of the woman, Max?"

Maximus wasn't ready to divulge what was in his heart yet, and certainly not to an audience. He glared at Tiberius. "Keep your mouth shut," he growled. "My behavior is none of your concern."

Tiberius was trying not to grin. He was sitting next to Maximus but stood up and moved away from him, fearful that he would be the recipient of a fist to the jaw. Maximus wouldn't hesitate if provoked.

"There is nothing to be ashamed of," Tiberius said, chewing his bread from the other side of the table where Jeniver and Gallus sat. "She is a beautiful, sweet woman, Max. Had you not met her first, I might have pursued her. In fact, if you are not interested, mayhap you will let me have her?"

It was the wrong thing to say. Maximus bolted up from the table, going after Tiberius with a vengeance. None of the knights moved to help Tiberius, mostly because they didn't want to be in Maximus' line of fire, but Gallus stood up and quickly put himself between his brothers as Maximus made a swipe for Tiberius' neck.

"Enough, Max," Gallus commanded softly. "No fighting with my wife present. And when did you become so sensitive? Go sit down and finish your meal."

Maximus was red in the face. He had hold of Tiberius' collar and wouldn't let go. "You put Lady Courtly out of your mind, do you hear?" he snarled at his younger brother. "She is not for you."

Tiberius was torn between being amused and defending himself. "Since when do you take me seriously?" he asked, trying to pry his brother's hand off of his tunic. "Let go of my tunic. You are going to tear it."

Maximus barred his teeth and tightened his grip but Gallus shoved at him, breaking his hold on Tiberius. As Tiberius made his way over to Jeniver and sat down beside her, knowing Maximus wouldn't go after him if Jeniver was nearby, Gallus frowned at his middle brother.

"Go sit down and eat," he told him. "He was just being as insufferable as usual. Why are you being so serious?"

Maximus didn't say another word. He turned and left the common room, heading out to the livery through the back door. Tiberius and Gallus watched him go, as did Jeniver. She looked at Tiberius.

"You have struck something within him by speaking of Lady Courtly," she said quietly. "I have never seen him behave that way before."

Tiberius was coming to see that he probably should not have teased his brother on the matter of the lady because the truth was that Maximus had paid an inordinate amount of attention to her the night before. It had been rather astonishing to watch, as Maximus wasn't known to pay attention to women on a conversational level. But Lady Courtly had his brother's undivided attention.

"I did not think he would react so violently," he admitted. "They were as thick as thieves last night. I have never seen my brother smile so much. If I had to guess, I would say the lady had thoroughly enchanted him."

Jeniver, a sensitive and caring woman, began to feel badly for Maximus, perhaps the most reserved of the brothers. She was coming to think that Tiberius' teasing had embarrassed him.

"Mayhap I should go and speak with him," she said, climbing off the bench and bracing herself against Tiberius' shoulder as she moved. "Mayhap he needs a woman to speak to and not his judgmental brothers."

Gallus was standing behind his wife, taking her arm to help her away from the table. At four months pregnant, she was moving rather stiffly and gingerly, as her belly was growing and she was just starting to become the slightest bit uncomfortable with her changing body.

"You had better let him calm himself first," he told her. "Sit down, sweetheart, and eat your meal."

Jeniver shook her head, moving for the door that led out to the livery yard beyond the inn. Already, she could smell the strong scents of horses and hay upon the cold, early morning breeze.

"He must not be left to stew about this," she said. "If he truly feels something for the lady, then it was wrong to tease him about it. I will see if I can ease the man."

Jeniver heard her husband's weak protest as he called to her but she ignored him. Something told her that Maximus did, indeed, need someone to talk to who wasn't going to tease him about his feelings if, in fact, he felt something for de Lara's daughter. Jeniver had a good relationship with Maximus and she loved him dearly, as a brother. He was a good man with a good heart that he kept buried deep beneath that warring exterior. As she wandered across the livery yard, shielding her eyes from the early morning glare, she caught sight of him just inside the stable.

Maximus was bent over his black and white stallion, inspecting the right front foreleg. Jeniver came up behind him, quietly, watching the man as he tended his horse.

"Max," she said softly. "Are you well? I am sure Tiberius did not intend to be cruel. You know how he is. He likes to tease."

Maximus looked up from his horse to see his lovely sister-in-law standing a few feet away. Jeniver was truly a wise and gentle soul, a lady that Maximus' mother loved dearly. Honey had accepted Jeniver from the beginning of her relationship with Gallus, and that was something that made Maximus respect his brother's wife greatly. Lady Honey's respect was not given lightly. Maximus smiled thinly at her, without humor.

"Aye, he does," he said. "Someday it is going to get him into trouble. And in answer to your question, I am well. You needn't worry about me."

Jeniver studied the very big de Shera brother. "I do not worry," she said. "But I would like to hear about Lady Courtly without Tiberius making jest of everything you say. Gallus told me how you two met. How very brave it was of you to save her life from a burning building. Truly, Max, that was an amazing effort."

Maximus sighed faintly, leaning on his horse and averting his gaze. Jeniver was one of the very few people he could let his guard down with and he could feel his control slipping, wanting to confide in someone about what he was feeling. He just didn't really know how.

"I just happened to be there," he said. "Anyone in my position would have done the same."

Jeniver smiled gently at the very modest warrior. "I am sure she and her father are very grateful."

Maximus nodded. "They are," he said. He hesitated a moment before continuing. "I will admit, I was quite astonished to know that she cooked the evening meal last night. She said she did not want her father to be embarrassed in front of his guests. She did it because it needed to be done. Most women would have lamented the fact that they had no cook and simply let everyone go hungry, but she did not."

Jeniver could see the soft reflection in Maximus' eyes as he spoke of de Lara's daughter. "And you admire that?"

He nodded. "I do."

Jeniver's smile grew. "Is she pretty, too?"

He looked at her, then, prepared to give a vague answer but he found that he couldn't. In all honesty, he simply couldn't diminish a woman who, in his opinion, was quite special. She was pretty, indeed. All that and more.

"Aye," he replied. "She is the most beautiful woman I have ever seen. She is excellent at conversation as well. Evidently, de Lara schooled both of his daughters in military matters and there was much that she and I could discuss. At least, a little bit. She seemed to want to speak of things like flowers and art, mostly."

Jeniver was quite intrigued by the way Maximus was speaking of Lady Courtly and she could see that Tiberius was right. Maximus, the consummate warrior, was indeed enchanted by the woman. It warmed her heart to see it.

"I think that is marvelous," she said sincerely. "She sounds like a wonderful woman. I would like to meet her."

Maximus shrugged and turned back to his horse, slapping the beast affectionately on the withers. "Mayhap you will," he said. Then, he eyed her a moment before breaking down in awkward snorts of laughter. "I will admit to you, and only to you, that I would like to see her again, too."

Jeniver laughed softly and went to him, leaning up against his horse. "We will have to find an excuse to visit her," she said. "Mayhap I should call upon her, as Gallus' wife, and you can ride escort. Would you like that?"

He wouldn't look at her, grinning like a fool. "Mayhap," he said. "I… I was thinking of sending her some fabric and other things that ladies might like. All of her possessions were burned in the fire, you know. She hasn't anything left to wear. She said that she does not even have a comb to use."

Jeniver was dismayed. "Is this true?" she gasped. "Then we must go to town immediately and buy her some material. I will take it to her as a gift from the House of de Shera. It should come from me, you know, at least until you are formally courting her. Then you can provide her with all of the gifts you wish."

Maximus looked at her, feigning shock, although he wasn't doing a very good job. "Who said I am going to court her?"

Jeniver could see that he was very interested in the idea in spite of his protests. "Would you have someone else court her, then?" she asked in a threatening manner. "Ty, mayhap? He would willingly do it."

Maximus' eyes narrowed. "I would kill him if he did," he said, watching a knowing smile play on Jeniver's lips. He shook his head, knowing that she now understood how he felt about Lady Courtly. He had given himself away with the death threat against his brother. Therefore, he signed in resignation. "Very well, you little vixen. You may bring her the gifts and I will ride escort. But do you feel well enough to do it?"

Jeniver nodded firmly. "Of course," she said. "I feel much better today, thanks to the licorice root and chamomile you brought me. You are a very sweet and thoughtful man, Max. Do not let Ty or anyone else make you feel ashamed because of it."

Maximus was back to looking at his feet, away from her knowing and praising gaze. "I am not ashamed."

"But you were ready to throttle your brother when he teased you about it."

Maximus frowned. "That is because Lady Courtly is not to be trifled with," he said, growing frustrated. "She is not an average woman, not in the least. I will not let Ty make sport of her."

Jeniver patted his big arm comfortingly. "I believe you," she said. "Shall we go into town and buy her a few things? I will take them to her with my compliments."

Maximus was still looking at the ground, now kicking absently at it. It was a few moments before he answered. "Aye," he said, casting Jeniver a sideways glance. "I would like to see her again today. It seems as if she is all I can think about. I could not even sleep last night because every time I closed my eyes, she was there. Truthfully, Jeni, I have never felt anything like this in my entire life. It is frightening and wonderful at the same time."

Jeniver was thrilled by his admission. "Then I wish you the very best of luck in your pursuit of Lady Courtly," she said. "I will do all I can to ensure there is another Lady de Shera. It gets rather lonely at times with no womenfolk to talk to. I miss your mother's company very much to that regard."

Maximus sobered. "I miss her very much as well," he said. "After de Montfort's meeting in two days, we are leaving immediately for home. Although I very much want to see to my mother's health, now it seems as if I am reluctant to leave Oxford because Lady Courtly is here. I do not want to go away from her because I am afraid I will never see her again. It is a strange dilemma, indeed."

Jeniver didn't seem to take it too seriously. "Mayhap when we leave for Isenhall, Lady Courtly can go with me," she said. "Mayhap I will speak to her father and tell him that I am in great need of a lady-in-waiting. I am a countess, after all, with only menfolk about me. That is reason enough to ask for her to come."

Maximus was overwhelmed with the thought. "You would do that?"

Jeniver nodded firmly. "Indeed, I would, if it will please you."

Maximus stared at her a moment, trying to imagine returning to Isenhall with Lady Courtly as company. He was nearly overcome with the joy and excitement the mere thought seemed to provoke.

"It would," he finally confessed. "You have no idea how much it would. But if she comes with us, then I should speak to her father about courting her. I… I do believe I would like to marry a woman such as Lady Courtly. I never imagined I would have a marriage that was anything other than a convenience, but when I see you and Gallus together, I realize that I hope for such happiness, too. Mayhap Lady Courtly would bring me such joy. It would be a miraculous thing, indeed."

Jeniver smiled at the man who seemed to have deeper thoughts than she believed him capable of. Was it true that, perhaps, there was a bit of a dreamer in Maximus de Shera? It seemed impossible from his usually warring manner but from his words, now it was seemingly probable. She squeezed his arm encouragingly.

"I hope so, truly," she said softly, sincerely. "It is wonderful to wake up every morning next to the person you love most. I pray you know that feeling, Max. I truly do. Meanwhile, do not let Tiberius upset you so. I believe that if he truly knew the depths of your feelings on the matter of Lady Courtly that he would not be so quick to taunt."

Maximus grunted unhappy. "I hope so," he said. "I do not wish to kill my own brother, but if he continues along his path, it may come to that."

Jeniver laughed softly. "Let us pray it does not," she said. "I will make sure he understands that there is to be no mention of Lady Courtly from his lips. I am sure he will see reason."

Maximus cast her a long glance. "You will not tell him what told you?" he asked hesitantly. "I… I do not wish for him to know what I am feeling, at least not yet. I will tell him in time."

Jeniver shook her head firmly. "I will not breathe a word of it," she said. "But may I tell Gallus? He will want to know. He will not taunt you. Moreover, he will want to know why I am going into town to buy gifts for a woman I have never met."

Maximus was forced to agree. "Then you must tell him," he agreed. "He will not be able to go with us because de Montfort has sent for him this morning. Did he tell you?"

"He did."

"I do not want Tiberius going with us, either."

Jeniver laughed softly. "As you say," she said. "He can go with Gallus to meet with de Montfort."

"De Montfort called for Gallus only. Tiberius can remain here for all I care. Whatever he does, I do not want him going with us."

"I will make sure he does not."

Satisfied, Maximus turned back to his horse, slapping the big neck affectionately. "Let me tend to my horse first and then we shall gather gifts when I am finished. Will you be ready in an hour?"

Jeniver was already moving from the stable. "I am ready now," she said. "But tend your horse. I will tell Gallus where we are going."

Maximus watched Jeniver as she moved halfway across the yard before coming to a halt. Slowly, thoughtfully, she turned back in his direction.

"Max," she said pensively, as if she were stewing on a great idea. "What if I was to invite Lady Courtly to come shopping with me rather than taking gifts to her? Your time with her would probably be better spent. How much will you really be able to speak with her if we take gifts to her home and her father is around? What if we deliver the gifts and he asks us to leave immediately? You will not be able to spend any time with her at all."

Maximus cocked his head curiously. "What makes you think her father will not let me speak to her?" he asked. "I spent a good deal of time speaking to her last evening."

Jeniver shrugged. "But if we bring her with us to town, then your time with her would be... uninterrupted, I would think," she said, rather slyly. "You may even take her shopping, alone, while I go about my business. You could not do that if her father was around. I am simply suggesting that you might like some time alone with her."

Maximus liked her idea very much. "And you would be correct," he said. "Very well, then. We shall go to Kennington and invite her to go to town with us and shop for her needs."

With a clever grin, Jeniver turned back for the inn, and Maximus watched her until she disappeared inside. Then, he turned back to his horse, bending over to feel for the swollen tendon he felt last night. All the while, his thoughts were lingering on the anticipation of shopping with Lady Courtly. He didn't tell Jeniver about the rose oil. He didn't know why. Perhaps because it was the first gift he had ever given a woman and it seemed like such a deeply personal thing, just between the two of them. He wanted to keep that memory private for the moment, something to savor.

As he headed back into the inn to make a poultice for his horse's swollen leg, he imagined all of the grand things he would purchase for Lady Courtly. He was eager to see her expression when he bought them for her, lavishing gifts upon a woman who had lost everything. He hoped that de Lara wouldn't be insulted by the gifts but he told himself that de Lara's angst didn't matter. He planned to ask for permission to court Courtly and he was sure Kellen would have no reason to deny him. He had, after all, saved the woman's life and Kellen had declared that they were all in Maximus' debt. Perhaps it was time for the debt to be paid.

As he thought on the joys of seeing Courtly again, he could not have imagined a very different scene happening that moment at Kennington. Had he known, he would have stopped what he was doing and raced for the manor.

He didn't know he was about to lose Courtly before he ever truly had a chance to gain her.

"BUT, PAPA... I do not understand," Courtly pleaded. "Why are you sending us home? What have we done?"

It was after sunrise following the evening with Maximus de Shera as their guest. The morning was bright if not cold, and somewhere during the night rain had fallen, leaving the bailey a soupy mess of mud. De Lara's men were milling about, starting cooking fires to warm over the remains of last night's pork stew, but along with those men going about their duties, there were about ten of them forming a traveling party near Kennington's iron gate.

It was this traveling party that Courtly was referring to. Standing in the doorway of the lower level of the wing where the bedchambers were, she was wrapped in a woolen coverlet against the morning's chill. She had nothing else to use against the cold. Her father had awoken her and Isadora just after dawn, telling his daughters that they were returning to their home on the marches that day. Then he had turned and walked away, but the news had Courtly on her feet and running after her father to confront him. Now, the confrontation was here as Kellen turned to answer his daughter's question.

"You have not done anything," he said stiffly. "I am sending you home because I do not believe Oxford is a good place for you. With the fire yesterday, now you have nothing at all by way of possessions, and I do not see Ellice providing anything to you so it is best to send you home. It is safer and better for you there."

That wasn't the truth behind the directive and Courtly knew it. She suspected from the onset what was behind her father's sudden decision to send her home and she would not tactfully couch her accusation. It came out in force as her father tried to turn away from her.

"That is not true," she hissed. "Could this have something to do with Maximus de Shera, Papa?"

Kellen paused to look at her, eyes narrowing. "I do not know what you mean," he said, trying to turn away again. "Make sure Isadora is ready to leave within the hour."

Courtly bolted out of the doorway and grabbed her father by the arm, stopping him from going any further.

"We are *not* going anywhere," she said. "I knew you were watching Maximus last night when he spoke with me. You were watching him from the moment he entered the hall, weren't you? From the very moment the man said his first word to me, you were watching him with suspicion. How could you do that, Papa? How could you show such mistrust for the man who saved the lives of your children?"

Kellen grunted. "The man didn't talk to the rest of us – only to you."

"He was our guest! Was I supposed to ignore him?"

Kellen yanked his arm away from her grasp. Their first conversation of the day had become very brittle, very quickly, and he was caught off-guard by it. He didn't like fighting with his precious Courtly and wasn't very adept in handling his emotions where it pertained to her.

"I never said this decision had anything to do with Maximus de Shera," he insisted, although it was weakly done. "Why would you accuse me of such a thing?"

His denial angered her. "Because it is true!" she fired at him.

"You always behave the same way when any man comes within ten feet of me. You think every man in England is out to ravage me. It simply isn't true!"

Kellen was trying not to lose ground in this argument. Maximus' attention towards Courtly had him up all night and by morning he'd made his decision what to do about it. He knew he couldn't chase a de Shera away as he'd done with other suitors. Therefore, it stood to reason that if he couldn't send the man away, he needed to send his daughter away where the man could not get to her. Still, he would not admit to her accusation. He didn't like having his decisions questioned.

"I have no idea what you mean," he said, again. "I am sending you back to Trelystan because you and your sister have nothing and your aunt has not yet returned this morning, so it is doubtful you will have anything you need to replace what you lost."

Courtly threw up her hands in a gesture of utter frustration. "We can just as easily go into Oxford to purchase items to replace what we lost in the fire," she pointed out. "You would rather send us home, more than two weeks on the road, with absolutely nothing to our name? We would have to stop somewhere, at some time, to purchase something to tide us over. Why not purchase it here?"

Kellen's jaw ticked angrily and he was having a difficult time looking at his daughter. "You will be safer at home," he said, avoiding her question. "I should not have brought you with me to Oxford. There is too much danger here."

Courtly grunted with frustration. "There is no danger here," she said. "You have made up any danger in your mind. Admit it, Papa – you want to send me home because Maximus de Shera was kind to me. He showed me attention. Every time a man shows me attention, you do your very best to send him away. Now, you are sending *me* away because you cannot send a de Shera away. Admit it!"

Kellen growled and turned away from her. "You are mad."

Courtly watched him march away. "Mayhap I am," she called after him, furious. "But I am *not* going home!"

With that, she stomped back into the building, slamming the door behind her. When she returned to the small, dark chamber she shared with her sister, Isadora was sitting up in bed, sleepily rubbing her eyes.

"Why were you shouting?" Isadora wanted to know, yawning. "Why was Papa here?"

Courtly was hurt, frustrated, and angry. She sat heavily on the end of the bed, near tears. She knew what her father was capable of but this was one suitor she did not wish for him to chase away. Speaking with Maximus the night before, it was as if they were the only two people in the entire hall. Her father had been right. Maximus had *only* spoken to her for most of the night. He had been attentive, kind, and humorous. It was true that she had done most of the talking, but he had listened most carefully. And when he spoke in that deep, melodious voice, it was enough to send bolts of excitement coursing up her spine. She could have listened to that voice forever.

But she knew her father had been watching. He'd been watching both of them since the moment they came back from the kitchens. Although Maximus' brother was able to engage Kellen in conversation, monopolizing the man for the entire evening, it was clear that Kellen had been distracted by the conversation going on between Maximus and his daughter. Courtly had been fully expecting her father to make a comment about it but she certainly hadn't expected the man to make an attempt to send her home. Well, she wasn't going no matter what he said.

"Papa wants to send us back to Trelystan," she finally said, answering her sister's question. "I told him we are not going."

Isadora appeared puzzled. "Why does he want to send us back?"

Courtly looked at her sister, then. "Because he wants to send me away from Sir Maximus," she said. "He did not like the attention the man paid to me last night. We knew this would happen, Issie. It always does."

Isadora yawned again although she was becoming more lucid. "I saw Papa," she said. "He watched you and Sir Maximus all night."

Courtly sighed heavily and hung her head. Her frustration and anger was wearing off, being replaced by a powerful sense of disappointment. *Not this time, Papa. I will not let you do it this time!*

"Why does he do it, Is?" she sighed. "I did not much care when he chased away my first two suitors, old men who had summoned me because they had heard I was beautiful. I did not even care when he chased away that young knight who had been traveling from Ireland. What was his name? De Royans? And if Papa knew that Kirk St. Héver has tried to show me attention, he would dismiss the man forever. But with Sir Maximus, I do not want to go home and never see him again."

Isadora watched her sister's sad expression and felt very sorry for her, as sorry as a child could feel. She didn't yet understand the allure of men and of marriage, but someday she would. She didn't want to face what her sister was facing. Climbing out of bed, she went to her sister, snuggling against her, trying to give the woman some comfort.

"Papa is afraid," she said simply. "He is afraid someone will take you away from him."

Courtly sighed. "I wish it was that simple," she said. "It seems as if there is something more than that, something...."

She was cut off when the door to the chamber suddenly swung open, revealing Ellice in the doorway. Isadora gasped with fright at the unexpected sight of her aunt, who looked damp and disheveled, as if she had been running all night long. Her eyes had an edgy gleam to them. Courtly, however, did nothing more than meet the woman's gaze. She was in no mood for the woman's games, now appearing as if Lazarus had just returned from the dead, when she had been missing all night.

"Greetings, Auntie," she said without enthusiasm. "We missed you last eve."

Ellice eyed her niece. "I was told you cooked the meal," she said. "Is this true?"

Courtly looked away. "I had little choice," she said. "You ran off and took your servants with you, including the cook. We could only find one girl to help. I suppose she was the one who told you that I cooked."

Ellice remained in the doorway, the stench of moldering leaves wafting into the room, so much so that Isadora actually put her fingers to her nose. Ellice smelled as terrible as she looked.

"There were others," Ellice said vaguely. "I will commend you for doing what needed to be done. I did not know you had such strength in you."

It was as close to a compliment as Ellice had ever come, a surprising comment, but Courtly was unimpressed. "It does not matter," she said. "Papa wants to send us home so you will not have to worry over us any longer. I am sure Papa will leave Kennington, too, so you can return to your normal life without all of us underfoot."

Ellice was only interested in a small part of that statement. "Why is he sending you home?"

Courtly simply shook her head. She had no intention of telling the woman the truth, but Isadora, being unable to keep her mouth shut, spoke.

"Because Papa does not like that Maximus de Shera paid attention to Courtly," she told her aunt. "Sir Maximus was our guest last night at the feast. He is the one who helped save us from the fire. Papa wants to send us home so Sir Maximus will forget about my sister."

Ellice stared at the girl. At that moment, something shifted in her eyes. A twinkle, a glimmer, perhaps an inkling of remembrance came to the woman's expression. Her pale, damp face seemed to change also and her cheeks began to grow pink. Flushed, even. Coming into the room, she slammed the door behind her and focused on Courtly.

"Tell me everything," she demanded quietly. "What did my brother do?"

Courtly wasn't sure why her aunt was asking such questions, questions she surely didn't want to answer. She glanced at the woman but made no real move to respond.

"He did not do anything," she said, looking away. "Papa simply said he wants to send us home."

Isadora jumped into the conversation because Courtly didn't seem apt to tell their aunt what she knew. She didn't stop to think that it was because Courtly didn't want the woman to know.

"Papa does not like it when men pay attention to Courtly," she said. "He has sent away six suitors already and last night, Sir Maximus was very kind to my sister. Papa does not like that and he wants to send us both home."

Ellice digested what Isadora told her. "Did he say anything to your guest? To Sir Maximus?"

Isadora shook her head. "I do not think so," he said. "Papa spoke with Sir Maximus' brother all night long. I do not think he spoke to Sir Maximus at all."

"What is this to you?" Courtly asked, interrupting Isadora. Her gaze was both pleading and frustrated upon her aunt. "This is not your business, Auntie. This is between Papa and me. You do not need to know these things. Surely you do not care."

Ellice gazed steadily at her niece, her lips twitching with a shade of a snarl. She was very good at snarling when provoked, something that was both intimidating and frightening. But instead of snapping off a bitter retort, she abruptly turned for the door, muttering to herself as she moved.

"He will *not* do this again," she hissed. "Not again. I will not let him do this again."

With that, she was gone, leaving Courtly and Isadora looking rather perplexed by her abrupt departure. But the mumbling had Courtly on edge and she stood up, going to the door and watching as her aunt disappeared through the doorway that led out into the ward. She could still hear the woman muttering.

"What is wrong with Auntie?" Isadora wanted to know.

Courtly shook her head, puzzled. "I do not know," she said. "But mayhap I should follow her and find out."

Leaving Isadora still upon the bed, Courtly followed her aunt's trail, pursuing the woman out of the building and into the ward of Kennington. The day was deepening and the sun had risen, casting its golden rays across the land. The mud, which had been so heavy in the early morning, was starting to dry up a little. Smoke, heavy from the cooking fires, blanketed the complex. As Courtly looked around for her aunt, she began to hear yelling. Following the sounds, she came to the northwest corner of the two-storied building, noting her aunt and father several feet away. Ellice was clearly livid as she spoke to her brother.

"Will you do this again, Kellen?" Ellice was saying. "First with me and now with your own daughter? Will you be the one to drive men away from her so that she grows up embittered and lonely? You cannot do this to her."

Kellen's back was to Courtly as he angrily waved his sister off. "You speak of things long past," he said. "You are speaking of things that happened twenty years ago."

Ellice was nearly shrieking. "Twenty years, aye!" she cried. "But to me, it was yesterday. It was yesterday when you sent my love away and he never came back. Don't you realize what that did to me and to my life? I had to hear that he married another and I wanted to die from the sorrow I felt. And now you will do the same thing to your own daughter? I cannot allow it. You are a selfish, cruel man to want to keep the womenfolk in your family alone and unattached and utterly dependent upon you. Still, I am dependent upon you and ever will be. I hate you for it!"

Kellen shook his head, trying to move away from her. "I will not discuss this with you."

Ellice followed. "If you do not, I will follow you around and speak of terrible and private things until you listen to me. Do you want your men to hear how you chased off every suitor I ever had until no one came? Do you want them to hear how you controlled me and used money to either reward or punish me, so long as I did what you wanted?"

Kellen whirled on her, bellowing. "You are chattel," he roared. "You are my responsibility and I did what I felt best for you. I will do it for my daughters as well and you will not question me, you ungrateful cow."

Ellice had that snarling expression upon her lips again as she watched her brother yell at her but, at this point, Courtly stopped listening. She'd heard far too much already. It was shocking to hear how her father had treated his sister, how he had chased away the man she loved. Now, so much was clear as to why Ellice behaved the way she did. If what she said was true, and Kellen's answers seemed to support it, then Ellice's manner was a direct result of Kellen's control over every aspect of her life, even suitors. It was little wonder why Ellice was the way she was. Now, it was all starting to make some sense. And that thought scared Courtly to death.

*I do not want to be like my aunt,* she thought to herself as she scurried back for the door that would lead back inside the structure. *Is it really true? Did Papa chase off all of Auntie's marital prospects?* But even as she thought it, she knew it was true because her father behaved the same way with her. Old patterns repeating themselves, now with his own daughters. But if Courtly had anything to say about it, the pattern would not be the same. She intended to destroy it for her sake as well as for Isadora's sake. She couldn't let the man deliberately turn them into spinsters. The mere thought was sickening.

As she headed back to the house and to her sister, she heard commotion at the gate but she didn't pay any attention. Soldiers were calling to one another and somewhere in the middle of it she heard St. Héver's distinctive bellow. But she entered the building after that and heard no more, moving into the small bedchamber where Isadora was pulling on her stockings and shoes. The girl looked up from her right foot when her sister entered the room.

"Where did you go?" Isadora asked. "What is Auntie doing?"

Courtly was lost in thought, mulling over what she had just heard and the implications of it. She looked at Isadora, shock and confusion on her face.

"She is talking to Papa," she said. "Oh, Issie, you would not believe what they are speaking of. Auntie said... she said that Papa chased away all of her suitors and that is why she is so unhappy and nasty. She said she is lonely and bitter and that Papa is the cause."

Isadora's brow furrowed. "Papa chased men away from her, too?"

Courtly nodded. "That is what she said," she replied. "He is doing the same thing to me and will do the same thing to you. I do not want to end up like Auntie, old and alone and mean."

Isadora was still a bit too young to fully grasp what Courtly was saying. Suitors and men had no real meaning in her world. But she knew that someday, they would mean a great deal.

"What will you do?" she asked, concerned.

Courtly shook her head, trying not to become despondent. "I do not know yet," she said, running her hand over her hair, which was mussed from sleep and also from the fact that she had no comb. She began to run her fingers through it, trying to smooth it down. "But I know that I will not become a spinster. Why does he do it, Is? Why does he chase men away? He knows that I want to marry someday. Why is no man good enough?"

Isadora didn't have an answer for her. She put her other shoe on and stood up, going to her sister and running her hands over Courtly's hair. She liked brushing her sister's hair, and braiding it, so she took over the duties as her sister stewed about their father's predilection towards running off suitors. It was of much greater concern to Courtly than to Isadora, especially since there was now a knight that Courtly was interested in. She could sense her sister's sadness and disappointment.

They fell silent as Courtly brooded and Isadora brushed her sister's hair with her fingers. She was able to smooth it enough so that it looked moderately combed and then she braided it into an elaborate braid. Having nothing to secure it with, she ended up tearing a strip of linen off the end of the coverlet and using the piece to tie off her sister's hair. Having no clean clothing, soap or water to wash with, it was the best they could do in order to groom themselves. As Isadora finished with the braid, there was a knock on the chamber door.

Isadora scooted over to the panel and opened it. One of their aunt's servants was standing in the darkened corridor outside, an older woman, and she looked directly at Courtly.

"M'lady," she said. "Lady Ellice asks you to come to the ward."

Courtly sighed heavily. She was so depressed that she didn't even question the servant's instructions. She simply stood up and left the room, following the woman out into the ward.

Courtly could feel the chill as she stepped outside but she had left the coverlet wrap back in the bedchamber and she pondered returning for it. However, it occurred to her that there were a great many unfamiliar people in the ward and her focus was diverted to the crowd. It took her a moment to realize that there were soldiers in the bailey bearing colors of black and yellow. She had noticed those colors on one of the knights who had accompanied Sir Maximus on the previous evening and her heart suddenly leapt into her throat. She could hardly breathe. Was it possible that Sir Maximus had returned? Suddenly giddy with excitement, yet with some confusion, she made her way towards the group.

As she drew closer, she could see that her father was standing next to a carriage, speaking with a beautiful, young woman inside it. Her aunt was standing several feet away, watching the entire circumstance suspiciously, but Courtly headed in the woman's direction. It was her aunt who had sent for her, after all. She wanted to know why.

"Auntie?" she said as she approached. "What is happening?"

Ellice, hearing her niece's voice, whirled around and reached out, grasping the woman by the wrist and pulling her close. That was an unusual move for Ellice who usually kept everyone at arm's length. Courtly was hit with the smell of rotten, moldering leaves as she drew near her aunt. The woman smelled of compost.

"Your Sir Maximus has returned and he has brought rein-forcements," Ellice hissed at her. "See the woman in the carriage? That is the Earl of Coventry's wife. She is asking for you."

Shocked, Courtly looked at the carriage. It was very fine, paint-ed in colors of yellow and black, and the woman inside was quite elegant and lovely. She had very dark hair and a porcelain-like face, now speaking very politely to Kellen. Courtly couldn't hear the words but she could see that the lady was smiling at Kellen, obviously engaging him in pleasant conversation. Courtly had no idea what to make of the situation.

"But why is she here?" Courtly asked. "Where is Sir Maximus?"

Ellice shook her head. "I do not know him on sight but I heard the lady mention him," she said quietly. Then, she gave Courtly a shove towards the Coventry carriage. "Go, now. Show yourself. The countess wishes to speak with you!"

Courtly stumbled as her aunt pushed but she caught herself and moved towards the carriage as instructed. She was fixed on the lovely woman speaking to her father, quite curious about her appearance here at Kennington. But she was eager to see Sir Maximus again and her eyes darted about, trying to find him in the group of Coventry men, but they were all dressed in armor and tunics that made them all look alike.

Her hunt for Sir Maximus abruptly ended when she finally locked eyes with the Countess of Coventry and Kellen, seeing the countess' shift in focus, turned to see that his daughter was nearly standing next to him.

Startled by Courtly's unexpected appearance, Kellen's initial reaction was one of anger. He almost ordered her away but realized that he could not, not in front of all of these people. In truth, he had been preparing to tell Lady de Shera that his daughter was unavailable when Courtly appeared. Therefore, he did the only thing he could do. He hastened to make introductions.

"Lady de Shera," he said, sounding displeased. "This is my daughter, Lady Courtly. It is she who you have been inquiring about."

Kellen would look back on that moment as the day that changed his life forever.

# CHAPTER SIX

I N THE MUDDY, cold, and bright bailey of Kennington, Jeniver studied Courtly intently, very curious about the woman who had captured Maximus' heart.

Lady Courtly was about the same size and shape as she was, with bright, blue eyes and long, dusky lashes. Her hair was a lovely shade of blond that had been swept into a braid, complimenting her sweet, oval face. In truth, Jeniver was not disappointed in what she saw. She could easily understand Maximus' attraction to the luminous lady.

"Greetings, my lady," Jeniver said. "I am honored to meet you. As I was telling your father, my husband's brother, Maximus, told us of your harrowing adventure yesterday and also of the wonderful feast he attended last night. He is most impressed with your father's hospitality and also by your culinary skills."

The countess had a sweet, honeyed voice, and Courtly curtsied smoothly. "I am the one who is honored, Lady de Shera," she said. "Sir Maximus surely saved my life and the life of my sister. Providing him with a meal was the least we could do to thank him for his efforts."

Jeniver laughed softly. "And he was very thankful for it," she said. "We are staying at The One-Eyed Raven in town and the food there has not been particularly good, unfortunately. I think he was very grateful for an excellent meal by your hand."

Courtly smiled because Jeniver was. Already, the woman had a way of making her feel at ease. She didn't act like any countess Courtly had ever met. Lady de Shera was friendly and warm, and given that Courtly spent nearly all of her time with either her father or sister, she didn't have much opportunity to make new friends. Immediately, she felt drawn to her.

"As I said, we were honored to provide it, my lady," she said. "I am very glad Sir Maximus enjoyed it."

Jeniver nodded. "Indeed," she said. "Wherever did you learn to cook?"

"I fostered for a time at Prudhoe Castle, my lady. Lady d'Umfraville learned the culinary arts in France and taught us."

Jeniver watched Courtly as she spoke. She was well-spoken and polite. She could see how the young woman had entranced Maximus. She knew for a fact that her brother-in-law was behind her, grouped among the de Shera men, waiting very impatiently for Jeniver to make her move and ask for Lady Courtly's company on a shopping excursion. The time for small talk and meaningless chatter was over. It was time to move to the point of their visit before the situation became awkward.

"Lady d'Umfraville taught you very well," Jeniver said. Then, she eyed both Kellen and Courtly as she spoke. "In fact, that is why I have come. Lord de Lara, I am alone in Oxford save my husband and his brothers, with no lady to attend me. It has come to my attention that your daughter is cultured and knowledgeable, and I wonder if I could beg you to allow me to take Lady Courtly with me into town. I must do some shopping and I very much need a lady by my side. For my position, after all, it is unseemly that I do not have any ladies-in-waiting. I pray upon your good graces that you will allow me the company of your daughter for the duration of my stay in Oxford."

Kellen looked at Jeniver, shocked and speechless by the request. He knew the request was one of honor. For the wife of an earl to ask for the service of a daughter was honorable, indeed, but Kellen wasn't sure he could agree for two very good reasons – the first being that he did not like his children out of his sight where he could not keep a watchful eye over them. That was the main reason he had recalled Courtly from Prudhoe Castle, in fact. True, he wanted her home, but it was mostly so he could watch over her and keep his daughters under the same roof. *His* roof.

But the second reason, of course, was that Maximus de Shera was Lady de Shera's brother-in law. If Courtly was around Lady de Shera, then Maximus would be there, too. Nay, he could not allow that, not in the least. He struggled to refuse without insulting the countess.

"That is a most gracious offer, Lady de Shera," he said, stumbling. "But… you see, I have a younger daughter and Courtly must tend her. I surely cannot let her go or I will have no one to tend my younger child."

"I will look after her."

They all turned around to see Ellice standing a few feet away. It was she who had offered. Kellen scowled at his sister.

"You?" he asked. "*You?* You do not know anything about tending children, Ellice."

Ellice's expression upon her brother was one of abject hatred. "And that is your fault, is it not?" she volleyed, with Lady de Shera listening. As Kellen struggled not to explode at her, Ellice walked up beside her niece and looked to Lady de Shera. "My niece would be an excellent companion, my lady. There is no reason why you cannot take her right now, in fact. I will look after the younger girl."

Kellen was beside himself with outrage but he dare not vent his anger in front of the countess. As it was, he was straddling a very fine line of courtesy versus insult. He knew Lady de Shera was watching him, awaiting his answer, but he was having a very difficult time giving one.

"This is all so sudden," he finally said, backing away from the carriage so he would have more room to think and to breathe. He couldn't do either with Lady de Shera's attention on him. "My daughters' stay in Oxford has not been a pleasant one. You heard of the fire yesterday, no doubt, and all of their possessions were lost. I was preparing to send them both back to Trelystan Castle, this morning in fact. They will be much safer at home."

He was speaking quickly, as if he were scrambling for a reason to deny Lady de Shera's request, and Jeniver was coming to sense something more than mere reluctance in the man. Her request for the company of Lady Courtly had rattled him deeply and she didn't understand why. Surely any father would have been happy for his daughter to be taken into the house of a countess as her lady, but it was clear de Lara didn't think that way. There was something very odd with the man, indeed.

"You do not have to decide at this moment, Lord de Lara," she said, trying to salvage the situation somehow, "but at least let me take her to town with me and shop. I require her company and her opinion on many things. Will you please do this for me? My husband will be very pleased if you do."

She purposely brought up the husband to force de Lara's hand. Gallus de Shera was not only the Earl of Coventry, but he was also the right hand of Simon de Montfort. To have connections to such a man during this dark and turbulent time would be a prideful thing, indeed. Jeniver was also, not so subtly, telling Lord de Lara that Gallus would be quite displeased if the man denied her request. Therefore, Kellen had no choice and he knew it. His jaw began to tick, struggling not to become angry over the situation and over Lady de Shera's control. He didn't like a woman, any woman, to have control over his decisions.

"Very well," he said, smiling thinly. "You may take her to shop but I would have her returned home before nightfall. I will insist, my lady."

Courtly, who had been watching the exchange carefully, was so relieved and excited when he gave permission that she nearly shouted, but she managed to keep control. If her father saw that she was too happy, he might do his best to go back on his word. Therefore, she remained demure and polite as a de Shera knight opened the door to the cab and Courtly quickly climbed in. She looked to see if it was Maximus who had opened the door but it was not. It was a very young knight with brilliant, blue eyes.

The carriage pulled away without another word to Kellen, as if they were anxious to get away from him and remove themselves from Kennington's bailey. The de Lara escort formed loose ranks and followed the carriage, thundering out of the ward. As the big, iron gates lurched closed, Kellen turned to his sister.

Gazing into his hard eyes, it was the first time Ellice had every truly been afraid of her brother.

*Oxford*

NOT A WORD was spoken between Jeniver and Courtly until they were well away from Kennington. In fact, the carriage was awkwardly quiet for several long minutes. Courtly would not speak until the countess did and Jeniver wasn't sure how she was going to start the conversation. They were strangers, after all, and Jeniver had essentially abducted the woman from her father. She had given the man no choice, but she wasn't sorry in the least. As she observed Courtly as the woman watched the passing landscape through the cab window, she was coming to think there was something rather downcast about the woman. She was both concerned and intrigued.

"It is very kind of you to accompany me, my lady," Jeniver finally said, smiling when Courtly looked at her. "It looks as if the weather will hold. It should be a fine day."

Courtly nodded. "Indeed, Lady de Shera," she said, returning her gaze to the carriage window. "I... I would like to thank you for inviting me to attend you. I have never attended a fine lady before. Well, except for Lady d'Umfraville, but she had several ladies-in-waiting and a half-dozen wards. I was one of many."

Jeniver grinned. "It sounds as if she had an entire court at her disposal."

Courtly laughed softly. "She did," she agreed. "And she behaved much like a queen would. She was gracious and generous, but she was not afraid to take a switch to you if the situation warranted."

Now it was Jeniver's turn to laugh. "God's Bones," she said. "That is positively tyrannical."

Courtly shook her head. "Not really," she said. "She was a very kind woman. Having lost my mother at a young age, I appreciated her guidance."

Jeniver's smile faded. "Then you and I have a great deal in common," she said. "I lost my mother at a young age, also."

It was common ground that immediately bonded them. "Do you remember your mother, my lady?" Courtly asked. "I was fostering when my mother died. My memories of her are distant, almost as if I have dreamt her."

Jeniver understood. "I have very little memory of my mother," she said. "I was very young when she passed away. It was only my father and me for many years until I met my husband."

Courtly was feeling comfortable with the conversation and with Lady de Shera. It was very rare when she had the opportunity to converse with women and, as she'd felt almost immediately upon meeting Lady de Shera, she was drawn to the woman's warmth and kindness.

"We have more in common than you realize, my lady," she said. "It has only been my father and my younger sister all of these years."

Jeniver cocked her head curiously. "What of the woman who offered to tend your sister?" she asked. "Who was that?"

Courtly lifted her eyebrows in an ironic gesture that only she understood. "That is my father's sister, Lady Ellice," she said. "My aunt and my father do not get on well. They fight constantly. She did not have a hand in raising me."

There was something both ironic and bitter in that statement but Jeniver ignored it without making it seem too obvious that she was. "I am sure your father did a fine job on his own," she said. Then, she shifted the subject a bit. "Your name is very pretty and very unusual. Is it a family name?"

Courtly grinned. "It is not," she said. "My mother named me Courtly Love because she was a woman who was quite enamored with all things romantic and chivalrous. I cannot tell you how much I detest my own name, however. I had always wished for something elegant and lovely, like Elizabeth or Eleanor."

Jeniver shook her head. "Pah," she scoffed softly. "Boring names, both of those. Your name is unique and lovely. It is very regal, I think."

Courtly shrugged, flattered. "My mother chose the name because she said that every woman should know courtly love and thought that the name would bring me great love in my life."

Jeniver giggled softly. "Has it?"

Courtly immediately thought of Maximus and her cheeks flushed unexpectedly. Startled at her reaction, she looked at her lap, trying not to appear too embarrassed.

"Not yet," she admitted. "But I hope it will, my lady."

Jeniver watched the woman, her head lowered with her pink cheeks, and she could see that perhaps the lady was as taken with Maximus as Maximus was with her. The red cheeks, the sudden inclination to demure... it was just a feeling she had. And it gave her great hope for Maximus' sake.

"Surely you have more than one prospect, my lady," she said leading.

Courtly shrugged. "I have had suitors," she said, fighting off the giddy flush that thoughts of Maximus provoked. "Unfortunately, my father is not keen to me having a suitor. He has chased them all away. But I hope that someday there will be a man he will be unable to chase away."

Jeniver studied her carefully as she delivered her reply. "Do you have anyone particular in mind?"

"Mayhap."

"Have you considered Maximus?"

Courtly's head shot up, her eyes wide. "Why... why would you ask, my lady?" she asked, almost fearfully. "I have never... that is to say, Sir Maximus saved my life yesterday and I have the utmost respect and gratitude towards him. I have never indicated anything else."

Jeniver could see, quite clearly, that she had struck a nerve. Courtly had the same look that Maximus did when the idea of attraction between the two had been broached. She put up her hand to ease the woman.

"I know you have not been improper with him," she assured her. "That is not what I mean. What I meant was... if Maximus was to call upon you, then I doubt your father would be able to chase him away. No one chases Maximus de Shera away, in any case. He is a fine, noble, and compassionate man, and he is the greatest warrior in England. Aside from my husband, that is. Maximus will make some fortunate woman an excellent husband."

Courtly was back to looking at her lap as Lady de Shera's words rolled over and over in her mind. Her fingers were fidgeting but beyond her slender fingers and chapped skin, she could see the dusty, dark green dress that she had been wearing since yesterday. It didn't smell too much like smoke any longer but it was still rather dirty and worn. She sighed faintly, brushing at the dress.

"I am sure he will, my lady," she said quietly. "But why should he want to call upon me? Did he tell you how we met?"

Jeniver nodded. "He said he saved your life when your hostel burned."

Courtly rolled her eyes, rather miserably. The way she and Maximus had met wasn't something she ever envisioned herself speaking of, but at this moment, it was on the tip of her tongue. For whatever reason, she felt the need to confide in Lady de Shera, perhaps because she had never really had anyone to confide to in all of her life. This was all very new to her.

"I fell on his head, my lady," she said, embarrassed and distressed. "I was climbing down a rope I had made of bed linens and the rope gave way, so I crashed down on his head and… and my skirt went over his head, trapping the top-half of him within my skirts when we fell to the ground."

Jeniver's eyes widened. She opened her mouth to say something, perhaps offer her condolences on such an undignified meeting, but she ended up laughing. She slapped a hand over her mouth.

"It is not true!" she hissed, stifling her giggles.

Seeing that Lady de Shera was laughing should have upset Courtly greatly, but it didn't. She, too, saw the humor of the situation, now a day after it happened. At the time, it was the worst possible thing that could have happened but now, in hindsight, it *was* rather funny. She struggled not to smile.

"I am afraid that it is," she said, remembering the entire event with great clarity. "But... but that was not the worst part. He became entangled in my skirts with his head... where it should not have been, my lady, and I swear I thought he was a beast, a fiend at the very least. As his head remained trapped in my skirts, I... I beat his head through the fabric."

Jeniver couldn't help it, she burst out laughing, so much so that Courtly started to chuckle whether or not she wanted to. Jeniver's laugher was contagious and, as Courtly thought on the situation, she realized just how funny it really was. She began to scream with laughter, too. As they rolled along the rocky, hole-prone road towards Oxford, the entire carriage was echoing with laughter.

"God's Bones," Jeniver gasped, wiping tears from her eyes. "That is the best thing I have heard in weeks. You say you really beat him around the head?"

Courtly was still snorting. "I did, my lady."

Jeniver was off in gales of laughter again until she was weak with it. Struggling to catch her breath, she was leaning back against the cushioned side of the cab when a very big horse and an armored leg appeared near the cab window. There was a very big hand, too, gloved, and as the horse plodded along, the man astride it bent over so he could look into the cab window.

"What is happening in there?" Maximus asked. "All I hear is screaming."

Jeniver glanced at Courtly, who had the look of absolute surprise and absolute elation on her face. But Courtly abruptly looked at her, horrified that the woman was going to tell him why they had been laughing and Jeniver subtly shook her head.

"It is not of your affair, Maximus de Shera," she told the man. "We are speaking of womanly things. You would not be interested."

Maximus flipped up his three-point visor, of the latest style, and looked between Jeniver and Courtly. Mostly, he was looking at

Courtly. His eyes lingered on her, like a gentle caress, something that didn't go unnoticed by Jeniver. She'd never seen that expression on Maximus' face, ever.

"I suppose you told her why she is here," he said to Jeniver.

Jeniver, a sly smile on her face, shook her head. "I have not," she said. "Now you have ruined the surprise. Go back and ride behind the carriage, Maximus. You are spoiling all of my fun."

Maximus grinned, flashing those straight white teeth framed by the beard. "Hurry and tell her before we arrive," he said. "Oxford is up ahead. I can see it now."

Courtly was looking at Jeniver very curiously at this point. Jeniver, seeing the woman's expression, sighed dramatically.

"Oh, very well, Maximus," she said, even though she was looking at Courtly. "It has come to our attention, Lady Courtly, that all of your possessions were burned in the fire yesterday. Is that correct?"

Courtly nodded, although she was somewhat confused by the question. "They were," she said. "That is why I must apologize for my state of dress. This is all I have to wear and...."

Jeniver cut her off, gently done. "I know," she said. "Maximus and I discussed your predicament and he would like to take you shopping for a few things to replace what you lost."

Courtly was hit with a wave of utter delight, of utter shock. "But why?" she asked, to both of them, but ended up looking at Maximus. "Sir Maximus, it was not your fault that my possessions burned. You certainly do not have to replace anything."

He was bent over his horse, looking at her through the cab window. "I know," he said. "I want to do it. It would give me great pleasure, my lady. Please do not deny me."

Courtly stared at him, unsure of what to say to that. She didn't want to be rude, but she wasn't sure what her father would say to all of this, either. He might be offended by others paying for what his daughter had lost. Perplexed, she looked at Jeniver.

"I thought we were going to shop for items *you* needed, my lady," she said.

Jeniver lifted her slender shoulders. "I am going to shop for items I need," she said. "If you are agreeable, Maximus will take you shopping for a few items that *you* need."

Courtly still wasn't following her meaning. "Then you and I are not going together?"

Jeniver shook her head. "Maximus will be perfectly behaved, I assure you," she answered. "It will be quite safe to go with him alone. Unless, of course, you would rather come with me, in which case, Maximus will accompany us. The choice is yours."

It was a wide-open question, the answer of which could have implications on both Maximus' life and Courtly's. The opportunity was presenting itself for a potential suitor to have some time with Courtly, away from her father, and the realization was almost too much to comprehend. In fact, it was too *good* to comprehend. Courtly could hardly believe it, but it was becoming readily apparent to her that this had been planned all along – Maximus wanted to spend time alone with her, much as he had done in the kitchen the previous night, and Lady Jeniver was helping him accomplish that. Overwhelmed with the scandalous joy of such a thing, all Courtly could do was nod.

"Aye, my lady," she replied softly, with emotion in her voice. "I will go with him, alone. I would be honored."

Jeniver smiled. "It could be considered quite unseemly by others," she warned gently. "Surely you understand that."

"I understand."

Jeniver was pleased that the lure of being alone with Maximus was worth the risk of gossips. That showed that Lady Courtly had some bravery in her and it also showed that perhaps her feelings for Maximus were indeed genuine. In any case, the woman was agreeable, as they had hoped. Jeniver turned to Maximus.

"Max?" she said, catching his attention. "Hurry us along to Oxford, now. You and Lady Courtly have shopping to do."

Maximus didn't need to be told twice.

*Oxford Castle*

"GALLUS, WE MUST move. We must convene at Westminster."

The ominous words came from Simon de Montfort. Leader of the baron's rebellion against Henry III, he had essentially been in control of the country since the end of April when the king had been virtually overthrown by de Montfort and his most powerful barons, Hugh Bigod and Gallus de Shera included.

Hugh Bigod was also in on this meeting along with Peter de Montfort, of no relation to Simon, Hugh's brother Roger, John Fitzgeoffrey, and Richard de Clare. These were some of the most powerful men in England at this time, men who ruled alongside de Montfort, but Simon's latest words had Gallus furrowing his brow.

"Why?" Gallus asked, perplexed. "I thought we were meeting here, with all of our supporters, in two days?"

De Montfort shook his head. A big man, he was older but he was still quite strong and healthy. He sat heavily in the nearest chair, one of oak with a silk pillow on the seat, and one that happened to be the closest to the pewter decanter of wine that de Montfort was so fond of. As the man poured himself a draught of wine, he spoke.

"Our main goal last month when Hugh wrested power from the king was that a council be set up to govern the country so the king does not have absolute rule," he said. "You know this, Gallus. You were there when Henry agreed to surrender his absolute rule in favor of a council of twenty-four men, chosen equally by him and by us."

Gallus snorted. "The king did not have much choice with Maximus standing over him," he said. "He was afraid he was about to be arrested or worse. Maximus has that effect on people."

Simon's lips flickered with a smile as he remembered the incident. Henry had been caught off-guard by a mutiny of his barons and, fearful of being thrown in the Tower, had agreed to their terms. That was essentially how de Montfort had come to power, but the struggle wasn't over, not in the least.

"So he does," Simon agreed. He took a long swallow of wine and wiped his lips with the back of his hand. "I have received word that Henry has chosen his representatives for the council and, unfortunately, I agree with none of them. Most of them are damnable Poitevins, Henry's relatives from France that seem to be infiltrating our country by the hundreds. Those men have no right to rule England."

It was serious news, indeed. The king's French relatives were one of the main points of contention between Henry and his barons.

"What do we do?" Gallus asked quietly. "Henry was free to choose his representatives, as we were free to choose ours."

Simon eyed him. "Henry was free to choose men who *belong* in England," he snapped softly, "not mercenary relatives who will only govern for their own good and not for England's. That is why we must go to London, Gallus. My sources tell me that they are convening at Westminster and we must be there."

Gallus understood. "Very well," he said, though there was disappointment in his tone.

Simon caught the inflection. "What is it?"

Gallus hesitated a moment before speaking. "I was hoping we would be finished with our business in Oxford quickly so that I could return home and see to my mother," he said. "I realize that seems like a trivial thing when the fate of the country hangs in balance, but certainly it is not trivial to me."

Simon sobered, eyeing Hugh Bigod, who was standing several feet away. Hugh and Gallus had shared a contentious relationship for the past several months, culminating last month in what could have been a rather violent circumstance. The truth was that Hugh had not forgiven Gallus for refusing to marry his daughter and the situation, and Hugh's pride, had veered out of control. It was only redeemed when Gallus saved the man's army from an attack from the king's forces, although Simon was still unclear as to how, exactly, Gallus had known the king was moving against Bigod. It was still a mystery but one Simon couldn't spare any thought to. At the moment, he had quite enough to deal with and he worried that Hugh might press Gallus on the very touchy subject of his dying mother, so it was a situation between the men that continued to bear watching.

"Lady Honey has not improved, Gallus?" Hugh asked politely.

Gallus knew that Hugh did not approve of him, arguably the rebellion's greatest warlord, being so inordinately attached to his mother. It was one of many points of disagreement between them. Lady Honey de Shera was a daughter of England's greatest champion, Christopher de Lohr, and by sheer association she was greatly respected among fighting men.

Still, Hugh had always seemed to disapprove of the fact that all of the de Shera brothers were very attached to her. He'd even spread gossip about boys being curtailed by their mother's apron strings. That being the case, it wasn't a subject that Gallus was willing to be pressed on by Bigod and he could feel his temper rise.

"She has not," he turned to look at Hugh as if daring the man to say more. "If we are moving to London, then my brothers and I will go, but I would like to take time to see my mother first."

Simon tried to be tactful. "Gallus, Coventry is three days north of Oxford," he said. "Even if you ride like the wind, it will still take you almost two weeks to ride north to Coventry and then south to London. Henry is gathering his council representatives next week. We cannot wait so long for you to see your mother. I am dreadfully sorry to say so, but it is true. If you go to Coventry, then we go to London without you."

Gallus sighed sharply and turned away from de Montfort, wandering over to the hearth in the great solar of Oxford Castle, a solar that had seen more than its share of war conferences. It had seen more than its share of strife. As Gallus leaned up against the hearth, debating on his course of action, Peter de Montfort made his way over to him.

Peter was an older man, wise and calm, and he and Gallus had an excellent bond. He put his hand on Gallus' shoulder.

"Your mother has been ill for quite some time," he said quietly. "Will she know you if you go to her?"

Gallus was reluctant to answer. "She has been mostly unconscious for the past month," he said. "I am sure that when we return, her condition will be the same. The cancer is claiming her one day at a time."

Peter squeezed his shoulder. "Then you go to satisfy yourself," he said as Gallus looked at him curiously. "You go to say your farewells to a woman you have already bid farewell to. It is not your mother lying in that bed, Gallus. Your mother has already gone. It is simply her body that lingers. But that, too, shall pass, whether or not you go to see her while she yet still breathes."

Peter made sense even though Gallus didn't want to agree with him. He forced a weak smile at the man. "I will discuss it with my brothers and my wife," he said. "If we return to Coventry, it will be briefly. Even though you say that my mother is already gone, there is still life there. I want her to know… I must see her one last time."

Peter merely squeezed his shoulder again and moved away,

passing by Simon as he went and lifting his eyebrows at the man as if to beg patience on behalf of Gallus. It was a difficult time for him, indeed. Simon, however, was exhibiting more patience than he felt.

"Go and speak with your brothers, Gallus," he instructed. "Tell them what I have told you. It is imperative that we leave for London on the morrow in order to make it in time for Henry's council meeting. I want you to ride at the head of the armies, Gallus, but I will allow you to make that choice. I will not force you to do it."

Gallus simply nodded his head as he turned back to the group. "I am grateful," he said. "Meanwhile, let us discuss what to expect in London. Surely your spies have intelligence for us, Simon. What do we know about the situation we are about to face?"

He was changing the subject away from his mother and on to the focus at hand, which pleased Simon. He needed Gallus. He needed the man's political wisdom as well as his military might. As Richard de Clare, Earl of Gloucester, began to speak of the Lusignan relatives that the king had selected for his representatives on the governing council, Simon watched Gallus lose himself in what he did best – strategizing.

This was the Gallus he loved and the Gallus he needed if they were going to establish a new government and a new England. He needed all of the de Shera brothers if they were going to accomplish what they intended. Men that fought for England, men who controlled the reins of power and might. The de Sheras were all that and more.

The Lords of Thunder *were* England.

# CHAPTER SEVEN

*Oxford, City*

OBLIVIOUS TO WHAT had been discussed between this brother and Simon de Montfort at Oxford Castle, the muscle of the Lords of Thunder, surprisingly, had other things on his mind, things that didn't involve the state of the country or preparation for battle. Maximus' mind was on a woman.

Leaving Jeniver with Garran de Moray and Stefan du Bois to do her own shopping, Maximus took Courtly with him as he liveried the carriage and the horses in a small livery near St. Clement's Church. The day, which had dawned clear but cold, was showing distinct signs of brilliance as the sky overhead bled bright blue from horizon to horizon. A few puffy clouds scattered across the expanse, pushed around by a gentle breeze.

Once the carriage was parked, Maximus dismounted his steed and opened the carriage door, extending a polite hand to Courtly who was still inside. He waited with anticipation until she put her small hand in his big, gloved one and he was able to assist her from the cab. Even though a heavy layer of leather was between them, he swore he could feel the heat from her hand against his flesh. It was enough to set his heart racing, an effect she seemed to have on him with very little effort. When their eyes met, he couldn't help but smile.

"I do apologize if this all seems rather scandalous and forward, my lady," he said. "But in speaking with you last night, I felt very sorry for the fact that you had lost everything in the fire. In fact, I feel somewhat responsible – I should have tried to help you save what you could. In any case, since you made no mention of your father replacing any of your possessions, I thought to make the offer."

Courtly gazed up into the handsome face of the very big de Shera brother, feeling so giddy that she was breathless with it. It was a struggle not to feel faint.

"It is very kind of you, Sir Maximus," she said sincerely. "But you are clearly not responsible. Please know that when I spoke of losing my possessions, I did not say it to play upon your sympathies. I was simply stating facts."

He nodded. "I realize that," he said. "That is why I hope you do not think me too forward for sending my brother's wife to lure you into a shopping expedition."

Courtly grinned. "I think it was a very generous thing to do."

He smiled because she was smiling All he wanted to do was smile when he looked into that lovely face. "Shall we continue, then?" he asked, holding out his elbow to her. "I was on the Street of the Merchants yesterday and found a stall with all manner of goods. We shall go there first."

Courtly nodded, eagerly took his arm, and promptly stepped straight on into a massive puddle of urine. It splashed up and got on her already dingy dress, causing her to gasp with horror. But the damage was done. Her right foot, right lower leg, and the hem of her dress were soiled. Maximus, seeing what had happened, pulled her even further back, away from the puddle.

"I beg your forgiveness," he said, genuinely concerned. "I did not even look to see where you were stepping. This is my fault."

Courtly was looking at her soaked foot and dirty skirt. She

sighed heavily. "Nay, it is not," she said, resigned. "It is my fault. I should have looked where I was walking. Honestly, Sir Maximus, I cannot possibly see how you would want to pay even the slightest attention to me. When we first met, not only did I fall on your head, but I beat you, too. Last night when you came to sup, you found me cooking the meal, looking like a common servant in the only dress I have. Now, I make a mess of myself again. I should apologize for all of this and tell you that I am not normally this slovenly or this clumsy, but so far, that is all you have seen from me. I will admit that I am ashamed."

Maximus was watching her closely as she spoke. She seemed so dejected and sorrowful, but her words of apology only made him smile. Reaching out, he took her left hand and brought it to his lips for a warm, gentle, and thoroughly wicked kiss.

"And do you know what I have seen from you since we met?" he said, holding her hand against his bearded chin. "I have seen an exceptionally resourceful, intelligent, and determined woman who makes the best of whatever situation she is in. Instead of waiting for someone to save you from the hostel fire, you found a way to escape it. Instead of allowing your father to be embarrassed in front of his guests last eve, you cooked the meal yourself regardless of how it would make you appear. You sacrificed your dignity and reputation to ensure your father was not shamed. You may feel as if you have presented nothing but the worst you have to offer, but I assure you, I see the exact opposite. You are like no woman I have ever met."

By the time he was finished, Courtly was looking at him with some astonishment. More than that, his bearded lips to her hand were making her heart race wildly. She'd never known such excitement in her life.

"I... I do not know what to say," she breathed, watching his lips move over her fingers, "except that you are a very strange man if a foolish, dirty woman appeals to you."

Maximus broke down into laughter. He kissed her hand again, wishing he could do much more but knowing this was not the time nor place for it. Besides, he'd already been bold enough and a move like that might scare her off. So he dropped her hand, bent over, and swept her up into his big arms to carry her through the puddled livery yard.

"Then I accept the fact that I am a strange man," he said, "because a certain foolish, dirty woman does appeal to me. I am sorry if that shocks you, but you may as well know of my intentions now rather than later."

Aloft in his arms, Courtly's hands were around Maximus' shoulders for support as he carried her through the yard. It was the safest, strongest place she could have ever imagined. The only man who had ever touched her had been her father, so to be in the arms of another man, a man she was wildly attracted to, was a new and thrilling experience. More thrilling still were his words.

"Intentions?" she repeated. "Will you explain your intentions?"

They had reached the street at this point and Maximus set Courtly carefully to her feet. "Is it not obvious?" he asked. "I just said that a dirty and foolish woman appeals to me, and you have called yourself those things."

Courtly had indeed realized what he meant when he had first spoke the words, but she needed confirmation even if he didn't want to give her a straight answer. It was nearly beyond her comprehension to realize that this man, this man she had dreamed about since the moment she had met him, was actually interested in her.

"Be plain, Sir Maximus," she said. "Tell me plainly what you are declaring."

He looked at her, his eyes crinkling with mirth. Reaching out, he grasped her gently by the elbow.

"I just did," he said. "And I give you permission to call me, simply, Maximus. Or Max. I will answer to whatever you choose to call me. Now, have you eaten yet this morning? Are you hungry?"

He was pulling her along, out into the street, but Courtly was still reeling from their conversation and unprepared for a change of subject.

"I... I suppose that I am," she said, now thinking on the fact that he had not only declared his interest but that he had given her permission to address him informally. Perhaps even affectionately. "I have not yet eaten this morning. Have you?"

Maximus shook his head. "I have not," he replied. "But we will find a seamstress first because you need something clean to wear. Then, we will find a baker and a *bagnio*, or bath house, which is undoubtedly attached to it so that you may eat, bathe, and dress at the same time."

Courtly looked at him, both hesitant and intrigued. "When I fostered at Prudhoe, Lady d'Umfraville said that bath houses were almost always located next to bakers because they used the big ovens to warm the water," she said. "I have never visited a bath house, however. Do you truly intend to take me to one?"

Maximus pointed to her soiled right foot and the bottom of her skirt. "Unless you intend to walk about smelling like a livery, I do," he said. "And you cannot wear this soiled garment any longer, so we must find you a clean one."

Courtly wasn't sure what to say to all of that. It was generosity beyond measure. "You seem to have everything planned," she said. "I do not suppose there is one thing you have left out."

Maximus shook his head. "There usually isn't," he replied, watching her grin. Her smile struck him, like an arrow straight to the heart, making him feel warm and giddy. "For a lady who has fought so hard to survive and thrive over the past day, I would not dare disappoint her on her trip to town."

Courtly laughed soft at him. She very much like the feeling of his hand on her elbow. "I do not suppose you could ever disappoint me," she said. "Except when you do not give me a straight answer."

His brow furrowed. "When did I do this disgraceful thing?"

She looked up at him, eyes twinkling. "I asked you to explain your intentions," she said. "You did not."

"I did."

"Nay, you did not."

He sighed heavily, feigning annoyance. "Can a man not work up his courage to discuss such a thing?" he asked. "Suffice it to say that I have pulled my sister-in-law into my scheme of having you all to myself on a shopping trip. Shouldn't that tell you my intensions?"

"It tells me that you are going to buy me bread, some manner of garment, and take me to a bath house."

He pursed his lips wryly. "Does it not tell you that I wish to be alone with you, as we were briefly last night?"

Courtly picked up her skirt as she hopped over a water puddle, although she didn't know why she bothered to try and keep her dress out of it. The garment was already ruined.

"It does," she said. "But let us be clear. Simply because you offer to buy me things, does not mean that I will be less than proper with you, in any fashion."

"What does *that* mean?"

"It means that if you expect some manner of physical demonstration of my gratitude, then I will not do it."

He fought off a grin. "A simple word of gratitude will suffice," he said, eyeing her. "I do not want anything else. In fact, I would refuse it."

Her expression washed with insult. "You would?"

He could see that he had her miffed and it amused him. "Aye, I would."

She paused, frowning at him. "That is a terrible thing to say," she said. "If you do not want a physical demonstration of my gratitude, then why are you taking me on a shopping trip?"

His grin broke through and he took her hand, bringing it to his bearded lips once again. He kissed her fingers tenderly.

"Well," he said softly, hesitantly. "Mayhap I *do* want a physical demonstration of your gratitude. Just a little."

Courtly could see that he was teasing her, quite flirtatiously. The man could be very charming when he wanted to be. She fought off a grin.

"I may or may not give you one," she said, turning her nose up at him and pretending she wasn't interested in the least. "I have not yet decided."

Maximus laughed softly and tucked her hand into the crook of his elbow again. He resumed their walk down the street.

"Then I may have to steal such a thing," he said, eyeing her to see how she was reacting.

But Courtly kept her serious demeanor. "If you do, you may not like my reaction."

"We shall see."

"Aye, we shall."

They turned a corner on the avenue and entered the Street of the Merchants. It was bustling at this hour, with people going about their business, children and dogs running up and down the avenue and contributing to a busy sense of purposeful chaos. Already, he had his eye on the merchant where he had purchased the rose oil yesterday because the man had many wonderful things in his treasure trove. It was their very first stop.

The old, white-bearded merchant was thrilled to see Maximus again and even more thrilled to see the lady. Women usually meant that copious amounts of money would be spent and he wasn't wrong. Maximus and Courtly inspected nearly every item he had in his stall. Maximus would pick out a soap or a comb, show it to

Courtly and, depending on her reaction, turn it over to the merchant for purchase.

Using this method, Maximus picked out two bars of hard, white soap, one bar of lumpy white soap that smelled of lemons, and another bar of lumpy yellowish-colored soap that smelled of roses. He also came across an oil, meant to soften the skin, that smelled fresh, like dewy grass, so he passed that to the merchant, too. He found a tray of combs, both to brush the hair with or use as an adornment, and from the tray he selected a large, bone comb for Courtly along with two big, butterfly combs meant to both affix the hair and decorate it.

All the while, Courtly simply followed along behind him, either nodding to approve an item or shaking her head at it. Shifts, scarves, and hair adornments became part of her growing booty. She was coming to see that whenever she thought something was pretty, he would buy it, and she was becoming very concerned with the amount of money he was already spending, so she began rejecting nearly everything he found after that.

Maximus caught on to what she was doing and began making arbitrary decisions with some fairly gaudy choices, which forced Courtly to speak up. He was very clever about eliciting an answer from her, something Courtly was also coming to see. But it was part of his charm so she truly didn't mind. Maximus was, if nothing else, manipulative in the best sort of way.

But there was more to come. The real money was spent when the merchant indicated that his wife had loosely basted together several garments, selling them to fine ladies who then had their maids make the final touches on them, and that was exactly what Maximus had been looking for. The old merchant had called forth his wife from the rear, dank depths of the stall and the woman began producing all manner of simply constructed dresses made with some of the spectacular, exotic fabrics that the merchant imported.

Courtly had never seen such beautiful dresses, coats of the most elegant material. There were greens and yellows, blues and reds, and delicious shades of violet. Maximus didn't know anything about women's clothing but he knew when he saw a pale, shimmering green fabric and a silken dress the color of amber that he liked those the best. Courtly liked them, too, and very shortly she had four dresses in a pile and Maximus was examining a fifth.

But Courtly begged him off, assuring him that what she had was quite enough, and he politely surrendered to her wishes even though he would have liked to have purchased more. The intended of Maximus de Shera must be well-dressed. At least, that was what he was thinking – he had yet to voice it. The merchant even had small, embroidered slippers with all the colors of the rainbow that matched the simple gowns and, with that, Maximus made his enormous purchase complete.

Leaving the merchant to count the small pile of gold coins Maximus had paid him in, Maximus and Courtly left the stall with Maximus carrying the enormous bundle all wrapped up in a lavender-colored, linen surcoat. On the next avenue was the Street of the Bakers and Maximus headed in that direction, winding through the crowds of people. Courtly, holding on to his elbow, tried to keep pace.

"Where are we going now?" she asked.

Maximus slowed down so she wasn't running after him. He usually moved very swiftly and wasn't used to having to consider someone else's pace.

"The Street of the Bakers is on the next street," he said. "I do not recall seeing bathing houses there, but the last time I was there I was not looking for any. Let us see what we can find."

Looking up at him, Courtly shielded her eyes from the mid-morning sun. "Truly, my lord, you have done quite enough for me today," she said. "I do not know how I am to explain all of this treasure to my father."

Maximus cast her a sidelong glance. "I told you to call me Maximus in private," he said, his voice low. "As far as your father is concerned, I will explain to him why I bought these items for you. And then I shall ask for his permission to court you. So, you see, these will be considered gifts for my intended. Surely he cannot disagree with that."

Courtly came to an abrupt halt and Maximus with her. When he looked into her face, he could see that her eyes were growing moist with emotion.

"So you have found your courage and now you are plain with your intentions," she said. "Is this truly your desire, then? To court me?"

"It is."

"Do you realize that you have only known me less than a day?"

He failed to see what had her so upset. "Of course," he said. "Why are you so distressed?"

Courtly looked at him, *really* looked at him. There was so much joy and sorrow in her heart that it was difficult to isolate just one particular feeling out of the maelstrom. Why *was* she so distressed? *If he only knew....*

"Are you truly serious about seeking my father's permission?" she whispered.

"I never say anything I do not mean," he said. Then, he began to think that something was seriously wrong. "Is there another, my lady? If there is, then...."

Courtly cut him off. "Nay," she said quickly. "There is no other. But let me be clear. What you have just told me brings me more joy than you can possibly comprehend. Last night, in spite of everything, was the most marvelous night of my life and although I should not be thankful for such a thing, I find myself very thankful that the hostel burned, because if it had not, I more than likely would never have met you. You are a kind, wonderful man, Maximus, and I am deeply honored by your attention."

Maximus was greatly pleased to hear that she was receptive to his suit. Not that he believed otherwise because, based on the time he had spent with her, he felt very strongly that she was interested in him just as he was interested in her. Once, he'd feared that was not the case but clearly he had been wrong. He was glad, for once, that he had been wrong. But it seemed to him that there was something more that Courtly wasn't telling him.

"But… *what?*" he asked, seeing the myriad of emotions in her face. "What is the matter?"

Courtly sighed heavily. "If you are truly serious about asking my father for permission to court me, then know it will not be an easy task," she said. "I do not want to tell any more than that for fear that you will change your mind, but I find that I cannot withhold such information. You must know that my father has chased off every potential suitor I have ever had. He is fanatical about it. The fact that you and I were so attentive to one another last night, engrossed in conversation as we were, was enough for him to make the decision to send my sister and me back to Trely-stan Castle. Before you and Lady de Shera arrived this morning, my father and I were arguing over just that very thing. He wants to send me away from you."

Maximus' expression grew serious. "Is this so?"

"It is," she replied miserably. "I realize that my father is an ally of de Montfort and you more than likely do not want to disrupt that allegiance. If that is the case, then as much as it pains me to say it, I understand."

He cocked his head. "Understand *what?*"

"That you will not ask permission to court me and risk disturbing the alliance, of course."

He frowned. "If your father allows a suit for his daughter to destroy an alliance, then it would be by his choice alone," he said. "I will still offer for you and he will accept if he knows what is good for him."

Courtly sensed something ominous in that threat. "What does that mean?"

Maximus could feel himself getting worked up over the fact that his suit for Courtly was evidently going to run into an issue in the form of the lady's father. It could prove to be a formidable obstacle. He began to prepare his answer with all manner of threat against de Lara but, looking at the lady's face, he realized that he couldn't do that. In spite of everything, the man was still her father. Uncertain now, Maximus simply took her by the elbow and continued on their journey through the alley.

"Come along," he said, somewhat quietly. "We will speak on it later."

"Please do not think me forward, but there may not *be* a later once you return me to Kennington."

"That remains to be seen."

Courtly didn't question him further. He said it with such finality, as if he had no doubt that he would emerge the victor in whatever tussle there might be for her hand against Kellen de Lara. Therefore, she simply followed the man through the narrow passage and out onto the road beyond.

The Street of the Bakers wasn't quite as crowded as the Street of the Merchants but it was still fairly busy. Maximus paused before taking a direction of travel, inspecting the buildings surrounding them to see if he could spot a bath house. He finally poked his head into the nearest bakery and asked the proprietor, who directed him to the next street, a smaller avenue, where a bath house was indeed attached to a neighboring bakery. There was no name on the bath house but there was a piece of wood hanging over the door with a crude flower painted on it. Opening the heavy, awkward door, having swelled from the heat and moisture inside the bath house, Maximus ushered Courtly inside.

It was very dark inside the structure and the ceiling was low, causing Maximus to have to duck his head. When the proprietress was summoned by a hovering servant, Maximus explained that his lady needed to be bathed and dressed, which the proprietress was more than happy to do. But rather than simply leave Courtly off and allow her to be tended by strangers, Maximus insisted on inspecting the bath house to make sure there were no hidden threats like lascivious men or any other danger to threaten a lady. As the proprietress stood by, rather shocked, Maximus carefully handed Courtly her bundle of possessions, unsheathed his broadsword, and went on the offensive.

He quickly learned that there were only five rooms to the entire structure; a small greeting room at the door with an attendant and three big dogs, then a room for men and a room for women. Off of each of these rooms were smaller rooms used to dress in. Maximus marched right into the men's bathing room where two fat merchants were lingering in one of four big, barrel-shaped tubs of lukewarm water. The tubs could each hold two to four men, and serving women attended the bathers by rubbing oil into their skin and then scraping it off with a pewter instrument meant for such a thing. In the corner, a young man played a mandolin very badly, meant to be an entertainment while one bathed. But Maximus didn't like the fact that it was a bathing house for both sexes if Courtly was going to be in the other room, so he ordered the merchants to put their clothes on and leave.

Of course, the men didn't take well to this in the least, so Maximus reached into the bathing vessel and pulled one man out by his neck. Seeing his companion being roughly handled by the enormous knight, the second merchant fled the tub and, with both men dressing hastily, Maximus chased them from the bath house without them as much as having time to put on their shoes. Courtly, in the reception room, watched the barefooted men flee with great curiosity until she saw that Maximus was pursuing them with his enormous broadsword in hand. It made for a very comical situation but she dare not laugh. In fact, she rather appreciated Maximus' sense of propriety. He didn't want naked men in the same building with her, and she was deeply flattered.

With the merchants having been chased out, Maximus then went into the women's bathing room and was greeted by three women in various stages of undress. They screamed when they saw the knight with the broadsword and it was enough to chase Maximus out of the chamber as abruptly as he had entered. He was fine in a room full of naked men, but a room full of half-dressed women had him somewhat unsettled. He stood at the door and tried not to look too embarrassed.

"There are already three women in there," he said to her. "Are you comfortable bathing with other women?"

Courtly grinned at him. She couldn't help it. She knew that if she told him that she wasn't, then he would chase the women from the chamber just as he'd chased the men. Therefore, she nodded.

"Perfectly comfortable," she said. "What will you do while I am bathing?"

He shrugged those wide shoulders. "Wait here until you are finished."

"You have nothing else that you could be doing?"

He shook his head. "I will not leave you unattended."

Courtly didn't have an argument for that. "I see," she said thoughtfully. "I feel rather guilty that you will be waiting for me to bathe. It will take an hour at the very least."

"I will wait."

"Why not go and find us something to eat? By the time you

return, I should be finished. I will hurry."

"Are you famished, then?"

"I am."

It gave Maximus something to do other than hang around a bath house, so he agreed, but not before he explained to the proprietress that Lady Courtly must never be unattended and must be given the best of everything. The woman agreed, especially when Maximus paid her handsomely for her troubles. With a wink to Courtly, he quit the bath house in search of a feast fit for a queen.

*His* queen. And he would dare her father to deny him.

# CHAPTER EIGHT

GARRAN DE MORAY had accompanied Lady de Shera on her shopping trip into Oxford but she had quickly become exhausted, and ill, so he'd quickly returned her to the inn where they had been staying. He hoped Gallus was already returned from his meeting with de Montfort but the man was not yet back by the time they returned, so Lady de Shera went up to her rented bedchamber to lay down for a while as the knights settled down in the main room to eat the nooning meal.

No one seemed to find it odd that Tiberius wasn't there. He'd been banned from accompanying either of his brothers on their various plans that morning, so the last anyone saw of him, he had been in his bedchamber on the second floor, mending a piece of armor that had pulled loose. Garran, who was close to Tiberius, as well as to Maximus, didn't give his absence much thought as he delved into a meal of boiled mutton, carrots, beans, and vast quantities of bread. They were halfway through their meal when Tiberius made an appearance.

Entering the inn from the main door, Tiberius kicked the roving dogs out of the way as he made his way deeper into the room that smelled of smoke, dirt, and unwashed bodies. When he saw the de Shera knights hunched over a table, sharing a meal, he headed in their direction. More specifically, he headed for Garran.

"De Moray," he said, sounding surprisingly serious. "How long have you been here?"

Garran had a mouth full of carrots. "Not long," he said. "Lady de Shera was not feeling well so she wanted to rest. Maximus is still on the Street of the Merchant's with de Lara's daughter and we plan to collect them shortly and then return the lady to her father so it looks as if they have not been alone all afternoon. Quite a plan, is it not?"

He was grinning, as was Stefan. Only the two of them had gone with Maximus and Jeniver, as the de Wolfe brothers had gone with Gallus. But Tiberius wasn't interested in what Maximus was or was not doing. He was preoccupied with something else. He leaned down to Garran.

"I must speak with you," he said, his voice low. "Come with me."

Garran swallowed the carrots in his mouth as he stood up, pausing only to down a swallow of wine to wash the vegetables down. He proceeded to follow Tiberius until they were near the entrance to the inn. There was no one around there. Only then did Tiberius stop and turn to him.

"After you left this morning, you received a visitor," he said quietly. "Your father is in town. Did you know this?"

Garran's eyes widened. "I did not," he said, immediately fearing the worst. "What is wrong? Where is he?"

Tiberius held up a hand to quiet him. "He came specifically to find you," he said. "Evidently, he arrived in town yesterday and began asking for the de Shera party. He was able to find someone who had seen us and he was directed to this inn. Garran, I know your father is a supporter of the king. We have never truly discussed it with you because your father's loyalty is his own business and your loyalty is to us and, consequently, de Montfort. But your father needs to speak with you now and I will take you to him."

Garran was trying not to panic. "Is he well?"

"He is well."

"And my mother – is she well?"

"He did not speak of her so I can only assume so."

Garran felt some relief at that but not much. There was a sense of urgency in the air, something he did not understand. In fact, the entire situation was puzzling and Tiberius' words were only making it worse. Still, he was on the move, as he'd been asked. Already, he was returning to the table to collect his possessions before riding out with Tiberius. As he moved, Tiberius followed.

"Have you just come from him?" Garran asked Tiberius. "Where is he staying?"

Tiberius shoved another dog out of the way when it came too close. Dogs tended to flock to him for some reason. "He is towards the south side of town at an inn called The Bruised Thistle," he replied. "When he first came to The One-Eyed Raven, we spoke here for some time before moving to his hostel. We have actually been speaking quite a bit."

Garran eyed Tiberius curiously as he collected his sword. "What about?"

Tiberius simply shook his head, unwilling to elaborate with the other knights and a few soldiers eating around the table. He waited until he and Garran were outside in the bright sunshine and heading for the livery before speaking.

"Your father mostly spoke of the old days," he finally said. "He knew my mother as a young woman, you know. He never courted Honey but he knew her. He also knows Davyss and Grayson de Winter, which I'm sure you already know. The de Winters are close friends of the de Sheras and have always championed the king, much as your father does."

Garran already knew all of this. "None of this tells me why he has come to Oxford to seek me," he said. "He has traveled all the way from Dorset, which took him weeks at the very least. Did he come alone?"

Tiberius nodded. "He had four men-at-arms with him," he replied. They entered the livery, sending a pair of servant boys running for their horses. As they paused to wait for the animals to be brought out, Tiberius spoke again. "Garran, from the conversation your father and I had, it seems to me as if he has come to Oxford before heading on to London. You know that the king has summoned the council he intends to represent his interests in de Montfort's parliament. Although your father did not tell me directly, it is my suspicion that your father intends to sit upon the king's council."

Garran's brow furrowed as he looked at Tiberius. "What makes you think so?"

Tiberius shrugged. "Simply the way he was speaking about the king and his advisors," he said. "He mentioned bringing balance to London. Mayhap that is what he intends to tell you, that he is sitting on the king's council. That means he will be sitting opposite Gallus and Maximus and me. We will be on opposite sides."

Garran thought on the greater implications of that. He loved his father dearly but he did not like the king nor support the man's ideals. He was much more supportive of the government that de Montfort was trying to establish. Still, he loved his father in spite of his politics. And there was a reason why Bose de Moray was so supportive of the king. After a moment, he sighed heavily.

"My father is an old and wise man," he said. "He is the most rational and unselfish supporter the king has."

"I know. God would be on our side if de Moray would pledge allegiance to de Montfort."

Garran shook his head, as if such a thing would never happen. "There is a very good reason why he supports the king so stringently," he said. "But his reason is not my reason. I do not support

Henry and probably never will."

Tiberius was listening carefully. "What is the reason?" he asked. "Will you tell me?"

Garran nodded faintly. "When my father first met my mother, he wanted very much to marry her but my grandfather would not have it," he said, his voice softening as he spoke of his beloved father. "In fact, my grandfather somehow managed to cast my father in a very negative light and he was actually slated for execution. The only thing that saved him was King Henry and ever since then, my father has unwaveringly supported him. The man saved his life and he would never side against him."

Tiberius registered mild surprise. "I never knew that."

Garran shrugged his big shoulders, glancing at the horses as they were brought out to be saddled. "As you said, we have never spoken of my father's allegiance to the king, but that is why the man is so supportive of him," he said. "My father was Captain of the King's Guard in his younger years, when Henry was also quite young. They became friends and they share a special bond, even to this day."

Tiberius didn't have much to say to that, although the elder de Moray's loyalty to the king now made much more sense. He fell silent as the horses were saddled and then moved to help the stable boys secure his gear to his saddle. He and Garran left the livery and headed south, towards the inn where Bose de Moray was staying. There wasn't much chatter between them as they moved through the city streets, some crowded and some not, until they reached the southern tip of the town.

This portion of the town was seedier, dirtier, with several brothels and bath houses posing as brothels. Crime was rampant. Tiberius and Garran pulled their horses to a halt in front of The Bruised Thistle, a very big building of waddle and daub amongst small and run-down wooden structures. There were several young boys standing around and Tiberius paid two of the boys well to have them tend the horses. Taking their saddlebags with them, the knights proceeded into the inn.

The common room of the tavern was, literally, a big pit in the floor. And it was very crowded, mostly with people drinking or gambling or fornicating in the shadows. As the knights passed through the room, women approached them, offering to service their needs for a few pences. Tiberius ignored them, as did Garran, and they headed to an old, unsteady staircase that led to the second floor of the structure.

It was quieter up here but smelled badly of urine, from men relieving themselves against walls and in corners, with no one bothering to clean it up. Tiberius headed for the last door on the left, rapping softly when they reached it. He was preparing to rap again when the door jerked open and a mountain of a man stood in the doorway. Garran barely had time to recognize his father before the man was pulling him into his enormous embrace.

"My son," Bose de Moray breathed. "You cannot know how pleased I am to see you."

Garran hugged his father tightly. "Papa," he said with satisfaction. "It has been a long time."

Bose let his son go long enough to cup his face between his two big hands, gazing into features that looked very much like his own.

"Garran," he murmured. "Are you well, my son?"

Garran nodded, smiling at his father. The man didn't change much from year to year. With black hair and black eyes and the big scar on his left cheek, Bose de Moray was a legendary knight who had dominated the tournament circuit for many years. Now, he lived a quieter life, but he was still dangerous and formidable when the occasion called for it.

"Well, Papa," he said. "I am well. And you? Have you been well? And how is Mother?"

Bose kissed his boy on the cheek and dropped his hands. "Your mother is very well," he said. "She sends her love. I have been well also."

Bose was moving back into his room and Garran and Tiberius followed. As Tiberius closed the chamber door and bolted it, Garran spoke.

"I am very glad to hear that," he said. "What a surprise to find you in Oxford, Papa. Why are you here?"

Garran had been given several minutes to think on his father's unexpected appearance on the ride over from The One-Eyed Raven so he would not waste any time getting to the point. Bose didn't reply right away. He sank into a stiff chair positioned next to the hearth and held out his hands to the blaze, warming them.

"Many reasons, my son," he said. Then, he glanced at Tiberius. "I had a long and pleasant conversation with Tiberius. Did he not tell you?"

Garran nodded. "He said you came to The One-Eyed Raven looking for me," he replied. "He did not say why. What is the matter, Papa? What makes you hunt me down in Oxford?"

Bose scratched his head, looking at Garran as the man sat down on the floor next to him. In the tight and cramped room, there was nowhere else to sit. Bose reached out a big, calloused hand and patted his son's cheek.

"Many reasons," he repeated softly. "I had heard that de Montfort was convening in Oxford and assumed you would be with the de Shera brothers. I am pleased to see that I was correct."

Garran nodded. He couldn't help notice that his father, so far, had not directly answered any of his questions. "Aye, you were," he said. "But why do you need to speak with me?"

Bose glanced over at Tiberius, who was sitting on the small cot in the room. "My lord," he said. "Would you mind giving me a few moments alone with my son? If it would not be too much trouble?"

Tiberius was already on his feet, moving for the chamber door. "Of course not," he said. "I will be right outside should you need me."

Bose watched the tall, dark-haired de Shera brother as the man opened the door. "Thank you," he said.

Tiberius quit the room, shutting the old, oak panel softly behind him. When he was gone and they were alone, Garran returned his attention to his father.

"Why did you ask him to leave?" he asked quietly. "Papa, what is happening? Why do you need to speak with me alone?"

Bose gazed down at his son, his only son. He and his wife, Lady Summer, had four children. Garran was the eldest and the man had three younger sisters. It had been very hard for Bose to allow Garran to leave his home and swear fealty to the House of de Shera, but Bose understood that Garran was his own man and needed to do what he felt best. Now, as he gazed down into his son's eyes, he began to feel very possessive of him. He wanted him back.

"Henry is convening a council in London next week," he said quietly. "Surely you know of all of this, Garran. Your lords were instrumental in nearly wresting the country from Henry. The man was only able to save himself by agreeing to share power with de Montfort and the barons. I do not think it was right of the barons to do this. The king is the monarch and his rule should be absolute, not shared with a group of power-hungry barons. That is all this is, Garran; a grab for power."

Garran pondered his father's words. He knew the man was passionate about supporting Henry but he didn't particularly want to get into an argument with him about it. They had differing philosophies.

"Is that why you came, Papa?" he asked softly. "To scold me for siding with the de Sheras?"

Bose shook his head. "Nay, my son," he said. "I did not come to scold you. I have come for a reason more powerful than that. I have come to tell you that I will be sitting upon Henry's council. The king has asked this of me and I have agreed. That being said, I have now come to ask you where your true loyalties lie. Do they lie with your family or with the House of de Shera?"

The gentle expression faded from Garran's expression. "What do you mean?"

Bose lifted his black eyebrows. "Exactly that," he said. "You know that I have tried to stay out of whatever was happening between Henry and de Montfort. I do not like power struggles but I also do not like to see a gang of sword-heavy barons threaten the king."

"We are not threatening him."

"Then what do you call it?" Bose wanted to know. "Your beloved de Shera brothers are inciting another Anarchy, just like the one that nearly destroyed this country when Stephen and Matilda were fighting, and if the de Sheras are fighting against Henry, that means *you* are fighting against Henry. If Henry pulls me into this war, which he has done, then it means you are fighting against me. Will you raise your sword against me, son?"

Garran looked horrified. "Of course not."

Bose could see how upset Garran was becoming. He put his hand on the man's cheek again to both comfort and calm him.

"I am afraid it will come to that," he admitted. "Henry has asked for my sword and I have sworn to give it."

Garran's horror was growing. "No offense intended, but you are an old man, Papa," he said. "You do not need to be fighting the king's wars."

"Yet, I am," Bose countered quietly. "He has asked and I have agreed. Now, I have come to tell you this personally. I have also come to ask you to side with your family and return with me to London. If you do not, then at some point, you and I will face each other in battle. I do not want this, Garran. It will surely kill me."

Garran's onyx-colored eyes were filled with sorrow. He could hardly believe what he was hearing, yet upon reflection, he wasn't surprised in the least. He was only surprised with the fact that it had taken his father this long to ask for his loyalty. *Family or de Shera*. Those were his choices. He was a man torn. With great effort, he stood up and moved away from the hearth, lost in thought.

"I do not agree with the king's politics, Papa," he finally said. "How can I side with a man I do not agree with?"

Bose watched his son carefully, the movements of a distraught man. "You are siding with *me*," he insisted quietly. "I must support the king. You will support me and the de Moray name."

Garran shook his head. "It is not that easy and you know it," he insisted. "I believe in what de Montfort is doing."

"Enough to side against your own father?"

Garran sighed heavily, putting his hands to his face in a gesture of utter confusion and defeat. When he opened his eyes, all he could see was his father gazing back at him, with hope in his eyes, and he couldn't stomach that look. He knew what he *had* to do, yet he also knew what he *wanted* to do, and they were two different things. Greatly torn, and greatly grieved, he went to his father and put his arms around the man's shoulders.

"Papa," he whispered. "I would not raise a sword against you, but you must give me time to think about this. What you ask… it would be the greatest decision of my life."

Bose patted the arms that were around him. "I know," he said. "It is not an easy choice, but you must decide what is more important to you – your family or your convictions. As much as I would convince you to come with me, ultimately, you must make the decision that is right for you. I understand that."

Garran lay his cheek on the top of his father's head. "And if I choose to remain with the de Shera brothers? What then? Will you disown me?"

Bose squeezed Garran's arm. "I will not," he confessed. "But my heart would be broken. Imagine if you were in my position, Garran. Would you not want for your son to be at your side in all things? That is what I want – I want my son back. I want you supporting me and supporting your family. I do not believe that is too much to ask."

Garran thought on the words. Nay, it was not too much to ask, but it was a decision that would change Garran's life one way or the other. All he knew was that he could not lift his sword in battle against his father, yet he could not support a king he did not like. With a sigh, he kissed his father's head and let him go.

"I must think on it," he said, moving away from the older man. "I cannot give you an answer right away. I must think on what you have said and reason it out in my own mind."

Bose watched his son as the man sat heavily on the small cot. "I am leaving Oxford tomorrow morning," he said quietly. "I would like you to leave with me, so do not wait too long to give me your answer."

Garran felt dull inside, dull and torn. His mind was in turmoil as he glanced up at his father. "Why so soon?" he said. "You can make it to London in plenty of time if you wait a day or two to leave Oxford."

Bose shook his head. "I am meeting up with Grayson de Winter and his sons," he replied. "You know Grayson and Davyss and Hugh, of course."

"I do."

"Grayson has asked that I join with them in two days just outside of London. I have agreed."

It was more stunning news. The de Winters were the muscle for the crown, much as the de Sheras were the muscle for de

Montfort. Now, Garran's father was going to be part of the king's muscle, too. Garran simply shook his head, astonished.

"You know that Grayson and Davyss are very close to the de Sheras," he said. "Grayson de Winter is Gallus' godfather and Davyss is Gallus' best friend. And now *you* join them?"

Bose nodded faintly. "I do," he said. "My son, as I said before, you do not have to agree with Henry's philosophies. I am not even sure I do. But the crown must be kept intact from these men who are attempting to destroy it. To destroy Henry will destroy England. Is that what you want? More anarchy and a fractured country?"

Garran wasn't sure what he wanted. It was too much information, too much to think about, and his mind was reeling. He lifted his hands, shaking his head as if to ward off what his father was telling him.

"You must give me time to think," he begged softly. "Can we not put this aside for a few hours and share a meal? I would like to hear of my mother and sisters. I miss them. Can we not speak on more pleasant things, at least for the next few hours?"

Bose relented, mostly because he didn't want to force Garran into making a quick decision that they would both regret. He had said all he wanted to say and there was nothing more he could do. Garran would either side with him or he wouldn't. So he nodded, smiling weakly.

"This place has terrible food and even worse company," he said. "We should go somewhere with better food and less whores."

Garran burst out chuckling. "Why did you pick this place to stay, anyway?" he wanted to know. "This is the worst tavern in the city."

Bose shrugged. "I was tired when we arrived in town this this was available," he said. "But if I receive another proposition by a woman who wants to kiss me where I pee, then I will collect all of my possessions and flee the city entirely. But please do not ever tell your mother I stayed here. She would then kick me where I pee and I should be a very sad man."

Garran was laughing so hard that he could barely breathe. His father was usually such a stately, austere man that to hear him speak so crudely, and so humorously, was one of the best things he had ever experienced. He put his hands to his face as he howled with laughter.

"You are becoming very funny in your old age, Papa," he snorted, wiping the tears from his eyes. "Very well, then. We shall find a better place to eat with less whores. I do not want Mother to go on a rampage against you. Shall we invite Tiberius to go with us?"

Bose was standing up, laboriously, as his old muscles tended to tighten up on him. "Of course," he replied. "I rather like young Tiberius. He is a wise and witty man."

Garran sobered as he helped his father gain his cloak. "Aye, he is," he replied, thinking on the de Shera brothers, men he was very attached to. "He is a good friend."

They were heading for the door when Bose stopped, putting a hand on Garran's arm. His expression was sincere in its sorrow and resolve.

"Please know that I am sorry I had to come to Oxford with all of this," he said quietly. "I would not have come had I not felt strongly about it."

Garran gazed into the face of the man he loved very, very much. "I know," he muttered. "But let us not speak on it, at least for the afternoon. I want to become reacquainted with my papa again with the threat of war hanging over our heads."

"Agreed."

With that, Garran and Bose headed out into the corridor, finding Tiberius standing over near the old staircase. Tiberius went along with the de Morays as they went in search of a better place to feast, having no idea what had transpired between father in son. It was better that way. Had he known, he would have been just as unhappy as Garran was.

This was a situation that no one could win.

# CHAPTER NINE

*She is an angel.*

THAT WAS WHAT Maximus was thinking as he walked down the avenue with Courtly on his arm. He had returned to the bath house promptly an hour later, with a good deal of food, only to be met in the reception room by the most Godly angel he had ever laid eyes on. Dressed in a gown the color of amber, it was silky, simply cut, and emphasized everything good about her. She looked absolutely magnificent.

And she smelled strongly of lemon and lavender. It was exhilarating. With her clean hair, braided and styled, and a scrubbed face, Maximus knew, at that moment, that he had passed beyond simple infatuation with the woman. He was entering a realm he'd never before entered, something deeper and more meaningful. But it scared him, and thrilled him, so much to think about it, that he wouldn't verbalize it, even to himself. He simply settled down to enjoy the view.

So he took her in one hand and her possessions in the other, and went outside to find a place to eat the food he had brought. Somewhere down towards the big square where the church was located, he found a small garden between buildings that had a bench made from rough-hewn logs. Putting their meal of bread, fried pork, and little pies made from meat and raisins onto the bench, he set Courtly down beside it and they both plowed into the food, starving.

"A lovely meal, Maximus," Courtly said after swallowing her first gratifying bite. "Are you fond of fried pork, then? Some people do not like it because it is dry and crispy."

Standing over Courtly, Maximus had a mouthful. "I adore it," he said, chewing. "My mother, much like you, learned the art of cooking. When I was very young, she would have the cook fry pork skin in lard and it would puff up, crispy and delicious. She would make other things, too."

Courtly was shoving the soft center of the bread into her mouth, being careful not to get crumbs on her dress. "Like what?" she asked curiously.

Maximus thought as he chewed the pork. "Well," he said reluctantly, eyeing her as he chewed. "I will not tell you unless you promise not to laugh at me."

Already, Courtly was grinning but she fought it. "I swear."

"Swear again."

"I do," she said sincerely. "A million times, I do."

That was good enough for him and he shoved another piece of pork into his mouth. "As I said, my mother has collected many recipes over the years," he said. "My older brother has a favorite – Cheese pie. My mother would make it for him quite a lot. As for me, I too had a favorite dish – a tart that she would call 'Maxi's Tart'. I do not even know if it has a real name because she always called it *my* tart, but it is onions boiled in beef broth and then mixed with butter, salt, cheese, raisins, and spices. It is baked in a crust and is absolutely delicious."

Courtly went back on her promise and grinned at him. "It sounds wonderful," she said. "Mayhap your mother will give me the recipe if I ask her."

Maximus' good humor took a hit. "That would be very difficult," he said, his tone considerably softer. "She has been quite ill for the past month. She does not seem to awaken any longer. She simply sleeps."

Courtly sobered dramatically. "Oh, Max," she breathed softly. "I am so very sorry to hear that. Where is she?"

"At Isenhall Castle, my brother's seat."

Courtly's brow furrowed as she thought of Maximus' mother dying without her sons around her. "Then why are you here?" she asked, though not unkindly. "I should think that if my father was ill, I would want to be by his side every moment."

Maximus nodded, sadly and wearily. "I am here because in my mother's brief moments of consciousness," he said, "she dictated that the good of the country was more important than sitting around, waiting for her to die. We had to come to Oxford after that. You see, my mother is not someone to be crossed. Had we not come to Oxford, I promise that she would have risen out of her deathbed to box our ears. But it was not an easy decision, I assure you."

Courtly was sad on his behalf. Speaking of his mother seemed to dampen his good humor significantly and for that she was sorry. Reaching out, she grasped his wrist, squeezing gently.

"I am truly sorry," she said. "I am sorry that you felt you had to come to Oxford rather than be with your mother. Will you be able to see her soon, I wonder?"

Maximus felt her flesh against his like a searing brand. Her hand was soft and heated. He took it in his hand and lowered his big body onto an uprooted stump next to her. Still, he held her hand, gazing into her beautiful eyes.

"When I go home, I want you to go with me," he said, quite impulsively. "I will speak with your father today when I return you to Kennington. I want him to understand that I will marry you right away. I… I cannot explain myself any more than that. This is not impetuous or foolish, Courtly. I do not give my feelings away easily, but I know what I want. What I want is you."

Courtly couldn't help the smile of genuine elation that crossed her features. "My heart is overjoyed," she exclaimed. "I know that others would think you very hasty, but I do not. When you feel something very strongly, then it is the right decision for you."

"Then you agree?"

Courtly gazed into the face of the man she knew she would marry. It was nearly too much happiness for her to digest. Was it really true? Was all of this truly happening? It seemed as if she were living a dream.

"I do," she murmured. "Indeed, I do."

"Then tell me how to approach your father. If he does not agree, I shall take you anyway, so it is best if he agrees. How can I accomplish this?"

It was a complicated question, coming from a man who was unused to being denied his wants or wishes. She lowered her gaze, watching his big, rough hand as it toyed with her fingers. There was something so incredibly warm and safe about his touch, yet she knew they were hands that had killed. Everyone knew of Maximus de Shera and his reputation for being a ruthless battle lord. *The Thunder Warrior*, he was called. But at the moment, those hands were nothing short of tender. She must have been looking at him rather strangely because Maximus smiled when she didn't answer him right away.

"What is it?" he asked. "Why do you look at me so?"

Embarrassed that she had been caught daydreaming, Courtly grinned. "I am sorry," she said. "I do not mean to stare at you. But it was only this time yesterday when we met and now, already, you speak of marriage. I must say that when you make a decision, you move swiftly with it. But what about your family? Mustn't your brother and mother give permission? You are a great lord, Maximus. Surely there are protocols you must go through."

Maximus continued to caress her fingers even as he ate more fried pork. "Although my brother is the Earl of Coventry, I am a lord in my own right," he said, chewing. "I am Baron Allesley, a title I inherited from my father. I have lands far to the north near Chester with two smaller, manor homes and a small castle that is manned by de Shera men as a garrison against the Welsh. The land is very rich, the soil good, so the crops are always plentiful. Moreover, the castle guards a road leading in and out of Wales, and tolls are taken. I have a very good income from my lands and will be able to provide extremely well for you, as my wife. As for me needing permission from my brother, I supposed that I do, but he will do whatever I want him to do. If I tell him I am to marry you, he will have no objections."

Courtly was rather surprised to hear all of this, although in hindsight, she should not have been. She knew the de Sheras were powerful. But she also knew that a title and lands would not overly persuade her father to give his permission to a marriage. In fact, she was fairly certain the title of Lord Allesley wouldn't impress Kellen one bit.

"If you say that is true, then I will believe you," she said, "but I fear that my father will not think it so simple."

Maximus took a drink out of the wine bottle he had brought along. "And why not?" he asked. "I have everything he could possibly want in a good husband for his daughter."

Courtly nodded, sighing as she set down her food. She found she wasn't particularly hungry any longer, thinking about her father and how he would surely reject Maximus' offer of marriage. Knowing her father as she did, it was a given.

"You would make any woman a fine and honorable husband," she said, forcing a smile. "You are perfect in every way. But my father... I am not entirely sure what drives him but, as I told you, he has chased away every suitor I have ever had. Earlier today, I discovered that he has done the same thing to his sister, which is why she is a spinster. Or, at least, she blames my father for her state. I had no idea he had done that to her but I suppose I should have guessed something like that was amiss. My father and his sister cannot stand the sight of one another and surely there is a great reason behind that. Hatred such as that is not innate."

Maximus took another drink of wine and squeezed her hand before releasing it, picking through the food he had brought and offering her something small, baked, and pie-shaped.

"Here," he said. "It is custard. Surely you have not finished eating yet."

Courtly shook her head, took the custard, but didn't bite into it. She noticed that Maximus had not replied to her statement. As he rummaged around for more little custard pies, she spoke.

"Please tell me your thoughts, Maximus" she said. "If you have changed your mind, I do not blame you."

He looked at her, frowning. "Why do you keep saying that?" he asked. "I have not changed my mind. I will never change my mind, so you can put your fears to rest. I am simply thinking on how to approach your father with all of this. You have given me a good deal to think on."

Courtly pondered the situation, watching him down two small, custard pies. She took a tiny bite of hers. "Do you want my suggestion?"

He nodded. "I asked you, did I not?"

Courtly sighed faintly and set her custard pie down onto the bench beside her. "Send your brother and his wife to ask on your behalf," she said. "My father both respects and fears Gallus de Shera. He is greatly impressed with the man. If your brother will plead on your behalf, my father may consider it. Truly, with the earl making the approach, he may have little choice in the matter."

Maximus looked at her, seriously. "I would be a poor man indeed if I sent my brother in to plead for your hand on my behalf," he said. "I am not afraid of your father. If I do not ask for your hand directly, what manner of respect do you think he will have for me? Nay, love, I will not hide behind my brother, although I understand your position on the matter. When I offer for your hand, it will be directly to your father."

She smiled at him. "My apologies," she said softly. "I did not mean to ask you to be any less than you are. I simply meant to suggest a way in which my father could surely not refuse."

Maximus reached out again and took her hand, holding it tightly in his big mitt. "I know," he assured her quietly. "But this is between me and your father. Now, eliminating my brother as an intermediary, how else would you suggest I approach him?"

Courtly thought on that. "As you said," she replied. "Approach him directly and forcefully. Be firm but polite. My father respects strong men, of which you are clearly one, so the best way to handle him is to be stronger than he is. It is my suggestion you tell him what your intentions are rather than ask him. If you simply ask him, I can promise you he will deny you."

Maximus lifted his eyebrows in thought. "Then I will not give him the opportunity," he said. "But if he denies me, then I hope you will like living on the run, because that is what we shall do."

Courtly giggled until she realized he was serious by the expression on his face. Then, she was rather stricken. "But… but you cannot do that," she said, somewhat passionately. "What of your family? It will reflect poorly on them. And what about you? You have a great reputation, Maximus. You cannot ruin that by absconding with a woman. That is no way for a man like you to live your life. You cannot throw it all away simply because you cannot have the woman you want."

He didn't like her reply even though he knew, deep down, that she was correct. He brushed the crumbs off his breeches, looking around to see if there was more food.

"Do you want anything else?" he asked her, utterly avoiding her statement.

Courtly could see he was putting her off. Because a man's life was at stake, no matter how much she wanted to be his wife, she couldn't let him ruin himself because of her.

"Maximus," she said softly. "Listen to me. If you and I run away together and you forsake everything, eventually, you will grow to resent me. That is no way for a marriage to exist. Once it is done, it cannot be undone. Your mistake cannot be undone. I will not let you destroy the rest of your life because of me."

He paused in the hunt for anything further to eat. When he looked at her, it was with uncertainty and sorrow.

"You would not leave your father and go with me?" he asked.

Courtly reached out and put her soft hands on his bearded face, looking him in the eye. "There is nothing I would want more than to go with you," she whispered, touching the magnificent face of Maximus de Shera and feeling his bristly heat against her flesh. "I have known you less than a day and, already, you are under my skin. Your humor and generosity and good character has endeared itself to me. Would I go with you? Without question. But I could not have you ruin your reputation because my father denies your marriage suit. Mayhap in time, he will relent if you continue to ask him and demand he change his mind, but for us to run off without his permission… you will ruin everything you have ever worked for. It will reflect badly on your family. What would your mother say?"

He was in the process of being thoroughly hypnotized by her luscious eyes and full lips, but the moment she brought up Honey, he stiffened.

"You will not bring her into this," he said.

Courtly didn't back down. "Why not?"

He wanted to pull away from her but couldn't. Those eyes had him within their grasp and there was no escape.

"Because…," he said hoarsely. "Because she would possibly say the same thing you have just said. If my mother were of health, I would send her to your father in my stead. My mother and no other. No one denies Honey de Shera, of anything."

Courtly smiled gently. "I pray I have the opportunity to speak with her one day," she whispered. "I would be deeply honored."

Maximus smiled at her but the pull was too strong. Reaching out, he grasped her and pulled her against him, his lips slanting hungrily over hers. He could feel Courtly resist at first, startled by his action, but he wrapped his muscular arms around her and refused to let her go. She was sweet and warm and delicious, tasting like the custard she had just eaten. He could taste it on her lips. He kissed her slowly, with a purpose, experiencing her scent and taste and texture. It was intoxicating.

Maximus lost all sense of time as he gently suckled Courtly's lips. She had stopped fighting him and was now collapsed against his chest, cradled in his arms as he feasted on her. Maximus had been with women in his lifetime, of course, losing his virginity when he was seventeen to the young women he had once described to Garran – *She was the smithy's daughter. When my father found out, he sent both her and her father away. I heard that she died later that year of a fever.* Aye, that was all he really knew of love. He knew the pain of losing it before it even started.

As he nibbled on Courtly's chin, he vowed that this love would be different. Already, it was stronger than he had ever imagined it could be. This love, he would not lose. As he began to suckle Courtly's lips again, he heard someone clearing their throat softly.

"Maximus?"

Maximus knew the voice so he wasn't particularly startled as he looked up from Courtly's flushed face. Stefan du Bois was standing several feet away, looking rather embarrassed that he had been forced to intervene. Maximus, however, was consummately cool.

"Stefan," he said evenly. "How did you find me?"

Stefan didn't look at Courtly as she pulled herself from Maximus' arms, her back to Stefan as she struggled to compose herself. Stefan, like any good knight, was focused on his liege.

"Lady de Shera has sent me for you," he said. "She told me I could find you in or around the Street of the Merchants. Lady de Shera says that it is time to escort Lady Courtly back to Kennington."

Maximus stood up, realizing that his manhood was a slightly aroused as the result of his heated kisses with Courtly, but he simply shifted his tunic under the guise of repositioning the sheath for his broadsword to cover it up. He was still reeling from their kiss, however, so much so that he was having difficulty focusing on what Stefan was saying. But he forced himself.

"Where is Lady de Shera?" he asked.

Stefan threw his thumb in the direction of The One-Eyed Raven. "She is not feeling well so we must return for her before we take the lady home," he said. "She says that she must accompany you back to Kennington so the lady's father will not think her irresponsible for leaving the lady alone with you."

Maximus was already collecting Courtly's possessions as the woman stood up, still wiping her lips, which were very red from Maximus' bristly beard. Maximus took her by the elbow and politely escorted her to where Stefan was standing.

"Did you just come from The One-Eyed Raven?" Maximus asked the knight.

Stefan nodded. "Less than a half-hour ago."

"Has Gallus returned from his meeting with de Montfort?"

"Not yet."

"And Tiberius?"

"He and Garran went off together. They have not yet returned."

Now that Maximus knew the status of his men and his brothers, he turned to look at Courtly, who smiled up at him wanly. She still wasn't over Stefan having stumbled upon them. Maximus could see the embarrassment in her features and it made him smile. He found humor in her chaste shame. It was very charming. He extended an elbow to her.

"Shall we go, my lady?" he asked politely.

Courtly forced a smile, accepting his elbow and refusing to look at Stefan as Maximus led her past him. He headed for the livery, taking his blushing lady with him as Stefan followed behind. They had to cross a couple of busy avenues before they arrived at the livery, the yard of which was crowded by a merchant and his traveling party. Maximus simply plowed through the group, but they gave him a wide berth. Maximus was not a man to be ignored, in any case.

Inside the stable, the de Shera carriage had been removed when Jeniver had been taken back to The One-Eyed Raven. The only thing left was Maximus' muscular jennet plus Stefan's big, white rouncey. Maximus quickly realized that there was no transportation for Courtly so he sent Stefan to hunt down the livery owner. As Stefan went on the prowl, Maximus turned to Courtly.

"I should apologizing for that unseemly display," he said softly, a gentle smile on his lips. "I should not have lost control as I did but I could not seem to help it. Worse yet, I cannot promise that it will not happen again."

Courtly broke into a bashful smile. "I suppose you must sample that which you intend to marry."

Maximus laughed softly. "I must," he agreed, sobering. "And I am pleased."

Courtly gazed up at him. "As am I," she whispered. "But... but I truly fear what will happen when you return me to Kennington.

My father was clearly unhappy this morning when I went with Lady de Shera and I am afraid of what he will do upon my return. I suppose I am in for a row."

Maximus' expression grew grim. Deadly, even. "He would not hurt you, would he?"

Courtly shook her head. "Nay," she assured him. "He would never do that. But he will be… angry."

Maximus considered that scenario. Not that he blamed the man, to be truthful. His daughter had all but been wrested away from him. With a sigh, he gently stroked her hair as he leaned forward to kiss her on the forehead in a gesture of comfort.

"It is not your fault that we took you from Kennington," he said. "But I understand your point. Hopefully my brother's wife can soothe any anger your father might feel when we return you home, because angry or not, I intend to speak to him tonight."

Courtly wasn't entirely sure that was a good idea. When her father's mood was foul, there was no reasoning with him. To broach a marital contract would certainly not be well-met. She wasn't convinced that tonight would be the appropriate night for such a thing but, on the other hand, she supposed there would never be a good time for such a thing in her father's eyes.

"Be mindful of his mood, then," she said with a sigh. "I know you wish to speak with him sooner rather than later, but since you will not send your brother on your behalf, all I can say is that you must be mindful of his mood."

Maximus eyed her with some amusement. "I believe I can handle the man."

He was confident. Courtly appreciated a man with confidence, but she hoped he wasn't in for a massive shock when her father denied him. In Maximus' world, there was no such thing as a denial to his wishes. She could see it in his face. He had every confidence that he could convince Kellen to allow him to marry Courtly. She feared that would not be the case.

Maximus, however, also harbored those secret fears in spite of his outward appearance. The lady had fairly convinced him that his pursuit of her hand would not be an easy task and, as much as he had told her he would not send his brother in his stead, now he was starting to reconsider. If Gallus could get him what he wanted, then he was willing to consider it, but on the other hand, he was a very prideful man. He wasn't accustomed to sending others to do his tasks. As Stefan returned with the livery owner leading a small, gray palfrey, Maximus hoped that Gallus was returned to the inn by the time he got there.

He needed the man's counsel on a most serious matter.

"MAX, I AM glad you are here. Plans have changed and we must discuss them."

Maximus had entered the smelly, stale inn only to run straight into his brothers, both of them. The words had come from Gallus, who had been standing next to Tiberius in quiet discussion over by one of the leaning, abused, tavern tables. But the appearance of Maximus had Gallus and Tiberius moving towards him, only to realize that on Maximus' arm was a petite, rather beautiful woman. Both brothers came to a halt, focused on the lady.

"My lady," Gallus greeted. "Please excuse me. I did not see you when my brother entered the room."

Courtly smiled at the very handsome man with black hair who slightly resembled Maximus. "That would not be difficult, my lord, considering that Sir Maximus fills up the entire doorway when he enters a room," she said, watching the brothers snort in agreement. "There is nothing to excuse, in any case."

Gallus was smiling openly at the woman. "You must be Lady

Courtly," he said. "My wife has told me about you and has spoken quite highly of you. I am Gallus de Shera and I believe you already know my brother, Tiberius."

Courtly dipped into a practiced curtsy. "My lords," she greeted, noticing that the youngest de Shera brother was smiling at her quite broadly. It was almost comical. "It is a pleasure to see you again, Sir Tiberius."

Tiberius moved to take her hand but Maximus threw out a big arm, blocking his brother. "I would not if I were you," he threatened, eyeing Tiberius. As Tiberius shrugged, good-naturedly, Maximus returned his focus to Gallus. "What plans have changed, Gal? Can the discussion not wait? I must speak to you most urgently."

Gallus was having a hard time keeping his attention strictly on his brother. He was mostly focusing on how tightly Maximus was holding on to the lady, which wasn't like him at all. Gallus' wife's words were coming back to him now, words she had spoken that morning when Maximus had stormed off after his confrontation with Tiberius. *If he truly feels something for the lady.* Already, Gallus could see that it was true, astonishingly so. He'd never even considered that Maximus was capable of such a thing, although there had been a young woman in his youth that he had believed himself in love with. Still, Maximus was the last man he would ever have thought to have fallen for a woman.

"I am afraid it cannot wait," Gallus finally said. "Jeniver is prepared to escort the lady back to her father. I will send my wife with a full escort to Kennington and you will remain here with me. We have much to discuss."

That was not what Maximus wanted to hear. "Gal, whatever you wish to discuss is not more important than my news," he said. "I have asked the lady to be my wife and she has agreed. But her father may prove to be a very large obstacle and I require your counsel on the matter."

On the balcony above, where the sleeping rooms were, they heard a familiar cry. "Oh!" Jeniver was overhead, looking down at them. "Max, I heard you! What thrilling news!"

They could then hear rapid footfalls as Jeniver ran across the catwalk and took the stairs at the far end very quickly. Gallus was already moving in her direction.

"Slow yourself," he admonished. "You will fall and break your neck."

Jeniver, moving swiftly, waved him off. She rushed right past him and straight at Maximus, throwing her arms happily around his neck. Maximus, grinning, accepted his sister-in-law's congratulatory hug, but Gallus was not so happy. He held out his hands as if to ease the force by which his wife was hugging.

"Easy, sweetheart," he begged. "Max, if you squeeze her, you will have to answer to me. Do nothing!"

Maximus started to laugh, holding his arms out as if to show he wasn't squeezing his brother's pregnant wife. "I am not touching her, I swear it."

By this time, Jeniver had released him and was moving to Courtly. Forgetting protocol, she hugged the woman happily.

"My heartiest congratulations," she said, squeezing Courtly before releasing her. "This is the best possible news, my lady. Welcome to our family."

Courtly was touched and pleased by Jeniver's enthusiasm. "Thank you, Lady de Shera," she said sincerely. "In truth, it has happened rather swiftly since Maximus and I have only just met, but… well, I am most pleased with his proposal of marriage."

Jeniver was ecstatic. "Of course you are," she said. Then, she looked between Maximus and Gallus. "I heard what you said about the lady's father. Do you plan to approach him tonight when we return her to Kennington?"

Maximus nodded. "That is my intention," he said. "I do not wish to wait."

Jeniver was in full agreement as she looked at Gallus. "Absolutely not," she said. "Gal, you will ride with us to Kennington and ask Lord de Lara on Maximus' behalf. He cannot refuse an offer of marriage if it comes from you."

Gallus threw up his hands. "Wait," he commanded softly. "I cannot go to Kennington tonight. We agreed that you would return Lady Courtly. I have serious matters to discuss with my brothers and I need them both with me."

Jeniver frowned. "Nothing is more important than a marriage, Gallus," she said. "Your business can wait. Go with us now to Kennington and then you may discuss your business later tonight after we have settled with Lord de Lara."

Gallus eyed his wife, displeased. He could see that she was being quite stubborn and he didn't want to upset her, but his matters had priority over Maximus' betrothal at the moment. Still, he could see by the expression on her face that it would be very difficult to convince her otherwise, especially in her emotional state. The pregnancy had wreaked havoc on his normally calm and sweet wife. It had made her a crazy woman at times. With this in mind, he drew in a calming breath and crooked a finger at both his wife and Maximus.

"A moment with you both, please," he said. "Ty, please take Lady Courtly in hand. I must speak with Max and my wife, alone."

Tiberius was more than happy to escort Courtly even though Maximus was literally growling at him. He ignored his brother and took the lady over to a table where they had wine and fruit and cheese. Meanwhile, Maximus and Jeniver went to Gallus, who pulled them to the edge of the room so they could have a bit of privacy.

"Max, I... Max, look at *me*," he said, noting that his brother's attention was on Tiberius and Courtly. When Maximus reluctantly looked at him, he continued. "You know I had a meeting with de Montfort today. We will be leaving for London on the morrow and we must discuss plans and logistics of such a move. I do not have time to enter marital negotiations with Lord de Lara. Moreover, I am sure he has the same news that I do and will be moving to London tomorrow as well. His daughter, I would assume, will go with him. Can we not discuss marital contracts once we reach London?"

Maximus was clearly, and deeply, unhappy. "London?" he repeated. "Why are we going there? I thought de Montfort was convening a big gathering at Oxford tomorrow?"

Gallus grunted. "As I said, plans have changed," he replied. "De Montfort received word that the king is convening his supporters next week and he wants to be there. Therefore, we move to London."

Maximus rolled his eyes in exasperation. "That is all well and good, but it is quite possible that my business cannot wait until we go to London," he said. "Courtly has said that her father intends to send her and her sister back to Trelystan Castle, mostly to separate Courtly from me. Evidently, he has chased away every suitor she has ever had and he did not like the fact that I paid his daughter attention at the feast last eve. It would seem that her father has an aversion to men when it comes to his daughters."

Jeniver was listening serious as Gallus exhaled sharply, with impatience. "Max, listen to me," he muttered. "I am very sorry to say that Kellen de Lara's approval of your betrothal is not the most important issue we face at the moment. There is something even more critical than all of this. Because de Montfort wants us in London by next week, we cannot go home and visit Honey. We cannot spare the time to see to her."

Maximus was distracted from Courtly and Tiberius now with

the mention of his dying mother. He hissed. "Damnation," he growled. "Can we not even spare a few days, Gal?"

Gallus shook his head. "You know I am as unhappy as you are about this, but we have no choice," he said. "Moreover, my sorrow is deepened because I do not believe it will be safe to take my wife into London, either. It is a dangerous place at any given time and we will be spending most of our time with de Montfort and the allies, which would leave Jeniver alone a good deal of the time. It is my intention to send her back to Isenhall. I feel I have little choice. She will be safer there."

With that, he reached out and took Jeniver's hand, pulling her gently to him. As Gallus kissed his wife on the temple, Maximus was watching the two of them.

"Then in your sorrow from being separated from your wife, surely you can understand my desire to seek a betrothal with de Lara," he said quietly. "You do not want to be separated from the woman you love and I... I do not want to be separated from Courtly. I must know she is mine, Gal. Can you not understand that?"

Gallus could, somewhat, but Maximus' behavior had him frustrated. He struggled not to explode. "Of course I do," he said with some anger. "But, Max... why you? Why now? You are my rock, my most dependable warrior. You are an immovable object, but now, suddenly, you are pleading like a childish squire, bleeding all things soft and silly about wanting a woman. How can you do this now when you know how badly de Montfort needs our focus?"

Maximus stiffened at his brother's words. "I am allowed to be a man in all ways," he said, struggling not to snarl in front of Jeniver. "I am allowed to have feelings for a woman. You've had the opportunity twice and I have not had it at all. Now, when I have found a woman I want to marry, you begrudge me the same happiness you have known? Are you truly so selfish?"

The situation was starting to get ugly and Jeniver put herself in between the two of them so they wouldn't start throwing fists. "Max, he does not begrudge you happiness," she said to calm the situation. "He does not mean it the way it sounds."

Maximus was so angry that his lips were starting to turn white, tense with rage. "He means it exactly that way," he said, both to Jeniver and to Gallus. "I will not let him ruin my chance for happiness. If her father will not allow us to marry, I have no qualms about abducting her and leaving England for good."

Shocked, Jeniver and Gallus looked at him. "Max, you wouldn't," Jeniver gasped. "You would not leave us!"

Maximus opened his mouth but Gallus reached out and grabbed him by the collar of his tunic. "You are mad," he hissed. "You do not even know what you are saying. I did not say that I would not speak with de Lara on your behalf. I simply asked you to wait. How is that destroying your chance at happiness? If the lady loves you now, she will love you next week or next year. Why is it so urgent that you marry her this instant?"

Maximus didn't like to be grabbed, not even by his brother. Jeniver could see his fists balling and she shoved him back, smacking her husband's hand so that he would release him. Pushing the men apart was strenuous and she was already feeling sick and weak, but she jabbed a finger at Maximus in a stunning show of strength.

"You will not fight him, do you hear?" she commanded. Then, she looked at Gallus. "And you know very well that family loyalty supersedes everything. Your loyalty is to your brother most of all. You will listen to me well, both of you. Gal, we will all take Lady Courtly back to Kennington now, whereupon you will speak with Lord de Lara about Maximus. You will get the man's consent to a marriage this night or we will stay at Kennington until you do. Once you have his consent, Lady Courtly and I will return to

Isenhall while you and Maximus go to London. Lady Courtly will be of great assistance to me, as you know I am not feeling my best as of late. We will remain with Lady Honey and your daughters until you and Maximus return from London. Maximus will then marry the lady the moment he returns. Now, will that convince both of you that the situation is not worth fighting over?"

Gallus didn't like to see his wife so upset. Her pregnancy had been very taxing on her, and even now as she scolded them, he could see that she was rather pale. Nay, he didn't like it at all, not one bit. He looked at his brother.

"She is right," he mumbled. "Family is the most important thing. I did not mean to make you feel guilty for your feelings towards the lady, but you must understand that there is a great deal of pressure on me to mobilize our army and move at the head of de Montfort's force. And you… you are my warrior. You are the knight that all men hope to be. I cannot lose you, Max. I simply cannot."

Maximus was softened by his brother's words and he, too, didn't like seeing Jeniver so upset. He was feeling a great deal of remorse that he had upset her so, but mostly, he was fixed on what she had said.

"I know," he said after a moment. "You will not lose me. But I need your help, Gal. Lady Courtly says that her father has chased away every suitor she has ever had and I do not want him to chase me away. I have a feeling I cannot intimidate him into agreeing to my demands. Therefore, I need your help. Badly."

Gallus relented, mostly because he knew he had no choice. He looked at his wife. "Very well, sweetheart," he said. "We will go to Kennington now and open negotiations on behalf of Max. I suspect I should just turn you loose on de Lara because we shall have his agreement much sooner."

Jeniver grinned, relieved that Gallus and Maximus were no

longer fighting. "I would not be opposed to that," she said, although she was seriously thinking of resting for a little while. She was beginning to feel quite weak now. Still, this situation would not wait. She needed to be strong. "Allow me to go and gather my things and then we shall depart. Kennington House is not far from here, truly. We should make it there in little time and, depending on how soon we can gain de Lara's agreement, we should be back this evening in plenty of time for you to discuss business with your brothers."

Gallus cocked an eyebrow at his wife as she turned for the stairs she had so recently come racing down. "It is not that simple and you know it," he said. "Negotiations could take more than just a few moments of your time."

Jeniver cast him a glance, giving him a wink. "Not if you turn me loose on him."

Gallus lifted his shoulders. "If you feel up to the task, you may try," he said. "He may respond better to the soft overtures of a woman."

Jeniver's only reply was to smile as she turned back for the stairs. The moment that she did so, however, the entire room began to rock unsteadily and she began to feel very weak and dizzy. Grabbing for the banister was the last thing she remembered before everything went dark.

# PART THREE

## WINDS OF WAR

# CHAPTER TEN

*Kennington House*

"WHERE IS MY daughter?"

At sunset, Kellen was standing at the gates of Kennington, waiting for his child to be delivered and already, the situation wasn't going well. He was gathered with a group of his men, including St. Héver, armed to the hilt and appearing as if he were looking for a fight.

Maximus' heart sank when he saw the offensive posturing that Kellen was presenting. He looked at Gallus, who appeared terribly strained and grossly impatient with de Lara's demeanor. Having just left his ill wife, Gallus was in no mood for foolery. He couldn't even present a semblances of politeness at de Lara's question.

"She is with my wife," he said flatly. "My wife became ill this afternoon and your daughter has been kind enough to tend her. Given that my wife has no ladies about her and I do not want serving women touching her, I accepted your daughter's offer. That is what I have come to tell you, de Lara."

Kellen looked unhappier than he had when they'd first arrived. He eyed Gallus and Maximus, and the host of de Shera soldiers behind them. There were about thirty, including three very big knights. Jaw flexing, Kellen took a few steps towards Gallus as the man sat astride his volatile, red jennet.

"I am sorry that your wife fell ill, my lord," he said through, Gallus was sure, clenched teeth, "but you can surely afford great care for her. I want my daughter returned home."

Gallus wasn't going to let de Lara bully him. More than that, the man was being plain rude. Bracing his big, gloved hand on his thigh, he leaned forward and looked the man in the eye.

"I can afford the best care in England for her," he said. "But that is not the point. The point is that your daughter graciously volunteered to sit with her and tend her so that my wife is not being attended by people she does not know. Your daughter is a generous and giving individual, qualities you do not seem to have. Kindly tell me why you were so hospitable and kind to my brother last evening and then today you treat us as if we have done something unspeakably wrong. Well? I am waiting."

De Lara eyed Maximus as the man sat, emotionless, astride his black and white steed, waiting and watching for Kellen's reply. Kellen, however, was reconsidering his attitude after Gallus' scolding. Nothing the man had said was untrue. He simply didn't like anyone to point it out. It was his prerogative to behave however he wished, especially with his daughter at stake.

"I am grateful to Sir Maximus for saving my daughters from a burning building, my lord," he finally said. "But you must understand that I am very protective of my children. I do not like it when they are out of my sight. I worry just as any father would. The fact that your wife promised to bring my daughter home at sunset, yet she is not here, concerns me greatly."

Gallus scowled. "Why should it?" he said. "You know where she is. You know she is with my wife. She is safe and comfortable. Why on earth should you be concerned for her safety?"

Kellen was starting to become flustered. "You do not understand," he said. "Since my wife died, it has only been me and my girls. I am naturally protective of them."

Gallus waved him off impatiently. "My first wife died two years ago this summer," he said. "I have two small daughters and I am protective of them as well, so do not speak to me of being protective of your children. Your daughter is safe and I need her help. I will bring her back to you as soon as my wife has sufficiently recovered."

Kellen wasn't happy with that directive, not in the least. "*Where* is my daughter?" he demanded one last time. "You will take me to her immediately."

Gallus sighed sharply. "She is at The One-Eyed Raven Inn," he told him. "If you want to go to her, then you will do it on your own, but if you go near my wife in your attempt to get to your daughter, know that I will strike hard and strike fast. No man goes near my wife. Is that in any way unclear?"

Now, threats were being leveled and Kellen was forced to back down. He didn't need the Thunder Lord as an enemy but he was rapidly heading in that direction. He glanced at St. Héver, standing next to him, seeking the man's silent support, but all he received was an impassive expression in return. At that point, he was coming to think that perhaps he was looking like a fool for being so demanding and rude. After a moment, he lifted his hand in a gesture that implied a reluctant surrender.

"It is clear, my lord," he said. "I am not attempting to offend you. I simply want my daughter returned to me, as your wife promised."

Gallus would not accept the man's apology. "What you have done is insult my honor and my wife's honor," he said coldly. "You have implied great distrust in us as if we have done something to deserve it. Do you always treat people this way, de Lara? It is a wonder you have any allies at all."

Kellen could see that he had, indeed, insulted de Shera a good deal. He would have to attempt to mend that state if he wanted to keep his standing in de Montfort's rebellion. Insulting the Lords of Thunder was not a way to get ahead in life, or at least in de Montfort's world. With a heavy sigh, he struggled to appear submissive, at least as much as he could. He was a stubborn man, however, and it was difficult.

"You will forgive me, my lord," he said, laboring to spit out the words. "Will you please come inside and enjoy some refreshments? Allow me to at least make amends for my slander against you and your wife. That was truly not my intent."

Gallus glanced at Maximus, who was more than willing to go with the man. They both realized that this would be the perfect opportunity for Gallus to present a marital contract to de Lara, especially now that they had the upper hand against him. De Lara had been scolded and now he was being rather docile because he had tried to stir up a battle he had no chance of winning. Maximus intended to take advantage of his surrender because, in those first few tense moments after they'd arrived, he could see what Courtly was talking about when she described her father's protectiveness over his daughters. *I am not entirely sure what drives my father to chase away all suitors,* she had said. Maximus could clearly see what she had meant. Kellen was a zealot when it came to the protection of his daughters. Therefore, he knew to proceed carefully.

"Then we accept," Gallus finally said, only when he received Maximus' imperceptible nod. "Lead the way, de Lara. Let us see if your hospitality is enough to ease my anger against you."

Kellen had his soldiers open up the big, iron gates and usher in de Shera and his men. Gallus had his soldiers take up station near the gate, away from the bulk of de Lara men who were across the bailey and closer to the great hall. Scott, Troy, and Stefan had accompanied them to Kennington and when Gallus and Maximus entered the hall that Maximus had feasted in the night before, the knights followed with a somewhat suspicious manner. Having seen de Lara's fit, they weren't entirely sure that they weren't in enemy territory and were on their guard.

The big hall of Kennington was cold and dark when they entered and Kellen immediately set about starting a fire in the hearth, but he had to do it himself because Ellice was still keeping her servants hidden. Gallus thought it was all rather odd until he remembered what Maximus had said about the night before, how Lady Courtly had been forced to cook the entire feast because of a disagreement between her father and his sister. As Kellen tended the hearth, which must have been embarrassing for him, Gallus leaned in to his brother.

"I see what you mean about the de Lara's sister absconding with her servants," he muttered. "Was it like this last eve, too?"

Maximus nodded, looking around. "It was," he said. "But the aunt was here this morning. In fact, it was she who insisted that Courtly attend Jeniver on her trip. De Lara tried to tell us that he needed Courtly to tend her younger sister but the aunt volunteered. I wonder where the aunt is?"

Gallus lifted his eyebrows in agreement. "Excellent question," he said quietly, then spoke louder as he addressed Kellen. "I understand your sister lives here, de Lara. Will she join us?"

Kellen threw more pieces of kindling on his infantile blaze. "She will not," he said. "She is tending my younger daughter."

"Where are they?"

Kellen looked over his shoulder at Gallus. "In their chambers, I would think," he said. "I do not expect them to join us."

Gallus turned back to his brother although he was eyeing Kellen oddly. "So he keeps the women hidden when male guests arrive," he muttered. "Strange."

Maximus shook his head. "He did not keep them hidden last night."

"That is because he did not view you as a threat. Now, he evidently does, to any and all women in his family."

Maximus was fairly certain that was the truth, which worried him for the marital negotiations to come. But he sat down when Kellen indicated for him to sit at the same feasting table he had occupied the previous evening, and even in the same seat. But instead of Gallus on his right, last night it had been Courtly. Already, he missed her and the growing bond they had. Her smile, the warmth of her hand... he missed everything. He wished very much that she was sitting beside him.

Kellen's soldiers apparently had kitchen duty this night because two of them came from the small door that led to the kitchen yard bearing trays of cups and two big pitchers. But it was clear they resented the duty because they weren't very polite or even very competent when distributing cups and setting down the pitchers. Wooden cups tumbled and rolled, and wine splashed from one of the pitchers, set down heavily, and splashed on Scott's tunic. The de Wolfe brother was visibly displeased at the dark purple stain on his shoulder.

If Kellen noticed that his soldiers were being rude, he didn't speak up. He poured himself a full measure of wine and drank deeply before Gallus had even been served. Casting Maximus a long glance indicative of his feelings on de Lara's bad manners, Gallus passed the wine pitcher to his brother before taking a drink of the tart, cheap wine.

"Your younger daughter," Gallus started the conversation. "How old is she?"

Kellen looked up from his cup. "She has seen eleven years," he replied. "Why do you ask?"

Gallus shrugged his shoulders. "Simply to make conversation," he said. "Why is she not fostering at that age?"

Kellen was starting to look displeased again. "Because I never sent her away," he said snappishly. "She was quite young when her mother passed and I never had the heart to do it. You said you had two daughters. How old are they?"

Gallus didn't appreciate the man's rather confrontational tone but he let it go for the moment, especially since he wanted something from the man. "My eldest, Violet, is five years of age and her sister, Lily, is almost four," he replied steadily. "They are not old enough to foster yet if that is what you were going to ask."

Kellen simply downed more wine because that was exactly what he was going to ask and he was frustrated that de Shera was one step ahead of him. "See if you do not send them away when they come of age," he said knowingly. "It is more difficult than you think."

Gallus lifted his eyebrows in agreement. "I absolutely believe that," he said. "Sending your daughters away to foster is much like sending them off to marriage. It is quite difficult to let them go but it is necessary."

*Brilliant!* Maximus thought as he cast his brother a casual glance. Gallus was leading up to the subject of their visit. But Maximus kept his mouth shut and let Gallus take the lead. He was much better at negotiations than Maximus was. Maximus tended to swing a sword first and ask questions later.

Kellen, however, didn't think Gallus' statement was brilliant or relevant. He had nearly drained his wine cup by now and was moving to pour himself more.

"Why is it necessary?" he wanted to know. "I see nothing necessary about marrying off daughters. It is simply a way for a man to gain your money through a dowry. Moreover, once your daughter is married, she no longer belongs to you. She belongs to a stranger."

Both Gallus and Maximus were coming to understand a great deal of how Kellen thought of marriage in that brief statement. "Not necessarily," Gallus said. "If your daughter marries someone you know, a fine man that you approve of, who wants nothing from you including a dowry, that would be quite an excellent circumstance for your daughter. Not only does she have a fine husband, but you keep your money."

He laughed as he said it, hoping Kellen would, too. He was attempting to ease the man into the idea of his daughter being married. But Kellen saw no humor in the statement so Gallus wiped the smile off his face and took another drink of wine, thinking on his strategy.

"Men are only after money," Kellen reiterated as he started in on his second cup of wine. "They do not care for the women they marry."

Gallus shook his head. "That is not true," he said. "I love my wife dearly and I took her without a dowry, although when I married her, I inherited Anglesey from her father. It is a fine legacy to pass down to my son. Wouldn't you want a grandson to pass your legacy down to?"

Kellen frowned. "I have not thought on it," he said. "Although... although I will admit that I have been thinking on marrying again so I can have a son. Daughters are useless and expensive."

Gallus stopped drinking his wine. He was more interested in watching Kellen's guard come down the more the man drank. Before he drank himself into oblivion, Gallus needed to act. He was very careful in how he proceeded.

"They do not have to be," Gallus said. "Daughters could actually bring you some wealth instead."

He purposely said it to peak Kellen's curiosity, which it did. The man cocked his head thoughtfully. "How?" he asked.

Gallus had him where he wanted him. "Let me see if I can think of an example," he said, pretending to ponder the situation. "Hypothetically speaking, let us say that a man comes to you and offers for your eldest daughter. He is a wealthy man from a good family with excellent connections. Let us say that instead of expecting a dowry, he offers you lands in Cheshire that belong to him. The lands are part of a bigger estate, but what he will offer you is a gift of land that produces over a hundred acres of barley a year and has a small village attached to it, a town that you can draw revenue from. Now, for that kind of gift, you would gain quite a bit of wealth and keep your daughter's dowry. Would you not find that manner of offer attractive?"

Gallus and Maximus held their breath as Kellen mulled over the proposal. It was hard to tell just how seriously he was considering it because the wine was already having an effect on his manner – his face was flushed and his eyelids were droopy.

"Mayhap," Kellen finally said. "But I am not sure I can let my daughter leave me."

Gallus didn't let up. "But you said yourself that you were considering marrying again," he pointed out. "A house cannot have two queens. If you take a wife, your daughter will be unwanted in her eyes. You must allow your daughter to have a house and husband of her own."

Kellen's brows drew together. It was clear that he was considering that scenario but Gallus didn't want to give him too much time to think about it. He continued.

"My lord, consider this," he said. "I have found your daughter an excellent husband from an excellent family who will gladly give you a portion of wealthy lands in exchange for your daughter's hand. That is an offer any sane man would readily accept."

Kellen looked at Gallus, shocked. "You…?" he stammered. "*You* have found my daughter a husband?"

Gallus nodded. Then, he looked at Maximus, for it was time to bring him into the conversation. "My brother, Maximus, would like to offer for Lady Courtly's hand," he said with satisfaction. "He will make it a most attractive offer, my lord. You *will* consider it."

Kellen looked at Maximus. He simply stared at him, without much emotion at first, but then it was as if Gallus' words suddenly sank deep and he realized what had just been said. The man's mouth popped open in outrage and he slammed his fists down on the table hard enough to spill the wine.

"You!" he bellowed. "I *knew* you wanted her! I could tell when you came here last eve that you were determined to have my daughter. Well, I will not have it, do you hear? You cannot have her no matter what you offer. Do you think she can be bought like... like a cow? Is that what you think?"

His anger was not surprising but Gallus and Maximus remained calm, particularly Maximus. He wanted something and he wasn't going to leave without getting it.

"It is not a cow I am bartering for, my lord," Maximus said politely. "It is compensation for a daughter I am offering. I want to marry your daughter and I shall. It is your choice whether or not you accept any compensation for her."

Kellen was drunk and outraged. He stood up, falling over the bench in his haste to move away from the table as Gallus, Maximus, and the de Shera knights rose to their feet. Kellen finally stumbled to his feet, pointing accusing fingers at Maximus.

"Where is my child?" he demanded. "You have her! I want her back!"

Maximus, standing on the other side of the table, crossed his arms stubbornly. "Nay."

It was the only thing he said. Kellen, expecting something more by way of an answer, realized that it would not be an easy thing to get his daughter back and his hysteria went from bad to worse.

"Give her back to me," he seethed, going for the broadsword at his side. "Give her back to me or I will kill you!"

The de Shera knights unsheathed their swords as well. Kellen's bellows had invited the interest of his soldiers, just outside the hall, and when one looked in and happened to see Kellen with his sword drawn, more de Lara swords began to come out. The de Shera soldiers, across the bailey, then saw the de Lara men with weapons and their weapons came out, too. It was a chain reaction that had the de Shera men rushing the de Lara soldiers and, very shortly, the entire bailey deteriorated into a massive brawl.

"This is going badly," Gallus said, hearing the fighting outside. "Unless we want blood on our hands, I suggest we leave."

Maximus looked at his brother, stricken. "But…"

Gallus grabbed at him. "We will live to fight another day, Max. We cannot accomplish anything more tonight."

Maximus was never one to back down from a fight. Moreover, he had an emotional investment in this situation.

"I came to gain his consent in marrying Courtly," he pointed out as Kellen was fended off by Scott and Troy. "I am not leaving until I have it."

Gallus shot him an exasperated look. "Can you possibly be serious right now?" he asked. "Look at the man. He will not give his consent tonight. We must leave this place before one or more of us ends up impaled on the end of a broadsword."

Maximus was quickly growing furious as he watched Kellen do battle against the de Wolfe brothers. It was like watching two cats toy with a mouse. Kellen was a decent knight, but the de Wolfe brothers had their father's legendary skill. As Gallus tried to pull him away, Maximus yanked himself from his brother's grasp and charged Kellen, shoving Troy aside and knocking Kellen's broadsword away with his gloved hand. It was a very skilled, and very powerful, move. With a great shove, Kellen ended up on his arse, weaponless, as Maximus stood over him.

"Listen to me and listen well," Maximus growled. "I will marry your daughter with or without your blessing, so you may as well consent. This is not over, not in the least. I will give you until tomorrow morning to come to your senses or I will marry your daughter at first light and there will be nothing you can do about it."

Kellen tried to kick at Maximus. He was just that angry and frustrated and drunk not to fully realize what he was doing. Infuriated, Maximus stepped on the man's kicking leg, so hard that Kellen bellowed with pain. At that point, Gallus pulled Maximus off of the man and away from the confrontation. He began pulling his brother towards the door that led out to the kitchen yard.

"Rally the knights!" Gallus shouted.

It was the call that would bring all of his knights to him. Scott and Troy, leaving Kellen on the ground, were heading in his direction but Stefan was at the great hall entry, fighting off any de Lara soldiers who were trying to come inside. He was having a marvelous time with it but Scott whistled loudly between his teeth, catching Stefan's attention.

"Du Bois!" he called. "Come now!"

Giving one last de Lara soldier a poke, Stefan broke off and ran after the de Wolfe and de Shera brothers, following them out into the kitchen yard. There were no soldiers here, yet, but it was only a matter of time. There was a gate the connected the kitchen yard to the bailey and Gallus made his way towards it. Before he could reach it, however, a woman emerged from the shadows of the yard.

"Sir Maximus!" she hissed.

All five knights came to a halt as Ellice emerged from the darkness. She knew Maximus on sight, as she had seen him earlier in the day when he had come to Kennington along with Lady de Shera. Maximus peered at the woman he recalled seeing that morning.

"You are Lady Ellice," he said. "Your niece told me who you are."

Ellice nodded quickly, nervous as she heard sounds of fighting. "I am," she said. "Where is Courtly?"

Maximus wasn't entirely sure if the woman was foe or ally so he answered carefully. "She is safe," he replied.

It was a generic answer, one that Ellice didn't have much to say to. It was clear that Maximus didn't want her to know.

"What is the fighting about?" she asked. "Did my brother attack you?"

Maximus shook his head. "He is not happy because I offered for Lady Courtly's hand," he said. "I shall have to ask another day when he is calmer and not so drunk."

Ellice sighed heavily. "It will not matter if you ask another day," she replied. "His answer will still be the same."

Maximus frowned as the sounds of fighting began to draw closer. The de Shera knights were keeping watch but it was clear that they would soon need to flee.

"What do you mean?" Maximus asked. "Why is he so opposed to me marrying his daughter?"

Ellice shook her head. "It is not you in particular," she said. "Kellen has done it to every suitor. He even did it to my suitors when our father died at an early age. Kellen feels that he is protecting the women of the family when, in fact, he is ruining us. Did he tell you how his wife died?"

Maximus peered at her curiously as men spilled out from the hall, fighting, and the de Shera knights went into battle mode.

"He did not," Maximus said even as Gallus unsheathed his broadsword to fend off the deadly tide that was creeping towards them. "What happened?"

Ellice swallowed hard. "A knight who came to court me," she said, struggling through it. "He made advances to Kellen's wife when Kellen was elsewhere. She rejected him and he killed her. Kellen has blamed me ever since and he has chased away every suitor that has ever come for me to punish me. He is repeating the pattern with Courtly. He will chase you away, too."

Maximus' jaw flexed with sorrow, with determination. Sorrow for what had happened to Courtly's mother and determination that he would marry Courtly regardless.

"I am sorry that happened," he said, unsheathing his broadsword because he could hear the fighting close behind him. Even though he was facing Ellice, he could still hear it. He knew the sounds of Gallus' sword. "Courtly does not know this, does she?"

Ellice shook her head. "She must never know," Ellice said. "She was away fostering at the time. Kellen told her that her mother died of a fever."

The fighting was nearly upon him. Ellice was starting to back up, fearful of the men with swords, but Maximus followed her. He had to know something more. Answers were coming forth from an unexpected source and he needed them.

"If Kellen will not consent to marriage, then I will take her anyway," he said. "I am telling you this so you will know. I... I am very fond of your niece. I am sure I will grow to love her. I will make her happy and comfortable for the rest of her life, I swear it."

Ellice's dark eyes glimmered at him, a moment of peace and joy amidst the turmoil of the battle surrounding them.

"Then you have my approval," she said. "Let Courtly know happiness where I have not. Do not let her father's burdens become her own. *Take her.*"

Maximus could see that the woman meant it. But the fighting drew too close and she ran off, back to the shadows from whence she came, leaving Maximus somewhat reeling from the conversation. *Courtly's mother was killed by a rejected suitor.* Now, Kellen's attitude was starting to make some sense. Maximus was eager to share the information with Gallus but they had to get out of this predicament first.

De Shera and de Lara men were fighting all throughout the kitchen yard, in the hall, and in the bailey. The de Wolfe brothers and Stefan had entered the fight in the kitchen yard and de Lara men were beginning to die. Gallus had even entered the fight and he had already dispatched two soldiers. Maximus, sword in hand, began to move towards the bulk of the fighting and the de Lara men, knowing the Thunder Warrior on sight, began to back off. Sometimes, all Maximus had to do was show himself in order to strike fear into the hearts of men. But Maximus had another purpose. He was looking for someone.

*St. Héver.* De Lara's big, blond knight was not in the kitchen yard so Maximus moved through the kitchen gate and out into the bailey beyond in search of the man. He finally spied him over near the doorway leading into the great hall and he shouted the man's name above the combat. He had to call him three times before St. Héver finally heard him. Then, the blond knight headed directly for Maximus, his sword leveled.

But Maximus didn't want to fight him. He wanted to speak with him. As St. Héver drew near, Maximus held up a hand.

"Stop," he commanded. "You know a battle between us cannot end well, so lower your sword and order your men to do the same. Your lord attacked us first. By God's word, I swear that is the truth. Tell your men to lower their weapons."

St. Héver didn't hesitate. He knew Kellen de Lara well enough to know that the man wasn't shy about striking the first blow or even attacking his own guests. He'd seen it before. Moreover, he'd seen how Kellen had treated the de Sheras when they first arrived. Immediately, he lowered his sword and emitted a piercing whistle, one that the de Lara men evidently recognized because they all seemed to slow their assault. When St. Héver saw that he had his men's attention, or at least most of them, he held up a big fist.

"Cease," he roared. "Gather the wounded and dead in the hall!"

It was a simple command but one the de Lara men followed. They simply lowered their weapons and walked away from the de Shera men, who were quite confused by the abrupt cessation of hostilities. Maximus called out to his men.

"Gather at the gates!" he bellowed. "We leave!"

Weapons lowered or sheathed, the de Shera men did as they were told by their commander. They began picking their wounded up from the ground, carrying men back to their horses. The de Shera knights, including Gallus, had heard the command and they began to emerge from the kitchen gate and out into the bailey. Gallus, without a scratch on him, headed for Maximus.

"What happened?" he asked his brother as he drew near. "How did you convince them to stop?"

Maximus pointed to St. Hévér, who was over near the entrance to the great hall. "See that knight?" he said. "That is Kirk St. Hévér, de Lara's knight. I sought him out and told him what happened. He is the one who gave the cease command to de Lara's men."

Gallus sighed heavily, wiping some sweat off his brow as he sheathed his broadsword. He looked over the bailey, seeing that there were several wounded and perhaps just as many dead. It was quite a bit of carnage for so short a fight.

"We had better leave immediately," he said. "We must return for Lady Courtly and...."

"Nay," Maximus cut him off, looking at him. "I am not returning her to Kennington, Gal. I am marrying her first thing in the morning."

Gallus closed his eyes softly, briefly, in a gesture of great regret. "I knew it would be too much to ask you to wait," he muttered. "If you marry the woman without her father's consent, this could get ugly. Surely you know that."

"I know that."

Gallus eyed his brother in the dim light of the bailey. "You know that I would never deny you your heart's desire, Max, but are you sure about this?" he asked sincerely. "Do you truly want to travel this path or can you wait until the lady's father has calmed sufficiently and seek his permission?"

Maximus was serious. "You heard what the aunt said," he replied, lowering his voice so the de Shera men gathering around them wouldn't hear. "Kellen will never give his permission. This is a chance I must take, Gal. I am as sure about this as I have ever been, about anything, in my life."

Gallus wouldn't argue with him but it was clear that he was disappointed. He was disappointed that de Lara was so resistant, disappointed that Maximus was so determined. It would make the entire situation quite edgy for years to come, and they would forever be at odds with Viscount Trelystan when the man should be their ally. Nay, it wasn't a good situation at all. But he knew if he denied Maximus that his brother would do it, anyway. He might even do as he had threatened and flee the country. If that happened, Gallus would be devastated.

"Very well, then," Gallus said, putting a hand on his brother's shoulder and turning him for the horses gathered near the gate. "Then let us return to the inn and retrieve the women. We must find another place to stay this night, as de Lara knows what inn we are housed in. He could very well regroup his men and come after us."

Maximus nodded, relieved his brother was not going to fight with him on the matter of Courtly. Gallus may not have agreed with his decision but at least he wasn't going to argue with him. He would support him, no matter what.

"I will send Stefan out to find us new accommodations," he replied. "Let us leave this place now before something else happens."

Gallus didn't have to be told twice. He and Maximus and their men mounted their horses and fled into the night, leaving Ellice watching from the corner of the kitchen yard.

God's Bones, how she wished that the man she had loved those years ago had been determined to have her as much as Maximus was determined to have Courtly. She was happy for her niece, at least as much as she could be, but she was also jealous. Jealous that her time for such things had come and gone.

As the de Shera men headed north towards Oxford, Ellice didn't even both to go and check on her brother. She was more concerned with Isadora, as the young girl was now quite alone with her sister being taken in marriage. Ellice had never felt very maternal towards her nieces but she found that she rather felt that way now towards Isadora. The child would miss her sister greatly.

Ellice, for the first time in her life, would attempt to give the girl comfort but, more than that, she intended to give her brother counsel. It was time for him to stop feeding on old fears because it was clear that his burden was beginning to affect them all; first Ellice, now Courtly, and soon Isadora. The man had to be made to understand that what happened to his wife had been an isolated incident. The women in the family had to be allowed to have lives and loves of their own. If they didn't, they would grow to be just as bitter as Ellice was, and Kellen had to be convinced of that fact.

Beating some sense into her brother's head would be the most difficult task of all.

# CHAPTER ELEVEN

THE ROOM WAS quiet and dark but for a glowing fire in the hearth. It also smelled heavily of rosemary, that crisp fragrance that assaulted one's nostrils in a most glorious way. Jeniver was very fond of it, as the scent seemed to help her pregnancy-related illnesses. It soothed her. As Gallus entered the chamber he shared with his wife at The One-Eyed Raven, his gaze eagerly sought the woman out. When he finally found her in the darkness of the chamber, what he saw was not what he had expected.

Jeniver was dead asleep on the bed. He knew this because she was snoring softly and she always snored softly when she was exhausted. Courtly was lying on the bed, too. The woman's lower half was in a chair next to the bed but the upper half of her was lying down next to Jeniver. She, too, was sleeping soundly, weary from her exhausting day with Maximus.

Maximus was standing behind Gallus as the man lingered with the door half-open, surveying the room. Maximus opened his mouth to speak but was immediately silenced by Gallus when the man put a finger to his lips. Gallus pointed at the bed and Maximus slipped in behind him to see what he was indicating. What Maximus saw brought a smile to his lips. Silently, the pair slipped out and softly shut the door.

"We cannot allow them to sleep much longer," Gallus whispered. "As soon as Stefan returns with new accommodations, we must be ready to leave. I fear that de Lara is already amassing men to come here and wrest his daughter from us, so time is of the essence."

Maximus rubbed his bearded chin, thinking on the situation. "It is," he grunted. "But it concerns me greatly that there will be no defense from an attack of armed men if we go to another inn. No walls, no moats, no measures of defense – de Lara can simply walk into the common room and from there, we will be left defending doors that any normal man could kick down."

Gallus was forced to agree. "I am not entirely sure we have much choice," he said. "But I will admit that I am worried that my wife will be caught up in the maelstrom. She would not be able to take such excitement in her present condition."

Maximus knew that was true and he was coming to feel the least bit guilty about everything, but only for Jeniver's sake. "Mayhap it would be best if I take Courtly and go," he said. "At least take her out of Oxford. We can meet up with you later in London. That way, Kellen will have no cause to go after you and, subsequently, put your wife in danger. I would never wish that upon her, Gal. You know that."

Gallus nodded. "I know," he said. "But even if you flee, de Lara will still have cause to move against me. That does not solve the problem."

Maximus struggled with increasing guilt. "Then I will marry Courtly tonight," he said. "That way, even if Kellen manages to get to her, he cannot take her. She will be my wife and the Church will side with me in any dispute."

It was a technicality that Maximus was relying on. Gallus knew it was foolish to assume such a thing and, deep down, Maximus did, too, but he was not going to admit that he had perhaps acted rashly in all of this. He had made his choice, and his decision, and he would stand by it.

"Possibly," he finally said. Then, he slapped his brother on the shoulder. "In any case, let the women sleep for a little while longer while you and I share a meal. I am famished. De Lara provided absolutely nothing by way of a meal. He was a terrible host."

Maximus snorted as he allowed his brother to direct him back downstairs to the common room. "That is because he did not have his daughter there to cook for him."

Gallus grinned, moving with his brother down to the common room where Tiberius and the rest of the knights were already congregated around their usual table. The inn was rather full this night, as a storm was rolling in from the east, and many people were seeking shelter from the coming rains. Gallus knew this would make Stefan's job more difficult of finding another place for them to stay, but he remained hopeful. Still, they would have to discuss other options in case Stefan was unable to locate something suitable.

As they took their seats at the table below, Jeniver's chamber door quietly opened. Courtly poked her head out, looking to see if Maximus or even Gallus were anywhere nearby. She had awoken nearly the moment Gallus had opened the chamber door and she had heard what was subsequently said. She heard everything.

As she knew, her father had not been receptive to Maximus' offer of marriage. That was no surprise. But the attack Gallus and Maximus spoke of was indeed a surprise, at least against the two de Shera brothers. Her father was aggressive, that was true, but he usually was careful with his aggression. He picked fights that he knew he could win. Clearly, the man could not win against the de Shera war machine, but she could imagine how irate he must have become when the question of marriage had been introduced. She had no doubt that he was indeed amassing a raiding party to come and claim her.

Closing the door quietly, she looked at Jeniver, sleeping heavily upon the bed. The woman had been good to her, at least in the short time she had known her. She liked Jeniver a great deal and after Jeniver had fainted in the common room, she was greatly honored that Gallus allowed her to sit with his wife and tend her. Jeniver had come around, briefly, but she had fallen back asleep again and even now, remained sleeping heavily. It was clear that the day in general had been very taxing for the woman.

But a party of armed men would tax her even more, de Lara men that were after one thing – Courtly. They would come for her and even though Courtly was positive that Maximus and Gallus and Tiberius could fight them off, it would not end the situation. Her father would come and come again in his attempts to regain her. It would truly never end until one of them was dead – her father, or Maximus, or even Courtly. Kellen de Lara would never give up. She knew her father well enough to know that.

Therefore, there was truly only one solution – she had to return to her father of her own free will. Only then would Kellen consider the matter settled, as he would have no reason to continue his aggression against Maximus. Tears sprang to her eyes as she thought of the situation and of her life with Maximus that would never be – no sons in his image, no life of love and joy in the de Shera household. Much like Ellice, Courtly was destined to be a spinster because of Kellen's unnatural fear of men who would pursue the women in his family. At the moment, all she could do was hate her father for it. God Bones, she hated him so much. She hated him because he did not want to see her happy or in love, with Maximus or with anyone else.

She stifled a sob as her gaze fell upon the new possessions that Maximus has purchased for her that day. She would take none of it, of course, except for the garment she wore. She had nothing else to wear so there was little choice. Dear God, was this really to be her life? Living alone and unloved, without the man she had very quickly fallen in love with? Aye, she loved Maximus. There was so much to love about the man that her heart was full of it. They had shared special moments and a kiss that had spoken of untold passion, quickly ignited between the two of them.

But it would be passion unrealized. It would be love unrealized and un-nurtured, but she knew her love for him would never die. It was a part of her, permanently, as he would be. She wished she could tell him that before she left, but she knew she had to leave without his knowledge. He would never let her go and that would only cause his family great pain. She didn't want to be the cause of great pain to people who had been quite kind to her.

As she wiped at her eyes, her gaze fell upon a small table that contained pieces of vellum, an inkwell, a quill, sand, and a seal of some kind. She knew that Gallus had been conducting business from the inn so she assumed they were the earl's possessions. Given that Courtly could both read and write, it occurred to her to borrow a scrap of vellum and leave Maximus a note. She had to. She simply couldn't leave without telling the man what he meant to her. She couldn't leave without begging him not to pursue her for the good of all. She hoped he would obey her wishes. There were things in life that simply weren't meant to be and, because of Kellen de Lara, this was one of those things. Her love for Maximus was over before it began.

Quickly, she pulled forth a small scrap of vellum and dipped the quill into the inkwell. Carefully scripted letters began to appear on the page, a short note for Maximus that would be the only thing left from a marriage that was not to be. She tried not to weep while writing the note, keeping her attention focused on Lady de Shera to make sure the woman remained deep in slumber. Courtly didn't want to explain what she was doing or why she was leaving. It would have simply been too painful.

She finished the note without sanding the vellum. She was in too much of a hurry, too fearful that her plans would be discovered. As Jeniver snored softly on her rented bed, Courtly opened the shutters to the window that overlooked a livery and alleyway behind the tavern. The ground was uneven here and a portion of the yard backed up to the wall, meaning that the drop between the window and the ground below was eight feet or less. In her new lavender gown of heavy brocade, Courtly climbed from the window and hung from the sill by her fingertips, finally letting herself drop to the ground below.

She landed awkwardly and fell over, but she was able to regain her footing quickly and run to the stable where her borrowed palfrey was stabled. The little gray mare they had acquired at the livery near the Street of the Merchants was in her stall, fat and happy, and Courtly collected the animal, putting a bridle on her but nothing more. She didn't want to take the time to put a saddle on the little beast, so she quickly mounted the animal bareback and proceeded from the livery, losing herself in the collection of buildings of the town before finally finding the road south.

As the storm finally rolled in and the rain began to pour, Courtly made her way towards Kennington House, praying she was in time to prevent her father from doing something very, very foolish. The rain poured and the thunder rolled as if reminding her of that which she would never have: the Thunder Warrior in the flesh. He would be hers only in memories now.

*Farewell, Max... my love....*

ST. HÉVER WASN'T sure he was seeing correctly.

Standing at the gates of Kennington House, he had been called forth by a soldier who swore he saw something moving in the darkness along the road, something small and distant. The storm had fully engulfed the land with whipping winds and lightning, and St. Hévér stood out in the elements with several other men, watching the road for signs of the mysterious wraith he had been told of. He stood there for several long minutes, waiting, until the lightning flashed again and, for a brief moment, he could see what the soldier had been indicating – there was something approaching.

Whatever it was, it was a solitary figure. St. Hévér saw no threat in that, so he continued to stand by the gates, those oddly built, iron slat gates, and waited until the figure drew close. Then, and only then, could he see that it was a small figure astride a sopping palfrey. As it drew closer still, a flash of lightning illuminated it yet again and he realized it was Courtly. In a panic, he ordered the gates opened.

Soldiers threw the bolt and began heaving the gates open, made difficult because of the mud build-up from the rain and further made difficult from the rusting joints on the hinges. But it opened enough so that St. Hévér managed to get through, racing to Courtly and realizing she was without a cloak or any protection whatsoever. She was soaked through and through. He pulled her off the palfrey and carried her in his arms back through the gates as another soldier went out to capture the palfrey and bring it in. By the time St. Hévér reached the great hall, he was bellowing for food, wine, blankets, and servants. His loud cries woke up the entire house.

St. Hévér set Courtly down on a bench near the hearth with only a few burning embers in it. She was half-unconscious and so cold that her skin was nearly blue. St. Hévér began to stir up the fire, coaxing forth a blaze, as Courtly sat there and shivered. As the heat from the fire began to reach her, she began to come around a bit.

"Wh-where is my father?" she asked, teeth chattering.

St. Héver was working furiously to build up the blaze, which was growing fairly large the more he stirred it. Sparks flew into the air, drifting out into the great hall. "In his chamber, my lady," he replied. "The last I saw of him, he was sleeping off too much drink."

Courtly pushed the wet hair out of her eyes, focusing on the fire that St. Héver was so vigorously stoking. She slid off the bench and crawled on her hands and knees to the hearth, closer to the warmth. She held her shaking hands out against the heat of the blaze. She'd never been so cold in her entire life.

"What about his army?" she wanted to know. "Why is his army still here?"

St. Héver looked at her in confusion. "What do you mean, my lady?"

Courtly looked at the young knight. "Is he not going after the de Sheras?" she asked. "I know what happened tonight. I assumed he would be amassing his army to attack them."

St. Héver was trying to piece together what she was talking about and began to understand. "Your father was very drunk, my lady," he said. "What happen with the de Sheras… your father will indulge in a fight at the slightest provocation, you know that. After they left, he wanted to pursue them but I convinced him it would not be wise, especially with the storm coming. We would be trying to battle them in their own element and we would surely lose."

Courtly was trying to stop her chattering teeth. "What do you mean?"

St. Héver smiled thinly. "The storm, my lady," he said quietly. "Have you not heard of the Lords of Thunder? They use the storm to their advantage in battle. It is their preferred medium. Some say the lightning does their bidding. I have heard from more than one man that it is true."

Courtly was warming up, becoming more lucid, and her mind began to mull over St. Héver's words: *the Lords of Thunder*. Aye, she knew that was what the de Sheras were called, everyone knew. But now she understood why. Thoughts of Maximus filled her brain and the tears that had flowed since nearly the moment she left The One-Eyed Raven returned with a vengeance. She turned her face to the fire, unwilling to let St. Héver see her tears of utter sorrow.

"Courtly!"

A cry caused her to turn away from the flames, wiping tears from her face, as Isadora burst into the hall and ran to her sister. The little girl nearly pitched herself into the fire in her haste, prevented from doing so by St. Héver's quick actions. Courtly and Isadora hugged fiercely.

"You have come back!" Isadora gasped, holding tightly to her sister. But she soon recoiled, wiping off her damp hands. "But you are so wet. You must put on something dry!"

Courtly shook her head, kissing her little sister on the cheek. "I have nothing else," she said. "Remember that all of our possessions burned. I must dry out what I am wearing."

Isadora's attention moved to the garment her sister was wearing, a dress she had never seen before. "Where did you get this?" she asked, fingering the lavender material. "It is so beautiful."

Courtly wasn't sure what to tell her sister. *My love purchased this for me and it is the last thing I shall ever have to remember him by.* But she didn't voice her thoughts. Isadora didn't need to know such things. As she prepared a generic reply, Ellice entered the hall.

Courtly's guard went up, watching her aunt as the woman shook off the wet cloak she was wearing and left it by the entry. As Ellice approached, their gazes locked and something odd filled the air between them. There was understanding and remorse and sorrow there, intangible sensations at best. But, clearly, Courtly felt no hostility from her aunt whatsoever, a rare condition, indeed. Ellice didn't come any closer than the feasting table and she made no move to embrace her niece as she planted her wide bottom on the bench near Courtly and Isadora. Her dark gaze was on Courtly.

"Why did you come back?" she asked. "You had no call to."

Courtly wasn't sure how to answer, unsure how much to say in front of Isadora. "I had to," she said simply.

"Why?"

Ellice was pushing her. Not wanting to speak of such things in front of her little sister, Courtly put her hand under Isadora's chin and looked her in the eye.

"Will you go into the kitchen and see if there is warm wine for me?" she asked. "I am in need of something warming."

St. Hével stood up. "I ordered wine," he said. "I shall see what is keeping it."

He walked away, taking with him Courtly's excuse to remove her sister. Even so, she patted the little girl on the shoulder.

"Go with him," she said. "You can help him."

Isadora trailed after St. Hével without an argument. When she and the knight disappeared through the door that led to the kitchen yard, Courtly spoke to her aunt.

"Because I heard what happened her," she hissed. "I heard that Papa denied Sir Maximus' marriage proposal and I heard about the fight. I came back to prevent my father from attacking Maximus and his brother. If I am home, there is no reason to attack them. They were very kind to me, Auntie. It would be appalling if Papa attacked them because of me."

Not strangely, Ellice could see her point. She sighed heavily. "You should not have returned," she said. "You were with the man who wanted to marry you. What must he think now? That you are a silly fool who has run off?"

Courtly shook her head. "I left him a note," she said. "He will know that I did this to protect him and his family. Auntie, Papa is a ridiculous fool for behaving the way he does. He has no cause to deny Maximus' marriage offer and certainly no cause to attack the man."

"You should not have come back."

"I am protecting the man I love!"

"Love him, do you?"

Ellice and Courtly turned to see Kellen standing in the entry, dripping from the rain. He didn't seem drunk in the least. In fact he seemed furious and lucid. He yanked the door shut behind him and stomped into the room, glaring at Courtly as if she were his worst enemy.

"Answer me," he boomed. "Do you love him?"

Courtly had never heard her father speak to her like that and she had to admit that he was frightening her. He didn't look like the same father she had known all of these years. He looked different, edgy, like a man possessed. It was a struggle to maintain her courage.

"Aye," she replied steadily. "I do. He is a kind, generous man and you had no reason to deny him his marriage proposal. Why did you do it?"

Kellen's teeth were clenched with rage as he faced off against his daughter. "You will not question me," he snarled. "I will do what is best for you, even if you are too stupid to realize it."

His fury had Courtly's dander up. "I am not stupid," she fired back at him. "You have no earthly reason to deny Maximus' suit. He is a good man from a good family. What would possess you so? Why would you want to make me lonely and bitter for the rest of my life?"

Kellen's jaw flexed, indicative of his level of emotion. "You are too stupid to realize when your father is protecting you," he said. "You have no sense at all, girl. Maximus de Shera has bewitched you somehow. What else has he done to you? What personal favors have you granted him?"

Courtly wasn't exactly sure what he was asking but she knew

that she didn't like what he was possibly implying. "What do you mean?"

Kellen took a step towards her, his dark eyes blazing. "Whore favors, girl," he growled. "What whore favors have you granted him?"

Courtly lashed out and slapped her father across the face, so hard that the man's head snapped back. He staggered back a step as well, startled that his beloved Courtly should actually strike him. For a brief moment, it occurred to him just what he had accused her of and he was remorseful, but only for a moment. Immediately, his anger and suspicions swamped him, stronger than before, because he was sure that he was correct. She *had* granted the man favors. He looked at his daughter, his eyes wide with shock and outrage, as Ellice moved to stand between the two.

It was a surprising move by the woman who usually kept well away from her brother and nieces when it came to family business, but in this case, she was taking a stand. She had to. She pointed a finger at Kellen.

"You will not touch her," she threatened. "Get out of here, Kellen. Go back to your room and leave Courtly alone. You have no reason to accuse her of such things. You are a foul man with a foul mind."

Kellen's venom focused on his sister. "This is none of your affair, Ellice. I would advise you to move out of the way."

Ellice refused to move. "I am not moving," she said. "If you want your daughter, you will have to go through me to get to her and I promise you that I will not make an easy victim."

Kellen stood there looking at his sister and his daughter, his expression wrought with turmoil. He was beyond furious at this point. He was flirting with the edge of madness. Courtly was rebelling and Ellice, of all people, was siding with her. There was only one thing to do. He had to remove his daughters from

Kennington. He had to get them away from Ellice and away from Oxford in general. They had to leave.

"You are a wicked, bitter woman," he muttered to his sister, backing away towards the entry door. "I should never have brought my children here. I knew you were a bad influence on them but I am only coming to realize just how bad. I am sending my daughters back to Trelystan tonight and if you stand in my way, I will kill you. Is that clear?"

Courtly let out a shocked gasp. "Papa!" she cried. "You would send us home in this weather? How can you do that?"

Kellen roared at her. "Silence!" he said. "St. Héver will return you home this very night. God damn de Montfort, I must remain here because of his foolish gathering, but I will trust St. Héver to take you home. You will obey the man, Courtly, or I will give him permission to beat you. Is that clear? I will have him beat Maximus de Shera right out of your head!"

Courtly didn't say a word, she was afraid to. She looked to Ellice, however, who was rooted to the spot, between Kellen and Courtly, watching her brother as he staggered out of the hall and back out into the rain. When the heavy door of the hall slammed shut, she turned to Courtly.

"I can hide you," she said to Courtly. "Come with me."

Courtly was still reeling from her father's words. In his current mental state, she couldn't be sure that he wouldn't carry out his threat against Ellice. She went to her aunt, grasping the woman by the arm gently. She'd never done that before. She'd never even really touched her aunt before, but at the moment, she felt closer to the woman than she ever had. In this moment of darkness, there was a ray of light.

"Nay, Auntie," she said softly. "If you do, he will punish you. I cannot let that happen."

Ellice was softened by Courtly's tender touch although she

would not admit it, not even to herself. She liked to think of herself as hardened to any emotion, but she really wasn't. Like anyone else, she craved a human touch.

"You heard him," Ellice said. "He is going to send you and Isadora back to Trelystan tonight."

Courtly sighed. She loathed the mere idea. "I have no choice," she murmured. "If he sends me and my sister back home, then mayhap he will cease this madness that he has suffered over the past day. Mayhap he will calm down and become himself again. The situation with Maximus has seemed to drive him right to the brink of madness."

Ellice began to feel a sense of desperation on behalf of her niece. "If you return to Trelystan," she said softly, "chances are that you will never see Sir Maximus again. Are you willing to risk that?"

Courtly gazed at the woman, her eyes filling with tears. She simply couldn't fight them off as Ellice reminded her of the heart and soul she had left back at The One-Eyed Raven. Her features crumbled and she sat heavily at the feasting table, right in the same spot she had sat the night before with Maximus at her side. She remembered that night clearly, word for word, and her hand moved over the seat next to her where he had been. She could still see him sitting there, strong and proud. The sobs came.

"I have no choice," she wept quietly. "If I do not do what Papa says, he will take it out on innocent people. He may even take it out on you or Isadora. I could not live with myself if he harmed all of you because he was angry with me."

Ellice was moved by her tears. She remembered another young girl, years ago, with similar tears where it pertained to Kellen de Lara. Ellice had been so very young when Kellen had chased her last suitor away, a man she had loved. God's Bones, but she remembered those tears. She remembered the pain. Courtly's sorrow cut her deeply.

"Then you are giving up," she said hoarsely. "You are letting your father win."

Courtly shook her head, wiping at her cheeks. "I am doing what I must in order to save those around me," she said. "If something must be sacrificed in all of this, I would rather it be me than Maximus."

Ellice watched her niece quietly weep, each tear driving the nails of grief deeper and deeper into her heart. She had so wanted to help Courtly so the woman would not suffer the same lonely life she had, but Courtly was convinced that she had to obey her father in order to keep those she loved safe. It was the truth, in fact, and the noblest sacrifice Ellice had ever seen. She felt so very helpless because she knew she couldn't help Courtly. But she knew who could, perhaps the only person in all of England who could.

"Where is Sir Maximus?" Ellice asked. "Where is he staying?"

Courtly wiped at her nose. "In Oxford," she sniffled. "At a tavern called The One-Eyed Raven. Why do you ask?"

Ellice avoided the question. "When he discovers you missing, he will come here. You know that."

Courtly shrugged. "I asked him not to," she whispered. "I told him not to come after me."

Ellice snorted. "Do you think he will listen?" she said, glancing up at one of the tall, lancet windows at the top of the room when the lightning flashed overhead. "He is more than likely on his way here."

Courtly looked up at her, disturbed by the suggestion. "I asked him not to," she repeated, with concern in her tone now. "He must not come, Auntie. It will be a horrible situation if he does."

Ellice nodded, pretending to agree. "Aye, it will be," she said. "Mayhap… mayhap I should go and warn him not to come."

Courtly stood up, her expression eager. "Will you?" she asked hopefully. "I know the weather is terrible, and I would not ask this of you under normal circumstances, but I am afraid of what Papa will do if Maximus comes for me. Papa might even try to kill him."

Ellice was indeed thinking of riding to warn Maximus, but not for the reasons Courtly was concerned with. Ellice had her own plans.

"I will ride into town and speak to him," Ellice said. "He must know not to come. He must know… what is happening."

Courtly nodded her head, deeply thankful for her aunt's selfless attitude. "Please, Auntie," she begged softly, "Please go to him. I will be forever grateful."

Ellice waited until Isadora returned with warmed wine before leaving the hall and heading to her chambers to don clothing that would be somewhat resistant to the terrible weather. She'd spent so much of her life feeling worthless and restless that to actually have a purpose fueled her with confidence and new hope.

She was going to ride to find Maximus de Shera, that was a fact. But it would not be to warn him not to come to Kennington. It would be to tell him that Kellen was sending his daughters back to Trelystan. Her suggestion would be that Maximus should intercept that escort and take back what rightfully belonged to him. Kellen, who had to remain in Oxford because of de Montfort's gathering, might not know for weeks or even months that his daughters had been taken by Maximus de Shera. By the time he found out, Courtly would be Lady de Shera and Kellen would be too late to do anything about it. Aye, it was a brilliant plan.

For the marriage Kellen had denied his sister those years ago, Ellice would finally make her brother pay.

She would have the last laugh.

# CHAPTER TWELVE

**m**AXIMUS RECOGNIZED THE woman the moment she walked into the inn, drenched and sputtering.

He had been standing at the usual de Shera table, the one near the barkeep, discussing Courtly's disappearance and her subsequent note that they had discovered a few minutes earlier. Thinking the women were sleeping, they had left them alone until Stefan had returned to tell them that he could not find one hostel or inn that had room for all of them. Then, there was no point in waking the women at all and they'd found the note only by chance when Gallus had gone to look in on his wife again and found her very much alone in the chamber. Courtly's note had been on the table nearby. They had been preparing to go after her when Lady Ellice walked through the tavern door.

Maximus crossed the room in seconds. Perhaps he even flew. He wasn't entirely sure. All he knew was that, suddenly, he had his hands on Ellice as if she alone held all of the answers to Courtly's disappearance.

"Where is she?" he demanded savagely. "Where is Courtly?"

Ellice was somewhat caught off-guard. Having charged blindly into the inn to get out of the rain, she suddenly found herself in the hands of a madman. She yelped with surprise, looking up into a very angry, very worried face.

"Sir Maximus!" she gasped.

Maximus' grip on her arms tightened. "Where is she?" he repeated.

By this time, Gallus and Tiberius had joined Maximus and were attempting to pull his hands off the woman.

"Max," Gallus said softly, urgently. "Let her go. Come, now, release her."

Maximus managed to get one hand off of her but he still kept a grip on her arm, even as Gallus and Tiberius led them over, in some odd-looking group clutching at each other, to the table where all of the de Shera men were gathering. Someone extended a cup of warm wine to Ellice, which she gratefully accepted. She was soaked through. But Maximus had to let her go in order for her to lift the cup to her lips and he did so, though reluctantly. Ellice drank deeply before speaking.

"Courtly is at Kennington," she said, licking her lips. "She came back because she was afraid my brother was going to launch an attack against you. She believed that if she went back to her father, then he would cease his hostilities."

Maximus already knew that, more or less. "Is she well?" he demanded. "Did she make the journey safely?"

Ellice nodded and took another long drink of wine. "She is well," she replied, hearing the great concern in Maximus' voice. "You needn't worry over her health. But I have come to tell you that my brother is sending her back to Trelystan this very night. There is no time to waste. If you want to reclaim her, do it when she is on the open road with only a few soldiers as protection."

Gallus and Tiberius, as well as Maximus, were listening carefully. Maximus, who was usually the calm one in all situations, was having a difficult time keeping his bearings under these circumstances. When he had discovered Courtly missing, he had felt panic as he had never experienced in his life. All he could think of was the woman, alone, traveling back to Kennington in such terrible weather. Moreover, she was heading straight for her abusive, crazed father. But hearing that she was safe, at least for the time being, soothed him like nothing else could have. She was safe and whole. That was truly all that mattered to him. The rest, he could deal with as long as she was healthy.

"De Lara is sending her back *tonight?*" Gallus repeated what he'd just been told. "How is that even possible? He would do such a thing in this weather?"

Ellice looked around the table at the host of powerful knights, de Shera knights. These were the heart of the de Shera war machine, but the truth was that she'd hardly been out of Kennington in years and certainly not enough to find company with men she did not know. Looking into the faces of the de Wolfe brothers, of Garran, and finally into Stefan's very handsome, young face stirred her female blood somewhat. She had almost forgotten what it was like to be around attractive men.

"As I said earlier, when you were at Kennington," she said, tearing her eyes away from young Stefan, "my brother believes he is protecting his children and will do what he feels necessary in order to do that. At this moment, he is only concerned with removing them from Oxford and, in particular, separating Courtly from Sir Maximus. The weather does not matter. All that matters is that they leave as soon as possible. He wants to put as much distance as he can between Sir Maximus and his daughter, and do it quickly."

"Tonight?" Gallus clarified.

Ellice nodded. "Tonight," she confirmed softly. "But be advised that my brother will not be part of the escort. He must remain here for de Montfort's gathering, as I am sure you are all well aware, so he will not be returning with his daughters to Trelystan. He will send an escort of de Lara men to take them. It may be your one and only opportunity to reclaim her if you truly wish to do so."

Maximus was much calmer now than he had been only moments earlier. "Do you know what road they are taking?"

Ellice lifted her shoulders. "I can only assume the north road that skirts the edge of Oxford and heads north towards Evesham," she said. "It is the only one they could possibly take."

"Do you know when they are leaving?"

"The men were beginning to mobilize when I left Kennington. It is possible they will leave within the next hour or so."

Maximus digested the information a moment before turning to Gallus. "We can take thirty men and intercept them on the road north," he said. "But the issue is this – if we leave any of them alive, they will run back and tell de Lara that I have his daughters. But if we kill all of the soldiers, it will look like any manner of massacre at the hands of outlaws and the women will be missing. De Lara will not know what has become of his daughters and he will more than likely refrain from coming after me, at least for a time."

Gallus sighed heavily as he sat back in his chair, looking to Maximus. "As a father myself, I am not entirely sure I can condone leaving de Lara to believe that his daughters have been abducted by bandits. That would be a most painful thing."

Maximus cocked his head, almost defiantly. "Then do not ride with me and you can disavow knowledge of the entire situation," he said. "Either way, I am riding to intercept that escort and I am going to kill every one of them because any man I leave alive will run back and tell de Lara that I have abducted his daughter. That will bring the House of de Lara down upon us ten-fold."

Gallus could see that he was about to enter into an argument with his brother and he forced a smile at Ellice. "A moment, please, my lady," he said, standing up and pulling Maximus with him. "A word with my brother is all I need."

Ellice let them go, watching as the tall, youngest brother joined his two siblings. As the men huddled together, Gallus spoke in hushed tones.

"Max, I realized you want this woman," he said quietly. "I told you before that I want to see you happy. I was more than willing to allow her to remain with us here at the inn and then fight off de Lara when he came for her. But now you are speaking of intercepting her father's escort, killing every man there so they cannot give you away, and then abducting not only Courtly, but her younger sister as well. Now you will have both daughters and you want de Lara to think that they've been abducted by unknown outlaws? There is something less than honorable about that."

Maximus' jaw flexed unhappily. "Then do not go with me," he snapped. "I will go myself. I do not need you."

Tiberius reached out and grabbed his older brother. "Wait, Max," he said, trying to soothe the man. "Gallus did not mean it the way it sounded. I believe what he is saying is that a situation like this will only create a bigger mess with de Lara."

Maximus was furious and struggling to calm himself. "If either one of you ever asked the same thing from me, to help you regain the woman you love, then I would do it without question," he hissed. "But I am evidently not afforded the same courtesy. Unconditional, brotherly love means unconditional support, in all things, but if you do not want to be a part of this, then I will go it alone."

Gallus grabbed hold of him, too, before he stomped away in anger. "Nay, you will not," he sighed, relenting. "Ty is correct. It is my sense that going about it the way you are suggesting will only create more of an issue with de Lara. God's Blood, Max, if you marry the woman, de Lara will be your father-in-law for the rest of your life and grandfather to your children. Do you truly wish to have an adversarial relationship with him forever? How do you think that will wear upon his daughter and, eventually, your marriage? Could she even grow to resent you?"

He had a point. Maximus stopped his angry posturing and took a deep breath, laboring to ease his anger. He pulled upon that reasonable and steady demeanor that was his usual manner. Where his emotions were concerned, where Courtly was concerned, he was coming to see that he could be very volatile.

"I am too emotional about this," he conceded, raking his fingers through his dark brown hair. "I am sure you are both correct. Forgive me for being so angry about it. But I intend to intercept that escort. I will rely on the two of you to decide how, exactly, we extract Courtly. All I want to do is kill them all and leave no trace. Mayhap it is not the best way, but it is my way."

Gallus slapped him on the shoulder. "And we may yet have to kill them all," he said. "But only if we have no other choice. For now, let us muster the knights and a party of thirty soldiers and ride out to intercept the de Lara party. Ty, summon the knights over. We will tell them what we are about to do."

Tiberius produced a low whistle, catching the attention of the knights standing around the table where Ellice was drinking the last of her warmed wine. The men gravitated over to the de Shera brothers, expectant of the orders that were about to come forth. Gallus didn't keep them waiting.

"We are going to intercept the de Lara escort," he said, stating the obvious. "Scott and Troy, you will muster the soldiers. Make sure they are mounted and well-armed. Treat this incursion as you would a battle. Stefan, we will travel light, meaning no provisions wagon. You will ensure that every man has rations and also ensure that every horse is sound. If the beast is not, then this weather will surely ruin him and weaken our war party. Garran, I am sorry to say that I will have you stay with my wife while we are gone. She needs at least one competent knight and you would honor me by remaining with her. Are there any questions so far?"

The knights shook their heads and Gallus dismissed them. He was turning back for Max and Tiberius when he realized that Garran was still standing beside him.

"Do you have an issue, de Moray?" he asked, thinking that Garran was going to argue about being left behind with Jeniver. "State it."

Garran's gaze was somewhat uncomfortable as he looked at Gallus. He had been uncomfortable all day, ever since seeing his father, and the discomfort had only grown worse. He'd spent most of the day at the inn, as he was there to protect Lady de Shera while her husband had dealings with Kellen de Lara, and he'd therefore had a good deal of time to think on what his father had asked of him. He eventually came to the only conclusion he could come to and it was time to let the de Shera brothers know. Perhaps this wasn't the best time, but it might be his only opportunity. He cleared his throat softly.

"My lord," he said to Gallus. "I must speak with you, but not about anything involving your wife. I am always agreeable to protecting Lady de Shera. I must speak with you about something different."

Gallus glanced at Maximus and Tiberius. Maximus had impatience on his features but Tiberius appeared rather suspicious. Wary, even. It was an odd expression but one that Gallus didn't give much note to. He tried not to appear impatient, too.

"Must we discuss it now?" he asked Garran.

The man nodded. "We must, my lord," he replied. "It is important. I will only take a moment."

Gallus lifted his shoulders. "Very well," he said. "State your business and be quick about it. We must mobilize."

Garran knew that. He found that he was nervous to speak with de Shera. He hoped the man would understand his decision, as heartbreaking as it was. He took a deep breath.

"My father is in town," he said, looking to Tiberius. "He came yesterday and paid a visit to the inn when we were away. Tiberius was here, however, and he and Tiberius spoke. I went to see my father at his lodgings on the south side of town to find out why he was in town. I had no knowledge of him visiting Oxford. I am sure you all know that my father is a staunch supporter of Henry but I do not believe you know why. When he was younger, the king saved his life and he has, therefore, always felt a life debt to him. That is why he cannot side with de Montfort. In any case, it would seem that the king has summoned my father to London and has asked him to sit upon his council. I know you were afraid that the king's council would be full of Poitevins, but it would seem that my father will be among them. My father... he understands that I do not agree with the king or his policies, but my father has come to ask for my support, as his son."

Gallus, Maximus, and Tiberius were listening intently. "So that is what your father came to Oxford for," Tiberius said. "You did not give me a direct answer when I asked you. Now, I know why."

Garran nodded, looking somewhat sad and disappointed. "Henry has asked not only for my father's counsel, but for his sword," he said quietly. "My father has agreed. At some point, we will be facing Henry in battle and, consequently, my father. I hope you understand when I say that I will not fight my father on the field of battle. I would never lift a sword to him, ever, no matter what I believe. I must therefore ask you to release me from my oath of fealty, Lord de Shera, because I have made the decision to support and, if necessary, fight alongside, my father."

Gallus, Maximus, and Tiberius were stunned to varying degrees, but each brother understood, implicitly, what Garran was staying. They would not have expected him to fight against his father. Gallus put a hand on the young knight's shoulder.

"You are certain of this?" he asked softly.

Garran nodded with remorse. "I am, my lord."

Gallus thought on his reply a moment. "Your father is a legend," he said. "He is a fine and honorable knight. Although I am deeply saddened to lose your sword, I understand completely. I could not fight against my father, either."

It was a sorrowful moment for them all, especially for Tiberius. Garran was his good friend.

"When will you go?" Tiberius asked softly.

Garran looked at his friend, his liege, with great sadness. "I will go to him as soon as you return from intercepting de Lara's escort," he said. "I will not leave Lady de Shera unattended. Please… please know this was not an easy decision for me. It is mayhap the hardest choice I have ever had to make, but in this instance, understand that my choice is not in favor of Henry – it is in favor of my father. It will always be my father."

Gallus patted him on the shoulder again. "I know," he comforted. "As it should be. Godspeed and fair winds, Garran. May we never meet up in battle, my friend, but if we do, then I pray we both survive it."

There wasn't much more to say, from any of them. Garran forced a smile, silently thanking Gallus and his brothers for their friendship and trust, before turning away and heading back over to the table where Ellice was still sitting, now on her second cup of warmed wine. The knight sat down at the end of the table and simply hung his head.

It was a desolate moment. Gallus, Maximus, and Tiberius watched Garran as he slumped at the table, shocked and saddened by the turn of events. But they couldn't linger over them. They had a more pressing engagement looming and they would need all of their focus for what was to come. They could fully worry about the loss of a knight, and good friend, at another time. But now was not the time.

Eventually, Gallus turned away to prepare himself, followed by Maximus. As they went about their business, Tiberius remained where they had left him, his gaze lingering on Garran and feeling a distinct sense of loss. He wasn't entirely sure he could face the man in battle, either. He knew he couldn't strike him down. But family loyalty superseded friendship. He understood that well.

With a heavy heart, he followed his brothers as they prepared to intercept de Lara's escort and regain Lady Courtly.

JUST BEFORE NOON on the following day, outside of the sleepy village of Begbroke, north of Oxford, the de Shera army was waiting.

The rain had stopped for the most part, revealing clear skies above, but the ground was still soaked and muddy, making traveling difficult. Roads were impassable in some spots and farmers with wagons, trying to get to town, had been thwarted by the holes and puddles.

The de Lara party was heavily armed as they moved along the sludge-filled road. Courtly and Isadora were both astride the small gray palfrey, bundled up with a coverlet stolen off of a bed from Kennington, as they made their way very slowly along the muddy road. St. Héver was at point, leading the party along beneath cold, blue skies and as they passed on the outskirts of Begbroke they eventually entered a wooded area where the road was surprisingly better. The canopy of trees had protected the road from the driving rains somewhat. As the exhausted women plodded along the dark-mudded road, the trees around them suddenly came alive.

Men were pouring out of the woods, men with weapons, from both sides of the road. There were dozens of them, certainly more than the twenty men that surrounded Courtly and Isadora, and when the harrowing cry of men went up as they burst from the trees, the little, gray palfrey bolted, dumping both Courtly and Isadora onto the wet, soft earth.

As Courtly leapt to her feet and pulled Isadora up beside her, St. Héver bellowed commands for his men to surround the women and made his way back to them to protect them. But he was a lone knight with only twenty men-at-arms as six very big knights on very big horses came bursting out of the trees, heading directly for them. St. Héver was no fool. He saw the fine weaponry and the seasoned horses, especially a distinctive black and white jennet. He'd seen that horse before, most recently at Kennington House, so he knew who the men were. He ordered his soldiers to drop their weapons and surrender on the spot because there was no use in fighting the Lords of Thunder. He gave up without a struggle.

Without a fight to be had, the de Shera men came to an uncertain halt, surrounding the de Lara party as the six massive knights rode up. Maximus, leading the charge, flipped up his visor and fixed on St. Héver.

This was not the situation Maximus had planned on. He had expected fighting and killing, and in spite of what he told Gallus, he intended to do most of the killing, unwilling to leave witnesses to his abduction of Courtly. What he didn't expect was for St. Héver to surrender before the fight even began. It was a brilliant move on St. Héver's part, knowing that the de Shera war machine wouldn't murder men who had surrendered. It simply wasn't done. Now, the situation Maximus had hoped for was already going awry. Now, he would have to out-fox St. Héver.

"I do not wish to kill you, St. Héver," he said, his voice loud and steady. "I simply want Lady Courtly and I will be along my way."

St. Héver was a young knight, that was true, but he was exceedingly clever. He moved to Courtly in a gesture that suggested to Maximus that he could easily do what he wanted to with the woman before Maximus could stop him, up to and including killing her. It wasn't what he intended to do but he knew he was at a distinct disadvantage. He had to show that the de Sheras didn't have him completely defeated. There was still fight in him and, consequently, room for negotiation.

"I am deeply regretful that I cannot comply, my lord," he said to Maximus. "I have been instructed to take Lady Courtly and her sister back to Trelystan. Those are my orders."

Maximus looked at Gallus, who was focused on the young and strong knight. Gallus knew that Maximus had been hoping for a fight. He wasn't a fool. He knew how his brother thought, and he also knew that St. Héver's surrender had upset Maximus' plans for a murder spree. Not to say that he wasn't impressed by St. Héver's move, but now he had some quick thinking to do before Maximus began swinging his sword like a madman. Gallus flipped up his visor to better see St. Héver.

"I understand your orders, St. Héver," Gallus said. "But we intend to make it so you do not carry them out. We can do this peacefully or we can do it violently. The choice is yours."

St. Héver was in a bind and he knew it. "You know that I simply cannot turn her over to you, my lord."

"I know."

"Then I suppose you are going to have to take her by force."

Gallus looked at Maximus, who immediately dismounted his steed and unsheathed his broadsword, a wicked looking thing with a serrated edge on one side. It was designed to slice and cut, and surely there was no more feared weapon in the arsenal of Simon de Montfort. Everyone knew of the Thunder Warrior's horrific sword that was known to cut men in half. But Maximus paused a moment, looking at St. Héver.

"Are you sure you will not surrender her peacefully?" he asked.

St. Héver knew what was coming. God help him, he knew and

he was calm. "I cannot, my lord."

"St. Hévér," Gallus said. "Swear fealty to me. You are an honorable and strong knight. I could use you in my stable."

It was an attempt to diffuse the situation but St. Hévér, remorsefully, shook his head. "I have sworn fealty to Lord de Lara," he said. "I would not be an honorable knight to switch lieges so quickly at the first sign of a threat. I regret that I must decline, my lord."

Maximus cocked his head. "I do not want to kill you," he said. "But know that in order to achieve my wants, I will kill you and all of your men without hesitation."

St. Hévér nodded steadily. "I realize that, my lord. You must do as you must."

Courtly, who had so far been standing silent and shocked throughout the entire exchange, spoke up.

"Nay," she said, putting herself between St. Hévér and Maximus. Her focus, beseeching, was on Maximus. "Please do not kill him. He is only doing what he was told to do."

Maximus cocked an eyebrow at her. "I will speak with you when all of this is settled," he said, rather ominously. "I will tell you just what I think of your running off and returning to your father."

Courtly sighed heavily. "Maximus, I had to," she said. "I explained everything in the note I left you."

Maximus glared at her. He wanted nothing more than to spank her and then hug her, in that order. To have her so close and being unable to pull her into his arms was sheer torture. But he didn't want to get into a big discussion with her for all to hear, so he moved to the horse next to him where Tiberius was mounted. He faced away from Courtly, and consequently St. Hévér, as he spoke to his brother.

"I do not want to kill St. Hévér," he said to Tiberius. "I did not expect to find him here leading the escort. He is an honorable and good knight, but it is clear he will not turn her over. What do I do?"

Tiberius had his eyes on St. Héver and the rest of the de Lara men. He, too, dismounted his horse, standing next to his brother, still facing the de Lara group.

"You have two choices," Tiberius muttered. "Either kill the man and all of his soldiers like you planned to do all along, or…."

Maximus scowled at him. "I never said I planned to kill them all along."

Tiberius shot him a wry expression. "I know you, dear brother. I know how you think."

Insulted, Maximus looked away. "I did not count on St. Héver," he repeated. "What else can I do?"

Tiberius cocked an eyebrow at him. "I was getting to that," he said. "Or we can take them someplace and imprison them so they cannot return to de Lara and tell them what they know."

Maximus was interested. "Imprison them for how long?"

Tiberius shrugged. "Until you give de Lara grandchildren, at least."

Maximus pursed his lips wryly in response but he understood the man's point. There was no knowing how long they would have to keep the men imprisoned. Before he could reply, Gallus came around the back of Maximus' horse.

"What are you two muttering about?" he demanded quietly. "To see you in conference makes you look indecisive. What are you talking about?"

Maximus and Tiberius looked at their brother. "Tiberius suggests we take St. Héver and his men and imprison them somewhere," Maximus said. "At least for a time. I am agreeable to this because I do not want to outright kill St. Héver. He is a good man."

"He is also a very good fighter," Gallus said. "There could be a chance of you losing to him, but we will leave that discussion for another day. Imprison them, you say? I would be agreeable to that as well. We can take them back to Oxford Castle and put them in the vault there. De Montfort was staying at the castle but, as of this morning, he is moving on to London. I will speak with the castle constable and have him hold these men for a month or so, at least until we can figure out what to do with them."

It was the best of terms all three of them could come up with. Maximus looked over his shoulder to see St. Héver still standing very close to Courtly. "But before we can do any of that, I must remove Courtly from St. Héver's custody," he mumbled. "There may be a bitter battle here today yet."

Gallus looked over at the de Lara knight as well. "Your only hope of not fighting him is to convince the lady to come with you peacefully," he said quietly. "Mayhap she can convince St. Héver not to try and stop her."

Maximus lifted his eyebrows. "Mayhap," he said, his gaze still on Courtly and St. Héver. He began to move towards them. "Let us find out."

With that, he broke away from his brothers and moved towards Courtly, with St. Héver standing a few feet away from her. His sword was still in his hand and could be raised quite swiftly should he decide to go on the offensive. He hoped he didn't have to, at least not against St. Héver. That being the case, he had to make his proposal plain for all to hear. He focused on Courtly.

"It is my intention to take you with me, my lady," he said. "That is why I have intercepted this escort. I understand St. Héver has his orders, but the fact remains that I will take you one way or another. I will give you a moment to convince St. Héver not to fight back. Make it clear to him that I will kill him if he does."

Courtly gazed at Maximus, seeing the beautiful, bearded face that she loved so well, her heart breaking into a million pieces of sorrow.

"Max," she breathed, admonishingly. "I went back to Kennington for a reason. It was to keep my father from attacking you and wreaking havoc. Do you think I want to put you at risk because of him? Do you think I want to put your brothers or your men or even Lady Jeniver at risk because of my father? Of course I do not. You have all shown me the most wonderful time of my life and I cannot jeopardize all of you like that. I made this clear in the note I left for you. I told you not to come for me."

Maximus was starting to feel some anguish. He couldn't quite grasp that she wasn't instantly eager to go with him. She was still speaking of protecting all of them from her father's madness.

"I cannot help but come for you," he said, quietly, knowing that he was speaking for all to hear and struggling not to become embarrassed about it. Maximus de Shera was a warrior with no emotion. Now, he was showing emotion and in unfamiliar waters. "Asking me not to come for you is like asking me not to breathe. I realize you thought you were saving us all from your father's wrath, but some things are worth fighting for and risking one's self for. I thought we had a love that was worth these things, but if I am wrong, please tell me. I do not want to fight for something that you do not feel strongly about."

It was a shot to the heart. Courtly felt tears popping to her eyes, blinking rapidly to chase them away.

"I feel more strongly about it than you can know," she said quietly. "It is not about fighting for something. It is about protecting people I have come to adore. It is about saving *you*."

He was gladdened by her words, touched beyond measure. He smiled faintly. "I do not need protecting, although I thank you for your concern," he said. "I have been fighting for many years, love. I can handle the Kellen de Laras of this world. But what I cannot handle is being away from you, not even for a moment."

It was such a sweet thing to say, now in front of everyone, for all to hear. Now, everyone knew what Maximus felt but he realized that he hardly cared. It was the truth and now was the time for total truth. Men's lives, *his* life, was at stake.

"Do you feel that, already, we have a love worth fighting for, then?" Courtly asked softly. "We have known each other so short a time."

He knew there were scores of men, standing around, listening. At that moment, he didn't care.

"I knew I loved you within the first few minutes of knowing you," he said. "I am a man of firm beliefs and firm decisions. I cannot do anything without my whole heart. You already have my whole heart, Courtly. I cannot walk away from you."

Even though Courtly was grinning broadly, the tears came. She laughed at herself, at the situation, and at her unmitigated joy in general. As she wiped the tears off her face, Isadora moved over to St. Héver.

The child was looking at the big, blond knight, even going so far as to slip her hand into his big, gloved one, the hand that wasn't holding the sword. When he looked down at her, she gazed up at him with her big, blue eyes.

"Can you not simply let her go?" she asked the knight. "I know you like her very much but she likes Sir Maximus. You want to see her happy, don't you?"

St. Héver's expression remained steady as the child divulged some very private information. He had no idea how she knew what he felt, although he supposed, in hindsight, that he hadn't been very good at hiding his feelings, once. About a year ago, he'd been fairly obvious about it to Courtly but, fortunately, Kellen had not caught on. But his infatuation with her was over. There had never been any hope between them.

He wasn't bitter about it. But in listening to the conversation between Maximus and Courtly, he was starting to feel a sense of defeat. Defeat because he knew love was something he could not fight. There was no defense against it. Courtly de Lara had been a fairly lonely lady for several years, thanks to her father. St. Héver had watched the man chase away at least two very good, marital prospects for his daughter among the six or seven that had come to vie for her hand. Even if St. Héver didn't have feelings for her any longer, it still wasn't right that she should be denied what he himself had been. He knew he shouldn't relent but he was starting to topple. He squeezed Isadora's hand as he spoke to Maximus.

"My lord," he said. "May we have a word without weapons present?"

Maximus immediately complied. He handed his sword over to Tiberius and walked away from the group, down the road, as St. Héver paralleled his path on the opposite side of the road. When they were several yards from the group, they came together in the middle of the muddy, uneven path. Maximus faced St. Héver expectantly.

"It would seem that we have something to discuss, my lord," St. Héver said quietly. "You want Lady Courtly but I am bound to take her to Trelystan."

Maximus' expression held steady. "You love her?"

St. Héver wasn't surprised by the question but he struggled not to be embarrassed by it. "No longer," he admitted. "There was a time I did but she did not return those feelings. Still, she has remained kind and considerate towards me. She is a very kind and gracious woman in general."

Maximus turned to look down the road where Courtly was standing, now with Isadora next to her. The little sister had her arms around the big sister's waist and the two stood there, hugging.

"I have come to learn that about her as well," he said, returning his attention to St. Hével. "What did you wish to speak of?"

St. Hével drew in a deep, contemplative breath. He shouldn't be proposing what he was about to say but he found that he couldn't help it.

"If I allow her to go with you, then twenty de Lara soldiers will have seen the exchange," he said. "It will get back to de Lara and I am not in the habit of disobeying orders."

"Understood."

"But I do not wish to fight you over it, either."

"That is wise."

St. Hével chuckled at the man's arrogance. He couldn't help it. "However, if the lady were to run off," he continued, "tonight, mayhap, when we stop in the town of Woodstock for the night, I would not know about her disappearance until the morning, at which time it would be too late to go after her. Moreover, I have my orders, to return de Lara's daughters to Trelystan. I would still have Lady Isadora to return, and that would take weeks. By the time I return to Lord de Lara, Lady Courtly could be… anywhere. Long gone, in any case."

Maximus was coming to understand his meaning, quite clearly, and he was both relieved and grateful.

"What a coincidence," he said. "We were planning on being in Woodstock tonight."

"I thought you might be."

They understood one another. Maximus cleared his throat quietly, glancing off again towards Courtly and her sister.

"There is a tavern in Woodstock called The Buck and Bounty," he said. "The owner is a friend of mine. I think I shall visit him tonight. I will be there *all* night."

St. Hével nodded in understanding. "That is good to know."

"It is."

With that, St. Hével silently begged his leave with a bow of the head and moved off towards the de Lara party. Maximus headed back to his men, bellowing for his soldiers to mount their horses. Tiberius and Gallus watched him with some curiosity, Gallus going so far as to reach out and grasp Maximus' arm as the man gave the order for the soldiers to move out and south. All Maximus did was wink at him and give him a hint of a smile.

Confused, Gallus and Tiberius followed their men southward, leaving the de Lara party to continue along their way. It wasn't until they got down the road and out of sight of St. Héver and his men that Maximus pulled his animal to a halt and explained to his brothers what had taken place. Then, and only then, did they understand.

When Courtly appeared at The Buck and Bounty Inn towards dawn the next day, Maximus was waiting for her.

# CHAPTER THIRTEEN

*The next day*

I T WAS MID-MORNING in Oxford as Maximus and Courtly, both of
them upon Maximus' black and white jennet, made their way to
St. Clement's Church. Courtly, exhausted from the events of the
past two days and having very little sleep, was sitting across
Maximus' lap, sleeping quite soundly against him. He held her with
one hand and controlled the horse with the other. Even when he
pulled the horse to a halt at the livery they had been using when in
Oxford, he still didn't have the heart to wake her. But it was
necessary.

"Courtly?" he whispered, giving her a gentle shake. "Wake up,
love. We have arrived."

It took Courtly one or two more shakes before she roused.
Yawning, she sat up, rubbing her eyes and looking at her surroundings. It took her a moment to recognize their location.

"We are back in Oxford," she said as Maximus dismounted his
steed and lifted her off the horse, setting her carefully to the
ground. "Why did you choose to come back here? It is too close to
my father, Max."

He shook his head. "I would not worry about it," he said. "In
any case, I do not see him coming to this section of Oxford and,
more specifically, St. Clement's any time soon."

She looked up at him with her sleepy eyes. "Is that where we are going?"

"Aye."

"Why?"

"To get married."

She gave him a half-grin. "We may has well," she said, feigning sarcasm. "We have gone through an awful lot of trouble in order to be together. You had better marry me if you know what's good for you."

Maximus laughed softly. "I would have told you this at The Buck and Bounty last night only you came in the door, threw yourself into my arms, and promptly fell asleep."

Courtly yawned again. "That is because I was up the entire night before and all day, too," she said. "I am still so sleepy that I could lay down right here on the hay and go back to sleep."

He put his arm around her. "I know, love," he said quietly. "But let us be done with our business this morning and then you can sleep."

Maximus gathered his saddlebags and weapons before allowing a stable boy to take his horse away. With his weaponry and bags slung over his left shoulder, he took Courtly with his right hand and led her from the strong-smelling livery and out into the cool, bright day beyond.

The Street of the Merchants was immediately to their right and St. Clement's to their left as they emerged from the yard. Before he went to the church, however, Maximus returned to his favorite merchant to see if the man had any manner of gift to give his bride on the event of their wedding. Maximus' mother, Honey, had been given a beautiful necklace from their father at the wedding and she wore it always, but in later years, Antoninus de Shera had given his wife a ring. Maximus liked that symbol very much because, to him, it looked like a golden shackle by which to keep his wife bound to him. Therefore, he was specifically looking for a ring, which the white-haired merchant was more than happy to sell him.

After a looking at several choices, Courtly selected a golden ring with a beautiful, yellow stone in the center. A yellow diamond, the merchant had said, and Maximus had paid handsomely for the thick-banded ring. He also paid for a well-made, dark blue cloak for her also, as she had nothing of warmth to wear. The cloak, lined with gray rabbit, was warm and beautiful, and with that, Maximus and Courtly headed over to St. Clement's.

The morning mass had come and gone, and the church was relatively empty as Maximus went in search of a priest. He found two of them in the back of the church, behind the screen that separated the rear of the church from the major part of the sanctuary. As Courtly wait patiently on the main floor of the sanctuary, watching an occasional worshiper move past her, Maximus conducted business behind the screen.

Courtly could hear muted voices, at least two unfamiliar ones and then Maximus' deep tone. She couldn't quite hear what was being said but she was sure, much like any other type of obstacle Maximus de Shera faced, he was beating the priests down stone by stone by sheer force of will. She smiled as she thought of the man who was to be her husband, thrilled beyond measure that the stars had aligned enough so that she was able to marry the man without immediate fear of her father. It was almost too good to believe.

*My father.* Courtly tried not to think too much of Kellen and what his reaction would be when he discovered what she had done. Ellice had been so instrumental in making sure Courtly and Maximus were together that she seriously worried about the safety of her aunt, wondering if her father would somehow find out the extent of what she had done and punish her.

Courtly had never particularly had any use for her normally-taciturn aunt, but the situation with Maximus had changed that opinion. Ellice would not let the same thing happen to Courtly that had happened to her. She had been most determined that her niece not be a spinster. Perhaps in some way, she would share in Courtly's happiness, knowing she had contributed to it. Courtly certainly hoped so. Many people had risked many things in order to see her and Maximus joined, not the least of which was Kirk St. Héver.

As Maximus and a priest emerged from behind the carefully-carved screen made from Yew, Courtly briefly reflect on St. Héver and his selfless act of disobedience. Courtly remembered back to the previous year when St. Héver had impressed upon her his feelings for her and she clearly remembered, with some sadness, how she could not reciprocate them. St. Héver had been disappoint-ed but he'd take it in stride and had never mentioned it again.

Even last night, when their party had reached Woodstock and, under the guise of helping bed down Isadora, he'd hypothetically presented a story to Courtly about a young woman who ran off from her escort and ended up at The Buck and Bounty Inn to rendezvous with her lover and had made no mention of his past feelings for her. All he had said was that he hoped she was finally happy. St. Héver was taking an enormous chance incurring her father's wrath and they both knew it, but St. Héver didn't seem to care. He simply opened the rear door to the inn they happened to have been staying at and told her that The Buck and Bounty was down the avenue. Stunned, Courtly had kissed him on the cheek before running like the wind.

But thoughts of Kirk St. Héver faded as she focused on Maxi-mus, who was smiling at her as he approached with a short, thin man in heavy, woolen robes. The priest took them both back behind the screen and, with Maximus' generous payment of five gold crowns, performed a marriage mass, the end of which saw Lady Courtly Love de Lara become Lady Courtly de Lara de Shera.

It all seemed so surreal and dream-like as Maximus put the beautiful, golden ring on her finger, the big stone glistening in the weak light. Once the mass was complete and the marriage recorded in the big book that the priests kept of births, marriages, and deaths, Maximus took his new wife out of the church and headed back to the livery to collect his horse. And with that, a whirlwind courtship had finally become a marriage. It was done.

But there were no thoughts of consequences or angry fathers after that. There was only joy. As they crossed the busy road towards the livery, Maximus held Courtly's hand tightly, so tightly, in fact, that he was cutting off her circulation. By the time they reached the stable, she was forced to extract her hand from his grasp. When he looked at her, questioningly, she grinned and held up her hand.

"I was losing feeling in it because you were holding on so tightly," she said, showing him the red-marked fingers. "What are you afraid of? That I'm going to run away?"

He grinned. "Nay," he said. "I apologize, love. I did not realize I was trying to crush your hand."

Courtly laughed, watching as Maximus sent a stable boy on the run for his horse. When the boy fled, she spoke.

"You did not," she said. "In fact, I welcome the way you hold me. It tells me that you will never let me go away again, no matter what."

Maximus turned to her, pulling her into his arms and gazing down into her sweet face. "I will always be with you," he said softly. "Just as you shall always be with me, until the end of time. We are forever joined, you and I. Not even your father can separate us."

Courtly relished the feel of his arms around her, the power and majesty that was Maximus de Shera. "I consider myself the most fortunate woman on the face of the earth," she cooed. "I was a fool to run from you, Max. I hope you understand that my motives were true."

He nodded, bending over to kiss her on the nose although he wanted to do much more than that. She was his wife now and with her warm, soft body pressed against him, the arousal was instant. Everything about her was consuming him already.

"I know," he whispered. "I told you on the road outside of Begbroke that I was going to tell you just what I thought of your running off, but now I find that it is wholly inconsequential. There were a great many things I was going to tell you after I spanked you soundly for such a thing, but I have you back now and nothing else seems to matter."

Courtly bit her lip to keep from grinning. "Not even spanking me?"

"Not even that."

"Are you prone to spanking women, then?"

"Do you intend to test me and find out?"

She broke down into giggles, hugging the man tightly with her head against his broad chest. Maximus held her snuggly, savoring the moment as he had never savored anything so sweet in his entire life. He was very correct. Now that he had her back, things like spanking and fear and even Kellen de Lara had little meaning. As long as he had Courtly, he could move mountains.

The stable boy brought the distinctive black and white charger around and Maximus lifted his wife to the saddle before swinging on behind her. Paying the boy a few pences, he spurred his horse out onto the busy avenue.

The morning was late and the time was bearing down on noon as Maximus directed his horse towards The One-Eyed Raven. As they took a side street and ended up on a wider avenue, they came face to face with the burned-down hostel that had brought them together. There were scavengers picking through the ruins and Courtly seemed very interested in the activity as they rode by.

Maximus sensed her concerned focus.

"Do you want to see if any of your possessions are left?" he asked her. "I can stop and we can go through the ruins. Mayhap something is still there."

Courtly shook her head, although there was longing in her expression. "Nay," she said. "If there was anything left, I am sure it is gone by now. I am sure the vultures have been going through everything since the embers were cool enough to touch."

Maximus wasn't hard-pressed to agree with her so he continued on, noting that she remained focused on the hostel until they had passed well out of range and she was forced to turn around.

"You said it best," she sighed, watching the city around them as it passed by. "Although I should not be thankful for a fire such as that, I am grateful that it brought us together. Every time I see a fire I shall think of you."

He snorted. "It will remind you of how scorching and consuming I am."

She laughed, snuggling against him as they rode along. "You are indeed scorching and consuming," she said, turning to grin up at him. But her grin soon faded. "Please tell me what will happen now. Where will we go from here?"

He didn't even want to think about the separation that was coming but he had little choice. Moreover, he had to tell her what was to come. A gloved hand came up, touching her head tenderly.

"Now that I have you, I do not want to leave you," he said softly. "That does not please me, not in the least."

Courtly cocked her head curiously. "Leave me?" she repeated. "Where are you going?"

He sighed heavily, thinking on the events to come. He was quite certain she knew nothing about de Montfort other than the cursory information she had heard because of her father, and she more than likely was still under the impression that de Montfort and his barons, including de Lara, were in Oxford for a great gathering. She would have no way of knowing that those plans had changed. There had never been the opportunity to tell her.

"Yesterday, after we left you and St. Héver outside of Begbroke, I went on to The Buck and Bounty to wait for you while my brothers returned to Oxford," he began softly. "Even now, my brothers are preparing our men to move to London. We have been ordered to be there by next week. Since I will go to London purely on business, and I do not want you there in the midst of many different and opposing houses, you will be returning to Isenhall Castle with Jeniver. It will be safer for you there."

Courtly was extremely disappointed to hear what the immediate future would entail, but she didn't argue or cry about it. She wasn't the type. She simply accepted it, stoically. There wasn't much else she could do.

"What is happening in London?" she asked softly. "Can you tell me?"

Maximus thought on how to simplify things. "Last month, de Montfort wrested most of the power away from the king," he said. "The king was presented with a series of provisions, one of which outlined the manner of government we would have from now on. It is meant to be a more fair and autonomous way of governing. De Montfort will select twelve men and the king will select twelve men, and together that group of twenty-four men will form a council to govern England. We have received word that the king is prematurely convening his half of the council and de Montfort wants to be there when they do as a show of force."

Courtly understood quite a bit about politics, purely from her father. The man didn't have many people to talk to so, consequently, he talked to his daughter a good deal about the winds of political change currently enveloping England. She understood what Maximus was telling her and she also knew that this was a volatile situation. Wars had begun for less reason than this. But any war that started, her sweet Maximus would be at the head of it and she dreaded that thought. It punched holes in her belly, making her nauseous simply to think on it.

"My father did not say anything about going to London," she said after a moment. "I wonder if he even knows?"

Maximus shrugged. "He should know by now," he said. "As of yesterday, de Montfort was sending out messengers to all of his barons, telling them to congregate in London next week. That is another reason I will not take you to London. If your father is there, I do not want to chance you crossing paths with him."

Courtly was forced to agree. "Nor do I," she said. "But this council... are you sitting upon it?"

Maximus shook his head. "Gallus is," he said. "And many other great barons. It will truly be a sight to behold once convened."

Courtly thought on that scenario as they passed onto a street that would take them to The One-Eyed Raven. In fact, she could see the structure in the distance and her heart began to ache. Things were happening so quickly that it was difficult to grasp. But she knew one thing – she had married a warrior, the Thunder Warrior, and he would be fighting wherever there was a battle that involved him, or wherever de Montfort told him he should fight. She knew that when she met him, but the reality of it was still disheartening.

"When will you be leaving?" she asked.

His grip tightened on her, hearing the longing in her voice. "We should have left this morning," he said. "There will be a full moon tonight so it is my suspicion that we will move out under the cover of darkness. You and Jeniver will return to Isenhall in the morning after you have had a night's sleep."

Courtly struggled not to let depression overwhelm her. She clutched at Maximus' arm, the one he was holding her with, already missing the man tremendously. She simply couldn't help it.

"Tell me of Isenhall," she said to distract herself from the tears that were threatening. "What is it like?"

Maximus thought on his home in Coventry, feeling comforted knowing that Courtly would soon be within the massive, protective walls. "I was born there," he said. "It is an oddly shaped fortress. You will see for yourself. It is round and the keep and great hall are all jammed into the middle of it. The bailey is quite small but the keep is enormous. As a child, there were many places to hide. We used to torment my mother constantly with our disappearances."

Courtly smiled happily as she thought of Maximus as a devious child. "Please tell me about your mother," she said. "I know she is very ill. Would it be too much for you to tell me something of her?"

Speaking on Honey these days was much of a strain, but he found that he wanted his new wife to know about his mother, the woman he loved best in the world. At least, the woman he had loved best until Courtly came into his life. He wanted his wife to see the woman through his eyes.

"My mother is a de Lohr," he said. "She is the youngest daughter of Christopher and Dustin. Although my grandfather passed away some years ago, my grandmother is still alive. My mother is much like her, actually; feisty, strong, fearless, compassionate. Her given name is Charlotte but my father started calling her 'honey' early in their relationship, so that is what everyone calls her. She rules with an iron fist and loves beyond reason. She is a warm and wonderful woman and her illness has been very difficult for us."

Courtly digested the description of the Lady Honey de Shera. "May I ask you to tell me what ails her?"

Maximus grunted. "A cancer in her belly," he said. "She fell ill last fall and it has grown progressively worse. The physic believed she would be dead last month but still, she has lingered. My brothers and I were hoping to see her after de Montfort's meeting but, unfortunately, that will not be the case. I must go to London and you must go introduce yourself to her as my wife."

He said it with some humor, causing Courtly to turn and look at him. She smiled at the man, seeing in his eyes how sorrowful he was about his mother. She put a soft hand to his bearded cheek.

"I will introduce myself happily," she said. "I can only pray she finds me acceptable to be a member of the House of de Shera."

Maximus kissed the hand that was on his face. "She will," he murmured. "She will love you as I do."

The smile faded from Courtly's face and she tipped her head up, kissing him gently on his soft lips. Maximus leaned in and kissed her hungrily, suckling on her lower lips, struggling not to let his passion and arousal overwhelm him out in public for all to see. It was an effort to pull away as they came upon The One-Eyed Raven, but his thoughts turned to the inn itself and the bedchambers on the second floor. He fully intended to consummate his marriage before he left for London. In fact, it was nearly the only thing on his mind.

The livery behind the inn was crowded with de Shera horses and the big yard surrounding the livery was also jammed with them. Horses spilled out into the street, tethered, and being tended to by overworked stable boys. Maximus' attention was diverted from his luscious wife for a moment as he entered the livery yard and realized just how many de Shera men were present. His brother had brought fifty men with them to Oxford, men that had been spread out somewhat because they couldn't all fit in one tavern, but it was clear that all of them had now gathered.

Maximus tethered his jennet personally inside the livery so the stable boys could tend the sometimes snappish animal. Taking his wife with him, he proceeded into the rear of the tavern, noting that it was a hugely busy and crowded place inside. Men were eating, talking, yelling, and in general creating a bit of a ruckus. Over near

the barkeep's station, he saw Tiberius and Gallus around the usual
de Shera table and he made his way towards them, shoving aside a
soldier who came too close to Courtly. The man went flying,
bashing into a leaning table, which collapsed onto the floor.

Gallus and Tiberius looked over when they heard the crash,
seeing Maximus and Courtly approach. The both rose from their
seats, varied expressions of pleasure on their faces.

"Ah," Gallus said. "Maximus enters a room as only Maximus
can. So you have returned, my prodigal brother?"

Maximus gave him a half-grin, glancing over his shoulder at
the soldier picking himself up off of the broken table. "He is lucky I
only shoved him when he came near my wife," he said. "Next time, I
will break his neck."

Gallus and Tiberius looked straight to Courtly, the smiles fading from their faces as the reality of Maximus' words hit home.

"Wife," Gallus repeated softly. Then, he reached out to Courtly
and placed a very brotherly kiss on her cheek. "Welcome to the
family, Lady Courtly. We are very honored to have you."

Courtly smiled timidly at Gallus, thinking that the man was
perhaps lying. All she brought with her was uncertainty and
discord into a family that was strong and relatively peaceful. She
could only imagine that Gallus was already thinking of the long-
reaching implications with her father.

"Thank you, my lord," she said. "I am deeply honored to be a
member of the House of de Shera. I shall do my best to always be
worthy of my station."

Gallus' smile was back. "You are Lady Allesley now," he said.
"You are a baroness and most worthy of that title. My brother is a
very fortunate man."

Courtly looked at Maximus, surprise registering on her features. "I had completely forgotten about your title," she said. Then,
she teased him. "Be assured I did not marry you for your rank."

Tiberius entered the conversation. "Or his comely looks."

As Maximus scowled at his younger brother, Courtly laughed. "I did indeed marry him because he is the handsomest brother," she said. "No offense, my lords, but I am rather partial to him."

Tiberius kissed her on the cheek. "You have no taste in men," he said, "but I am happy to call you my sister."

Courtly accepted Tiberius kiss, watching Maximus push his brother away when he thought the man lingered too long around Courtly. But she could also see that it was in good-natured fun. The brothers clearly adored and supported one another, as she'd seen from the beginning. It was heart-warming to see such interaction from a powerful family that not only worked well together out of sheer family loyalty, but also liked one another. That was rare. Courtly grinned at Tiberius as the man made faces at Maximus, but Maximus was content to ignore the man soundly, at least for the moment.

"We were just married at St. Clements," he told Gallus. "It is my intention to send my wife back to Isenhall with Jeniver while we continue on to London."

Gallus nodded, watching Tiberius as the man continued to act the fool behind Maximus' back, much to Courtly's amusement.

"Agreed," Gallus said. "She will be safe there. As you can see, we have accomplished a great deal since we arrived back in Oxford yesterday. All of the men we brought with us to Oxford are mobilized and I have sent word to Isenhall for another four hundred. They have orders to move swiftly and meet us at Braidwood Manor in London, de Russe's place."

Maximus nodded. Hughston de Russe was part of the de Montfort ally network and his home outside of London, big and fortified, was usually where de Montfort's supporters gathered. It had become their unofficial headquarters. It was clear that the entire de Shera contingent was ready and waiting for Maximus. He was the lone straggler when usually, he was the first one ready to move.

Today, however, he didn't care about that. He could only think about the fact that he was soon to leave his new wife. Even though he knew he had to go, and he'd known it for some time, it wasn't sitting well with him.

"When do we leave?" Maximus asked reluctantly.

Gallus eyed Courtly, but now for a different reason. He cleared his throat softly. "How soon can you be ready?"

Maximus knew what he meant. He glanced at Courtly, seeing her laughing at Tiberius, and he sighed faintly.

"Give me an hour," he said softly.

Gallus nodded, watching as Maximus, aware of Tiberius' antics behind him, lashed out a big fist and caught his brother squarely in the chest. As Tiberius grunted and, laughing, nearly fell to the floor, Maximus took his wife by the elbow.

"I will meet you down here in an hour," he told Gallus. Then, he turned to Tiberius who was rubbing his chest where his brother had slugged him. "When my wife left last night, she left her possessions behind. They should be in Gallus and Jeniver's chamber. Will you please retrieve them and bring them to me?"

Tiberius nodded but Gallus spoke. "Jeni is sleeping right now," he said. "She has not been feeling well since yesterday. Can it wait until she awakens?"

Maximus nodded, as did Courtly. "Please do not disturb her, Lord de Shera," she said. "I can wait."

Gallus smiled at Courtly. "You will please address me as Gallus," he said. "You needn't be so formal with me. We are family now, after all."

Courtly nodded her head gratefully, humbled by the acceptance she was being given by these men who, quite possibly, would have to defend that acceptance against her crazed father when he found out what she had done. But no one seemed to care, and certainly no one had mentioned it. As Gallus had said, they were family now. And family defended and protected family, no matter what the circumstances.

With that, Maximus took his wife to the second floor chamber he had shared with Tiberius. It was the very first door at the top of the stairs and he shoved the sticky door open, revealing a rather small and messy chamber. There were two small beds, both of them jumbled and messy, and there were various things on the floor – a worn tunic, dirty hose, a pair of boots. In fact, Courtly tripped over a boot as she entered the room and Maximus kicked it away from her.

"Ty lives like an animal," he said. "I apologize for the state of the room."

Courtly grinned at him. "Isadora lives the same way," she said. "You should see our chamber at home – clothes, poppets – all manner of clutter. She likes to pick flowers but she feels terrible for throwing out old, dead flowers, so we have that issue to deal with as well. There are dried weeds everywhere."

Maximus smiled as he reached out and unfastened her cloak, pulling it off and revealing the lovely lavender dress beneath, which, in spite of all of the travel it had seen, was wearing very well. It also hugged her figure quite deliciously which reminded Maximus why they had come to the chamber to begin with. He had something to accomplish and not a lot of time with which to do it. As he lay the cloak on one of the beds, he spoke.

"I am afraid there is no tactful way to approach this subject, so I hope you will not be upset if I simply come out with it," he said as he turned to her. "Since I am leaving for London very shortly, there is the matter of consummating our marriage. We must do this so your father cannot ever separate us and if we do not consummate it now, I do not know when we will be able to. Therefore, it must be done before I leave Oxford. I wish I could take all of the time in the world with this, Courtly, and not rush it or make it seem so... cold... but the fact is that it must be done now. I am sorry if that seems uncaring."

Courtly wasn't upset by the realities of marriage. In fact, she was rather curious about the entire process. She was also a woman not given to ridiculous fears and had already shown her mettle for bravery. Therefore, she simply nodded her head as she sat down on the bed behind her.

"I understand," she said. "You needn't apologize. But I will admit that I know very little about what to do. My name may be Courtly Love, but the truth is that I am a virgin in every sense of the word. The first time a man kissed me was when you did it yesterday. Of course, I know the mechanics of mating. That is to say I know what is supposed to happen and what the results are, as Lady d'Umfraville made sure to educate her wards on such things, but beyond that... I will have to depend on you to tell me what to do."

Maximus was rather relieved that she was looking at the situation so calmly, but on the other hand, he wasn't surprised. Courtly had proven herself to be calm and resourceful since he first met her, something he was very much coming to appreciate about his new wife. The fact that she wasn't a hysterical female spoke volumes to him. He sat down on the bed beside her and began removing his boots.

"Well," he said thoughtfully. "It is one of those situations where you let instincts take the lead. I think your body will know what to do even if your mind does not."

Courtly pulled off her slippers because he was removing his shoes. It seemed like something she should do. "You have done this before?"

Maximus cleared his throat somewhat nervously. "Aye," he said. "I have had to. It would not do if neither of us knew what to do, would it?"

Courtly thought it humorous to see the man uncomfortable. "Who has taught you what you should know?"

He lifted his eyebrows, hoping he could bluff his way out of the question. "Too many women to count," he said flippantly. "Why do you ask such questions, anyway? Do you really want to talk about my experiences with other women?"

Her smile faded. "*Have* there been other women?" she asked. "Someone… like me? Someone you were fond of?"

Maximus thought back to his first love, that flame-haired lass of fourteen he had been so very caring of. He shrugged. "She was fourteen," he said. "I was seventeen. It was a very long time ago."

Courtly smiled at the thought of young Maximus in love with a sweet young girl. "Why did you not marry her?"

He shook his head. "My father sent her away," he said. "She was not of my station. It was not meant to be."

Courtly thought she detected something sad in those words. "I am sorry," she said softly. "It must have been painful."

Maximus looked at her, studying her face, the delicate lines of her jaw. He drew in a long, contemplative breath. "At the time, it was," he said. "I was young and impressionable. But it was a young love and nothing more. When I look at you, I am not sorry in the least that nothing ever came of it. Had I married her, I would have never known you."

Courtly smiled sweetly at him. "You may have known me," she said, humor in her tone. "I may have still fallen out of a window onto your head, but you would have already been married. God's Bones, what if I had married Tiberius instead? Although your brother is handsome and strong, I would have spent the rest of my life lusting after his brother. After you."

Maximus was torn between being wildly jealous over the thought of her marrying Tiberius and the thrill of her declaration of lust. He settled for the lust. Reaching out, he gently stroked her blond head, digesting this woman who was now his wife. He could still hardly believe it.

"Then it was fate that sent her away those years ago and not my father," he said softly. "What I felt for her was something young and giddy. What I feel for you is something deep and abiding. I do not know how it is possible to love someone so strongly after only a few days, but I do. You have embedded yourself into my very soul, Courtly. Whatever the future holds and whatever comes, know that you have all of me, forever."

Courtly was listening to his words, bewitched by them. Everything about the man was filling her, reaching in and anchoring itself deep. His hand on her head was soft and gentle, yet the heat from his palm was causing her heart to race. She remembered the kiss they had shared earlier, the flames of new and awakening desire that had licked at her. His bearded lips had been wildly exciting, more than she could have ever imagined. She found herself leaning into the hand on her head, watching his mouth as he spoke.

"Max?" she whispered.

His hand had moved to her face, his rough fingertips brushing over her lips. "Aye?"

"Kiss me like you did earlier. Kiss me again but this time, do not stop."

Maximus didn't need any further prompting. Her murmured request had him on fire and he cupped her face in his two enormous hands, bringing her lips to his. When he slanted over her mouth, it was hungrily, as he had never before kissed a woman until this moment. Everything he had even known about a woman, the feel or taste of one, was gone. It was as if she were the first and only, so strong his passion. As his tongue began to lick her, begging for an invitation into her warm, wet mouth, his hands move from her face and went to work on her clothing.

The lavender garment that he had purchased for her seemed to disintegrate under his hands and he had no idea why. He didn't think he'd pulled that hard on it but he failed to remember that it had only been loosely basted. The truth was that he didn't care much and even if he had remembered, it wouldn't have made a difference because he was quite eager to remove her from her clothing. Courtly didn't resist him. When he tugged on something, she helped him pull it off.

In little time, the shift came off as well and in the dim light of the chamber, Maximus found himself gazing at his wife's perfect, nude body. He couldn't remember ever seeing anything so utterly arousing but as he moved to pull her against him, he realized he was still wearing his clothing and, almost frantically, it began to come off.

The tunic went over his head and he tossed it to the ground, simultaneously untying his breeches. He had to let her go in order to yank those off and they ended up on the floor alongside the tunic. In all his naked glory, he turned back to Courtly only to see that she was sitting on the bed trying to cover her chest with her slender arms. She seemed rather embarrassed, and probably cold, and he felt guilty that he hadn't been more considerate of her. This was her first time, after all, and even though she was a remarkably brave woman, she still had her limits of bravery. Rather than try to move her arms, he simply pulled her into a tight embrace and covered her, shielded her, with his big body.

He literally could not wait to get the woman on her back. He couldn't remember the last time he'd had a woman, a paid woman to satisfy a man's needs, so his arousal was very stiff and almost painful. Even his testicles were inflamed and swollen, as tight as cat gut, so he eased Courtly down onto the bed with the intention of burying himself in her tender folds as soon as he possibly could.

She was compliant and his tender kisses helped a great deal. At least she had unwound her arms and now her naked breasts were against his broad chest. Maximus could feel them, soft and round, and it nearly threw him over the edge.

Once he had her on her back, his hands began to wander. He went straight for her beautiful breasts, listening to her gasp with surprise when a big hand closed around one. She even stiffened up in his arms, fearful of the new sensation, but he worked her breast gently but firmly, toying with her nipples until she began to relax underneath him again. He was fairly certain she was enjoying it from the kitten-mewling sounds she was making. But those sounds were driving him mad with lust. His roving hands move lower.

*Her skin.* Like silk it was beneath his rough hands. He almost felt guilty for touching such pristine, gorgeous skin with his rough and calloused hands. Hands that had killed. He was oh-so-worshipful of her as he touched her, however, knowing he hardly deserved this fine creature but grateful just the same.

*Her smell.* Like lavender and honey, or angel's hair. There was something sweet and pure about her smell, something unbridled and intoxicating. As his hand moved down her torso and to her right thigh, he grasped her gently behind the right knee and pulled her legs apart, wedging himself in between her legs. He began to drag his lips over her neck, tasting her beauty, feeling the warmth of her flesh against his tongue. It was too much to take. He had to have all of her. He had to quench this thirst he'd had for her since nearly the moment he met her. He well remembered the day she fell on him and how he'd come into contact with that beautiful, quivering flower between her legs, the sight and scent that was so utterly beautiful to him. Now, he would have it for his own. He would claim her.

He rubbed his arousal against her pink core, coaxing forth her warm wetness that would prepare her body for his entry. She was already wet. He could feel it, so he drew back and thrust into her firmly but slowly, pushing his way into her body, taking possession of this woman as he had never taken possession in his life. He could feel her tightness around him, giving way for him, those honeyed walls that would give him life's greatest pleasure and be the path by which his children would be born. It was a silken sheath meant only for him.

He drew back again, thrusting harder, making headway into her tight and virginal body. Beneath him, Courtly groaned, a sound somewhere between pleasure and pain. Maximus took it as pleasure and thrust again, harder, listening to her gasp as the sting of losing her virginity echoed throughout her body, but by now, Maximus was realizing the greatest coupling he could have possibly imagined. It was time to make his wife his very own and to put his seed in her, marking her. He found himself dreaming of blue-eyed sons in his image.

He began to move within her, stroking in and out, coiling his buttocks and thrusting again and again as Courtly lay beneath him and softly moaned. She didn't particularly try to touch him. She simply lay there with her legs spread open and her hands gripping the bed until Maximus took one of her hands and put it on his buttocks. Courtly took the hint and put both hands on his buttocks as something to hold on to, feeling his flesh in the palm of her hands and liking it, but the minute she squeezed, he spilled himself deep into her virginal womb.

But he didn't stop moving, at least not right away. He continued to move within her until withdrawing and rubbing the tip of his phallus over the wet, swollen exterior of her woman's core. It was enough of an action to cause the overly-stimulated woman to experience her first climax and the moment she started gasping, he thrust into her again, feeling her tremors around his manhood, loving the sensation of it. He remained embedded in her simply because he wanted to, because if felt good and it felt right.

Pinned beneath his massive warm body, Courtly wrapped her legs around his hips and her arms around his neck, holding him fast. For several long minutes, neither one said a word. Neither one had to.

They were one.

# CHAPTER FOURTEEN

*Sixteen Miles southeast of Oxford*
*Village of Watlington*

H E COULD SEE the army on the horizon, clear as day. Under skies that were clouding up, promising rain, Garran could see a good-sized army encamped near the village of Watlington. Riding with his father and his father's four men-at-arms, Garran eyed the gathering in the distance suspiciously.

"What is that?" he asked his father, pointing. "Can you see it?"

Bose, calm and collected and dressed in full battle armor, nodded. "I do indeed."

Garran was still looking at the cluster on the horizon but he couldn't help noticing his father hadn't answered his entire question.

"Papa," he said, turning to look at him. "What *is* that?"

Bose didn't answer for a moment. His black eyes were riveted to the same thing his son was looking at. Finally, he spoke.

"It looks to be an army," he said. "In fact, that is the army we shall be joining shortly."

Garran's eyes narrowed. "Henry's army?" he asked. "Are we traveling with them to London?"

Bose shook his head. "Nay," he replied. "At least, we are not going to London at this moment. We have a task to accomplish first. That is what the army is for."

Garran didn't like the sound of that. "*What* is the army for?"

Bose looked to his son. "The army is to retrieve something that belongs to Henry," he said. "Hughston de Russe's cousin, Christon de Russe, is claiming Warborough Castle for his own. Henry wants it back."

Garran was stumped by the entire conversation. "Christon de Russe has been constable at Warborough for years," he said. "Moreover, he is a great supporter of Henry and, if I recall correctly, also his treasurer. *Why* are we going to Warborough?"

Bose flicked a drop of sweat from his eyes. "Christon de Russe has decided to side with his cousin and, subsequently, de Montfort," he said. "The man has turned against the king and not only has he switched allegiances, he has taken some of the king's money with him. Henry wants his money, and his castle, back."

Garran was starting to understand quite clearly now. A battle. His heart sank. "How long have you known about this?" he asked.

Bose returned his focus to the army in the distance. "Since before I arrived at Oxford," he said. "Why do you think I came to Oxford, Garran? I have been called to fight with Henry's army against Warborough and I can promise you that all of de Montfort's supporter in Oxford, including the House of de Shera, will be arriving shortly to prevent Henry from regaining his castle. I knew we would be fighting on opposing sides, my son. That is why I wanted you with me."

Garran grunted with disbelief. Aye, he understood everything now. A battle had been looming for quite some time and Bose had used the opportunity to remove Garran from the de Shera stable. He did not want to fight against his son.

"I see," he finally said, sounding disgusted. "You could have told me. You did not have to make it seem as if you had come to Oxford for me alone."

"I did," Bose countered in a tone that left no room for debate. "I came to collect my son."

Garran simply rolled his eyes and looked away. Now, so much of this was making sense. Still, it was concerning. He was fairly certain that Gallus, Maximus, and Tiberius knew nothing about Warborough Castle because they surely would have said something. Their only concerns had been to resolve Maximus' issue with Lady Courtly and then move on to London for the king's council. It concerned him that the king's army was going to be laying a trap for those who would come to defend Warborough.

But he said nothing as they plodded along the road, heading for the army in the distance which soon became quite a large group. Hundreds at the very least, perhaps even a thousand or more. They were met by sentries on the outskirts of the encampment and when Bose announced himself, he was taken directly to a large tent bearing the de Winter crest. Garran recognized it, he knew it well. The House of de Winter and the House of de Shera, before the madness with Henry and Simon, were close allies and friends. In fact, they still were. But the divisions of state had their public loyalties known to opposite sides.

Grayson de Winter came out of his tent as Bose and Garran rode up. A muscular man for his advanced age, he smiled at Bose as the man pulled his steed to a halt and dismounted. As Grayson moved for Bose, a younger knight emerged from the tent and Garran immediately recognized Davyss de Winter. He was Gallus' best friend and had been since they had been children.

Davyss de Winter was a legendary knight with legendary skill, even at his young age. Handsome and well-built with dark, curly hair, he looked very surprised to see Garran standing with Bose. Davyss knew that Garran was a de Shera knight and his confusion was understandable. He also appeared as if he very much wanted to say something but he kept his mouth shut, his hazel eyes fixed on

Garran in a most perplexing way. Garran stared back.

"De Moray," Grayson said with pleasure, putting a hand on Bose's broad shoulder. "I was told to expect you soon. Your men arrived two days ago and told me you had business in Oxford."

Garran's attention moved away from Davyss, now focusing on his father with some shock on his features. It was occurring to him that his father had somehow duped him, playing on family sympathies in order to obtain his son's fealty. But Garran knew his father wasn't manipulative. He was a very truthful man. Still, he felt as if he had somehow been lied to by omission of certain truths. He felt as if his father hadn't been completely honest about the situation. But he said nothing as Bose spoke.

"Indeed I did," Bose said, looking into the face of an old acquaintance. "I had to go and retrieve my son. He was in Oxford."

Grayson turned his attention to Garran, a mirror image of his father, and the smile on his face faded somewhat. "Garran," he murmured, as if remembering things about the young knight. "You are a de Shera knight."

Garran shook his head. "I have pledged to my father, my lord," he said. "I have been released from my de Shera bond."

Grayson lifted his eyebrows. "That could not have been an easy thing," he said. "Once a de Shera, always a de Shera. You know the saying."

Garran looked at his father. "De Moray blood supersedes de Shera friendship."

Bose detected some bitterness there and he could imagine why. His son wasn't happy about committing to the king's cause. But he would get over it. He returned his attention to de Winter.

"You have quite an army assembled," he said. "How many men?"

Grayson looked out over his military empire. "Almost two thousand," he said. "Henry has provided French mercenary troops.

I have told the English troops to keep watch on them because they like to raid and steal from the countryside. I will not permit the French to run amuck even if Henry *did* send them. But now that de Moray has arrived, they will be forced to behave themselves."

He said it in jest and Bose smiled thinly. He didn't like the thought of French mercenaries on English soil, either, but he had to go along with what the king dictated. He would never admit to anyone that supporting the king these days had him the slightest bit disgruntled. He gestured to the tent.

"Let us retreat inside and discuss strategy," he said. "Warborough cannot be more than a few miles away. What are the plans?"

Grayson began to lead Bose into the tent. "Warborough is approximately seven miles away," he said. "Now that you have arrived, we have orders to move swiftly. De Montfort is distracted with the rumors of Henry's council convening in London so the time to move is now."

Bose looked at him, a light of understanding coming to his eye. "Are those rumors, then?" he asked. "Henry is not convening his council?"

Grayson nodded. "Not so soon, at any rate," he said. "We spread those rumors that the meeting was imminent because we knew de Montfort was in Oxford. It is a ruse to turn his focus away from Warborough, at least for now. There are many barons in Oxford and if they gather to defend Warborough, it could be very bad indeed. These French mercenaries would like nothing better than to kill English barons."

Bose sighed heavily. He couldn't help but look at his son now, realizing that he had not realized the full scope of the move against Warborough. But Garran was emotionless as he gazed at his father and Bose turned back to Grayson, realizing he might have some damage control to do with his son after all of this was over. Garran did not appear happy in the least in spite of his impassive stance. The man was heading straight into a battle against men he considered brothers. Nay, Garran didn't like it in the least.

As Bose and Grayson moved into the big de Winter tent, Davyss put out a hand and stopped Garran before the man could follow. In fact, he pulled him away from the tent flap so their fathers could not overhear their conversation. When they were a safe distance away, Davyss turned to Garran.

"What are you doing here?" Davyss hissed at him. "I thought you were with Gallus."

Garran cleared his throat uncomfortably. "I was until my father came to town and begged for my fealty," he said. "He told me he did not want to lift a sword against me in battle and that was what this entire situation was coming down to. What he did *not* tell me was that there was already a battle on the horizon that he knew about."

Davyss shook his head, his frustration evident. "My father has objections to attacking Warborough as well," he admitted, "but he leads the king's armies so he has no choice. He hates these French mercenaries under his command. They are vile, foul men. I feel as if they are the enemy more than de Montfort is."

Garran thought the entire circumstance sounded uncertain and dangerous. "If you will forgive me, your father made the choice to side with Henry," he said. "He is bound to do whatever the king wishes and fight whomever he is told to fight, and that also means commanding the men the king chooses for him to command. He has no right to complain."

Davyss eyed the knight. "The de Winters have served the crown since the days of William the Bastard," he said. "My father did not make that choice. It was already made for him two hundred years ago. He simply carries on the family tradition."

"As do you?"

"Gallus has asked that same question, many times."

Garran wouldn't argue the subject of free will. As far as he was concerned, the entire de Winter family had made the choice to serve a king who did not deserve their loyalty. They were great warriors, and very rich and powerful. It was nearly the only great power from England that the king could count as a supporter.

"Gallus and his brothers are in Oxford," Garran said after a moment, given that the subject of Gallus had entered the conversation. "You know when they hear of Warborough, they will be leading her defense. We will meet them in battle."

Davyss tried not to look sick about it. "I know," he conceded. "But there is nothing we can do about it. The path is set."

"Will *you* lift your sword against them?" Garran wanted to know. "Gallus and Maximus and Tiberius? Because I know for a fact I will not. I cannot. I will go kill French mercenaries instead."

Davyss smiled faintly. "As I will I," he confessed. "You know I cannot fight Gallus. My father knows it, too."

"What will we do, then?"

Davyss sighed heavily. Then, he gestured to the tent. "Go inside and listen to our fathers discuss what you and I will *not* do," he said. "Come along before they come looking for us."

Garran followed Davyss into the tent without another word. Inside, Grayson and Bose and a few other senior English commanders were bent over a leaning table with a map spread across the surface. As Garran listened to the talk of taking Warborough, one thing was certain. He would not fight against the Lords of Thunder. Perhaps it had been a mistake to pledge fealty to his father in the first place, but his choices, now, were both terrible – either fight against his father or fight against the de Shera brothers. Either way, the outcome, for him, could only bring him to heartache.

Already, he was aching.

*Oxford*

"IT IS A very large army, my lord," the soldier said. "Thousands, at least. Lord de Russe has sent word to de Montfort and de Montfort has sent me to find you to tell you that you must come to Warborough."

It was late in the afternoon at The One-Eyed Raven. About an hour before, Maximus had emerged from his chamber to discuss departure plans with Gallus. The problem was that Maximus had a lazy smile on his face and was having difficulty focusing, which set Tiberius off into a fit of giggles. Marriage, already, agreed with him. All Gallus could do was look at his middle brother, snort ironically, and shake his head as if to say, *I understand completely.*

Nonetheless, they had plans to make. With their departure imminent, Gallus had awoken his wife and, even now, Jeniver and Courtly were in Jeniver's room, packing their possessions in preparation for traveling to Isenhall. It gave the women something to do while the men finalized the plans for their journey to London. But those plans came to a grinding halt when an exhausted messenger bearing the colors of de Montfort arrived at the inn. The sight had been concerning enough since de Montfort was on his way to London, but the news the man bore was even more shocking.

"Clarify this for me," Gallus asked de Montfort's soldier after he had listened to the man's breathless story. "The Lord of Warborough is an ally of the king. He is also the king's treasurer and constable of the castle. And you are telling me this is no longer true?"

The soldier nodded. "Aye, my lord."

"He has switched allegiances and is now allied with de Montfort?"

"Aye, my lord."

Gallus was at a loss for words. He hadn't heard such a thing. He looked around to his brothers and trusted knights – Maximus, Tiberius, Scott, Troy, and Stefan – but everyone seemed to have the same expression – shock. He turned back to de Montfort's man.

"*When* did this happen?" he demanded. "I saw de Montfort yesterday and he made no mention of Christon de Russe."

The soldier wasn't sure what to tell the Thunder Lord. He was a man to be both respected and feared, and the soldier didn't particularly like upsetting him. Even worse, the man's brother, Maximus, was looking less than pleased at the information and the soldier knew that Maximus de Shera was a man to placate in all situations. He'd been known to rip men's heads from their bodies in battle. Or, at least that was what he had been told. It was, therefore, a struggle not to show any fear.

"Lord de Russe is now allied with his cousin, Lord Hughston de Russe," the soldier said. "Lord Christon kept Warborough Castle and also has some of the king's treasury in his possession. The king is sending an army to confiscate the castle and take back the money, but Lord Christon would keep it for de Montfort's cause. Lord de Montfort has sent me to ask you to join him at Warborough Castle to defend it from Henry's forces."

It was all quite puzzling and, if genuinely true, quite astonishing. Gallus couldn't quite grasp what he was being told. Christon de Russe was thick with the king, or at least he used to be, much to his cousin, Hughston's, dismay. The de Russe clan had always been the rather democratic type that fell in with de Montfort's ideals, but Christon had been with the king for many years and enjoyed the status of his job.

Now, evidently, the tides were turning. Had Gallus not known the soldier, or at least had seen him with de Montfort, he might have thought it was a trap because the information was truly surprising. Even so, he was wary. He simply couldn't help it.

"How soon does de Montfort want us to mobilize?" he asked the soldier.

The man wiped at the sweat on his brow. "Henry's army has been sighted to the east of Warborough, my lord," he replied. "De Montfort is coming up from the south. He will meet you in Wallingford."

Gallus scratched his head, looking at his brothers, who seemed equally astonished by the information. "I know where Wallingford is," he told the soldier, "but de Montfort was already on the road to London. Now he is turning around to fight this battle? It must be important to him."

The soldier nodded. "It is, my lord," he said. "De Montfort wants Warborough and he wants the coinage that de Russe has stolen from Henry."

Gallus could understand that; money, and property, was power. "How far out is he?"

"He should arrive by tomorrow morning."

Gallus' mind began working furiously. He only had fifty men with him. The bulk of his army had been called down from Isenhall to meet him in London, but it would be days before they reached the city. Therefore, he had no choice but to go with only the fifty men he had. Combined with the other armies, they would comprise an acceptable amount of soldiers and archers, but he was less confident than he would have been had his four hundred seasoned troops been at his command. If they were to defend Warborough against a thousand troops, the odds were considerably stacked against them.

"Who else has been summoned to Warborough?" Gallus wanted to know. "There were many barons in Oxford because of de Montfort's gathering but I do not have the latest information as to who has already left for London and who remains."

The soldier was thoughtful. "Bigod and Fitzgeoffrey moved out with de Montfort," he said. "There are several barons still in Oxford according to de Montfort's intelligence and there are several messengers, much like me, sent to seek them out and summon them – de Ferrers, de Burgh, de Lara, Fitzalan... when they are all gathered, de Montfort expects twice Henry's numbers. We should easily defeat them."

Gallus eyed Maximus at the mention of de Lara. "Kellen de Lara?" he clarified with the soldier.

The man nodded. "Aye, my lord," he replied. "Viscount Trelystan."

*This is going to be interesting*, Gallus thought. He was sure Maximus had the very same thought, fighting alongside a man whose daughter they had so recently stolen. That is what it would boil down to. Regardless, he wasn't so sure about having the numbers to overwhelm Henry's forces but he would never publicly express a negative opinion regarding battle odds. Something like that would get around and demoralize the troops. Therefore, he simply nodded.

"You will ride with me to Wallingford," he told de Montfort's man before turning to his men. "Ty, spread the word among the men of our orders. Scott and Troy, make sure the horses are sound and ready for battle. Stefan, you will stock the provisions wagon with items for the wounded and Max, we must discuss the de Shera women. They are going to have to remain here for the time being. I cannot spare the men to return them to Isenhall. All we can do is leave a small contingent here to guard them."

Maximus didn't like the thought of leaving Courtly and Jeniver minimally protected, but he understood. They were heading into battle and needed every available man.

"How many men will you leave with them?" he asked.

"Four."

Maximus winced. "Just four?"

"Do *you* have any better ideas about it?"

Maximus didn't. Even leaving four behind out of the fifty they had was not a particularly desirable prospect but there was little choice. He finally shook his head and broke away from the gathering with de Montfort's soldier and headed up the stairs to see to his wife. He had a good deal of preparations to make before departing and he had little time to do it, but until he bid his wife farewell, he couldn't think of anything else. He had to see her.

A separation to go to London with a non-military purpose had been bad enough, but now that he knew they were heading for battle... a battle where they were undermanned, no less... filled him with a heavy heart. He didn't want to even think on the fact that he might not make it out alive. He wanted to see his wife again and watch their children grow. He wanted to live a long, full life with Courtly by his side. He'd never wanted that before.

As he reached the door to the chamber, he could already hear the women behind it, laughing. It made him smile to hear Courtly's high-pitched giggles. Knocking softly on the door, he snorted with humor when it was swiftly opened and Jeniver stood there, a huge smile on her face.

"Isn't it true, Max?" she demanded. "Didn't you light your uncle's farts on fire?"

Courtly burst out in a fit of laughter and Maximus came into the room, grinning. "She already knows what an incorrigible child I was," he said. "I told her what we used to do. What I did not tell her was that the gas from his arse had saturated his breeches so the fire spread quickly and burned the hair all up his back. My mother was so angry that she took a switch to us. I think I still have the scars."

Jeniver and Courtly were beset with laughter as Maximus stood there and smiled at them. "That was the same uncle who would defecate in the bailey and then blame it on the dogs," he said. "He would make sure to do it when he knew my father would be passing along that particular path so that the man would step in it."

The women were far gone with laughter at this point. Jeniver finally put up a hand. "That is utterly disgusting, Max," she pretended to scold, snorting. "And you would say it in front of your new wife? I am shocked."

Maximus was making his way over to Courtly, who was gazing at him quite adoringly. He couldn't help but return the expression. "It is too late for her to get away from me," he said, his eyes devouring the woman. "I can say what I wish now."

Jeniver shook her head reproachfully but the truth was that she was watching the besotted expressions of both Maximus and Courtly. It was very sweet.

"I will tell you a secret," Jeniver said. "I do not think she wants to get away from you."

Maximus glanced at his sister-in-law, grinning, but his attention returned to his wife. In fact, he couldn't stop staring at her.

"I am glad," he said. Then, he sobered somewhat. "Speaking of getting away from me, I've come to inform you both that you will be staying here for the time being. You will not be going to Isenhall right away."

The women sobered quickly as well. "Why not?" Courtly asked. "Has something happened?"

Maximus shrugged, reaching out to take her hand. Courtly clung to him, gazing up into his handsome face and noting that he looked rather serious.

"We have received word that Warborough Castle is under attack from Henry's forces," he said. "De Montfort has personally asked us to defend her. Therefore, we cannot spare the men to take you two back to Isenhall, so you will remain here with a small guard until we can return from Warborough."

Courtly's expression was full of concern. "Where is War-borough?"

He squeezed her hand. "South of Oxford and south of Kenning-ton by several miles," he said. "The constable of the castle used to be Henry's ally but it would seem he has switched allegiances and the king is not entirely happy. De Montfort wants us to fend off the king's attempt to reclaim the castle."

Across the chamber, Jeniver sighed heavily. "War," she said simply. "You are going to war."

Maximus tore his gaze away from Courtly long enough to look over at Jeniver. "Aye."

Courtly felt as if she had been hit in the gut. All of the wind was sucked out of her as she realized what, exactly, Maximus was telling her. It had taken Jeniver's softly uttered words to make her understand.

"War," she breathed. "Oh, Max, is it true? Do you really go to do battle?"

Maximus squeezed her hand again, kissing her fingers. "It is not as bad as all that," he said quietly. "Usually, all it takes is for Henry to merely see the de Shera banners and the man runs off. I doubt that I shall even unsheathe my sword."

He said it simply to make her feel better. Perhaps it was a lie, perhaps not. Perhaps his sword would be out and bloodied from the very moment they arrived. In truth, he didn't know, but he'd been through enough battles to know that anything involving sharp swords and archers was dangerous. There was always a chance of him not returning and, in spite of his comforting words, Courtly must have known that as well. She was looking up at him with fear in her eyes.

"I hope that is the case," she said fervently. "I shall pray for your safety with every breath."

He smiled confidently at her. "That would be appreciated," he said. "I hope that God will hear you."

Courtly simply nodded, releasing his hand and wrapping her arms around his trim torso, hugging him tightly. Jeniver watched the two of them embrace and her thoughts turned to her husband. He was going, too. She instinctively put a hand on her belly, thinking of the child she carried, a child she very much wanted to know his father.

"Max, where is Gallus?" she asked. "Is he coming to see me before he leaves?"

Maximus, with Courtly pressed against his chest, looked over at her. "Of course he is," he said. "He is still speaking with de Montfort's man. He will be up momentarily."

Jeniver nodded, suddenly not feeling so happy. She was starting to feel nauseated again but this time it was because of her husband's imminent departure. *To war.* She sat heavily on her bed, her gaze on her packed possession, thinking on her husband's future and struggling against the dread in her heart.

"The de Shera brothers have been in a few skirmishes since I have been part of the family," she said softly. "You have always managed to come through unscathed. I pray that continues."

Maximus had his big hand on Courtly's head as she laid it against his chest. "As do I."

Jeniver glanced up at him, smiling weakly, before continuing. "I think it is the fear of the unknown that worries women so much," she said. "It is the waiting and the not knowing whether or not your husband is alive or dead. I have nightmares of Gallus dying on the field of battle, alone and in pain. They haunt me."

Maximus wasn't so sure he wanted Courtly to hear Jeniver's anxieties but it didn't much matter. He couldn't protect her from her own fears for his safety. It was a tale as old as time – women worry while men fight. He could remember, as a child, having the same fear for his father when the man would charge off to war in the early days of Henry's reign.

"I do not know if this will help, but I recall something my mother told me once when, as a young lad, I expressed the same fears for my father's safety," he said quietly. "She said that we cannot know what will come at the day's end but that whatever it is, it will indeed come, and then the end will be known. If we saw my father again at the end of that day, then we would smile and embrace him, but if not, then we would not dwell on his ending but on his parting well-made. We always made our partings with our father well-made. We smiled, we spoke of our love for him, so that when he went to battle, he went fortified and loved."

By this time, Courtly was smiling up at him. "Then I shall do the same thing for you," she said with gentle determination. "You have given me the greatest gift in life, Maximus. To have been your wife, even for a day, has made my entire life worth living. I could ask for no greater honor and for no greater husband. When you face your coming battle, remember that. My love, and everything else, goes with you."

Maximus smiled, deeply touched. "Never have I heard such beautiful words," he whispered. "You honor me."

With that, he bent down and kissed her, sweetly and lovingly, and Jeniver had to turn away. She suddenly felt as if she were intruding on a private moment so she made her way to the door with the intention of giving Maximus and Courtly some privacy, but the moment she touched the door latch, the panel opened and Gallus was on the other side. Startled, she yelped and jumped back at the unexpected sight.

"Gallus," she gasped, hand on her chest as if to soothe her racing heart. "You surprised me!"

Gallus grinned at his wife. "So sorry, sweetheart," he said. Then, he looked at his brother, standing near the window in an embrace with his new wife. "Did Max tell you what has happened?"

Jeniver nodded. "You are going into battle."

Gallus' smile faded and he reached out to pull the woman into his arms. Kissing her forehead, he hugged her gently.

"Not to worry," he said. "It will probably be over before we even arrive, so I do not want you to worry. I want you to remain here with Courtly and eat, drink, and spend my money to your heart's content. I cannot imagine we will be gone more than a few days at most."

He made it sound much less serious than it was on purpose, much as Maximus had done, but in Gallus' case, he simply didn't want to upset his pregnant wife. She'd had a rough enough time of it without the added burden of a husband at war. His light attitude towards the situation seemed to work because Jeniver's taut expression eased considerably.

"Are you sure?" she asked.

He nodded, kissing her forehead again. "I am," he replied. "And as soon as we return, I want to go to Isenhall, so be prepared to depart."

Jeniver cocked her head curiously. "You are going to Isenhall, too? But I thought de Montfort wanted you in London right away?"

He nodded. "Mayhap he does," he said, eyeing Maximus. "But I care not. I want to return home and see to my mother's health. De Montfort can wait."

Maximus listened to his brother, unsure if he was serious or not. It could simply be that he was trying to comfort his wife by declaring they would all go home after the skirmish at Warborough was over. Whatever the case, it seemed to be working. Jeniver's mood picked up somewhat.

"Good," she said firmly. "You should be able to go home and visit Honey if you want to. De Montfort cannot stop you from tending to your mother."

Gallus nodded once more and kissed her on the forehead one last time. "Now, Maximus and I have much to do before we depart," he said. "We will come and bid you farewell before we go, but for now, we have things to do. You will stay to our chamber and relax. I do not want you downstairs. There are too many men and horses and you may get hurt."

Jeniver nodded. "Courtly and I can keep busy."

Gallus smiled and touched her cheek before letting her go. "Excellent," he said, motioning to his brother. "Come along, bridegroom. We have much to do."

Maximus pursed his lips irritably at his brother's taunt before kissing Courtly and following the man from the chamber. After that, they lost themselves in the familiar preparation for battle, something that was second nature to them. Whether they were mobilizing fifty men or a thousand, the preparation was always the same – logistics, a plan of action, and making sure the men and horses were sound to move out. It was what they were best at and excelled at. It was a procedure that brought about confidence.

They moved as an efficient team and their men were ready to move out, including a provisions wagon, in less than an hour. When they finally returned to the chamber to bid farewell to their wives, that confidence they were building up for the men was something that seemed to take a hit once they beheld their women. Women both of them wanted very much to see again and women who were much braver than they had expected. After sweet and loving farewells, Gallus and Maximus left The One-Eyed Raven with heavy hearts.

Maximus wasn't ashamed to admit that, already, the separation was killing him.

# CHAPTER FIFTEEN

*Wallingford*

ARRIVING THE FOLLOWING morning, mist was hovering over the ground just as sunrise began to turn the land shades of blue and pink. The de Shera banners were hanging heavy and wet in the new day but there was no mistaking the de Shera crimson and black, distinctive, with a great eagle in the center of it that reflected upon the House of de Shera's Roman origins. It was said that the family descended from a lost Roman legion somewhere up near Chester. Therefore, the family crest was an eagle. Gallus, and his forefathers, flew the standard proudly.

The camp was mostly awake at this time and word began to spread that the Lords of Thunder had arrived. Men began to rouse, to stand up and take notice, as the crimson and black standard moved through camp, heading for de Montfort's tent. The thunder of horses filled the air as Gallus and his brothers announced themselves as only they were capable of doing. The entire camp paid attention. The muscle had arrived.

*Bigod. Fitzgeoffrey. Gloucester. De Lara. Canterbury. De Ferrers. Fitzalan. De Wolfe.* All of these standards came to notice as Gallus, Maximus, and Tiberius came to a halt near de Montfort's big yellow tent. One of de Montfort's soldiers greeted them and directed them to set up camp directly to the east of de Montfort's cluster. Tiberius went with the men to establish their camp while Gallus and Maximus, along with their knights, dismounted. As men took the horses away, Maximus turned to Scott and Troy.

"I saw your father's standard," he said. "I am relieved that he is here. Things should go much smoother with The Wolfe leading the charge."

The de Wolfe brothers nodded. "Indeed," Scott said. "I should like to go to my father, with your permission."

Maximus waved him off. "Go," he said. "But do not be gone over-long. We intend to meet with de Montfort directly and find out what his plans are, so I will have need of you shortly."

The de Wolfe brothers nodded, heading off towards the distant standard bearing de Wolfe's dark green and black colors. Maximus was about to turn around but noticed that Stefan was standing beside him, his young face excited.

"I saw the Canterbury standards, my lord," he said. "May I go and see if my father has arrived?"

Maximus nodded. "The great Maddoc du Bois," he said, smiling at the young knight. "He is one of the few men left that are directly connected to the legends – your grandfather, your granduncle, Rhys du Bois, and Gart Forbes among them. Please give your father best regards from the House of de Shera and tell him that I look forward to seeing him again."

Stefan nodded eagerly and bolted off into the faint morning mist. With his knights off to visit family, Maximus turned in the direction of the de Lara banner. He'd seen it when they'd arrived, a red and white banner that had been mingled with others. He knew it was Kellen and he certainly wasn't surprised to see that he had arrived. And he was positive that Kellen had either seen the House of de Shera arrive or, at least by now, been told of it.

Given that Kellen believed his daughter was on her way back to Trelystan and far away from Maximus de Shera, the man was probably feeling just the least bit victorious. At least, that's what Maximus thought. He would let the man feel that way, at least for the time being, and he had no intention of seeking him out or having any manner of conversation with him. In fact, he would make a point of avoiding the man as much as he could. He was fairly certain that, at this point, any conversation between them would come to no good end. It was best to avoid it altogether, at least until time had passed and Kellen had been lured into a false sense of security, thinking he'd managed to keep Courtly away from her suitor. Maximus knew he'd have to face the man at some point with what he'd done, but that moment would have to wait. Now was not the time.

With his thoughts lingering on how to avoid Kellen de Lara in the near future, Maximus caught sight of Gallus, who was standing in conference with one of de Montfort's knights. Maximus recognized the warrior immediately, the right hand and champion of de Montfort, a knight by the name of Sir Paeton de Royans who was, perhaps, more formidable than almost any man in England. Even Maximus, as seasoned he was, had a healthy respect for de Royans' abilities. He was a tall man, although there were taller, but the sheer breadth and muscle on the man was an impressive and intimidating sight. He was brawny, blond, handsome as hell, and he knew it. A humble man, de Royans was not, but he had every reason not to be. Maximus liked the man a great deal. He was brilliant, humorous, and they'd seen battle together many times. As they approached, Paeton caught sight of Maximus and lifted a hand.

"And the God of War in the flesh arrives," he said, his blue eyes glimmering. "I have not seen you in months, my friend. I have heard all manner of wild tales over the past several months, mostly with you and your brothers involved in them."

Maximus laughed softly. "I have *not* been involved in anything," he stressed. "And even if you think so, you cannot prove it. Where have you been, Pete? We literally have not seen you in months."

Paeton smiled. "Drumming up support for de Montfort in the north," he said quietly. "The north is very fickle. If de Montfort cannot bring in a few of the more powerful barons, then we may have real trouble on our hands."

Maximus thought on that statement for a time. After a moment, he shrugged. "We are, after all, leading a rebellion against the king," he said. "I am not surprised that you have had difficulty finding allies. Speaking of allies, tell us what has happened with Christon de Russe. Has he really pledged to de Montfort?"

Paeton nodded his head. "Indeed he has," he said. "Henry is none too pleased with it, either. He has convened a large army about seven miles from here and not a straggler army, either. Our scouts have seen de Winter banners and, they suspect, there are mercenaries involved. It is de Montfort's intention to move his army to intercept them before they can reach Warborough."

Gallus and Maximus were listening closely. "When?" Maximus asked.

Paeton shrugged, glancing back at the big yellow tent, damp and somewhat sagging from the heavy dew of the morning air. "Soon," he said. "We are simply awaiting word from our scouts. When they arrive to tell us de Winter is on the move, then we will intercept them."

*De Winter.* That was not what Gallus or Maximus wanted to hear. Fighting Davyss de Winter and his father was like fighting a beloved brother and uncle, although they knew that whenever Henry was convening an army that the de Winter troops would be there. Still, there was little choice. They had committed to de Montfort and would do as they were told.

Paeton, who had been fighting de Montfort's battles a very long time, must have sensed their thoughts because he knew, much as most of those close to the House of de Shera knew, that the de Sheras and the de Winters had very close ties. He could detect their melancholy.

"I am sorry about this," he said softly, looking to both Gallus and Maximus. "You know it is not easy on de Montfort, either. He is Davyss de Winter's godfather."

Maximus and Gallus knew as much. Gallus waved the man off. "Such things happen in war," he said, unwilling to elaborate. In fact, he changed the subject completely, mostly because he simply didn't want to talk about it. "Where is de Montfort?"

Paeton pointed to the tent. "Inside."

Thanking Paeton, Gallus headed into the tent but Maximus lingered behind. It had been a great while since he'd seen his friend and he wanted a few cordial words with him, perhaps to even tell him about Courtly. He found that he was proud and eager to speak of his new wife. However, Paeton spoke first.

"What will you do if Davyss lifts a sword to you?" he asked softly.

Maximus shrugged. "He will not."

"Would you stake your life on it?"

"I would."

Paeton didn't have the heart to dispute him. "If he does and you do not lift yours," he confided, "I will be there. I will not let him strike you down."

Maximus looked at him. "Davyss will not strike any de Shera down and neither will his father," he said. "But I appreciate your concern, Pete, I sincerely do. However, there is something else you should know, something I am sure my brother is telling de Montfort right now. We lost Garran de Moray to Henry's cause because the king has asked Garran's father, Bose de Moray, for his sword. Garran has chosen to support his father in this matter. Although I hate to even voice such a thing, it is my suspicion that

Bose and Garran are with the de Winter army. They were both in Oxford and have since left, so I can only imagine that they have gone straight for Henry's army."

Paeton's blond eyebrows lifted. "De Moray?" he repeated, aghast. Mulling over the revelation, he simply shook his head. "Then this will be a battle of legends because we have William de Wolfe and Maddoc du Bois among us. These men are beyond legend, Max. They are the immortals. And now they face each other in battle? I never thought I would live to see such a thing."

Maximus put out a hand to the man, shaking his head firmly. "Do not curse them so by calling them immortals," he said. "They are men of flesh and blood, just like us. They can die just as easily."

"Let us hope not."

Maximus drew in a long, deep breath, coming to grips with the power on both sides of the battle lines. It was truly quite remarkable. "I had better go inside and hear what de Montfort has to say," he said. "Are you coming?"

"In a moment."

Maximus threw a thumb out in the general direction of his encampment. "When you see Tiberius, send him on to me."

Paeton nodded his head. "It will be my pleasure."

"And no planning nasty tricks with him, at least until this skirmish is over and I can fight back."

Paeton started to laugh, thinking on all of the rotten things they had done to each other over the years all in the name of good humor. Once, they'd fixed Maximus' saddle so that it slid off his horse and Maximus with it. In retaliation, Maximus had tossed a hive full of angry bees into Paeton's tent and sealed the flap shut so the man couldn't escape. Pranks that had been good-natured but, in some cases, rather painful. Paeton still had an unnatural fear of bees as a result.

"I promise, no tricks," he said, holding up his hand to honorably vow. "I cannot think of any good ones, anyway. I fear I am all out of ideas."

Maximus rolled his eyes. "Then that is excellent news," he declared. "That being said, I am going inside. It is good to see you again, my friend, tricks or no."

Paeton waved him away, watching Maximus disappear inside de Montfort's tent. There were already barons in there, gathering, although there was no formal meeting. That would come soon enough now that the Lords of Thunder had arrived. Now, they could start planning in earnest.

The fate of a nation was hanging in the balance and legends on both sides of the battle lines would soon be at war.

There could only be one victor.

IT HAD BEEN a difficult morning.

More than that, it had been a difficult night. Maximus, Gallus, Tiberius, and their men had left at midnight under a bright and full moon, heavily armed and confident that they could reach Walling-ford by morning. Gallus and Jeniver had said tender farewells, with Gallus keeping his hand on Jeniver's gently rounded belly, while Maximus and Courtly simply clung together. But they were soon forced to separate, necessary if they were to make de Montfort's rendezvous by morning, so Maximus and Gallus left the women in their chambers, safe behind locked doors, as they headed out into the night.

Courtly had hardly slept at all after that. She kept seeing Maximus, dressed in full battle armor, prepared for a fight, and it made her sick to remember him like that. Although she knew the man was a warrior, and the very best England had to offer, she still didn't like the thought of him heading into battle where men would be aiming to cut him down. She wanted him here, with her, safe and warm. But that was not meant to be.

Morning dawned misty and cold, but once the fog of the morning had lifted, Courtly and Jeniver had taken their small escort and had gone for a walk down the avenue and then back up again. Both women were edgy, nervous, and Jeniver seemed to feel much better when she could move around a bit, and Gallus had permitted her to walk up and down the street that The One-Eyed Raven was located on. On this morning after the men had gone, Jeniver saw no reason to deviate from her usual schedule. Therefore, she and Courtly walked up and down the street, observing their surroundings with interest and trying not to think of their husbands as they headed into battle.

The inn was located on a street with two other hostels and residences, and people moved about their business in a great rush. Children and dogs ran about in the street, one of the dogs being quite friendly with the ladies. It was a very big dog, scruffy and underfed, but it seemed to take to Courtly a great deal. Never having a pet, she tried to leave the dog behind at first but it kept following her, so she brought it along and back to the inn with her, mostly because she couldn't get rid of it if she tried. And she had.

In truth, she needed the distraction, something to focus on other than the fact her husband was waging war, possibly this very minute. This was all so new and unfamiliar to her, a new world of worries that she'd never experienced before, so it was difficult to know how to deal with the emotions the situation invited. Jeniver wasn't much better, but at least she'd had some experience with it, and she approved of the dog as a distraction. At least it would give Courtly something to do other than sit and worry. Therefore, Courtly focused on tending the scraggly mutt.

The innkeeper, now having become very familiar with his best guests, provided Courtly with a big, wooden tub to wash the dog in because it was so matted and dirty. Courtly didn't actually wash the dog herself but she stood by as a stable boy did it, and the dog seemed to begrudgingly accept the fact that it was being bathed. He was calm enough, at any rate. He had a very big tongue and licked Courtly happily when she petted its head, assuring the dog that it was being very good and obedient as the boy scrubbed. When the dog was finally rinsed clean, she took it into the kitchen of the inn and dried it off near the big bread oven.

Courtly ended up with the dog in the common room, sitting at the designated de Shera table, feeding it scraps from the morning meal. The dog proved to be an excellent distraction, at least for a time, but thoughts of Maximus continued to infiltrate Courtly's mind. It was much like a leaky dam. She would plug up one flood of memories with a distraction, only to have the flood return greater than before. She played the game for a while, petting and feeding the big and now, fluffy, dog, using it to keep at bay memories of Maximus, but soon she gave up the fight altogether.

As the dog lay down next to her and went to sleep, Courtly sat at the table with her chin in her hand, depressed, watching the activity of the room as patrons came and left. She wished with all her heart that Maximus would be the next person coming through the entry door, but alas, it was not to be.

"Well?" came a voice behind her. "Did you bathe the bugs from the dog?"

Courtly turned to see Jeniver as the woman took a seat next to her. Courtly smiled weakly. "Indeed I did," she said. "He is a very friendly dog."

Jeniver eyed the mutt. "He is a very *big* dog," she said. "I am glad that he is friendly because he could certainly eat you for sup."

Courtly laughed, turning to pet her new friend on the head. "I have decided to name him Henry," she said. "I can order him about to my content, make him do my bidding, and feed him scraps from my table. It is a perfect name, truly."

Jeniver laughed. "Maximus and Gallus will love that," she said. Then, she set a small, wooden box onto the table, something she had brought down with her from upstairs. She began to open it. "I thought you might like to play a game to pass the hours."

Courtly looked at the box with interest. "What is it?"

Jeniver pulled forth a stack of wooden cards, elegantly painted. "These are cards that I purchased when I visited Paris a few months ago," she said. "My father bought them for my birthday. We can play games with them."

Courtly had played cards before. "When I fostered, the lady of the house had cards," she said. "She taught us to play Bone Aces. Do you know that game?"

Jeniver nodded. "I do," she said. "This is exciting. It is the first time I have been able to use my cards. Gallus will not play with me because all he wants to do is gamble and I refuse to take money from him."

Courtly's mood lightened as her focus shifted from thoughts of Maximus to those of a card game. As the barkeep brought the ladies some warmed, mulled wine, Courtly and Jeniver played round after round of Bone Aces. The object was, through accumulating numbered cards, to total thirty-one without going over that number. One could discard and accept new cards, but if they went over the limit, then a winner was declared and a new game began.

Fortunately, both Courtly and Jeniver could count and they played the game with relish. When their four-man escort saw what the women were doing, they showed great interest and Jeniver invited the head of the escort to join them. The man happily accepted but was greatly displeased when he won not one hand against the women. Insulted, the next man in the escort took over from him and he, too, lost every hand.

By this time, Courtly and Jeniver were having a grand time

beating their escort at cards. They finished soundly beating the second man and were starting in on his replacement when the door to the common room opened and a figure entered. Courtly, who was facing the door, happened to glance up as the figure moved deeper into the room. Recognition dawned and all humor left her face.

"Auntie!" she gasped.

It was too late to run and hide, for Ellice had already spotted her niece. Oddly enough, she didn't seem surprised to see her. Pale, and wet from the intermittent rain that was striking up this day, Ellice made her way over to the table. By the time she reached it, Courtly and Jeniver were on their feet, edgy, but Ellice only had eyes for Courtly.

"I hoped I would find you here," Ellice said to her niece. "I had hoped you had not yet left to go to the de Shera stronghold."

Courtly was torn between bewilderment and fear. "Oh... aunt-ie," she sighed, knowing her deception had just been discovered. There was great disappointment in her tone. "Why did you come here?"

Ellice grasped her niece by the elbow and the four-man escort rushed to pull the woman away. Only a swift word from Courtly stopped them from breaking Ellice's arm.

"Nay!" she cried, holding up her free hand. When the escort froze, uncertain, she turned to her aunt. "Auntie, why are you here? How did you know to find me here?"

Ellice hadn't grasped her niece to hurt her. She had grasped her to emphasize her point. "Because your father knows that you are with Sir Maximus," she hissed. "I came to warn him. Where is he?"

Courtly felt as if she had been hit in the chest. She exhaled sharply in shock and grasped the chair next to her, weaving unsteadily. She was overcome with astonishment and fear.

"Sweet Jesú," she breathed. "How did Papa find out?"

Ellice actually steered her niece into the chair and sat heavily next to her. The older woman's face was grim.

"One of the soldiers he sent on the escort to take you and Isadora back to Trelystan returned to say that you had escaped in the town of Woodstock, just north of Oxford," she said. "He also told your father how the House of de Shera had intercepted the escort and had demanded that you be turned over to them. According to the soldier, St. Héver chased them away but you escaped that night. It did not take a genius to deduce where you had gone, Courtly. Kellen knew you returned to Maximus."

Courtly was pale-faced as she listened to her aunt, sick to the core. "Where is Papa now?" she asked. "Is he coming for me?"

Ellice shook her head. "Nay," she said. "De Montfort summoned him to Warborough Castle. I was there when de Montfort's messenger arrived and I heard everything he told my brother. Your father specifically asked if the House of de Shera would be present and the messenger said that they would, that all of de Montfort's allies would be there. As your father was gathering his escort, he was mumbling about 'killing the true enemy' and I do not believe he meant Henry. I think he meant Sir Maximus. It is my belief that he somehow means to do Sir Maximus harm."

Courtly gasped, shocked and horrified. "He would try to kill him?"

Ellice nodded. This wasn't easy for her, either. Her brother was still on the brink of madness and with Courtly's disappearance from the escort meant to take her back to Trelystan, and to safety, Kellen only saw one person to blame –Maximus. All of the madness and blame was on the middle de Shera brother.

"I believe so," Ellice said. "Is he here?"

Courtly had tears in her eyes. "Nay," she breathed. "My husband has already gone on to Warborough."

It was Ellice's turn to look stunned. "*Husband?*" she repeated.

"You married him?"

Courtly nodded, wiping the tears from her eyes before they fell. "We were married yesterday," she said. "I love him, Auntie. I love him with all my heart. I cannot allow Papa to do this. I must got to Warborough and warn him."

She stood up with the full intention of charging off to Warborough but Ellice grabbed her, preventing her from moving. Jeniver, too, put her hands on Courtly to stop the woman from running off.

"Nay, Courtly," Jeniver said gently but firmly. "You will not go. We will send one of our escort to him. He will ride faster than you can, moreover, he will know where to find Maximus."

Courtly turned to Jeniver and burst into tears. "My father will try to kill him, I know it," she sobbed. "Mayhap he is already moving against him!"

Jeniver wiped at the woman's tears. "Maximus will be on his guard around your father," she assured her. "You know that he is on his guard around everyone except his brothers. He will not give your father the chance to cut him down. You must have faith."

Courtly was terrified, struggling to stop her tears. "Please," she begged softly. "Send a man to warn him. Send him now."

Jeniver swiftly turned to the head of the escort, but the man had already heard the tale from Ellice and was prepared. He selected a young, slender soldier, one who would be light on a horse and ride like the wind. Already, the plans were in motion. Maximus had to be warned that Kellen de Lara was out to kill him. As the de Shera soldier fled to the livery behind the inn to collect a horse, Courtly turned to her aunt.

As she gazed at the woman, she realized that she was seeing a completely different woman from the one she had known all these years. The frightening, bitter, old aunt had become a surprising ally and Courtly could only manage to feel deep gratitude. She reached out to clasp Ellice's rough, worn hand.

"You came to warn me at great risk to yourself," Courtly murmured. "Please know how grateful I am, Auntie. If Papa throws you from Kennington because you have helped me, then you may come to live with me at Isenhall Castle. You will have a place to go, I swear it."

Ellice's cheeks flamed a bit. She wasn't used to kind words and was very awkward with anything sentimental. The best she could do was squeeze Courtly's hand, struggling to find the words to respond.

"What my brother did to you was not right," she said. "Although his behavior has been inexcusable, please know that he had… reasons for his manner. I do not want you to think he is simply a selfish madman."

Courtly cocked her head curiously. "What reasons?"

Ellice wasn't willing to divulge all she knew. If Kellen wanted Courtly to know, he would tell her in his own time. Ellice didn't feel that it was her place to speak.

"Someday he might tell you," she said. "It is my genuine hope that he comes to see the error of his ways. Now that you have married Maximus, I hope that he will indeed come to accept your relationship with the man."

Courtly thought on that, her expression reflecting what she thought was a hopeless feat. "But you believe he goes to kill Max," she said. "I do not see how he can accept our marriage if he is mad enough to kill for it."

Ellice wasn't sure what she could say to that statement because it was true. If Kellen was mad enough to kill, as Ellice believed he was, then the situation would not end well. Maximus de Shera could out-fight anyone in England, Kellen included, so Ellice was fairly certain that Kellen would soon be dead if he wasn't already. But perhaps that was what the man had planned. To ultimately end the relationship between his daughter and Maximus, perhaps he would let Maximus kill him. After that, what woman would remain with the man who killed her beloved father? In a small way, perhaps Kellen would have the last word in all of this. Certainly, it was something to consider. Perhaps in death, Kellen could end a relationship he couldn't end in life.

Ellice wondered.

# CHAPTER SIXTEEN

*1.7 miles east of Warborough, near the village of Shillingford*

THE BATTLE LINES were drawn.

Almost two miles east of Warborough Castle, the army of Simon de Montfort intercepted the army of King Henry. In fact, the armies had known they were nearing one another for some time and the lines had already been drawn and the troops placed. Standards of great houses blew in the breeze as rain intermittently fell, punctuated by periods of bright sun and clear skies. It was all rather strange but it made for beautiful weather at times, at least clear enough to see the standards of opposing houses as they flew straight and firm in the wind. It was clear that a battle of epic proportions was lining up.

When all was said and done, Simon had more men but Henry had the advantage of de Winter archers. They were the best in England. As Maximus, Gallus, and several other knights watched from a ridge just above the troop lines, they could see the archers being placed. Maximus guessed that Davyss, or his younger brother, Hugh, was placing the archers because it was strategic. They were behind the infantry and when the sun would come out from behind the clouds, they could see the glint of the archer shields. This would make the battle more interesting.

As the knights sat and watched, trying to gauge what Henry's army was doing so they could better place their infantry, they were joined by several other barons. William de Wolfe was one of them. The legendary Wolfe of the North, father of the de Wolfe twins, Scott and Troy, had joined Simon's army with one hundred men he'd brought with him from the north. It wasn't a good deal of men but, given that they served The Wolfe, it was a crack-squad of soldiers. Just one of de Wolfe's men was as good as five regular men.

De Montfort was on horseback, watching the distant army and surrounded by Paeton de Royans, the de Shera brothers, and several other men as de Wolfe approached. When Simon saw William, he motioned the man towards him.

"My lord," Simon addressed him formally, purely out of respect. "Have you been watching our friends across the field? They have many archers."

William, a handsome, older man with dark hair, dark skin, and an eye-patch over his missing left eye, studied the army in the distance. As he did, his sons, who had been back behind Gallus, gravitated towards their father. The de Wolfe men gathered together for battle, strength on strength, and William acknowledged his sons before turning his attention to Henry's army.

"They are positioning the archers very far back, almost near the tree line," William said, and everyone was glued to every word he said. The mighty Wolfe was speaking. "If I were a betting man, it would tell me that the archers are going to cover the infantry as it moves forward."

On the other side of de Montfort, Gallus grunted in agreement. "De Winter has been known to do that," he said. "He will shower us with arrows while his infantry charges forward and then we will be fighting off a hail of arrows and unprepared for the infantry when they finally come upon us."

De Montfort looked at Gallus. "Then what do you want to do?"

he asked. "Have you seen enough?"

Gallus nodded, his eyes still on the distant army. He turned around, looking at the tree line about a quarter of a mile behind them. "Get the men into the trees," he said. "That will take the advantage of the archers away from them because the canopy will stop the arrows for the most part. We, however, will place what few archers we have at the very front of our lines to cut down de Winter's infantry as it approaches. That should give us a tactical advantage."

The Thunder Lord had spoken. Word began to spread back through de Montfort's lines and soon, eighteen hundred men were moving west by a quarter of a mile, forming lines just inside a long band of trees that stretched, north to south, for about two miles. As they moved, they could see Henry's army, with the de Winter banners flying, following them, hopefully to close the gap. Or it was even possible that they thought de Montfort was retreating. However, when Henry's army came to the crest that de Montfort had been on and saw the tree line in the distance, and de Montfort's men buried within it, they came to an immediate halt. Now, they understood why de Montfort had moved. The odds were now even – it would be infantry against infantry.

De Winter pulled the archers back and his men were given the order to draw swords, the flashes of which could be seen in the sunlight. Gallus and the other commanders, realizing that Henry was going to take the offensive, gave the orders for their men to draw weapons as well. The knights thundered back to their troops and unmuzzled the war horses, nasty beasts that would bite and kick and trample the enemy to death. The smell of battle was in the air as the knights slung their shields over their left knee, the usual place for them when heading into battle for easy access in close-quarters fighting. And, from the looks of it, they would soon be in the middle of exactly that type of battle. Blood was coming.

Maximus remained with de Montfort and de Royans as Gallus and Tiberius headed back to their men. William was to the south of the de Shera troops and the Lords of Canterbury, represented by Maddoc du Bois, were on the other side of de Montfort to the north. Maximus could see the great knight at the head of his men, in full battle armor, and he was rather regretful that he'd been unable to converse with the man before they rode to battle.

Maddoc and Stefan had spent most of their time together, in Maddoc's tent, while Maximus had spent his time with de Montfort. Even now, Stefan rode with his father, as Gallus had given him permission to do so. It seemed that all of the sons wished to see battle alongside their fathers, as the de Wolfe brothers rode with William as well. It gave Maximus reflection, wondering if he would ever know a son who would ride with him to battle. He truly hoped so.

But his thoughts moved back to the battle at hand, away from thoughts of a strong son and avoiding thoughts of his wife. He couldn't think of her now, knowing that a distraction such as that could be deadly in his profession, but it was inevitable to think of her and, in so doing, to also think of her father. Kellen de Lara had been placed to the extreme northern end of the battle lines, far away from the Lords of Thunder and far away from Maximus. Gallus had made this so, fearful of what would happen if the two men came together. Gallus has done such a good job of placing Kellen that Maximus hadn't even seen him or his troops. The man blended in with the rest of the infantry.

De Montfort, of course, knew nothing about any of this and probably wouldn't for quite some time. It was inconsequential, truly, when the fate of a country hung in the balance. In fact, thoughts of Kellen quickly faded as Maximus noticed the de Winter standard runner bearing the flag for the infantry, signaling them to advance. Now, the battle was to commence in full and he muttered the fact to de Montfort just as Henry's infantry, along with several knights, began to move across the field towards them. Maximus looked over his shoulder to Gallus, several feet away.

"They are moving," he boomed to his brother. "Do we ride?"

Gallus lifted his sword. "Signal all infantry and knights," he bellowed to the standard bearers who were behind the first row of infantry. "Charge them!"

The standard bearers spurred their horses, riding in front of the lines, two men heading south while one headed north, signaling the men to move. And move they did. Holding back a secondary, smaller line of infantry, the majority of de Montfort's troops charged Henry's army, who were moving rather slowly across the field. Once they saw the charge of knights and infantry coming at them, however, everything change. They ran right at them.

The clash was deafening when the two armies collided. The Lords of Thunder charged in full-force with Tiberius being the first one to cut down an enemy knight bearing Teutonic-designed armor. More than that, de Montfort's men saw very quickly that a good portion of Henry's troops were not English. By the design of their weapons, tunic, and mail, it was clear that they were either French or Teutonic. Foreign enemy troops on English soil simply made Gallus, Maximus, and the rest of them extremely angry. Then, it became a bloodbath.

William de Wolfe, astride his big, black charger, had gone after a group of foreign soldiers with a vengeance. Scott and Troy rode with their father, cutting down men and battling two big, enemy knights with fairly expensive armor. When an enemy knight managed to unseat Troy, Scott and William closed in on him and between the two of them, nearly gutted the man. He fell to the ground, dead, as Troy remounted his steed and took the dead knight's animal as a prize. But the fighting didn't end there.

Maddoc du Bois was a man who had inherited his father's

fighting skill. He also carried dual swords like his father used to, and his father had been famous for them. Maddoc managed to direct his horse with knee pressure alone, a very exacting skill, while the dual blades sailed through the air with deadly purpose, severing limbs and heads on occasion. Stefan, fighting alongside his father, managed to kill a pair of mercenaries that were trying to yank his father from his steed – one man, he used his sword on but the other man had the misfortune of having his head nearly ripped off when Stefan grabbed the man by the hair. It was a brutal battle as the du Bois men made short work of the mercenaries they encountered.

Maximus was in heavy fighting near the center of the battle. He was encountering both mercenary and de Winter troops and trying very hard not to kill the de Winter men. The sun had clouded over again and rain was beginning to fall and, at one point, he thought he caught a glimpse of a knight on horseback who then disappeared behind a group of mounted soldiers. He didn't think too much about it although he couldn't help wondering where Davyss and even Garran were in all of this, because he was positive they were here. He just hadn't seen them yet.

What Maximus didn't know, however, was that someone with ill intent, had him in his sights.

The Thunder Warrior was his target.

KELLEN HAD BEEN watching for Maximus ever since he had heard that the Lords of Thunder had arrived in de Montfort's camp. He knew the man would stay close to de Montfort, and he had, but now in the midst of a battle, Maximus was somewhat on his own. Tiberius and Gallus were fighting near him, as was usual with the de Shera brothers, but de Montfort was back in the trees with the second line of soldiers, letting his seasoned, battle commanders do most of the heavy fighting.

While Gallus and Tiberius engaged soldier after soldier, Maximus was going for the kill. He had a nasty-looking sword with a jagged edge that he used to slice men's heads from their bodies. There were already several headless bodies around, a tribute to the man's strength and skill. But Kellen wasn't concerned with that. He was simply concerned with making his way to Maximus and killing him in battle.

Death in battle was expected and Kellen was certain he could kill Maximus undetected. There were hundreds of men around but no one was paying attention to him and, certainly, Maximus and his brothers and friends were busy with their own private battles. Therefore, Kellen was certain he could accomplish what he had set out to do. With a crossbow in his grip, he began to make his move towards Maximus.

There was no other way, of course. He'd tried everything to keep Courtly away from the man but she was acting more and more foolish. He'd tried to send her home but she had run off, directly to Maximus, Kellen was sure. He was equally sure that his daughter was completely under de Shera's spell. She was more than likely his whore. He'd tried so hard to prevent it but, in the end, the lure of Maximus has just been too strong for his weak-willed daughter.

Now, Kellen would take away her weakness. He would take away Maximus and then things would return to the way they were before the introduction of Maximus de Shera. Kellen would make sure of it.

MAXIMUS HAS LOST track of how many men he had killed, but he knew he was up in the dozens at this point. Infantry was simply no

match against a mounted knight. Additionally, he had seen Bose de
Moray on the outskirts of the battle, fighting against a group of
Fitzgeoffrey men, and Maximus saw quite clearly when Garran
intervened and helped his father chase off those he hadn't killed. It
did Maximus' heart good to see Garran, whole and healthy, and
shortly thereafter, he saw Davyss fighting off a group of Fitzalan
troops.

Davyss' distinctive sword, named *Lespada*, the sword of his
ancestors, gleamed in the weak light as the clouds gathered and the
rain fell. Davyss was a fearsome fighter and after Maximus
dispatched a particularly aggressive Frenchman, he paused a
moment to watch Davyss in action. The man was impressive to
watch. But his appreciation turned to concern when a Fitzalan man
leapt onto the back of Davyss' horse and grabbed Davyss around
the neck.

The knight was at a distinct disadvantage from the way the
man had grabbed him and Maximus knew that if he didn't do
something, Davyss would be in real trouble. Removing a razor-
sharp dagger from the folds of his armor, Maximus charged
through the sea of fighting men, close enough to pull his horse to a
halt and launch the dagger straight at the Fitzalan soldier.

The result was instantaneous. At about twenty feet, Maximus
had planted the dagger into the neck of the soldier and the man fell
back, toppling off the horse and landing heavily on the ground.
Davyss, regaining his balance, turned around with shock to see the
man on the ground and a very fine knife hilt sticking out of his
neck. It was not the knife of a foot soldier. Lifting his eyes, Davyss
saw Maximus several feet away.

When their gazes met, Maximus simply lifted a hand to Davyss
and turned back around, returning to his corner of the battle, and
Davyss knew at that moment that he owed Maximus his life. The
Thunder Warrior had used that fine dagger with great skill to save

him. More than that, it was a friend saving a friend no matter what side they fought on. It would always be that way. With a faint smile, he resumed his battle.

Back in the midst of his fighting, Maximus was busy with a pair of de Winter soldiers who were trying to pull him off his warhorse. The black and white jennet was very nasty in battle and gave one of the men a serious bite wound. The horse had also managed to head-butt another man to the ground and proceeded to trample him. As Maximus kicked a man in the head and engaged another in a fairly dangerous sword battle, he had no idea that Kellen was coming up behind him. He had no idea that the man had his crossbow trained on him but hadn't had a clear shot at him because of the mad boil of men between them. When Maximus pitched forward to slug a man in the head who was grabbing for his horse's reins, Kellen let his arrow fly a little too late and the arrow sailed over Maximus' head.

Frustrated, Kellen reloaded and moved closer, but Maximus was still unaware. He was too busy fighting more French mercenaries that were now ganging up on him. As he used his feet, fists, and sword to fight them off, the thunder of hooves could be heard and Maximus looked up to see Bose de Moray bearing down on him. The man had a crossbow aimed right at him and as Maximus lifted his sword to fend the man off and hopefully deflect the arrow, Bose let the arrow fly.

Maximus threw himself sideways in the saddle to avoid being struck and the arrow sailed right past him, missing him by a fairly wide berth. It did, however, hit something behind Maximus because he heard the grunt as the arrowhead impacted flesh and bone. Turning briefly to see who had been hit, Maximus was startled to see Kellen laying on the ground behind him, an arrow in his throat. A crossbow was still clutched in his hand even though his life was rapidly slipping away as blood gurgled up out of his mouth. Maximus stared at the man a moment before turning his astonished gaze to de Moray.

Bose was several feet away with his crossbow lowered. He pointed a gloved finger at Kellen. "I watched him as he tried to kill you once," he told Maximus. "He shot an arrow at you but missed and he was reloading. I was not going to let him have a second shot at you."

With that, he reined his horse around and thundered off, back into the midst of the fighting. Stunned, Maximus didn't have time to dwell on Kellen. There was still too much fighting going on around him and he found himself swept up in the wave of battle, the surge of hand to hand combat where it was either kill or be killed. He didn't intend to be killed. His wife was already going to have to suffer through the death of her father now. Maximus wouldn't let her suffer through his death as well. Thanks to de Moray, she wouldn't have to.

The fighting went on into the night.

# CHAPTER SEVENTEEN

*Oxford*

"**D**O YOU THINK they might return today?"

Courtly asked the question. Four days after Maximus, Gallus, and Tiberius had left for Warborough, Courtly and Jeniver were sitting in the common room of The One-Eyed Raven, a platter of bread and cheese and small apples between them, but neither one of them felt much like eating. It was mid-morning and the common room was fairly full of smelly and loud people, all of them eating or drinking or both.

But the ladies weren't paying much attention to what was going on around them. They were focused on their missing husbands, the battle at Warborough, and a messenger that had arrived from Isenhall late last night. The news he bore had not been good. This morning, their depression on the situation in general ran rampant.

"It is difficult to say when they will return," Jeniver said, picking at her bread. "It is difficult to say just how long a battle will last. If they were fortunate, they chased Henry off straight away, but if they were not fortunate, then it is probably still going on."

Courtly sighed faintly. "But it has been four days," she said softly. "Surely the messenger we sent to Maximus regarding my father has found him. Surely Maximus knows by now."

Jeniver glanced at her friend, seeing how worried she was.

There was much turmoil and strife going on in their world these days. "I am sure he knows," she assured her. "I am sure Maximus is safe, or at least as safe as he can be in battle. You needn't worry so much."

It was a silly thing to say. They were both greatly worried and both trying to pretend that they weren't. Courtly's thoughts lingered on Maximus and on her father for a few moments before she happened to catch sight of the Isenhall messenger. The man was eating ravenously, having ridden very hard for five days to reach Oxford to deliver his news. Courtly thoughts shifted from those of her husband to the information the messenger bore, something that had compounded their strain and anxiety ten-fold. It was news they had been expecting yet dreading it just the same.

"What was Lady Honey like?" she asked Jeniver. "I am sorry I will never have the opportunity to meet her. I had hoped to."

Jeniver's eyes filled with tears at the thought of Lady Honey's passing. But her tears weren't for Honey. The woman had suffered from her cancer terribly in her later days and death had finally put an end to that pain. Jeniver's tears were for her husband and for Maximus and Tiberius, men who were very attached to their mother. She knew how hard this would be on them. She sniffled, wiping at her eyes.

"She was a small woman who ruled the House of de Shera with an iron fist," she said quietly. "She was very kind, very loving, and quite intelligent. She is everything you would think the mother of the Lords of Thunder would be. Her death is going to be a tremendous blow to them."

Courtly already knew that. She noticed that Jeniver was still fighting off tears and she reached out, patting the woman on the hand.

"I am very sorry for all of you who knew her," she said. "My heart breaks for Maximus. He has spoken quite fondly of his mother."

Jeniver nodded her head, grasping Courtly's hand and holding tightly to it. "He will need your comfort," she whispered. "They will *all* need our comfort. We have no right to grieve at all. We must be strong for them."

Courtly nodded. "I intend to be," she assured her. "Certainly, they will want to return home right away, to attend their mother's burial. Who was left behind at Isenhall who can make such decisions?"

Jeniver shrugged. "When we left, there were only soldiers, a majordomo, and a physic to tend Honey," she said. "We also left Gallus' young daughters behind with their nurses, but the children cannot make such decisions. I would imagine the majordomo has taken charge."

Courtly's thoughts lingered on Isenhall, the castle where she would live but had not yet seen. Based on Maximus' description, she imagined it to be quite a mighty fortress.

"I did not know that Gallus already had children," she said, eyeing Jeniver curiously. "You never mentioned it."

Jeniver thought of fair-haired Violet and lovely, little Lily. "Haven't I?" she asked, thinking. "I suppose it just never came up."

"They are not your children, too?"

Jeniver shook her head. "I am Gallus' second wife," she said. "Gallus' first wife died in a fall two years ago. Gallus has two daughters."

Courtly's heart began to ache for Gallus, now for a bigger reason. "Then he has already suffered great loss of a woman in his life," she said. "I am very sorry for him. He has much to bear."

Jeniver nodded, trying not to tear-up again as she thought of her husband and the death he had suffered through. "He is a strong man," she said. "He has had to be."

Courtly didn't have much to say to that so she simply squeezed

Jeniver's hand again, holding it to comfort her. As she pondered the suggestion of playing more card games simply to distract themselves, she noticed a figure on the walkway overhead as Ellice emerged from her sleeping chamber.

Since Ellice's arrival four days before, she'd not left her niece's side. She had been strangely comforting to Courtly as she began to experience a new relationship with her aunt, one that she could have never imagined. Ellice had been considerate, thoughtful, and wise, certainly not the bitter spinster Courtly had known all of these years. It was rather strange but also rather wonderful.

Courtly poured Jeniver a measure of boiled fruit juice and then poured some for herself as Ellice came to the table. The older woman eyed Isenhall's messenger as she sat.

"Good morn to you, ladies," Ellice said, hungrily reaching for the bread. "I see the messenger is still here. I had hoped, for your sake, that his arrival yesterday was all a bad dream."

Courtly moved to pour her aunt some juice but Ellice waved her off in favor of watered ale. "Unfortunately, it was not," Courtly said. "It is all very real."

Ellice took a big bite of bread. "Has the man you sent on to Warborough returned yet?"

Courtly shook her head. "Nay," she replied. "I fear we are in for another day of waiting and wondering."

As they sat at the table, resigning themselves to another day of anxiety, there seemed to be a great commotion in front of the inn. They could hear horses, people shouting, and a few startled patrons bolted in through the front door as if the devil himself were chasing them. It was evident that something great was happening out on the street.

The three-man de Shera escort, sitting at the table next to the ladies, stood up, eyeing the door with some concern. The man in charge of the escort turned to Jeniver.

"My lady," he said. "Mayhap you should retire to your room for the time being. It sounds as if there may be some trouble about."

Jeniver didn't argue with the man. She'd been through this drill before. Sometimes loud and obnoxious men came to the tavern and it was safer if the women weren't in the common room. Therefore, Jeniver stood up and Courtly stood with her, both women making their way to the stairs that led to the upper levels. Ellice, hardly caring if rough men were about to enter the tavern, simply picked up her food and moved to another part of the tavern, back in a corner that was hidden from view. As Jeniver and Courtly reached the bottom of the steps, the door to the inn flew open and a shout from across the room stopped them.

"Courtly!"

Maximus stood in the doorway. When Courtly realized her husband had returned, she nearly fell off the bottom step in her haste to reach the man. She cried out with surprise, with relief, as she ran across the room, being thwarted by tables and chairs and people in her attempt to reach him. Maximus, too, was dodging obstacles, but he met his wife somewhere in the middle of the room and threw his arms around her, lifting her into his massive, warm, and safe embrace.

Courtly wept as she clung to Maximus, her arms wound around his neck so tightly that she was very nearly strangling him. They stood there in the center of the room, holding one another, as Gallus rushed past them, sweeping his emotional wife into his arms as he greeted her. Tiberius entered the room as well, without a scratch, followed by Scott, Troy, and Stefan. Troy was sporting a rather large bandage on his neck but out of all the de Shera knights, he seemed to be the only one who was injured. More men piled into the room, exhausted de Shera soldiers, and began shouting for food and wine. They had returned from battle, safely, and it was time to celebrate the fact.

It was loud and chaotic as Courtly and Maximus held one another, re-affirming bonds, each assuring the other that their beloved was safe. Courtly finally pulled her head from the crook of Maximus' neck, beaming at him through her tears of joy.

"You are safe," she breathed.

He nodded, kissing her deeply. "I am," he confirmed, his lips on hers. "I am well."

Courtly ran a hand over his bearded face, partially covered by the mail hood he wore. "Did the messenger reach you?" she asked, breathless. "Did he tell you about my father?"

*My father.* Maximus' joy diminished somewhat as he set Courtly carefully to her feet, his hands moving to her arms, clutching at her. As he gazed into her happy but concerned face, he struggled to bring forth the words that would tell her all that had happened. There was a great deal to tell and he hardly knew where to begin.

"He did," he finally replied. "The messenger did not find me until after the battle, however, when it was all over."

Courtly sighed heavily, with great relief. "God be praised," she murmured. "Aunt Ellice thought that my father was going to try to kill you because he found out that I had fled the escort assigned to take me to Trelystan."

Maximus gazed seriously at her. "How did he discover this?"

"A soldier assigned to the escort returned to tell him that I escaped," she replied. "He also told my father about the de Shera men who had intercepted the escort and tried to take me away. My father could only assume that I had escaped to run off to you and Auntie thought that he planned to kill you because of it."

It was essentially what the messenger had told him. Maximus peeled back his mail hood, revealing wet, sweaty hair beneath. He seemed so weary, so very weary, as he grasped Courtly gently and began to pull her towards the stairs. He wanted to take her to their chamber to inform her of her father's death. He didn't want to tell her here for all to see where her grief would be public. But as he pulled her towards the stairs, he happened to see a man he recognized sitting at one of the tables. The man was a soldier he had left behind at Isenhall. He knew the man very well. He came to a startled halt.

"Why is Chambers here?" he asked, pointing at the man. He looked at his wife, his brow knitted with both curiosity and foreboding. "When did he come?"

Courtly looked at the Isenhall messenger, who had spied Maximus long before Maximus spied him. The man stood up, moving towards Maximus and speaking before Courtly could answer.

"My lord," the messenger said, appearing rather strained. "The majordomo sent me. He wants me to tell you that your mother, the Lady Honey de Shera, has passed away. He begs you and your brothers to come home immediately."

Maximus stared at the man, unable to react to the shocking news. Gallus, standing with Jeniver several feet away, had also heard him, as had Tiberius, who was on the stairs, heading up to a bedchamber because he was so exhausted. But the messenger's trembling words had all three brothers frozen in time and space, unmoving as they processed what they had been told.

In fact, it seemed as if the entire room had come to a halt, the messenger's terrible words hanging in the air as the Lords of Thunder were informed that their beloved mother had finally passed away. Months of illness and weeks of anxiety and worry had now come to a close whether or not they were willing to accept it. It was final, as only death could be. As the brothers continued to stand, paralyzed with shock, Gallus was the first one to move. The look of grief on his features was indescribable as he made his way, haltingly, to the messenger.

"When?" he asked hoarsely.

The messenger, too, was wrought with sorrow because everyone at Isenhall knew what Honey meant to her sons. The woman had been so ill for so long but had lasted longer than she probably should have.

"Seven days ago, my lord," he replied. "It has taken me five days to reach Oxford. I only arrived yesterday. I came as soon as I could."

Gallus stared at the man, digesting his words. "Was…?" he began, choked, and started again. "Was her passing peaceful?"

The messenger nodded. "She died in her sleep, my lord," he replied. "She had awoken, briefly, the night before to ask that your daughters be placed in bed with her. Then she went back to sleep and never awoke. She was not alone, my lord. Lady Violet and Lady Lily were with her. She was comforted with her grandchildren."

Gallus' eyes filled with a flood of tears. He sat, heavily, in the nearest chair and Jeniver rushed to him, wrapping her arms around his head and neck, holding him to her breast as he wept. Maximus was still rooted to the spot, his gaze on the messenger as if unable to move or speak at all. Courtly was gravely concerned for him but she was distracted when Tiberius, as the news hit him, sat down on the steps leading up to the second floor and openly wept. The Lords of Thunder were crumbling before her very eyes.

"Max?" she whispered, clutching his hand. "Will you at least sit down? Please sit, my love. Sit down a moment."

Maximus was in shock. His mind was a black, roiling void with only thoughts of his mother filling it. He saw her when he was young, a beautiful woman with a brilliant smile, and he saw her as she took a willow switch after him and Gallus when they had stolen their father's coins. He saw her holding Tiberius as an infant and then comforting Maximus when he'd been ill with an infection in his chest. So many memories were rolling through his mind and not one of them bad. Everything was joyous. But upon those joyful memories came darker thoughts, those of Kellen de Lara and the man's attempts to kill him. The man who had given Courtly life had tried to take his, and Maximus began speaking before he even truly thought about what he said.

"Your father tried to kill me," he said to Courtly, looking down at her with a rather perplexed expression on his face. "I had been trying to avoid your father since we arrived at Wallingford but the man sought me out in battle and tried to put in arrow in my back. Bose de Moray killed your father as your father was making an attempt to kill me. De Moray saved my life."

Courtly gasped, her hands flying to her mouth in shock and grief, and the tears began to flow with a vengeance. It was then, and only then, that Maximus snapped out of his trance and realized what he had done. He'd spoken before he really thought about what he was going to say. It just all came tumbling out, his common sense overwhelmed by the news of his mother's passing. So much death. As a warrior, he was conditioned to accept death but not when it struck this close to home. He was simply having difficulty processing it.

"I am sorry, love," he said, reaching out and grasping Courtly, his manner deeply apologetic. "I should not have been so blunt. I wanted to tell you in a much more gentle fashion… forgive me, please. I fear that news of my mother's death has upset my balance. I did not even realize what I was saying until it was too late."

Courtly was sobbing deeply as Maximus tried to comfort her. "Auntie said he was going to do it," she wept. "Damn the man for trying. Damn him for his foolishness. What did he think would happen if he failed? He tried to kill you but he was killed instead."

Maximus didn't know what to say to her. He was feeling particularly horrible at the moment, comforting his wife over the death of her father which, somehow, helped his own sense of grief. It distracted him by having someone else to worry about. Looking around the room, he could see Tiberius sitting by himself, weeping, and Gallus seated on a chair with Jeniver holding him tightly to her bosom. They were all stricken with sorrow, weeping for mothers and fathers, weeping for those they loved.

With a heavy heart, and struggling to remain strong for his wife, Maximus pulled her over to the table where Gallus was sitting. Setting her down carefully, he then went over to Tiberius and pulled the man up from the stairs and led him over to the table as well. Everyone was so terribly shattered, but in that crisis of grief and strife, Maximus was strangely level-headed, if only to be strong for Courtly.

Maximus stood between his wife and Tiberius, his hand on his brother's shoulder and his other arm around his wife. He caught Jeniver's eye as she looked up from Gallus, and he smiled weakly at the woman. All the while, words his mother had once spoken to him, words he had once relayed to Courtly, kept rolling through his mind. Now, more than ever, they seemed particularly appropriate.

"Do you remember what Mother would say when we expressed the fears for our father's safety when he would ride off to battle?" he asked quietly. "Gal? Ty? Honey would say that we cannot know what will come at the day's end but that whatever it is, it will indeed come, and then the end will be known. If we saw Father again at the end of that day, then we would smile and embrace him, but if not, then we would not dwell on his ending but on his parting well-made. What did we say to Honey the last time we spoke her? Do you recall?"

Gallus was wiping at his eyes, struggling to focus on Maximus' question. It had been weeks since they'd last spoken to their mother, weeks since she had been coherent, so it was difficult to remember. As they struggled through the cobwebs of memories, Jeniver spoke.

"I recall one that of the last times we spoke, she spoke of Antoninus," she said, her hands on her husband's shoulders. "She told me that she had dreamed of him and that he looked the same as he did when he was young and strong, before age and his health caused him to deteriorate. She said that he stood at the gates of Isenhall but he would not come in. He simply stood there and smiled at her. She was rather perplexed at that but do you know what I think? I think he was waiting for her to come to him and she finally did. Certainly, her passing is a sorrowful thing, but we must not be sad for her. She is with Antoninus now and she is happy, so very happy. Should that thought not comfort us?"

Maximus was smiling knowingly by the time she was finished. He looked at Gallus and at Tiberius, seeing that their tears were mostly gone. They, too, were deeply comforted by Jeniver's words because their parents, who had been quite devoted to one another, were now together for eternity.

"It comforts me a great deal to know that," Maximus finally said. "She has missed my father every day since his death. Mayhap... mayhap instead of lamenting her death, we should be happy that they are finally together. At least, that his how I intend to view it. She is with him now and that is all that matters."

Seated next to him, Courtly sniffled. "As my father is finally with my mother as well," she said, wiping at her eyes. She looked up at Maximus. "That is how I will look at it as well. The man towards the end of his life was not the father I loved. He had changed somehow. But he, too, missed my mother very much. He never remarried, even after all of these years. They are together again and it is what he would want."

Maximus bent down and kissed her on the top of the head, giving her a gentle squeeze to comfort her. "As I would want to be with you, too," he murmured. Then, he glanced at the group around him, the table of people he loved best in the world. "But we are still here and we are still intact, and it is up to us to ensure that future generations of the House of de Shera have a country to inherit.

Honey would have wanted it that way. That is why she told us to attend de Montfort, to be by the man's side as he fights for a better England. I will honor what my mother wanted. With the last breath in my body, I will honor her wishes."

Gallus and Tiberius would, too. As the brothers gathered to speak of returning to Isenhall, Courtly went to tell her aunt, still over in the shadows of the tavern, about Kellen's demise. Ellice wasn't particularly surprised to hear about it nor was she particularly grieved. The man who had caused her life's misery was finally gone and, for the first time in her life, Ellice felt free. Free to live the life she always wanted to live without being under her brother's controlling thumb. More than anything, news of Kellen's death gave her relief.

Courtly watched as Ellice left the tavern, heading back to Kennington House with a lightness to her step that Courtly had never seen before. They were the steps of a woman who had been freed from resentment and anger. Courtly's thoughts lingered on the woman, hoping that she would indeed find happiness. She wished her aunt, the woman who had made all things possible for her and Maximus, nothing less than the best. The old spinster, that bitter, old shrew, had turned out to be a blessing in disguise.

But the real blessing in Courtly's life was Maximus. As she turned towards the de Shera table, she caught sight of her enormous, proud husband as he stood next to Tiberius, his arm around the man's shoulders, comforting his younger brother now that the news of their mother's death had settled deep. Tiberius actually had a weak smile on his lips and even Maximus was smiling, listening to Gallus as the man spoke of things Courtly couldn't quite hear. She observed the men a moment and she knew that, wherever Honey and Antoninus were, they were very proud of the mighty sons they had raised.

Glancing upward, to the heavens above, Courtly hoped that

Honey and Antoninus de Shera were watching. Somehow, she knew they were, and perhaps somewhere close by, her own mother and father were looking down upon her. It was odd how she could feel their presence very strongly and with that presence came peace. Most definitely, she felt at peace, because standing before her were the Lords of Thunder, men who would help make England a fine place for future generations.

And her beloved Thunder Warrior who would pass into all things legend.

## THE END

*Next: The Thunder Knight: Book Three in the de Shera Brotherhood Trilogy*

# MAXI'S TART

(Lady Honey de Shera's special tart recipe for Maximus who was, in fact, a finicky eater as a child. Guaranteed to make all future knights very happy with full tummies)

4 Tbsp. butter, melted

½ tsp. salt

pinch saffron

6 eggs

½ medium onion, coarsely chopped

½ lb. soft cheese, grated

½ cup currants

1 Tbsp. honey

1 tsp. parsley

1 tsp. sage

1 tsp. hyssop (this is an herb with a minty-ish taste)

1 tsp. powder douce (equal parts ginger, cinnamon, nutmeg, and cloves)

Grind saffron with salt, mix with butter, and set aside.

Place onions into boiling beef broth and cook until just tender and drain.

Beat eggs and combine with saffron-butter, onions, and remaining ingredients, pour into pastry shell, and bake at 350°F for one hour.

# ABOUT KATHRYN LE VEQUE

## MEDIEVAL JUST GOT REAL.

KATHRYN LE VEQUE is an Amazon All-Star author, and a #1 bestselling, award-winning, multi-published author in Medieval Historical Romance and Historical Fiction. She has been featured in THE NEW YORK TIMES and on USA TODAY's HEA blog along with numerous other publications and blogs.

In October 2014, Kathryn was the 31st MOST READ author on Amazon and now she is finding success on other platforms. She is extremely prolific with over 50 published novels and 37 #1 Hot New Releases in Medieval Historical Romance since May 2012.

You can find Kathryn on Amazon, Barnes and Noble, iBooks, Kobo, All Romance eBooks, Google Play and Smashwords. Please visit Kathryn Le Veque's website for a complete list of books and ordering information.

On Amazon
www.amazon.com/Kathryn-Le-Veque/e/B004QF87Q4

On Facebook
www.facebook.com/kathrynlevequenovel

On Twitter
@KathrynLeVeque

On Tsu
www.tsu.co/Kathry_Le_Veque

Website
www.kathrynleveque.com

Made in the USA
San Bernardino, CA
29 November 2016